The Town House

NORAH LOFTS

HOUSE OF
STRATUS

This edition published in 2001 by House of Stratus, an imprint of House of Stratus Ltd, Thirsk Industrial Park, York Road, Thirsk, North Yorkshire, YO7 3BX, UK.
Also at: House of Stratus Inc., 2 Neptune Road, Poughkeepsie, NY 12601, USA.

www.houseofstratus.com

Typeset, printed and bound by House of Stratus.

A catalogue record for this book is available from the British Library and the Library of Congress.

ISBN 1-84232-145-5

Norah Lofts, best-selling author on both sides of the Atlantic, was born in Norfolk in 1904. She was educated at West Suffolk County School and Norwich Training College, and taught English and History at a girls' school for eleven years. In 1936 Lofts turned to writing full time, also writing under the pen name of Peter Curtis. A passion for old houses and their history inspired her Suffolk 'House' trilogy, *The Town House*, *The House at Old Vine* and *The House at Sunset*. Lofts wrote more than 50 books, including historical non-fiction and short stories. She died in 1983.

PART ONE

Martin Reed's Tale

I

F EW BORN SERFS, like me, could tell you their birthdate, but I was born in that memorable year of 1381 when the peasants, armed only with the tools of their trade, supported by a few soldiers back from the wars, and a few priests with hearts of compassion, rose up against their masters, against the laws and the customs that made a serf the property of his lord. They gave – according to the stories – a good account of themselves: the men of Kent reached London and forced the King himself to lend ear to their grievances. In the end, though, they were disbanded by trickery, sent away soothed by false promises, and the freedom they dreamed of did not come in their generation, nor the next. So, when I was born in the autumn of that year, 1381, I was born a serf, as much the property of my Lord Bowdegrave as the horse he rode, and – at least until I reached working age – of less value: for his horse had an Arab strain, far more rare and precious than my Saxon peasant blood.

My mother died at, or soon after, my birth, and although some woman must have suckled me, or fed me with pap, I have no memory of it. For me life began in the forge where my father worked and where I learned not to touch hot things because they burned, not to get in his way because his hand was heavy, and not to go too near the horses' heels. I was working the bellows – and doing it properly – when I was still so small that I had to stand on a great stone in order to hold them level with the fire.

For his work on my lord's horses and harness and field tools, and armour on occasion, my father, being a villein, received no wage. He had his hut, a strip of land in each of the three open fields, and the right to eat his dinner at the lowest table in the hall. When he worked for other people he could make his charge in coin or in kind and he was not unprosperous. Some years before the rising of 1381 there had been a great sickness in which many people had died; skilled smiths were not as common as they had been. On some manors my father could have hoped and tried, by industry and thrift, to have saved enough money to buy his freedom, but my Lord Bowdegrave was a lord after the ancient fashion and boasted that never, on any of his three manors, had he manumitted a serf for money. My father knew this and therefore, given the choice of a coin or payment in meat or drink, he would choose the latter, so in our hut we ate well and I grew taller and stronger than most of my kind.

Maybe my wits profited from the good food too, for when the time came for me to learn the Catechism and Responses our parish priest praised me often, and in the end was taken with the notion of making a clerk of me. He was himself the son of a serf, base-born like me and set free by Holy Church, and he hoped to push me through the same door.

To my surprise my father was in favour of the plan. He was already showing signs of the dreaded smiths' palsy, that ungovernable shaking of the hands which results from the strain of lifting the heavy hammer and from the jar and thud of its fall. It was, as yet, slight, just a tremor which increased towards the end of the day so that sometimes in the evening he would slop a little ale from his mug, but he knew what it heralded. He knew, too, that on the manor of Rede, the old and the infirm had little to hope for. He would, of course, be entitled to a place by my fire, a share of the food of my table, but it would be a place and a share measured by the size of my family and the generosity or otherwise of the woman I married. He rightly reckoned that as the father of a celibate parish priest he would fare better, so, looking ahead, he allowed me time to take my lessons.

Learning came easy to me. I was naturally idle as all boys are, and earned myself many a buffet, but the priest said I had the makings of a scholar and would do him great credit in later years. As time went on I would relieve the tedium of the lessons by concocting questions which I hoped he would not be able to answer; the hope was justified more and more frequently. He had forgotten much of what he had learned. At last, in the summer before I was ten years old, he went to Norwich and bespoke for me a place in the monks' school there, where he had got his own learning. After that there was only one thing needed to set me on my way to clerkdom, and that was the permission of my Lord Bowdegrave to leave the manor and his service. The priest never doubted that permission would be given.

'My lord boasts that he has never sold a serf his freedom, but he will not hesitate to make a gift of you to Holy Church,' he said.

My Lord Bowdegrave was seldom at his manor of Rede; he had two others, one in Lincoln, one in Kent. This last was his favourite, being within easier reach of London, but the others were visited each year immediately after harvest, at which time even the most trusty steward might go a little awry in his reckonings. Also, after harvest, when the great field was all a-stubble, was the best time of the year for hawking.

It was in the first week of October in the year 1391 that I first came face to face with the man who owned me. My face and hands had been scoured, my hair was newly shorn and I was wearing a clean smock. I was very much frightened. The priest, who must have been – I now realize – a very simple and unworldly man, had warned me that my lord would surely wish to test my abilities. I must be prepared for questions; I must not answer hastily and without thought, nor must I answer slowly and thus appear stupid. Above all I must speak up so that I could be heard, and with the very greatest respect.

The steward had plainly prepared my lord for our appearance, for as we entered the great hall, he said, 'Ah! The smith's son. I remember.'

Fright boiled in my throat. I knew I could never answer a question, no matter how simple. Fright laid a heavy hand on my neck, so that my head was bowed, my eyes fixed on the rushes, fresh spread for my lord's visit.

Above me the voice asked one question.

'How many sons has the man?'

The steward said, 'This one, my lord.'

'Then he cannot be spared. Bad clerks are plentiful; good smiths are few.' Thus briefly was my future, the priest's hopes, my father's old age comfort disposed of. From my lord's verdict there was no appeal.

I was able then, for some reason, to raise my eyes and look into the face of the man whose lightest word was to us, his villeins, weightier than the King's law or the edicts of our Holy Father, the Pope in Rome. It was a handsome, well-fleshed face, highly coloured; stern too, as befitted a man of consequence, but not ill-natured. From the height of his chair on the dais he looked down at me and his light hazel eyes took my measure.

'You're a stout, likely-looking lad,' he said, 'far more fitted to handle a hammer than a quill.' Having thus dismissed me he lifted and crooked a finger and said, 'A word in your ear, Sir Priest.'

What the word was was not for me to know, but I noticed that from that day onward the priest favoured me no more but seemed rather to avoid me.

The priest may have suffered some disappointment. Now that I am older and know more, I can see that having made the one great stride from serfdom to clerkdom, he had shot his bolt; he had ended as a priest in a small, poor parish. Had I become the scholar that he thought I had it in me to be, then he would have been more, for great scholars remember their teachers and many a man of small learning is immortal because he taught the rudiments to one who has become famous. But this, of course, I only guess at.

My father and I, on the other hand, suffered nothing so positive as disappointment. I had been dreading the discipline of the convent school and the break with everything I knew, the harder lessons, the competition with boys born free. And my father was consoled for the loss of a more secure old age by the thought that in the immediate future he would have my assistance at the forge. Also – and this I have seen proved many times in later years – it is seldom those who are oppressed who resent their oppression; they wear it as they wear their clothes. Serfs, when they rise against their serfdom, are always led by free-born men. There was nothing of resentment in us. My lord had spoken and as he said, so it would be. I went back to the forge and the anvil; I began to take great pride in my strength, and later in my skill. Smith's work is a man's work, and it was quite as much to my taste as the question-and-answer work with the priest who would drub my head if I erred.

So, year followed year; life went on in the old pattern. I grew and I learned, toiling on the working days and making merry on Holy days. I might well have lived and died at Rede, one of my Lord Bowdegrave's possessions, had I not fallen in love.

II

Love is not, it is rightly not, a thing for every day, for ordinary people. Love is for the minstrels and the singing men to make tales of. That way it is safe.

How often have I heard a singing man strum his lute and raise his voice –

5

A gracious fate to me to me is sent;
Methinks it is by Heaven lent.
From women all my heart is bent
To joy in Alyson.

There is a pleasant thought, set to a tunable air, and suitable for a singing man who means nothing by it. Pity the poor fool of a man who in this our life suffers such a fate; who goes mad and sets one woman above all others, above all else. I know whereof I speak, for such a poor fool was I.

Men of property choose women who will bring them good dowers: acres to link with their acres, coin to rattle with their own, or a good name to boast of, or some other advantage; poor men, when the itch comes upon them, take the wench who is handiest, or, if they are uncommonly prudent, have a care to pick one with sound limbs, sweet breath and – so far as such things can be judged aforehand – an amiable temper. And they all do very well, since any woman can bear a child or boil a dumpling.

But I...I must needs fall in love!

There was, at first sight, no reason why my love for my sweet Kate should cause any upset. She belonged to our manor of Rede and her father was, like mine, a villein. He was a shepherd and lived on the sheep run, over by the river in a remote and lonely place; and since Ancaster church was nearer his hut than ours of Rede, he and his family went to Mass there; so I was twenty and Kate was seventeen before I noticed her, and then it was only by chance.

I was by this time a skilled smith and more active than my father, so when there was a job to be done at a distance I was the one to go; and on an April afternoon I was coming home from Ancaster, walking downhill towards the river where the stepping stones were, when I saw, on the Rede side of the stream, a child – as I thought – washing some linen in the stream. That was an ordinary sight enough on an April day when the body-clothes worn through the winter could be sloughed off and cleansed, and

I took no notice until a woman came out of the shepherd's hut, walked towards the child, berating her as she walked, and then, snatching up a broken branch that lay nearby, began to lay on heavily.

That again was no extraordinary sight and it was not for me to interfere between parent and child; only the priest, or perhaps the steward, had the right to do that. The little girl took the punishment without outcry and, for all I knew, deserved it. But after a moment, I, who all my life had seen women beating their children, was struck by the ferocity with which this woman went about the job. I splashed over the stones and on the other side slowed my pace and at last stood still. The woman seemed to be in a killing rage, and the prevention of murder is every man's Christian duty. So I said, 'Have a care, good wife. Such heavy stripes might kill the little wench.'

From what Kate told me later I have no doubt the woman would, sooner or later, have done that, but not out in the open under the eye of a witness. She gave me a savage look and laid on three more blows as though to prove her right, but they were lighter ones, and then she threw down the branch and went stamping and grumbling away back into the hut.

My fate then made me go to comfort the child, and as soon as I was within arm's reach of her I saw that her smallness belied her years; inside the torn dress was the white curve and the pink bud of a girl's breast. I looked on it and was lost.

I am not a poet or a singing man to tell of love. When I think of what made her dearer to me than any other I can only say that she was so small, so light and thin and small, like a little bird, a little rabbit. To the end of our days together I never grew used to the smallness of her, and my hands – sometimes against my will – always went gentle when they neared her. For the rest, her hair was the colour of new run honey and her eyes as blue as a speedwell.

I held her close to me for comfort, and dragging down the end of my sleeve I dipped it in the water and wiped away the blood where the skin was broken. She cried then. That was ever her way: to bear the blow, no matter how heavy, with fortitude, and then melt at a word or touch of kindness. When she was quiet again I asked for what reason her mother dealt so ill with her.

'She is not my mother. She is my father's new wife and she wishes me out of the house.'

'To go would be better than to be treated thus roughly,' I said.

'I cannot. The steward orders me to stay. I help my father with the sheep.'

'Then he must stand between you and the woman.'

'Ah, but she lays about him with her tongue,' Kate said. 'I should think shame to tell you what she says of us if ever he even looks at me kindly.'

I held her in the crook of my arm and thought more rapidly than I had done for years, since I had done the last time the priest questioned me. Up to that moment the business of bedding and breeding had troubled me less than it does most men. One day, I had said to myself, I should marry and get a son to work in the forge when I, in my turn, began to shake and shudder, but it had never seemed an urgent or even a desirable business. There had never been a woman in our hut, and father and I had managed very well; we were peaceful and better fed than most. But now I knew…

'Be of good heart,' I said, 'and keep out of the woman's way as far as you can. I shall be back tomorrow, to see how you fare.' I dared not say more lest I should raise a hope which it would be cruel to cast down. Rede, though in many ways a manor far behind the times, was well run, and the priest kept the Kin Book in order to make sure that no marriage was within the forbidden degree. There were the laws of the Church to be minded and other, unwritten laws which ruled against the wedding of double cousins, that is, cousins related upon both sides. Experience had proved such unions to be bad alike for mind and body: hare-lips, fits, deafness, dumbness and blindness had been the penalties of such near-incest in the past. So, on all properly managed estates,

even the lowest hind had his 'Pedigree' and it must be consulted
before leave to marry was given.

When I left Kate I went straight to the priest's house. I told
him that I wished to marry Kate, daughter to the shepherd, and
he said something which I always remembered.

'I have watched you, Walter, my son, and it has vexed me lest,
all unwitting, I made a monk out of you when you were young
yet failed to bestow the benefit of clergy upon you. I was not to
blame.'

'I know that, Father. You had no cause to be vexed for me.'

'You are twenty years old. Half your life is sped.'

A cold thought for a man in love. I shuffled it off, looking at
him; he had been in his middle years when he taught me.

'Ah,' he said, 'clerks live longer. That is the rule. Measure your
years not by mine but by your father's. He lacks a year of his two
score and he is an old man.'

That was all too true. Oh hurry, I said in my mind; open that
Kin Book, give me leave to marry Kate, for twenty years is all too
short a time. And yet, if we cannot marry, twenty years without
her will last forever, they will last so long that I cannot live them
out.

He used his finger on the page of parchment which, with
other pages, all of slightly different size and tied by thongs on to
a stave of wood made up the book. Sweat broke out on my
forehead and around my mouth. Weeks, months, years went by;
and at last he lifted his head and said, 'You are no kin to her.'

I thanked him as though he, and he alone, had arranged it.

It was too late, that evening, to disturb the Steward; but early
next morning, before he went out on his rounds, I went to him.

'Ha!' he said, 'And about time too. By the Rood I don't know
what is happening to you young rascals. Too idle to breed! With
labour so scarce, too.' That reminded him of something else.
'The wench must stay at her work,' he said. 'So she does that,
nobody minds in which hut she sleeps. Except you, of course.'
He gave me a nudge and a leer. 'You can tell shepherd that the

9

bride fee will be two geese, rightly fattened. That being settled, I am sure you will have my lord's permission to marry. It is a pity that you must wait until his harvest visit.'

That day I whistled as I worked, and as soon as I could down tools, went, without waiting for my supper, over to the shepherd's hut and said to that weak-minded man, 'I have from priest and steward, permission to marry your daughter, Kate.'

The woman looked pleased, but he grunted, and said something about talk coming cheap; he was a poor man with a wife and two children younger than Kate: where was the merchet coming from? He supposed I had never even thought of that; young men in their heat never remembered that every time a girl married the lord exacted his due.

'But I have remembered. Steward said two fat geese, and them I will provide.'

'Three,' he said, 'can be fattened as easy as two. One for me, two for my lord and the bargain is made.'

'It is made,' I said, and struck hands on it. 'And now,' I said, stepping back and including the woman in my stare, 'any blow on Kate's body will be a blow on mine and I will repay it fourfold.' As I spoke I knotted my great fist and the muscle on my forearm leaped up and quivered. Shepherd bleated, like his own bellwether, 'The children have run overlong unmothered. Their new mother did not more than mend their manners.'

His other children were boys, aged about seven and nine, and hardy looking. They bore no marks of ill-usage that I could see, whereas my poor Kate was all swollen and marked from yesterday's beating.

'Any correction that Kate needs from this day forward *I* will tend to,' I said, smiling at her, and feeling my heart go soft. 'As for you boys, if the woman bears on you too hard, kick her back. You're two against one, or, if you, shepherd, had the courage of a louse, three. What did she bring as her marriage portion? A gelding iron?'

'Take your foot from my floor,' the woman cried, furiously.

'Gladly,' I said, and taking Kate by the arm I drew her out and we went to a place where a bent hawthorn, just coming into flower, leaned over the stream. And there I held her close and we talked. I said, 'My pretty one, you shall be safe with me.'

Safe with me. Yes, I said that. I looked down the years and saw her in our hut, eating fatly of food I had provided, growing smooth and sleek. She was so small and I was so strong, I would never even let her carry a bucket of water from the well. Her work as sheep-girl I could not order, but I would put fear into the shepherd, so that the hard tasks did not fall to her. She should be safe with me.

III

Now here is something which men born in free towns, or on the manors of more enlightened lords, may find hard to believe: or they will believe that it was true in times long past, not in my living memory. But I swear by all that I hold holy, it was true at Rede. It was a custom which our Norman masters brought with them. Having a little learning I can give it its proper name – *Jus primae noctis* – but we called it First Night's, and it meant simply that the lord of the manor had the right, if he so wished, to take any serf-born girl's maidenhead. Whether he exercised the right depended upon many things, the man's own lustfulness, age or disposition, the way the girl looked, the fashion in the district. On many manors it was regarded as outmoded, like the Twelve Days of the Lord of Misrule at the Christmas season: but in this, as in other matters, my Lord Bowdegrave was old-fashioned, and here and there about Rede manor, and about his others I have no doubt, the long straight Norman nose, the cleft chin, the bright hazel eyes which were the visible sign of the Bowdegrave breed, could be seen, incongruous in a peasant face, bearing witness that he had not only exercised his right, but done it potently. Of late years, however, age and an increasing heaviness – it took two stout men to heave him into his saddle by this time – had cooled his ardours and for several seasons past he had contented himself with kissing the prospective bride if she were comely, or giving her a smack on the rump if she were otherwise.

Occasionally, during the weeks that followed my be-speaking of Kate, I thought upon this matter. It seemed to me impossible that any man, however old, however much he weighed, could look upon my Kate and not desire her. Yet, strange as it may sound to any not serf-born, I was not unduly disturbed. This matter of acceptance of circumstance cuts very deep. Think of those born hump-backed, deaf, blind. They accept their fate and bear it. I was born a serf. If my services were required even in the next village, Ancaster, to shoe a horse or mend a plough, I must ask the steward's permission before I could step across the boundary between Rede and Ancaster. Think how irksome that rule would be on any free man. To me it was nothing. In the same way it was…well, almost nothing, that the unlikely might happen and my Lord Bowdegrave should claim his First Night's right upon Kate. She would be mine for the rest of our lives. He could not be prevented. There lies the whole crutch of the matter: what cannot be prevented must be borne, like unseasonal weather, mildew on wheat, murrain in cattle. Through May and June and the months that must drag until our lord's harvest visit, every time I thought upon the matter I told myself – There is nothing I can do; it is unlikely that he will claim his right, but, if he does, what is one night?

That was a year of most remarkable fine weather. With the new moon of June the heat set in and by mid-July the corn was ready for reaping. Without hitch or hindrance, without so much as a summer shower to halt it, the harvest went on and before the end of August, a full month early, the stubbles were cleared. My Lord Bowdegrave, informed of this, put forward his visit and my time of waiting was cut from October to September.

I had ruled myself well. To a degree the season had been in my favour; hay-time and harvest are busy times for smiths, and this

year, since they followed so hard on one another's heels, I was
doubly busy. Also Kate's father, resenting, perhaps, my words
about the gelding iron, had sent Kate farther and farther afield as
pasture became scarce. So I saw her but rarely. However, late in
August, the grass having grown again on the low land by the
river, the flock came home, and one night, under a lop-sided
moon, she and I lay together.

It was sin; but she was guiltless. God and all the saints are
witness to that. I did it deliberately, courting all blame. I had
heard that day, somewhere in the yard, that my lord was on his
way to Rede, and I thought, he is old and clumsy, and he does not
love her. She is very small. There may be hurt and it is better that
I, who love her... That was part of my thought, but not all. There
was the reined-in desire of the last five months, and there was the
wish to forestall, to be first, despite all custom.

Afterwards I took her face between my hands with their
calloused palms and blackened nails and I said, 'Now you belong
to me.'

So then my Lord Bowdegrave came to Rede and there was
much commotion, with the paying of the rents and the taking of
tallies of all his stacks and beasts and flitches and honeycombs.
Then, one fine morning, Kate and I were called into the hall, just
as, long ago, my father and I had been called when it was to ask
consent for me to go to the monks' school. Walking over the
fresh rushes, hand in hand with Kate, I was grateful that that
consent had been refused.

I had warned Kate not to make herself look pretty. I still, in
my serf's heart, admitted the old lord's right, but by the mere
action of forestalling him I had taken a step out of bondage. I had
risen up under the moon and said, 'You belong to me'; later I saw
the falseness of that. If you lay claim to a piece of land you should
be able to prove your right in the face of all men; if you cannot
do so any man who trespasses there does you more wrong than if
he walked on common land. I was anxious, therefore, that she
should not appear in the hall with her hair newly washed and

streaming over her shoulders, wearing the wreath of flowers which marked the bride-to-be. Kate had laughed and asked, 'Shall I smear wood ash on my face?'

Even had she done so, it would not have hidden the fine shapeliness of her bones, the thickness of her honey-coloured hair or the blue of her eyes. I saw the old man look at her; first with that pitiable, old-man lustful look, wishing he were ten, twenty years younger; then in another fashion. Even as the steward hastily named us, Walter, the smith's son, Kate, the shepherd's daughter, no relation according to the Kin Book, I saw the old man straighten himself and shift a little in his seat.

'Both of this manor which will neither gain nor lose labour thereby,' chanted the steward.

'Have done,' said my lord. He dragged his eyes away from Kate, and shifting a little more, turned to me.

'You're my smith, eh?'

'Yes, my lord.'

'Then this is an ill choice, surely. You need a wench capable of working the bellows for you at a pinch, and breeding good strong boys. This little maid is altogether too fine and delicate for your purpose.' His face had grown fat and purple since I last looked at him; in it his eyes shone, his lips were wet, with lechery. He leaned forward a little and reached out his great mottled hand to take Kate by the wrist.

'I can find you better employment; in the still room of my house at Abhurst. You'd like that, eh?'

Without giving her time to answer – for what did it matter whether she said yes or no? – he said to the steward, 'Have her ready to ride, pillion to Jack or Will, when I go.'

To describe a moment of boundless rage, folks often speak of 'seeing red'. A true word. I saw red then. My Lord Bowdegrave, the chair upon which he sat, the tapestry on the wall behind him, the steward standing by, were all gulped up before my eyes in a great red wave into which I plunged my fist with all my might behind it. I felt, but did not see, the smash of my knuckles upon the great leering face. The next instant something hit me across the back of my skull and the redness gave way to a burst of sparks and then to blackness.

The utter black pricked out with stars, and there I was, lying flat on my back with my face to the sky. There was not an inch of me that was not in pain. My hide had been broken in a score of places and the whole of my body was set stiff in a case of dried blood. Somebody had given me a monstrous fine thrashing. I moved myself carefully and found that none of my main bones were broken; then I rolled over on my face and was sick and felt better for it. Bit by bit I came to myself. I was stark, stripped of my hose and shirt, and I lay on the dung-heap. Left for dead, I thought to myself. Remembering what I had done, and why, it struck me that maybe I should have been better dead – which thought, naturally, brought me fully back to life. I gathered myself together, piece by piece, and reeled into the forge which was handy, and where we always kept a bucket of clean water to slake our thirst. Feeling my way to it I dipped the horn mug and drank again and again, taking in, with the cool blessed water, the full sense of the plight I was in. I must get away, and I could not go naked. I staggered to our hut.

There was a strong smell of onions, and the fire upon which my father had cooked his supper was still a small pink glimmer on the hearthstone. He lay in his bed. I threw a handful of dry sticks on the embers and as the flames leaped he moved, lifted his head, saw me and crossed himself hurriedly, saying, 'God betwixt me and harm.'

'It's only me, Father.'

'A ghost,' he whispered.

'My living self.' The flames gained power and he could see me, horrid as my ghost, stripped and all bloody.

'I gave you up for dead,' he said.

I was his son; we had lived together in fair amity for twenty years and of late I had carried the weight of the work. I did not blame him for leaving me where I lay: I had done an unforgiveable thing and he had his own safety to look to. But he had come home, cooked his onions, laid down to sleep. At the back of my mind something stirred, a whole thought in a breathing space. That was to be a serf. A serf had no right even to human feelings; it was only by throwing away all claim to human feelings a serf could support his way of life. I had, this very morning, acted like a man, not a serf; and with what result!

'Small thanks to those who beat me that I am not dead. And if I am here by morning dead I shall be.' I forced my bruised, stiff limbs to move more briskly. I had dressed in my best to wait upon my lord; so now I must don my stinking working clothes. Then, because our hoard was hidden in the earth under his bed, I had to ask him, 'Give me my share of the money we have saved.'

He got up grumbling.

'Less the price of the three geese your share is,' he said.

'But I am leaving the geese with you. Father, I must go faraway. Who knows what may befall me? A penny may mean life or death to me.'

'And who is to blame for that?' Recovering from his fear of being visited by a dead man's ghost he began to rate me. Mad, reckless, ingrate. That ever son of his should lift violent hand against his lord. Shame, shame, undying shame, and worse. Punishment for him for breeding and raising such a rogue.

'You showed your colours plain enough when you left me for dead on the dung-heap and came home and roasted your onions. You have nothing to fear. Who else, when I am gone, can shoe a horse within ten miles?'

'That is true,' he said, comforted again.

Yet, when he had unearthed our little hoard, he divided the coins into two heaps, then took from mine the sum I had paid for the three geese and added it to his own. I protested at that.

'The six pence for the geese should be laid aside first, then the sum should be divided. The way you have it now, you are twelve pence to the good.'

'You talk like the fool you are. You took out six pence in April to buy the three geese. Now we divide into fair shares and I take six pence from your share and put to my own since I did not buy geese.'

Nothing would make him see differently, and I dared not stay to beat it out with him. I took the twenty-one pence which was my share, put them, a half loaf, a piece of cheese, my knife and a length of good cord into the little bag in which, when I worked away from home, I carried my noon piece, and then I was ready.

'You never saw me,' I told him. 'For all you know the crows picked out my eyes and the dogs ran off with my bones. If any speak to you of me, rail against me as you have just done.'

I was on my way out, ducking at the low doorway, when he said in an uncertain voice, 'God go with you, Walter.' I remembered then that he was my father, growing old, and tremulous, his working days almost numbered and with no one now to depend upon. And he had taught me my trade without too much clouting. So I forgave him his supper, and the unfair division, and made him a fair answer.

'God be with you,' I said; and went out into the night.

IV

The river bank, near to the place where Kate had been washing that day, was dotted with clumps of gorse bushes. I chose one close to the path worn between the shepherd's hut and the stepping stones where the family dipped their water, and there I hid myself. The gorse made an uncomfortable hiding place, but I was so sore all over that a few scratches mattered little. It was in my mind that I was most ill at ease. I had no certainty at all that Kate had been sent back home; it seemed far more likely that she had spent the night at the hall, in my lord's bed most like. But there was a faint, faint chance that she had come home and I could not leave Rede forever without snatching at that chance.

17

Day dawned. A thin blue thread of smoke rose from the hole in the roof hut; the shepherd came out, eased himself by the wall, and went in again. Presently Kate herself came out, carrying a bucket. She must have cried all through the night; her face was swollen with tears. She looked stupid with misery and moved listlessly. When she was as near my bush as the path to the water would bring her I said, softly, 'Don't look round.' I had debated with myself whether to say that first, or 'Don't be frightened.' It seemed to me that a fright she would get over, whereas for me to be observed would be fatal. I quickly added, 'Don't be frightened; and don't speak.'

I cannot understand why all the mummers in the world – even when it is the Blessed Virgin to be represented – should be men. Women are natural mummers. Apart from a slight start when she first heard my voice, Kate gave no sign at all. She walked down to the river, dipped the bucket and came back, leaning sideways against the weight. Level with me she set it down and stood rubbing her arm and shoulder, at the same time yawning heartily.

I jerked out a few words, telling her that I meant to slip away to the woods.

'I'm not asking you to come. Every man's hand will be against me. And you could live soft at Abhurst. But if you *want* to come, I shall wait in Tuck's Oak till dusk.'

I was not being unselfish. At that moment, much as I loved her, I was not sure that I wanted her with me. I felt weak and sick and sore, and I was about to do something new and dangerous, something I had never heard of anyone else doing successfully. A man about to jump from a great height, or swim a wide stream in the dark, is better off without a woman clinging about his neck, however well-beloved she may be. Yet in my heart, if not in my head, I must have wanted her to come, else why had I not made straight for the woods and got away under cover of darkness; why was I prepared to risk waiting all day?

Kate took up the bucket and moved away and in a moment I heard the voice of her step-mother, intent now upon currying favour with one who shortly might have benefits to bestow.

'Give me that bucket,' she said, her scolding voice over-laid with forced good humour. 'You don't want blisters on your hands tomorrow.'

They went indoors; the thread of smoke thickened. Soon, I judged, they would be breaking their fast. I began to move. I went on my belly like a snake, from gorse bush to gorse bush, keeping alongside the river until I was out of sight of the hut. Then I went to the water's edge and laid down my leather apron and the little round cap which all careful smiths wear to save their hair from rubbing against the horses' hides and picking up the running itch. I walked into the water, careful to make clear footmarks in the mud. I waded downstream in the water until my legs were so benumbed that they failed me; then I climbed out and made for the woods. I hoped that I had broken the scent which the hounds and my lord's huntsman would soon be following. I hoped that my off-cast apron and cap would look as though I had drowned myself.

Once safe in the great forest I regretted having made tryst with Kate. 'All for love' sing the singing men and in their songs love risks all, conquers all, never doubts and never falters. But the Bible says, 'All that a man has will he give for his life', and for ordinary, frightened men like me, that is a true saying. I was in the forest by midday and could have made good progress during the hours of daylight, had I not promised to wait. I climbed Tuck's Oak and lay along a stout branch, sweating with fear at the thought of the hounds casting up and down the river bank. Would any see through my trick? Would the search be long enough and patient enough to pick up my trail again? I remembered the way my fist had smashed into my lord's face; he would feel the damage this morning; he would be after me for vengeance as well as for my value. The longest day's labour had never seemed so long as the few hours I waited; and they were few, for Kate came while it was still broad day. She brought a basket into which she had packed four goose eggs, some cold mutton, a loaf of bread and some apples. She had thought to bring her winter's cloak.

At the sight of her, the realization that she had chosen to be hunted with me, rather than to live at ease with our master, love leaped up in me again. I was glad that I had lain in the gorse and waited in the tree, and glad beyond all measure that she had come. I dropped from the bough, took the basket from her and holding her by the hand set off in a southerly direction. She told me that the huntsman and two brace of hounds had found my hiding place in the gorse, followed it until it ended, and then, after casting about for an hour, returned. The man was carrying my cap and apron.

'And how did you get away so soon?'

'I said I must carry my father's dinner – for the last time. And for once she did not stand over me, weighing with her eye all that I put into the basket.' She laughed. 'Father said goodbye and he hoped that when I was in the still room at Abhurst I should remember that he was a poor man with several mouths to feed. I said I would. Then, when I left him I came here.'

'The hounds. If they are brought out on *your* trail?'

She laughed again. 'The sheep always loved me. I had but to call and they would follow. They came after me almost to the wood's edge – Father too busy with his dinner to mind them. When I was ready I turned and scattered them. It would be a rare hound that could scent me on ground sheep had been over twice.'

'So it would. And you, my Kate, are rarer among women than that hound among hounds.' I slackened pace long enough to kiss her heartily and then pressed on.

'Where are we going?' she asked.

'The only answer I can give you is away from Norwich. That is where they will seek us. So we must walk in the other direction until we reach a walled town.'

20

That was another thing which every serf knew, it was part of his serf's heritage, the knowledge that if by some miracle he could ever escape from his manor and reach a walled town and there spend one year and one day, without being reclaimed, or committing any offence against the town laws, then he would be a free man. Alongside this knowledge – which one might think any serf would try to use to his advantage almost as soon as he could walk – lay other knowledge all concerned with the risks and the difficulties and the ferocious punishments which awaited any who made an unsuccessful attempt. Once off his manor without leave, a serf was a marked man; for miles around a rider on a swift horse would raise the hue-and-cry, and while that was on any stranger would be challenged and asked to explain himself. When he was overtaken, he would be brought back, whipped and branded. Such a fate few serfs were prepared to face in order to gain 'freedom', which was just a word to them. The dues and the duties of villeinage might be heavy or light – it depended upon the lord of the manor, upon his steward or bailiff, upon old custom – but whether heavy or light they had worn calloused places upon the bodies and minds of the bondsmen and unless something out of the ordinary disagreeable happened, as it had happened in my case, no man in his senses would throw himself out into the unknown world. At least, so it was at Rede, which, as I have said before, was much behind the times in every way. I had never known a man to run away, and should never have done so myself had I not been driven. Having run I intended, if possible, to make good my attempt.

I did not know then, though I know it now, that the great forest stretched, with but few large clearings, from the Wash to the Thames river, but I knew it was large and I hoped that Kate and I could stay in its shelter for a long time, and then, perhaps emerge at Colchester, which was the only town besides Norwich which I knew by name. I knew it because of its oyster beds; every year, when my lord made his after-harvest visit, great creels of them were hurried up on horseback to lay upon his table. Where this town lay I did not know except that it was southward and my hope of reaching it was only a hope. For the woods, while offering shelter from the hue-and-cry along the roads, had dangers of their own. In the densest thickets there were wolves, and the even more dangerous wild boars, and everywhere there were the game wardens. Merely by entering the forest Kate and I were committing a felony and making ourselves liable to savage punishment, if caught.

All this we knew, yet, having found one another, we walked along in good spirits. On this first day of our journey the wood was mainly of beech trees, which do not encourage undergrowth. The great grey tree trunks rose straight and smooth as the pillars of a church, and under our feet was a carpet of leaves dropped in the autumns of bygone years. We travelled until a grey dusk was thick amongst the trees. Then I remembered stories of men who had been lost in fogs, or in forests, or in great open spaces like sheep-runs and gone round and round, retreading the same path. Lest we do the same and find ourselves, in the morning, back at Rede, I called a halt. We threw ourselves down under a tree so old that its roots in places grew clear of the soil, making little low caves. We crouched in one, ate bread and mutton and apples, the first food we had ever taken together. I thought of that, blasphemously perhaps, thinking that it was a kind of communion; and as I did so Kate put up her hand and touched the twisted arch of root under which we sat.

'This is our very first house,' she said.

Something began in my belly and swelled and swelled until it reached my head; I forgot all my fears, forgot our present plight and the future's uncertainties. I felt brave and powerful, tireless, undefeatable.

'You shall have better, sweetheart. I will build it myself, a snug, trig house, as sound as this tree.' I reached out my longer arm and laid a finger on the tree trunk.

Kate laughed and said, 'I'm glad you were touching wood!'

I laughed too. Rede seemed faraway, here in the wood's quiet, with night gathering about us we might have been alone in the world, another Adam, another Eve in a new Garden of Eden. We finished our meal and afterwards slept in each other's arms.

V

The next four or five days – that is so long as the food lasted – were the happiest in my whole life. I can look back and see them, set apart, glowing with something more than sunshine. Since then I have never pitied idiots; for during that time Kate and I were touched by idiocy, not set free from the dangers and cares of ordinary living but somehow not properly concerned. It was as though we had ceased to be Kate, daughter of the shepherd, Walter, son of the smith, and become people in some minstrel's song, walking through the greenwood, loving one another. 'All for love.'

The nature of the woods changed; the clear-floored beech trees ended and we came to the thick forest, with undergrowth of hazels, brambles and bracken, all closely woven. Sometimes we could turn aside to seek easier passage, sometimes I had to go ahead, hacking a way through with my knife. Still we moved on, careful to keep the sun upon our left hand until it was high, walking into its eye for an hour and then keeping it upon our right until it sank. We were sparing of our poor provisions, eking them out with blackberries and unripe hazel nuts, with sloes and crab-apples that soured our mouths, but even so we came to an end and were face to face with the eternal problem of the poor, brought back to earth by the question which is for all but the rich the first and the last question – How shall we eat today? We learned, soon enough, that love is a business for those with full bellies. No, maybe there I wrong Kate and, through her, all women; I think they care more for love and less for their bellies than men do. She stayed cheerful long after I had begun to fret;

she spoke gently and lovingly while my words grew few and sharp from hunger.

We say, lightly enough, the words 'starve to death'. Put like that it sounds easy and brief enough, a man ceases to eat and he dies. The truth is that he does not immediately die. Death by starvation has many unpleasant stages. There is the belly pain, as though, within you, some strange animal hungered and, lacking other sustenance, gnawed at your vitals with sharp fangs. There is, following the pain, a constant desire to vomit, as though you would turn your empty belly inside out, like a beggar proving his pocket to be coinless. There is a shakiness in the bones, your hands fumble and grow clumsy, your knees give way. There is a ringing in your ears, as though bees hived there.

As our need to get out of the forest grew greater we made less progress. We were weaker and we were forced to hunt. From the cord I made a rabbit snare and we wasted hours sitting somewhere near, but out of sight, fretting over the loss of time and yet glad enough to have reason for inaction. I caught nothing.

Kate bore up bravely until we ate the hawthorn berries. They were plump and red and ripe and looked to us, in our hunger, as good as cherries. 'Birds eat them,' we told one another; and we ate them, in quantities. They did me no harm at all, but they turned Kate's bowels to water. Soon she was stumbling along, doubled over with pain and looking so wan that I was frightened. Up to that point we had been careful to make as little of ourselves as possible, but now I began calling as we went forward, cupping my hands to my mouth and uttering loud cries. Wood-cutters, charcoal-burners and game-wardens lived in the forest and now that we were starving the hope of falling in with some man with a heart of Christian charity loomed larger than our fear. Nothing answered me but my own voice, bouncing back from the trees. In all that time we saw nothing but one red deer which flickered away like something seen in a dream.

We found no more hawthorn berries, but Kate's infirmity persisted; the time came when she could no longer walk at all, so I carried her; and I did not go straight forward, I took the easiest way. She never weighed much, but now she was variable. I'd pick her up and it was like lifting a kitten, so light she was; but as I went on she grew heavy and heavier. Sweat broke out all over my body, my heart hammered, my sight clouded. In the end I would set her down and fall prone, and she would creep away a little distance, behind the nearest tree or bush and then emerge, more deathly pale than ever. Through the ringing and buzzing in my ears a stern voice would say clearly, 'Kate is going to die and you are to blame.' Presently I would brace myself and try again. Again. Again. Making no progress, and the forest going on and on, and nobody in it but us.

From hunger sleep is no refuge; the starving do not sleep; they slip from one kind of misery to another; the gnawing pain goes on and so does the worry. I would lie down and think, imagine, dream, that a fine fat rabbit was kicking in my snare, then I would struggle up, shouting, to find that the piece of cord was still twisted about my wrist because I had lain where I had fallen and never set the snare at all.

It was a nightmare time.

Once I lifted Kate, turned dizzy, and only just set her down before I dropped her. She said, in a weak voice, gasping, 'You can't…carry me…any more. Leave me. No need…for both…to die.'

If I had had a known destination or any real hope of finding help I might have been more tempted. But mere walking was not going to save me. Only a miracle could do that. I told her so.

'Only a miracle can save us now. And a miracle could happen here as well as at any other place.' So I lay beside her for a little, gathering my strength, and then staggered a little distance and set my silly snare. That was the miracle I expected, a rabbit in my snare. As I set it I prayed, not in the manner I had been taught but as though God were the steward and I were begging some small favour of him. 'God send a rabbit, please God. A rabbit, God, please.' The light was just beginning to fail; it was a time when rabbits were abroad.

When I got back to Kate she said, 'I can smell...herrings roasting.'

I almost wept then. I knew that delusion. It had been my companion for hours, days. As I walked I had smelt more food cooking than had ever been set on my lord's table; fat pork boiling with peas; roasting fowl; dried herring; new bread; seethed beef; dredged hare; onions.

'Poor Kate,' I said. 'My poor, poor Kate. Your hungry nose deceives you.'

'But I can...can't you?'

I sniffed. I could smell it. A mouth-watering smell at any time. After the harvest of the earth came the harvest of the sea and the dried herring would come in barrels to Rede. When the day's work was done father and I would toast them, on long sticks, by the fire. We could have been doing it now, while Kate ate venison and syllabub at Abhurst.

Call me heartless knave if you will. But first go hungry for uncounted days; then make your own choice, love or a roasted herring. Lie weak with hunger on the ground and stare death by starvation in the face, and choose. If you say, Love, then I will call you saint and you may call me what you will. I am honest with myself. I wished myself back at Rede with a herring spluttering at the end of a stick, and Kate safe and full fed in Abhurst.

I lay, wishing that, and the good smell continued. Presently I realized that never before in my delusions had the one kind of smell continued. Moreover it grew more powerful. This, I thought, was because I was growing weaker, slipping farther and farther from reality. Perhaps, I thought, before we died we should taste food as well as smell it, God's final mercy. And from that I turned to thinking about dying, as Kate and I must do, unshriven, with all our sins upon us. Even the joys of our few happy days had been stolen. Unconfessed and unabsolved they would weigh heavy in the scales. I was beginning, desperately, to try to recall the proper prayers for those on the point of departure when Kate nudged me.

'Go and...look. It can't...be...faraway.'

Even in that extremity my good strong body served me; lying prone, even in despair, had restored me. Standing up, without having to lift Kate, I found myself steadier than I could have hoped. Turning my head from side to side like a hound, and drooling water at the mouth, I set off in the direction from which the scent seemed strongest. A few paces brought me to a place where, in some time past, the forest trees had been felled. Where they had stood, a coppice of bushes, elder and wild rose and hawthorn, had grown up. Close pressed and fighting with one another, they had woven themselves into a living wall. The strong scent of herrings roasting came from its farther side. I walked along the thicket, seeking an entrance, but there was none, and the scent grew fainter. I turned back and walked the other way. The fence continued, and the smell again faded. I was vastly puzzled. No house could be completely enclosed.

I staggered to the spot where the smell was strongest and threw myself at the bushes, thrusting my way into them bodily, hacking at them with my knife in a frenzy. The last line of them gave way before my onslaught and I found myself standing at the top of a little bank, looking down upon a sight as astonishing as it was welcome. To left and right, as far as eye could see in either direction, ran a straight flat road, bordered on each side by thicket like that through which I had just forced my way. The road was thickly grassed and at the point immediately below me stood a jenny ass with her foal. Nearby was a fire and over it, slung on a cross bar, the herrings. Standing guard over the whole was a little old woman with a donkey stick in her hand and an expression on her face that was at once terrified and defiant.

'Keep your distance!' she said. 'I've nowt worth stealing, and if you come near I shall fetch you a clout.'

I must have been a fearsome sight, bursting through the bushes, knife in hand, the bruises of my beating turning greenish yellow, the broken places now well-scabbed, all in addition to my desperate, hungry look.

My wits were still with me, however. I did not move, but dropped the knife so that it fell down the bank almost at her feet.

'Good mother,' I said. 'I am no robber. We have gone astray in the forest and are like to die of hunger. Of your charity, let us eat.' Then I remembered that I had money. 'I am no beggar, either.' I took out a penny and threw it after the knife.

'We,' she repeated on a questioning note. 'How many are you?'

'Myself and my wife, she is in worse case.'

'All right then.' She stooped and picked up my knife and the penny. 'No tricks, though. I'm old, but I'm lively.'

I turned and pushed my way back through the gap, widening it as best I could, and walked to where I had left Kate.

'Was...it true?'

For answer I bent and lifted her. Hope had given me strength and I was able to carry her to the gap and pull her through it. The old woman was still on guard, but at the sight of Kate her manner changed.

'Poor creature,' she said, and coming forward helped me to bring Kate down the little bank and place her by the fire. Then she quickly slid the herrings from the stick, cut great slabs from a round brown loaf and said, 'Lay to. And God send Grace on the food.'

I ate as I had never eaten before, but Kate, after a bite or two, sickened again.

'Poor mawther. She has clemmed over-long. Her belly is shrunk. If only...' In her face, brown and wrinkled as a walnut, her faded eyes snapped and sparkled. 'God be thanked,' she said. 'We have it!'

She routed about amongst her belongings and found a little wooden bowl.

'You must hold the donkey steady,' she said to me. 'She's not been milked this way afore.'

If ever there should come a time when dancing bears are so common that they no longer draw a crowd, an old woman, a young man and a jenny ass in milk should go the rounds. I was too anxious about Kate to be other than vexed by the performance and the time it took, but even then I could see its comical side, especially when the little foal, shrewd enough to see that it was being robbed, came butting in. However, at last we had a cupful of milk in the bowl. Kate drank it and it stayed down. The old woman slipped some more herrings on the stick.

'Maybe St Christopher knew what he was about when he let my basket break,' she said. I then looked at the two osier baskets which stood by the fire and saw that the bottom of one of them had given way.

'I'd have been a mile or two farther along the road if that hadn't happened,' the old woman said. 'Couldn't go scattering the good fish, so I thought I'd stop and mend it up while I could see; then I felt hungry and reckoned I'd eat first.'

'And we smelt your supper and were saved,' I said, looking at Kate, who was holding the bowl in both hands and sipping slowly, but steadily.

'Slip a bit of bread down with it, afore your belly shuts again,' the old woman said, handing her a slice. Kate ate, obediently, and when that stayed with her too I knew the worst was over.

When I was full to bursting, I licked my fingers and offered to try my hand at mending the basket. I used a piece of the cord and some young hazel wands. Kate curled up under cover of her cloak and slept; the old woman and I sat by the fire. She had lost all fear of me by that time, and when I needed my knife for the work, handed it back with a grin.

'I was flummoxed to see you,' she confessed. 'Mostly I'm on the look-out for trouble, but on this bit of road I never seen another living soul, not in all the years I've travelled it. None else know of it, and I ain't likely to tell them.'

It was a strange road, like none I ever saw before or since. Under the grass, which was shallow-rooted, were large flat slabs of stone, set edge to edge. I scraped away the grass to have a better look at it.

'It's a wonderful good road for a loaded donkey,' said the old woman. 'Pity there ain't more like it. I blundered on it by accident.'

She told me how, years before, with another donkey, she had camped for the night on a common and waked to find that, despite his hobble, the donkey had strayed. She thought she could hear him moving behind some breast-high bracken, and looking for him, had found the road.

'That was the end, all grown over and known to none. But it looked to me to run the same way as the other, so I reckoned I'd try it. And I'm glad I did. It's ten miles of easygoing for the beast, and nice for a lone woman to have a spell with her mind at rest without fearing to be set upon. The ghosts I don't mind. They don't heed me, nor me them.'

'Ghosts?'

'Aye. The like of no mortal men they are. Marching men, with short skirts, like a woman's but up to the knee, and shining helmets with brushes atop. There's great silver eagles on poles going ahead of them. I've seen them many's the time. The first time I was too scared to breathe, but I crossed myself and they went by without so much as a glance.'

'You have a stout heart,' I said.

'For some things. I'm feared of robbers. And of the time when I cannot get around to sell my herrings.' She watched me work for a while. 'By your hands,' she said, 'you're a smith. I've an idea that you broke your time and ran off to get married.'

An apprentice who left his master before his time was up was in fault, but he was not the marked, hunted man that a serf was who had run from his manor, so I nodded.

'Ah well, there's good masters and bad. Was yours a beater?' I nodded again, thinking to myself that in the morning I must warn Kate to tell the same tale.

'There's a smith in Baildon who *might* take you – if you was well-spoke of by somebody he knew, like me.'

'Would you so speak?'

'I might. You seem to me a decent sort of chap. And it'd cost me nowt.'

'I should be grateful to you all my life,' I said. 'Is Baildon where you go to sell your herrings?'

'One of the places. It's a fine large town with the best market in these parts. And it's a long way from Norfolk,' she added slyly.

'How do you know that I am from Norfolk?'

'By your tongue. Hereabouts we talk different. We sing our words. Silly Suffolk, some call us, but in the old days it was Singing Suffolk. Still, don't worry about that, we'll fash up a tale to explain. There, you've done a good job on that basket; good as new.'

We were on the move early in the grey and rosy dawn, for the old woman was anxious to get on. She and I breakfasted on herrings, from which Kate still turned sickened away, but she ate heartily of the bread.

'The little mawther can ride the ass for a bit, you and I'll hump the baskets. We'll go faster that way.'

Old and shrunken as she was she set a fast pace, one which I, carrying one basket, could only just manage, and to which the donkey held unwillingly, urged on by a light blow now and again. The foal frisked along, light as a leaf, unaware that his unburdened days were numbered.

Three miles along the road we came to a wide open space, which had also been cleared in some past time and was now all grass and self-sown bushes. Above the tangle some white columns rose, one complete, twice my height and beautifully carved at the top. Others were broken.

'There's a good well here,' the old woman said briskly. 'This is where I aim to spend the night when I'm this way.'

There was a well in Rede manor yard, but nothing like this one, all buried in bushes and weeds. This was a basin of that same white stone as made the pillars and shaped something like a churchfont, but one side was higher than the others and had a horse's head carved upon it; the water ran in a clear steady trickle out of the horse's mouth, into the basin. We all drank from it.

'Now we'll load the donkey and go in proper fashion,' our guide said. That done she took the animal's bridle and dragged it forward through some bushes and a belt of trees and in a few minutes we stood on a piece of common ground, beyond which was a sight which to me was new and most marvellous. When I say new, I mean to my *eyes*. Inside my head a picture something like it had formed when I had heard anything about Jerusalem. But my imagination had been small and mean compared with this reality. This town was walled, though in places the wall had been neglected and allowed to crumble; inside the walls were the crowded roofs of a multitude of houses, and rising above them were some great towers, taller than the highest tree I had ever seen. One in particular seemed to soar into the sky, with buttresses and pinnacles of extreme grace and beauty.

'That is Baildon Abbey,' said the old woman, seeing me staring. 'Don't stand goggling now. If Armstrong takes you, you'll have plenty of chance to look at it.' She urged on the donkey and we left the common for the high road which was crowded with market goers. There were men driving cattle and sheep and pigs, women carrying fowls and eggs and baskets of fruit and vegetables, other laden donkeys, people on horseback, even a litter or two.

'I didn't know,' said Kate in an awed voice, 'that there were so many people in the world.'

'Any others with herrings; thass what I want to know,' said the old woman. She looked sharply about her. 'Not that I worry much,' she went on, contradictorily, 'bringing fish this far is more of a trudge than most folks'd face. We go this way.'

Directly ahead of us was one of the town's gateways; some people entered it, others swerved aside and followed a track worn close to the wall.

'A new order last year. Market dues used to be collected on the market place, but the poor fellows wore themselves out, walking round. So now us with stuff to sell walk round to the North gate and pay as we go in. They chose that gate because it's nearest the Abbey – not so far to carry the bag!'

A monk – the first of his kind that I had ever seen – stood in the archway, accompanied by two ordinary men. As each market-goer drew level with the monk he looked over the produce he carried and without a moment's hesitation decided whether the dues should be paid in cash or kind. He touched nothing: if cash were demanded one of the laymen received it. If the dues were in kind the other took it. It was all done swiftly and in order and in a singular silence. There was no haggling; the dues were paid in sullen silence and no-one said much until out of earshot of the monk. At a safe distance grumbling began. I later learned that there was a kind of justice about the dues, ruled by the law of supply and demand. The monk might take, for example, a fowl from one woman and a pound of apples from another, unfair on the face of it; but inside the market that day fowls were plentiful and cheap, apples scarce and dear. From the basket that I had mended he demanded a score of herrings. Once out of earshot, our friend said sourly, 'There's robbers in all shapes, but them in cowls is the worst. They say that some of their takings come back again as alms and such, but I never took charity yet and never want to.'

The market place was a great open square immediately in front of the Abbey's main gateway. Here on the cobbles some people took up a stand and began to cry their wares as a means of drawing attention; others moved to and fro amongst the townswomen who had come out to do their marketing. I saw several females of a kind new to me, well dressed, with rings on their fingers and elegant head-gear, followed by maid- or men-servants, carrying baskets. In my simple way I took them for great ladies, never having seen one, for if my Lord Bowdegrave had a wife he never brought her to Rede. It was a surprise to me to learn that all this grandeur appertained to the wives of burghers who had been successful in their various businesses, and an even greater surprise to know that these grave-faced, sedate women were, in many cases, breaking the law by dressing themselves so fine. In the towns ordinary folk had become so rich that they could afford to ape the nobility, and laws were passed saying at what rank one might wear velvet, satin or the better kinds of fur. The laws were not heeded. In fact that was one of the first things I noticed about life in the town: the ordinary people were far less humble and conscious of their state than even the freemen on the country manors.

There was no other herring seller in Baildon that morning so Old Betsy – as I heard her called – soon emptied her baskets. One man even made an offer for the donkey foal, to which she replied shortly that she'd think about selling it when the creature was weaned. Then she said to me, 'Come along, and I'll take you to Armstrong, and be on my way.'

Leaving the Abbey behind us we climbed a short steep street called Cooks Lane, in which almost every shop was a food shop, out of which came odours that set my mouth watering anew, and from there we turned left into a narrower lane that smelt of hot iron and scorched hoof-horn. The smithy was set back from the street and its wide thatch stuck out, supported by roughly trimmed tree trunks, so that the animals awaiting attention and the men with them were sheltered from the rain or sun. The space was crowded and the smith with three apprentices were working at full pelt. Old Betsy pushed her way in, leaving Kate to hold the donkey and beckoning to me to follow. When the smith, between jobs, straightened himself, he saw her and said, 'Thass no good, dame. You must wait your turn today. I'm too busy to draw breath.'

'Then I'm doing you a favour. I've brought you my young kinsman, a good smith, in his sixth year. His master died, poor man, and his forge was took over by a man with four sons, so he wouldn't take over the 'prentices.'

'You want I should take him, eh?' asked Armstrong, looking me over with a calculating eye.

'You'd be doing yourself a good turn.'

'In his sixth year. I don't like other men's 'prentices, they ain't trained to my ways. Besides, though I got work, I'm short of room. These three lay all in one bed as it is.'

'He'd find his own bed. He's married.'

'What! In his sixth year! Scandalous.'

'Thass different in Norfolk where he come from. They ain't so hard-hearted; they make allowances for human nature.'

'Let's see your work,' Armstrong said, speaking to me for the first time. 'Clap a shoe on this nag.'

My hands were less steady, my movements less sure than usual, because so much depended upon how I showed, but I did the best job I could.

'Passable,' Armstrong said, without enthusiasm, when I had done.

'Well, do you take him, or don't you?' Old Betsy asked shrilly. 'We can't stand about all day, waiting on you.'

'Tell you what I'll do,' the smith said, narrowing his eyes. 'I'll take him, but not as a six year man. He go back to five; that'll give me a chance to undo the bad ways he've learned in Norfolk where everything is so different. He find his own bed, I give him his dinner and his dole at Christmas and Whitsun. Are you agreed?'

'Thass for him to say,' Betsy said. She looked at me and managed to convey, without a word, that in her opinion I should be wise to accept the offer since one in my position was not likely to get a better.

'I agree,' I said, 'and I thank you.'

'Well you may,' Armstrong said. 'And all here will witness the agreement.'

All the men within hearing nodded and said, 'Aye, aye.'

'Start right in, then. How're you called?'

Mindful that I might even yet, even at this distance, be hunted, I renamed myself there and then.

'Martin, sir,' I said.

I know now that amongst sailors there is a superstition that it is unlucky to change the name of a ship. Perhaps it does a man no good either.

VI

So I was established and had a footing, however humble, in the town, and could not be driven out as a vagrant, and Kate found work the next day in a bake-house in Cooks Lane. The work was hard and heavy, the wages very small, but – and this meant much to us – she was allowed to bring away, at the end of her day's toil, a good quantity of unsaleable stale bread.

We started off our life in Baildon, in a lodging about which one of my fellow-apprentices told me, saying it was a cheap place. It was in a loft over a stable and contained six straw-stuffed pallets laid close together on the floor and a cooking stone under a hole in the roof. There was a trough in the yard below. The beds, at that time of the year, when people were on the move, were always occupied by travellers of the poorer sort, tinkers, drovers, tumblers and bear leaders, and by the humble pilgrims to St Egbert's shrine in the Abbey. The loft had a stench of its own, a mingling of the stable smell from below, of years of careless cooking on the greasy hearth, of sweat and foul breath and human excrement; Kate and I found this irksome, for though neither of us had been bred to be fastidious, we were used to fresh country air, and to stinks so accustomed as to be un-noticed. In this lodging place the stink changed from night to night and always, it seemed, for the worse. Still, it was a shelter, the cheapest one available, and had I been earning only a little, we should have stayed there. As it was, what Kate earned just sufficed to feed us, and week by week I had to pay the rent out of my small store of money. I was ignorant of town life and had imagined that I might earn a coin or two by doing odd smith jobs for people, as Father and I had done in and around Rede: two things defeated that hope. For one thing Armstrong was a hard master and we apprentices often worked far into the night; after the horses had all been shod and taken home we worked by fire and candle-light on plough-shares and harrows, and chains, and spits and iron sconces. The other thing was that in towns all labour was organized into Guilds, which were communities of craftsmen, governed by strict laws, all of them aimed at upholding a monopoly. An apprentice to the smith's craft, for instance, was forbidden to work for hire outside the place where he was apprenticed. If he did so he would be punished, and worse yet, it would count against him when, his apprenticeship completed, he applied for journeyman status and admission to the Guild. The person who employed him would also be in trouble, since every Guildman in the district would be against him, refuse perhaps to do the most urgent job for him for a period varying from a month to six, and, if the man himself were a Guildsman of another craft, his own members would regard him as a traitor. There were some forms of work which I would have been allowed to do: I might, for instance, have helped to drive cattle to market, or dig somebody's garden, but such jobs must be done in daylight, and I never had a daylight hour to spare. The smithy closed early on Saturdays, and then another rule came into force; every apprentice was bound to go and practise shooting at the butts on Saturday afternoon; so I had only Sunday, when nobody wanted cattle driven or gardens dug.

I had not been in Baildon long before I saw that I had exchanged one servitude for another; in place of my Lord

Bowdegrave I had a trinity of masters, Master Armstrong, the Guild, and money.

One wet October evening a man known as Tom the Juggler came to sleep in the loft. It was Saturday, one of the two market-days, and he was grumbling that the weather had ruined his trade; people were not going to stand in the rain to watch his tricks.

'Another day like this,' he said, 'and I shall be sleeping in Squatters Row.'

'Is that cheaper?' I asked, wondering whether all my inquiries had missed some useful piece of information. He laughed.

'It's free, you fool.'

'Where is it?'

'Down by the Town Ditch. Grant you it stinks, but not worse than this. Only trouble is, the roof leaks.'

'Maybe I could mend it. I'm handy,' I said. He laughed again, as though at some wonderful jest.

Next day, when he took me along to the place he called Squatters Row, I understood his merriment.

It was at the rear of the Abbey, on the side farthest from the market place. It was a street, a good deal wider than any other in Baildon; one side of it was bounded by the Abbey's eastern wall, the other by the backs of houses, some of them slaughter-houses. The street sloped towards the centre and there ran the Town Ditch, the drainings of all the gutters and privies in the town, the blood from the slaughter-houses, the overflow from pigsties. It had, at some time long past, been decently covered in by an arched hood of stone; stretches of the cover still existed, but in the main it had given way. The stench was loathsome, but as Tom the Juggler had said, not much worse than the loft when it was fully occupied.

'But I see no place to live hereabouts,' I said.

'Use your eyes,' he said, and pointed across the ditch to the Abbey wall. It was heavily buttressed, and the buttresses stuck out to within a few feet of the Ditch, making, as it were, compartments with three walls. I looked along and saw that several of these compartments were occupied; most were open to the sky and to the Ditch, some were roofed over by pieces of sacking or sailcloth, supported at the foot on poles.

A sick feeling of defeat squirmed in my belly and when Tom the Juggler laughed I could have hit him.

'The north wind's the sharpest,' he said. 'You want to get the wall between you and it.' I noticed then that he had brought along his pack. He crossed the Ditch at a place where the arch still held and chose his buttress, throwing the pack down.

'There's worse places. If you want to come back say so, and I'll keep you the stall next door.'

It was still raining, but the rain was coming on a wind from the west; I noticed that the tall wall of the Abbey sheltered the ground immediately below it to a distance of some feet. The buttress would keep off the north wind which brought the snow. I could do better than rig a flimsy bit of sailcloth on four posts; I could fix timbers to the wall and the buttress and lay a thatch over. I could make a fourth wall. With what little money I had left I could buy the materials for that work, and enough timber to make a table and two stools, straw and sacking for a mattress. All at once I could see the little hut completed, weatherproof, even snug. And ours alone. After the lack of privacy in the loft that in itself seemed a blessing.

'I shall stay. And I'm very thankful to you.'

'Then your wife can cook my supper,' said Tom the Juggler.

I hurried back to our lodging where Kate was doing some washing and told her I had found a place. I warned her that it was in a foul place and in the open, but that I had plans for it.

'Just so long as we can be alone at night,' she said. So, when the washing was done I led her to the spot and tried to make her see the little hut as I had seen it in my mind.

In our lodging we had been among the poor, now we had joined the destitute. Our permanent neighbours were a one-legged sailor who lived alone, a man who was deaf and dumb, his wife and four children who had not inherited his infirmity, an aged crone, who, when anyone would employ her, acted as midwife and layer out of the dead, and an evil-looking young woman who twice a year was whipped through the streets for harlotry. As well as these, Squatters Row had a drifting population of people who had failed to find, or could not afford to pay for, a bed for the night. As the weather grew worse these grew fewer in number.

Before winter set in I had made a hut, just as I had planned; we had a table and two stools and a mattress stuffed with sweet fresh straw, much better than our louse-ridden bed in the loft, and rough, humble and cold as it was, it was, as Kate said, 'our second house' and it became home to us. That we should be happy in such circumstances and that the meals we ate there – often no more than hunks of four-day-old bread thinly smeared with fat – should seem like feasts to us, may sound strange, but is none the less true. We were young, we had our health, love was still lively and so was hope. If we were lucky, in a year and a day we should be free. In two years I should have served my time and be a journeyman, working for a daily wage. Then things would change. We had a great deal to look forward to. We had another advantage, too, and one which is, I think, sometimes overlooked when people think of living in great poverty; the smallest thing extra, or nicer than usual, was a wonderful treat. I remember Kate coming home with a skip in her step because, there being a shortage of stale bread, her mistress had told her to take a fresh loaf.

'Feel it,' she said, thrusting it into my hand, 'smell it.' To the full fed it would be a rare dainty indeed which could bring such pleasure.

The year and the day, so important to us, passed. On a September Sunday evening we could look at one another and say, we are free. On the Monday Lord Bowdegrave could ride up to the forge where I worked, recognize me for his smith's son and no more lay claim to me than he could to Master Armstrong. Only the serf born can know or guess or even dimly imagine what that moment meant to us.

We were spending the evening as we, and many of our kind, spent all our free time in fair weather – gathering firewood on the fringe of the Common ground. The forest there belonged, like most of the things around Baildon, to the Abbey of St Egbert, and the Abbot granted the townspeople that privilege; any dead wood which could be found within thirty paces of the boundary might be collected and taken away. Kate and I were indefatigable wood-gatherers; often through the past winter our less active or less provident neighbours had come to warm themselves, sometimes to cook by our fire. On this evening we were making two faggots of what we had collected, a large one for my back, a smaller one for Kate's, when she said, 'Thanks to the Virgin, our child will be free-born.'

God forgive me for the way my heart went plummeting down. A first child, indeed any child, should be a wished for, a welcome thing. But I was earning no wage, nor should be for another year. It was Kate's meagre money and the bread she brought home that stood between us and hunger. And I had known all along that the work in the bake-house was heavy, too heavy for her frail body; how long, with another burden within her, could she stay at work? And what would happen when that time was out-run?

There was that side to it; and there was another. It went hard with me to think that our child would be born and live its first year in a makeshift hovel by the brim of the Town Ditch. As month had followed month since our arrival in Baildon, I had hoped that God in His mercy was seeing fit to withhold parenthood from us until we had a home ready for a child.

Now all the cheer that the day had brought me failed and faded. Walking home, bowed under my faggot, I knew the first faltering of hope. I looked into the future and saw, not the neat little house in some more habitable part of the town, but Kate and I and our family condemned to live our lives out in that stinking place of outcasts.

Kate said, 'Don't be angry.' And that made me ashamed, remembering how, on a like occasion, the deaf-and-dumb man had beaten his wife until she was black and blue.

'I'm not angry,' I said. 'How could I be? It takes two to make a baby. But Kate, I am worried.'

'God and St Katherine will take care of us – and the baby,' she said. 'They always have done. We've done very well so far.'

'That is true. But I was looking ahead. You can't stay in the bake-house when…'

'Then something else will turn up,' she said, with the utmost faith. 'You'll see.'

Hating to drag her down into my own state of discouragement, I said no more. I only hitched my load a little more firmly on to my shoulders so that I could spare a hand to ease hers a little, thinking, as I did so, of the flour sacks, the loaves, the firing of the oven which she must manage, with none to help.

VII

Kate must have known about her state for some time before she told me in September, for the baby was born in February. The baker's wife had kept her on until Christmas and then told her not to come back, because it worried her, she said, to see Kate straining herself to do the work.

'Once your belly is out beyond the point of your nose when you stand upright, you should be careful,' the woman said. 'If you don't the child'll come feet first.'

Kate had argued that in the country women worked in the field sometimes until the very day the birth took place.

'Maybe, but I don't have to watch them,' said the baker's wife.

All this Kate told me, making light of it and still saying that when one door shut God opened another. I could see, however, that she was a little dashed that another door had not opened already. And none did, just as I had feared. After Christmas was the worst time of the year to go looking for chance employment, even the markets grew small; there were few travellers and no pilgrims in the inns; housewives were saving their work for the spring. Everything was at a standstill.

Since September we had saved what we could, but it was pitiably little and we were once again on the very verge of starvation when that other door did open.

Ordinarily both Kate and I were out of our hut and away early in the morning, and did not return until late in the evening, so of the ordinary comings and goings of our neighbours we saw very little. Now, doomed to stay at home, Kate noticed that every morning the sailor with the wooden leg and one of the children of the deaf-and-dumb man left Squatters Row together just before midday and came back carrying food. She asked where they had been and was told, 'To the Alms Gate.'

'And the monks give you food? Would they give me some?'

'Brother Stephen would. Brother Justinius would not,' Peg-Leg said. He knew all the rules. He explained the situation to Kate in his own simple words. The monks had plenty to give away. Baildon was a very rich Abbey and had in time past been heavily endowed by wealthy men who had sought favour in the sight of Heaven by remembering the poor in their wills. There had been a time when anyone, needy or not, deserving or not, could present himself at the Alms Gate and be fed; but after the great upheaval of the rebellion in the year when I was born, people in high places had become alarmed at this 'indiscriminate charity' as they called it. They said it encouraged indolence and the habit of drifting from place to place. So a law was passed saying that alms were to be given only to those who were not able-bodied.

This was a law which admitted of varying interpretations. Some monks said that they had no time to waste on making a close physical inspection before handing out a bowl of pease-porridge or a hunk of bread, or would split a hair of logic by arguing that a man in the throes of hunger could not rightly be

43

said to be able-bodied. There were others who accepted the law as it read and made it an excuse for reducing the scope of their charity.

In Baildon, in the main, the law was accepted. Dummy, our deaf-and-dumb neighbour, for instance, could hope for nothing at the Alms Gate; he was able-bodied, that is, sound of wind and limb. Peg-Leg, on the other hand, was accepted as a responsibility, and so was Dummy's child because she had been knocked down by a bullock running wild from the shambles and she had grown crooked.

A woman like Kate was a debatable case, and, as Peg-Leg said, it all depended upon which of the two almsgiving monks threw up the hatch in the Alms Gate which lay just beyond the Bell Tower. Brother Justinius argued that pregnancy was a natural state and that a woman heavy with child was in no sense disabled; Brother Stephen on the other hand, counted heaviness of body and shortness of breath as a disability.

'There you are,' Kate said to me, after learning all this from Peg-Leg. 'I told you we should be cared for.'

She joined the miserable little crowd at the Alms Gate and came away empty-handed or happy according to which monk was on duty that day. Brother Stephen even carried matters so far as now and then to dole her out a double portion, saying, 'You must eat for two.'

I invented a tale that Master Armstrong had taken pity on me and offered me a breakfast piece in addition to my dinner. This meant that I went to work every day with an empty belly. In fact the dinners which our master provided were as scanty as he dared make them, and the weather being very cold and wet, I grew thin and low-spirited. Those who have never hungered think little of food, those who are hungry think of little else. I confess that there were many times between Christmas and the birth of my first son when I would have exchanged even my freedom to be back in the hut behind the smithy at Rede, with the fat pork cooking in the pot. I had to find another, a longer way home. Cooks Lane, the shorter way, was so full of mouth-watering smells; and then I would be home and Kate would have something left from her dole if it had been a good day with Brother Stephen at the hatch, and she would offer it to me and I could feel the wolf look come into my eyes.

However, the child was born, whole and sound. The old woman who was our neighbour – her name was Agnes – came and gave her assistance. And hardly was the baby born – it was a boy – before the old woman said, 'There, my dear, you've a fine lad and now you can claim your Trimble.'

It was so early in the morning that I was still there, and I asked, 'Her what?'

'Her Trimble,' said Agnes. 'God bless my soul. Where were you reared never to have heard of that saint among women, Dame Trimble?'

'Let me hear now,' I said.

So, what time she bound the belly-band firmly about my son's raw navel, she told me about Dame Trimble as the story had been handed down a hundred years or more. A young girl, one of a large family reared in dire poverty, had gone to work for an old wool chandler, who married her and soon afterwards had died, leaving her well-to-do. She had no children of her own, but was all too well aware of the hardship which childbirth means to poor women. She was shrewd, too, and dealt wisely with the fortune she had been left, so that she died rich. She had founded a charity, now known familiarly as 'The Trimble' by which any poor woman in Baildon – poor meaning any woman whose husband was not a full journeyman or its equivalent – could claim, upon the birth of any child, meat, bread and ale for forty days following, a woollen gown, a hood and a pair of shoes.

'Dummy's wife is still wearing the one she got with her first,' old Agnes said, 'she sold the others. There's a good market for such. And the food and drink are good too, very generous, enough for the woman, and her man, and a bit over for the midwife if the family ain't too large, as in this case.'

'Who hands it out?'

'The monks. At the Alms Gate. One of the parents has to take the child and show it. It's the father's job, though I've known mothers to crawl out on the second day, them with no men to rely on. Dame Trimble made no difference, she didn't even say *respectable* women.'

So, on the next day, I had to forgo my dinner and run home and take the child to the Alms Gate. I felt silly and sheepish, expecting to be the butt for jeers, standing there with a baby in my arms; instead I found myself an object of envy. And well I might be. Brother Justinius was doling out the usual pease-porridge and bread, but at the sight of me he called out to someone behind him and bade me wait a little. Kate's Trimble, when it came, was food for a family, more food and better than I had seen at one time since I left Rede.

'The gown,' Brother Justinius said, 'according to the rules, must be of the woman's own choosing, and the shoes made to her measure. So they must wait. By what name is the child to be baptized?'

'Stephen,' I said clearly. Kate had chosen the name, long ago, because Brother Stephen had been kind to her.

'These Norman names, how fashionable they grow,' said Brother Justinius, with something sour in his voice.

I put on my most stupid, dull-witted look and said, 'Norman is it? We thought it came from the Bible.'

He gave me a sharp look. 'It is to be hoped that you are not tainted with Lollardry, to be for ever referring to Master Wycliffe's Bible.'

'Master Wyciffe? I do not know him. Is he a Baildon man?'

'Oh, get along with you,' Brother Justinius said crossly, and slammed down the hatch.

I hurried home to Kate with all the good food, and a little tale to make her laugh.

Dame Trimble's sweet charity carried us bravely through the next weeks; there was enough for Kate and me, and most often

Old Agnes as well. Kate got back her strength and I gained some flesh. The baby throve surprisingly, and although he had been born a full year before my plans made me ready to welcome him, now that he was here I loved him very dearly.

April brought in the softer weather, with its one disadvantage to us who dwelt in Squatters Row: when the gutters of the upper town ran freely, the Town Ditch often brimmed over until its stinking waters lapped our doors. Still, summer was coming in, and by the first week in September I should have served my overlong apprenticeship and be earning. Hope stirred once more.

The town itself was growing; every market-day brought more people. A ship-owner from Bywater came inland and began to build a fine new house which employed a number of masons and carpenters. Master Webster, the chief wool merchant in the town, bought a new string of pack ponies. At the forge we were very busy. But when, at the end of six weeks, Kate began looking for work, she found it hard to come by. One reason was that she refused to leave Stephen in the charge of Dummy's wife who had offered to look after him with her own, for twopence a week.

'I know her looking after,' Kate said. 'One of hers has been run down by a bullock, and one drowned in the Ditch. Stephen goes with me.'

By that time I was beginning to be anxious again.

'If she had twopence a week for minding him it would be to her own interest to keep him out of the Ditch. In any case it might be as well to leave him while you hunt for work, even if later, having proved your value, you took him with you.'

Nothing however would persuade Kate from her course; she was sure the right job would turn up. And in mid-May she found work as a picker in Master Webster's woolsheds.

The fleeces were cut off the sheep in the spring and bundled up just as they were and brought into Baildon. Master Webster paid a price which took into account a certain amount of rubbish, burrs, caked dung, leaves, bits of stick and mud. The bigger merchants – many of them overseas in Flanders – paid so much a pound for clean wool, so the fleeces had to be picked over carefully. The picker knelt or squatted as she worked her way through the wool, and the unchanging position became tiring. The oil and odour of the fleeces saturated her clothes, her hair, her flesh even. Kate bore it cheerfully, saying that she was used to the smell of sheep, and that Master Webster had been kind about letting her take Stephen. When he could crawl, she pointed out, the woolshed would be a far safer place for him than the bakehouse would have been.

Alas, before Stephen could crawl, Kate was with child again. This time she was dismayed.

'There'll be only eleven months between them. If Stephen isn't walking I shall have to carry them both to work.'

'But I shall be earning,' I told her.

She smiled as though it hurt her.

'I know. But there will be four to feed then.'

She had carried Stephen cheerfully and willingly and never ailed much. This was different. She was sick, and miserable. I was little comfort. To me there was something wrong, almost obscene, about this begetting without being able to support. I was ashamed, and that made me peevish. It was at this time that something went out of our hut, something which had made it, despite its squalor, a happy home. Kate and I now seemed to take an unholy pleasure in making sharp remarks to one another. One day, when she was complaining, I said, 'I warned you, didn't I. You would have been better off at Abhurst.'

She swung round on me like a swordsman.

'You mean you'd have been better off as an unmarried apprentice, with your feet under somebody else's table.'

The weapon to wound was there, at my hand, and I seized it.

'If it comes to that, I *am* an unmarried apprentice,' I said.

Kate shot me a glance of hatred and then began to cry.

'That's right. Throw that in my face!'

We had never been married. We had arrived in Baildon as man and wife and never dared risk drawing attention to ourselves by offering ourselves to be wed. There was that question, ordinarily so harmless, to us so dangerous, 'Of what parish?' It would have been easy to lie, but Holy Church has a long arm. It might have occurred to the priest to make inquiries whether these unknown people were free to marry, and that would have been disastrous. Sailing under false colours we had come into Baildon, voiced for by Old Betsy, and under those same false colours we must go on.

Now, sobbing bitterly, Kate poured out all her hidden shame and doubts. No wonder, she said, everything went wrong with us, living in mortal sin, as we were. And if she died in childhood, as well she might, she would go straight to Hell as a wanton. She went so far as to ask whether being born free could make up to Stephen and the child that was coming for their bastardy.

Her distress distressed me. I said I was sorry for having spoken as I had, and we kissed and made up. But every quarrel – of which this was but a sample – took something from us which no reconciliation could fully restore. I understood, during the next few months, what makes men go and drink themselves silly in the ale-house. I should have done so, many a night, had I had any money.

VIII

The day dawned that brought the end of my apprenticeship. Nothing had been said overnight, but I had not expected any sign, for during my two years at Armstrong's I had seen an apprentice become a journeyman. (Journeyman does not mean a man who journeys to his work; it means a man who works by the day, *jour* being the Norman for day.)

It was one of those enchanted days of late summer touched by the first breath of autumn, golden and blue and heavily dewed, as I set out for work, carrying Stephen, as I had done for some weeks, and walking round by Master Webster's woolsheds. Even Kate was more cheerful this morning.

I went, as soon as I reached the smithy, to the nail where my apron usually hung. It was not there. I pretended great surprise and anxiety. Then the others gathered round me, chanting,

> 'He's grown too big for his *apron*
> He'll have to get another one.'

The reply to this sally varied with the nature and wit of the new journeyman. I said, 'How can I get another? I've earned nothing yet!' and that was well received, with more laughter.

I then went to take up my tools. They too were gone and again I pretended concern. They gathered round me,

> 'He worked so hard for a dinner a day
> He wore his hammer clean away!'

The next remark was prescribed. I must turn round and cry in mock dismay, 'What shall I do?'

Then they all bellowed, 'Become a journeyman!'

After that there was a moment or two of jollity, with good wishes and drinking, turn and turn about, from a jar of ale, which, according to rule, should be provided by the senior workman present. It was an understood thing that on such a morning, the master should allow ten minutes for the little ritual. On this morning my apron and tools were returned to me, and I was, at last, a journeyman of the Smith Guild in Baildon town.

Presently Master Armstrong arrived, stood by my shoulder while I finished a job and then said, 'Step across the road with me. I've something to say to you.'

The 'Smith's Arms' stood directly across the road from the forge; we took a seat on the bench and Master Armstrong called for ale. This, I thought, was another stage in the process of being recognized as a journeyman. When the ale came I expected him to speak some words of salutation, but instead he took a deep draught and then wiped his mouth on the back of his hand.

'You ain't going to like this, Martin,' he said. 'But thass no good blaming me, nor nobody. Rules is rules and they hev to be kept. Last Guild meeting I brung up your name and said you'd done your time and was a handy skilled worker; but they ain't taking you.'

The cobbled lane, the forge opposite with its smoky red fire and the haunches of the waiting horses and donkeys began to rock and swing before my eyes, slowly at first and then faster, until all I could see was a blur. I realized that my eyes had filled with tears; I was about to cry, like a child. My throat ached and felt wooden. I lifted my mug and took a tiny sip and swallowing it eased me so that I was able to say, 'In God's name, why, master?'

'You worn't born here. And do you go back where you come from, you'll fare no better. There they'll hold agin you that you didn't do your full time there. See?'

At that moment it seemed like a cruel blow aimed at me personally by malignant fate. Later on I understood better and knew that I was but one of many men of all crafts who were, in the towns, superfluous to requirements. All through my lifetime, ever since the great rising of 1381, on all but the most old-fashioned manors the serfs had been buying themselves free and had thus been at liberty to apprentice their sons how they would. So every year more apprentices qualified to become craftsmen than old craftsmen died or retired, and those safely inside a Guild were casting around for excuses to keep the young men out. Often the excuse was flimsy, invented. In my case there was no need. I was a 'foreigner'; my exclusion needed no cunning twist and would cause no searching of conscience on anyone's part.

'What's to become of me then?' I asked.

'Ah,' Armstrong said. 'Thass the question. But I got the answer. I'm sorry for you, Martin, and I'm making you this offer outa goodness of heart. You mind that. I brung this up at the

Guild meeting too, and they was all agreed. You can't be a full journeyman, nor claim the rate laid down for such. But you can go on as a *paid* apprentice, see? They looked up the rules, laid down in past years when there was a shortage of apprentices. They was paid then, anything between quarter and half the standard rate; and you being a handy sort of chap, I'd give you half.'

I looked at him, and quickly away, lest he should see the loathing in my eyes. I'd had, from eating at his table and a hundred other little things, evidence of his meanness and cunning. Pretending to do me a favour he had prolonged my apprenticeship for a year. Now, pretending to do me another, he was getting a skilled, finished workman at half rate.

But I had no choice. Half pay was better than no wage at all. I said humbly, 'Thank you very much.'

He jumped up quickly and said, 'Let's to work then.'

All that day, added to my own bitter disappointment, was the dread of the moment when I must tell Kate. She did not, however, weep, or rail against Armstrong and the Guild; only the deepening of the lines in her face, the increased droop of her mouth, betrayed how shrewd the blow had been. I had dreaded her tears, and yet now, perversely enough, I wished she had cried. I might then have been moved to take her in my arms and comfort her. Once in a hard winter I saw a tree entirely encased in a coating of ice. Our poverty and our worries and our defeated hopes were putting a similar casing around our souls. Soon we should have lost even the memory of love, and be dull, plodding work animals, no more.

Kate had said, miserably, that there would be but eleven months difference in the age of our children; in fact there was less than that, for Robin came into the world a little before time, a small, ailing baby, unlike Stephen. When I carried my second son to the Alms Gate I was the subject of coarse jests about being such a quick worker. 'Do you get any faster,' one man said, 'you can knock off work and live on your Trimble.'

This time Kate sold her woollen gown and the hood. Since her place in the woolshed had not been filled, she dragged herself back to work at the end of a week, frail as she was.

'That way we shall get something in hand,' she said fiercely. 'We can save my wage so long as the Trimble lasts. With two to feed – and God knows how many more on the way…'

'There'll be no more, Kate.' That was a promise which would cost me nothing to keep. I was not like my neighbour Dummy who could go through the performance which ended with a baby feeling nothing for the woman he bedded with. Yet, though our joy in one another had been lost, somewhere between Stephen's birth and Robin's, we were still a unit, we two against the world, as helpful to one another as we could be, a good wife, a good husband, good parents so far as our means allowed. Kate still washed and mended and cooked. I mended the roof and hunted for firewood, and every morning and evening I went to the woolshed so that I could carry the heavier child.

On one cold March evening, miserable with falling sleet, I found Kate awaiting me at the gate, with something of liveliness back in her face again. When I went to lift Stephen she stopped me, laying a hand on my arm.

'The ponies from Bywater have just come in,' she said, 'and without Old John. He dropped dead on the road. If you went to Master Webster now you might get the job.'

It was a sensible suggestion; and Kate knew that ever since September I had longed for a chance to leave Armstrong; for I held in my mind the certainty that if he had stood up for me strongly enough, saying that he *needed* me as a journeyman, his word would have carried weight, even against the rules. Yet pride is a curious thing and will pop up in the unlikeliest places.

'But I'm a skilled smith,' I said, without thinking. Those few words said it all. I'd strained and sweated, and waited and almost starved in order to be a smith, not a pack-whacker to a pony train.

'On half pay,' Kate said.

I knew the need to defend myself. 'Should I earn much more, if anything? Pack-whacking is an unskilled job; anybody can do it and that sort of job comes cheap.'

'They get about. They pick up things. They do errands for people along the road and get gifts that way. I've seen Old John come in with food for a week.' She tightened her arms about Robin and braced herself to move.

'If it's beneath you to care whether we eat or not...' she began sourly.

'I'll do it. Where shall I find him?'

'In his office. Through the yard, there, to the right, where the light is.'

'You take the baby home,' I said, 'I'll bring Stephen.' He could by this time walk a little, and holding his hand I went into the wool yard and knocked on the door.

The room inside served as office and living room, was well lighted and warm. Tally sticks stood in every corner. Master Webster stood by an open cupboard on whose shelves lay samples of wool.

'Well?' he said.

'I'm told that one of your pack-whackers is dead. I wondered if you would give me his job.'

He pinched his upper lip between his finger and thumb, pulled it out and let it go again.

'You're a foreigner. I'd sooner hev a man that knew the roads.'

'I could learn my way about, master,' I said, humbly.

'Wasting *my* time meanwhile. You're the smith they wouldn't let into the Guild, ain't you?'

I nodded, gritting my teeth together, for I saw in this the beginning of a hard bargain. The man nobody wanted.

'Pack ponies are hard on their shoes,' he said. 'Now *suppose* I rigged up a forge, right here in the yard. Could you shoe the ponies as well as drive 'em?'

'Of course I could.'

'It'd hev to be done on the quiet. Now and agin I'd hev to send a beast to Armstrong or Smithson, and if they queried why my trade dropped off, thass easy explained, ain't it? Pony's likely to cast a shoe anywhere.'

'That is so,' I said.

'Mark you,' he said, 'I'm doing you a favour. Making a job for you, you might say.'

'I'm truly grateful.'

'So you should be. Now, as to wages...'

I saw his fingers working as he reckoned. They tapped out a sum which was fourpence more than I was earning at Armstrong's. With a gallon loaf costing a penny it was an increase worth considering; and I bore in mind Kate's words about a pack-whacker's chances to earn a little extra here and there. So I sold myself into another bondage for an extra fourpence a week.

IX

Within a week I was well aware of the advantages in my new job. For a trained craftsman, who had mastered his trade and passed his apprenticeship, to become a mere driver of pack ponies was a comedown, but it had its compensations. As Kate had said, we got into the country and it was in the country that food was plentiful and cheap.

When I joined Master Webster's teamsters it was winter and we were not collecting the dirty fleeces from farms and sheep runs, we were carrying the picked-over wool down to Bywater.

Bywater was a small port, much smaller, we understood, than Dunwich or Yarmouth, but it had obtained, during the reign of the great King Edward the Third, one priceless privilege. It was allowed to export a certain amount of wool, in defiance of all the rules governing the Staple. This was because at some critical moment during the King's wars with France, this small town's fishing fleet had chanced to be in harbour, and had been able to offer the King eighteen vessels for the transport of troops to France, shortly before the great battle of Crécy. The privilege of being able to export wool freely was its reward.

The Bywater people often laughed and joked about the privilege, saying that when King Edward granted them the favour, the limit he had set on their export had been far in excess of all the wool shorn in East Anglia, for Norfolk and Suffolk were not then reckoned to be sheep-rearing districts. The favour was, they said, 'like giving a one-legged man permission to dance a jig'. But things had changed since then; sheep runs had been established on many a ploughland and in my time Bywater exported every bale of wool the licence allowed.

Ships that set sail laden with wool returned with other commodities, and there were goods to be found in Bywater that could be obtained nowhere nearer than London. On the very first journey I made to Bywater we were stopped by an innkeeper at Nettleton. His little daughter was ill and he wanted an orange for her. She had once eaten an orange and all through her fever had craved another. I was lucky and found four and when I delivered them into his hands on the return he almost wept with gratitude. He took me and my fellow-driver, a lively little hunchback called Crooky, into his house and gave us each a mug of his best October ale. Then he asked which would we rather have, sixpence apiece or our pick out of his store-room. Crooky, who had no family and was a drinking man, chose the sixpence. I went to the store-room and stared about at more stacked-up food than I had ever seen in my life.

'You mean I can have anything?'

'Anything you can carry. Could you have seen the little wench's face when I put the thing into her hands! Take what you like and call me still your debtor.'

I chose a great ham, which, sliced into pieces by any of the keen knives in Cooks Lane and sold piecemeal, would have been worth four shillings.

'And I'd sooner give you that,' said the innkeeper, when I had made my choice, 'than the sixpence yon fellow took. The pig it came off fed on the scrapings of the plates, and drunk the wash-up water, and the smoking was done by the fire that we cook on. So it cost me nowt.'

That was my first experience as a doer of errands. Others followed. Not all the people we obliged were so deeply grateful and wildly generous, but I always remembered a farmer's wife who had broken her needle. She lived a long way from the road we travelled and had twice walked the five miles and stood a whole morning in the biting wind to catch us on our way down to Bywater. She gave us the errand, and the money for two needles and asked us when we should be returning. We told her, and when we came clattering along, the unladen ponies trotting and thinking of their own stable, there she was, with two grey geese on long leads of plaited rushes.

She said, in a shamefaced way, 'Would you take these in payment? The needles had to be paid for in coin, and I have no more, nor shall till the calves are sold. But they're good geese, right fat.'

'A goose, for carrying a needle!' I said, in astonishment. 'Payment enough and over.'

'But I can't walk to Bywater – the calves would starve; nor I can't sew with a goose, and my poor man's hose all agape. I'm much obliged to you both. Besides,' she said, grinning, gap-toothed, 'the geese cost nowt. Gander do his work for pleasure, goose lay the eggs. All summer they keep the grass down so I can walk dry-foot to tend the calves. Whass to a goose?'

I could have told her. To a goose there were some feathers to add to the collection in order, one day, to have a feather pillow. Then there was a fine hot savoury meal, and fat to spread on our bread on many a cold morning; and bones to boil, with an onion or two, into a heartening broth.

Oh, and there was more to it than that. There was me saying to Kate, 'You were right. Snatching at Old John's job was the best thing I've done so far.'

And there was Kate, with some of the worry eased out of her face, smiling at me with some of the old sweetness.

To the poor so little means so much.

When the sheep shearing time began and we started making journeys to outlying farms and sheep runs to bring in the fleeces there were more errands and more rewards. Now, with both of us in employment and a good deal of our food costing nothing, we began to lay aside a penny here and there, in the renewed hope of being able to hire a house somewhere far from Squatters Row.

There seemed no real reason why the secret of the work I was doing for Master Webster in addition to my pack-whacking should ever have been discovered. He was a very cunning man. He knew that the other drivers would soon notice if, bringing in a horse with a loose shoe or an unshod hoof overnight, they found it wearing a bright new shoe in the morning. So he made a new rule: the teams were to be driven in rotation. In this way, in the course of a few days, I went out with each team, and on our return to the stable, would take careful note of the state of the hoofs of the ponies with which I had made that journey. Crooky was well known to be unobservant and unheeding; he would leave a pony with a strained fetlock, or a sore back, and walk straight away to his drinking. I always walked away just as light-heartedly, but, when there was a job to be done, I went back, late at night, was admitted by Master Webster and went to work in the forge which he had set up in a little shed to which only I had the key. Every now and then, just to avert suspicion, a pony would be sent for shoeing to Armstrong or Smithson.

So, for six months Master Webster saved himself money and all was well.

One night, late in September, I had been working and was on my way home when I turned a corner and ran into a man who was lolling there by the wall. He reeled and had so much difficulty in recovering himself that I judged him to be drunk and clutched at him, steadying him with my hands. His hands clutched at mine, and at the same time he fell against me, his face buried in the shoulder of my jerkin.

I said, 'Hold up, man,' or some such words and he pulled himself straight, let go of my hands and lurched off.

I thought no more about him until, four or five days later when I came in with a load of fleeces from Clevely and reached home, I found Master Armstrong sitting on one of our stools.

'I wanted to see you, Martin,' he said. 'Your wife said you might be back today, so I thought I'd wait a bit.'

Kate turned from the hearth where she was cooking supper and over his shoulder made a face at me.

'Master Armstrong came yesterday and waited a long time,' she said.

I had a wild hope that perhaps in the last six months he had missed me, had persuaded the Guild to admit me, or, next best thing, was now willing to re-engage me at full journeyman's wage and be hanged to the Guild.

'What is it, master?' I asked.

'Thass this,' he said. 'You're doing Webster's smith work; and thass agin all the rules.'

'Why should you say that?' I put on an astonished face.

'Now don't play no fool's game with me. We know. Smithson's first man, Nobby, ran into you the other night. Your hands was black, he'd washed his, but he gripped yours and blacked his, see? And you reeked of the forge.'

'I did indeed, after he'd reeled against me, and so would any man. As for my hands – I'd just helped to unload twelve ponies, three hundred pounds of filthy fleeces apiece, marked with tar some of them.'

Armstrong grinned. 'You're a sharp one. Then how do you explain *this*? Ever since March, when you took up with Webster, that look like his ponies don't wear out their shoes. I noticed, Smithson noticed, but it worn't till we put our heads together we knew we'd *both* been done. I reckoned he was doing the jobs, he reckoned I was.'

'Ponies don't mind where they cast a shoe,' I said. 'And you can't run a pack pony on three legs. We have to get work done at the nearest forge.'

'That seem a rare rum thing that only this summer them ponies cast shoes so far afield so often. Me and Smithson, we still got our memories, mark you. 'Twasn't this way last summer, nor the one afore. Where's the difference? The difference is that Webster hev now got, working for him, the rascal I took and trained out of goodness of heart and is now plying the trade I taught him to do honest men out of work.'

That, in a way, I could deny. I wasn't doing it to spite honest men. I was doing it to keep myself alive. So I said, 'That is not true, master.'

'Thass true. And you know it. And now I'm giving you fair warning. There's ways of dealing with fellows who run agin the rules. Either you stop doing Webster's smith work, or we'll find a way to make you.' He stood up and stamped out of our hut.

Kate pulled the pot to the side of the hearth and came and gripped my arm.

'Oh Martin, what will they do?'

'Tackle Webster. He's a Guildsman too. He'll be savage at having to give up his fine penny-saving scheme and sack me. He never wanted to employ me anyway. He called me a foreigner.'

'We never make any headway,' Kate said drearily. 'Every time we do a bit better and begin to hope, something happens.'

Next morning, as soon as Master Webster appeared in the yard I told him of Armstrong's visit and threat.

'Did you admit doing the work?'

'I denied it, but he is sure none the less.'

'Then his case stands on the word of a drunken apprentice who ran into someone in the dark. And that against mine, mark you. We'll take no notice. The next pony to need a shoe shall go to

Smithson and that will keep him from siding too hearty with Armstrong. For the rest we'll go on as we were. It suits me well.'

'It suits me. But Master Armstrong said there were ways of dealing with those who went against the rules.'

'He said truly. But they must first prove that I'm breaking a rule. And of that I'm not so sure. I never seen any rule saying a man may not employ his private smith if he wants. I ain't flaunting the business, as you well know, there's nowt to be gained by falling out with your fellows. But first they must prove thass agin the rules. And all that will take time. We'll go as we were.'

By mid-October all that year's fleeces were in and our journeys to outlying places ceased. From then on, until winter weather closed the road, we carried the picked-over wool to Bywater, Lavenham and Melford.

On our outward journeys, when the ponies were loaded, we never travelled after dusk. Wool was valuable and there was always the risk that the pony train might be set upon by rogues who could easily find, in any port, some ship's captain who was not too nice in his inquiries as to where the wool came from and whose it was. Our summer journeys were different: the raw dirty fleeces were not so immediately marketable, and to pick them over demanded some settled headquarters, which robbers lacked. In summer we often moved loads at night but in the winter we only travelled after dark when the ponies were unladen and we were making for home.

Crooky and I were doing that, rattling along at a good pace, coming back from Bywater one November night. He rode the first pony, I the last, and we were urging the string along because there was fog about. We rode easily, having nothing of value to care for; our one concern was to get back home as soon as possible.

We reached a place where a narrow bridge spanned the river, some five miles out of Baildon. It was the same river which ran through Baildon and turned the Abbey mill at Flaxham St Giles.

Once we were over the bridge the river ran alongside the road on our left hand and for us the bridge had become a landmark. Many a time Crooky and I, crossing it, had shouted to one another, 'Nearly home!'

This evening, Crooky, riding ahead of me, shouted back, 'Nearly home!'

'God be thanked,' I shouted back. I heard his ponies' hoofs sound hollow over the bridge, and the next and the next...I was almost on the bridge myself when something dropped in front of my face; it fell to my waist and there pulled tight and jerked me off the back of the pony, which kept up its trot. I shouted, 'Crooky! Crooky!' but he didn't hear, or took no notice. And as I fell over the pony's tail and hit the road, blows began to shower down on me. The rope which had lassooed me held my arms fast, I was utterly defenceless. I remember thinking that this was how they dealt with those who went against the rules. Then somebody hit me on the leg, causing such sharp agony that I cried aloud. Another blow fell on my head and the pain ceased.

When it began again I thought I was back at Rede. It was like waking from a dream, all about running away and trying to make a life in a place called Baildon, and having two children and a makeshift hut in Squatters Row. I was Walter, the smith's son, who had hit his lord in the face and must get away sharply if he wished to live. I tried to raise myself and a quiet voice said, 'You must lie still or you will undo my work.'

I opened my eyes then and saw, not the dung-heap in Rede yard, but a smooth white-washed wall. Yet there was a connection with Rede – that same thirst which had sent me staggering to the bucket in our forge.

'I'm thirsty,' I moaned.

'A good sign,' said the quiet voice. And in a moment my head was lifted a little and the cool hard rim of a mug touched my lips. Beyond it, hanging in space it seemed, above me, was an old man's face, pink fleshed, deeply wrinkled, with faded blue eyes, the whole enclosed in a monk's cowl.

'Brother...brother...' I said in a fumbling way.

'Sebastian,' he said. 'I am the Infirmarian. You are safe and not much hurt except that your leg is broken.'

He lowered my head and I lay still, thinking, my leg is broken. Broken bones will knot themselves together, but like a thread which has been tied they are shortened. I thought that. Then I remembered that what I had just lately thought to be a dream was real enough. I lived in Baildon, had a wife and two children, and had found it hard to make a living when I was whole and well. Henceforth I should be a cripple, a beggar.

'It had better been my neck,' I said.

'And who are you to be giving orders to God?' asked Brother Sebastian, in a humorously rebuking voice. 'You should lie there and be thankful. You could have lain in the road until you died, but for a mule's cast shoe. Brother Bartholomew was collecting the Nettleton rents and should have been home before Vespers, but he was delayed. So he found you. And here you are in experienced hands. I mended the leg of a lay brother who fell from a ladder two years since and a bad job I made of it. But I know where I went wrong and with you I have made good my error. Poor Edgar's set like a dog's back leg, but on yours I have tried a new trick. A broomstick, tied firmly in three places. Aha, that wayward leg may think to set all crooked, but governed by that broomstick it shall be.'

'I am thankful,' I said. Then I thought for a moment and asked, 'Is it Thursday still?'

'No. The bell for Matins sounded half an hour ago. It is Friday.'

'I have a wife. She expected me back for supper on Thursday. She will be worried.'

'She knows. Brother Stephen recognized you and a message was sent. So calm yourself; lie still and be thankful and let your wounds heal.'

Lie still, perforce, I must, but I was neither calm nor thankful. Brother Sebastian, along with his tender, careful ministrations to my body, tried to minister to my soul. He spoke often of faith in God, of the will of God, of the beauty and virtue of unquestioning acceptance. I listened with my ears, while my mind went its own way; it was all very well for him, who had never had to grapple with the world, who if he hungered did it voluntarily and would be rewarded for his abstinence in Heaven. He could look down along the years – those few that remained to him – and see his life, peaceful, neatly ordered by the ringing of bells, pottering along until he died. I lay there, a young man yet, a man with a wife and two children, and saw myself limping and starving through the years.

Brother Sebastian and every other monk who came in contact with me showed me kindness. Brother Stephen sent frequent messages, and alms sometimes, to Kate, and every time she sent back word that all was well. My most urgent question – Is Master Webster holding my job open for me? – was either never asked, or never answered, or the answer suppressed.

'Time enough to fret about work when you are fitted to do it,' Brother Sebastian would say.

Despite my fretting, my flesh wounds healed and my broken bone knitted. The day came when Brother Sebastian removed the broomstick and having allowed two more days for the limb to strengthen, helped me to stand up and test the virtue of his new experiment. Up to a point it was good. My leg was straight enough, but it had set quite stiff and about two inches shorter than the other. I walked, if anything, more clumsily and painfully than Peg-Leg.

The straightness was all Brother Sebastian cared about. Fingering my shin gloatingly he said, 'Thanks be to God who brought the broomstick to my mind. The stiffness will wear off with use, you will find. And I will myself make the shortness of that leg the subject of a Novena.'

'Do you hope for a miracle?'

'Why not? I shall pray, and so must you, and you must have *faith*. Many much lamer than you have been restored at St Egbert's shrine.'

That, I knew, was true. The wealth and fame of Baildon Abbey was rooted in the miraculous reputation of the saint; I knew his story by this time. In life he had been King of a tiny kingdom, part in Suffolk and part in Essex. This was in time long past, before one king ruled all England, in the dim ages, before the Normans came. Egbert's enemies had been the Danes, wild heathen men who had come to rob and burn and rape in that part of England that lay along the sea. In one of his battles Egbert had been captured; but he had been so doughty and valiant a foe that the Danes' leader had offered to make an ally of him, give him high rank in their order, provided he would abandon the Christian faith and worship the heathen gods. He had refused and been killed. The monks of Baildon – then a small, poor wooden convent – had sought for his body and buried it in their tiny church; and then the miracles had begun. Then had come the pilgrims in search of further miracles, and the gifts poured in. The miracles could hardly be disputed. During my three years in Baildon there had been several; a young girl had been led to the shrine, jerking and twitching in the throes of St Vitus' Dance, and walked away in full control of her limbs; a man set fast in all his joints, just able to put one foot before the other, leaning on two sticks, had hobbled into the Abbey church and walked out, firm and upright, leaving his sticks laid across one another in the form of a cross at the spot where he had prayed and been healed. There were others, all well vouched for. But – and this was what stuck in my mind – both my afflicted neighbours, the deaf-and-dumb man and the man with one leg, had, in their time, asked a miracle and come empty away. And it seemed to me that Peg-Leg, at least, had asked the impossible. Had he really expected a brand new leg to grow out of his stump. And how – all at once, or inch by inch? And had their failure been due to lack of faith in themselves?

I was not pondering these questions for the first time. I had often thought about them while I was working. I had come to the conclusion – which may be a blasphemous one – that St Egbert's miracles acted, not on the affliction, but upon the person who was afflicted. The jumping, jerking victim of St Vitus' Dance, for instance, might have stood by the shrine and prayed and believed that St Egbert was helping her to hold herself still, and in that belief held herself still and then known that if she could control herself for one minute she could do it forever. The same with the man who had stiffened. Maybe he had waked one morning a little stiff, and coddled himself and grown stiffer; maybe he liked to be pitied, maybe he welcomed and traded upon his affliction. Then a time came when he wished, for some reason, to be like other men, so he made his pilgrimage, and standing there, leaning on his sticks, thought that he could stand upright and unaided if he *tried*.

In such miracles I could believe. But in a miracle that would add two inches to my short leg, no.

However, all that day Brother Sebastian kept me on the move; two other beds in the Infirmary were occupied and he made me help to wait upon the invalids. After each clumsy walk he would say, 'Rest now,' and then, when I was rested, set me in motion again.

That evening he gave me an enormous supper.

'Eat heartily,' he said. 'Tomorrow I shall dismiss you and you will need all your strength.' When I had eaten he said, 'And now we will go and see what St Egbert has to say.'

I had noticed before that they always spoke of their saint as though he were alive and aware.

For me it was a tiring and worrying walk. The Infirmary lay in a remote part of the Abbey – rightly, for often it housed sufferers from diseases which could be caught by others. We went along passages, up and down stairs, once across a piece of garden; and as I walked, my hand on Brother Sebastian's shoulder, I thought miserably that if this were the best I could do, with aid, it did not matter whether Master Webster had held my place for me or not. I could never work as a pack-whacker again. And though I could perhaps at a pinch have stood on my toes on the short side, and plied my smith's trade, nobody would employ me now, even at half rate.

I was panting hard when we reached a great doorway with torches in sconces on either side, and with a small door set in the one half of the large ones.

'Get your breath,' Brother Sebastian said. 'And *pray!*'

We went up the steps and in at the small door. The vast church was but dimly lighted, just enough for us to see our way. The tall columns of the nave soared up into darkness, but at its end there was a light and a sparkle.

We walked towards it, side by side, Brother Sebastian silently in his soft cloth shoes, I going stamp and shuffle as I put down my good leg and then swung the stiff one round.

The light and the glitter came from two sources. There was the altar which lay beyond the reredos screen, and the shrine itself which was on this side, slightly to the left. There were candles innumerable and their lights were taken up and thrown back at us, many times magnified by a thousand shining surfaces. The shrine, and this is true, was invisible under a thick pelt of gold and silver ornaments and jewels of every colour. Hundreds of people every year through hundreds of years had lain their offerings there. It was like looking at the sun at midday in the summer; the eyes blinked and squinted, unable to take in any one thing because the whole was so dazzling.

I was speechless with awe but Brother Sebastian might have been in his own Infirmary.

'The Saint's real tributes lie there,' he said, after giving me a moment to stare and wonder. He pointed to a space beyond the shrine, where sticks and crutches, leather neck braces, slings and bandages lay all in a jumble.

'There, you have seen what he can do. Kneel down and ask him to act for you.'

I tried. I tried to force out the prayer for the cure for the shortness of my leg, but it would not be. I found myself praying, with the utmost urgency – Let me find some work that I can do. Let me not be a burden on Kate. No other thought would come into my head and I went on praying the same thing over and over until at last Brother Sebastian touched me on the shoulder.

'We must not tire him,' he said. And something impatient and evil moved in me, I wanted to cry – How can you tire someone who has been dead and at rest for hundreds of years? And I knew that there would be no miracle for me.

Brother Sebastian, after he had spoken to me, had moved away and was now on his knees on the step which led up from the nave to the choir stalls. I stood up and went, stamp, swing, shuffle, until I stood behind him.

The altar was a gold table, bearing a jewelled crucifix and two seven-branched golden candlesticks. It was backed by a screen, also of gold, divided into a number of oblongs, each one a picture, done in glowing colours and worked in some way I did not understand into the gold. There were three rows of them, twenty-six to a row. From where I stood it was impossible to see them clearly.

Brother Sebastian stood up. He knew he had failed, or I had failed, or St Egbert had failed, and his manner took on a curious resemblance to that of a workman, say a smith, who has done a bad job and knows it and uneasily tries to divert attention by mentioning the weather or inquiring after the health of the customer or his family.

'You are looking at the screen. It is interesting. Come and regard it closely. It is one of our treasures.' We went forward.

'Two hundred years old,' he said. 'You see, the pictures in the centre row represent scenes from the New Testament, those above and below, scenes from the Old. But each three have a common theme. How many do you recognize?'

I looked at the three pictures in the centre.

'In the middle,' I said, 'is the Crucifixion. Above it, Abraham is prepared to sacrifice Isaac, but sees the ram caught in the thicket, and below is Jepthah keeping his vow by sacrificing his daughter. These three pictures have sacrifice as their common theme. Is that right?'

'Go on,' he said.

I looked about. In many of the sections the light just shone back at me, off the surface of the gold and the inlaid colours, carrying no meaning. I was, after all, an ignorant fellow. Here and there a picture had meaning.

'On the left there. In the middle is Our Lord Jesus Christ feeding the five thousand. Above is the prophet Elijah and the widow woman of Zarephath with the unfailing barrel of meal and cruse of oil. Below, that same Elijah is being fed by the ravens.'

'You are right. And what is the theme?'

'That God, if He wills, can provide.'

'Right again. That is what I wished to point out to you, but you pointed it out to me. Bear it in mind. In a few minutes the bell will ring for Compline. Come, I will help you back to bed.'

On the way back we neither of us spoke about the miracle which had not happened. Brother Sebastian talked about the altar screen, saying that beautiful and valuable as it was it was in the wrong place. It should be in some parish church where the priest could teach those who could not read the Bible truths by its means. Then he said suddenly, 'You have more learning than most. Where did you come by it?'

'I always heeded what our priest had to say.'

'You should thank God for a good memory.'

The good memory which so often reminded me how I had said to Kate, 'You shall be safe with me.' Something to be grateful for indeed.

That was my last night in the Abbey Infirmary, and it was a poor one. I slept in snatches, each full of strange and sometimes sinister dreams. Once I dreamed that my leg, like Peg-Leg's, was cut off at the knee and that St Egbert answered my prayer for a miracle by causing me to grow a golden leg, very marvellous to look at, but too heavy for me to drag; I lay on Rede dunghill, unable to walk and lamenting the miracle. Then I dreamed that Kate and I and Stephen were *really* starving, sitting before our hut, bowed over with the pain in our bellies. A great bird came swooping down, carrying Robin's dead body in his bloody beak. Kate said, 'It will be all right to eat this meat. It is a gift from God.'

From these and similar wild dreams I woke sweating, to lie and face the old gnawing anxiety again until once more I fell into uneasy slumber. I was glad when the bell rang for Prime.

I rose and began to dress and found that my right shoe was missing. I hunted for it until the Infirmary servant brought the breakfast and then sat down to eat my porridge while it was still warm. I had almost finished when Brother Sebastian came hurrying in, carrying my shoe.

'The miracle!' he exclaimed. 'The miracle, Martin. It happened. In my old head! Look.' He held out my shoe on to which had been tacked, very neatly, another sole, two inches thick.

'Try it. Try it.' He was eager and impatient as a child. 'The thought came to me at Matins and I asked Brother Anthony, our shoemaker, if he could do the work. He stayed up and worked instead of going back to his bed. How is it now?'

I stood up and stood level.

'Most wonderfully easy.' I began to thank him, but he cut me short.

'Thank St Egbert who put the thought into my head. Now, when the stiffness has worn off, you will hardly be the worse for your mishap.'

Once more I tried to thank him. He stopped me again, tapping my hand with his finger.

'Wait. There was something else I had to tell you before you go. Now what could it be? Nothing to do with your leg or my work...that is why I have forgotten it. But I shall...Oh yes! Martin, you live in Squatters Row as they call it?'

'Yes.'

'Well, be warned by me. Begin to look for other accommodation. There is talk of clearing that wall and covering in the Ditch and making all tidy there. The Prior and the Cellarer were talking only yesterday. The Bishop of Dunwich came to visit and entered by the East Gate and made some unfavourable comment. They're bound to take some action.'

I'd had less than a moment to savour the joy of the shoe that mitigated my lameness.

'I don't suppose it will happen tomorrow or even next week,' Brother Sebastian said kindly. 'Our present Cellarer is too old to move quickly, but...well, I thought I would warn you.'

I suppose I should have thanked him for that, too. As it was I took leave of him sullenly.

X

Kate's greeting of me was proof that our sharp words towards one another, the way we now lived, hardly touching one another, and all the worry and all the woe had not really set us apart. When I hobbled home she cried, partly at grief to see me so lame, but mainly with joy at seeing me again. She said how much she had missed me, how greatly she had longed to come and nurse me herself and I in turn said that I had missed her very sorely, thought of her by day and dreamed of her by night. I could hardly tell her what form those thoughts, those dreams had taken.

Soon, however, I had to ask the question.

'And has Master Webster held my place for me?'

All the joy, the young-Kate look went out of her face, leaving the harassed, irritable one which was her everyday one nowadays.

'No. He put a new man on the very next Monday. I went to him, Martin, I spoke for you. I went on my knees, and I cried. He took no notice. Then I lost my temper and told him flatly he was ungrateful when you'd been hurt beating off robbers on his behalf.'

'They weren't robbers,' I said. 'There was nothing to steal that night – except the ponies, and they made no attempt upon them. They let Crooky go by, and the ponies, until the last that I was riding. I think even Crooky knew.'

'Knew what?'

'That I was to be set on. You were here, Kate, when Armstrong said they had ways of dealing with those who went against their rules.'

'But they might have killed you.'

'They probably meant to. In any case, lying out all night I should have died. It was only lucky chance that I was found.'

'Then they're murderers. And they should be punished.'

'Who by?'

'The law. The constable.'

'I have no evidence against anyone. Whom could I accuse? It was dark, and foggy. I never saw a face, or heard a voice.'

'Then if it was Armstrong's men it was because you were doing Webster's smith work and he should have stood by you.'

'Maybe in a way he has; maybe he put on the new man just until I was better.'

Kate shook her head.

'No, I made sure of that. And he seemed so against you, somehow. I think he would have sacked me, simply for being your wife, but Margit got married and left us short-handed on the floor.'

'Why should he be against me? I always served him well. I shall come along in the morning and see him.'

'I don't think it will do a ha'porth of good,' Kate said.

In the morning I dropped Kate and the children at the door of the woolshed and went to look for Master Webster. He was in the stables and the moment he saw me his face darkened.

'What d'you want?'

I forced myself to be meek.

'I've come back to work, Master.'

'Not here. I've no use for blabbermouth jugheads.'

'Me?' I was never more astounded. I was of sheer necessity the soberest man who ever wore shoe-leather, and I never talked to anyone. Even Kate hadn't known why I worked so late so often, until Armstrong had come and let it out.

'Yes. You. You got yourself tipsy in the Smith's Arms and bragged about what you were doing here after dark.'

'I haven't been in the Smith's Arms since the day Armstrong broke it to me I couldn't join the Guild. Who's the liar who said he saw me there? I'll break his neck!'

'Shouting at me won't mend matters. This was all gone into at a full meeting of Guild Aldermen.'

'What was? You know yourself, I told you at the time, that I was spied on and reported to Armstrong and that he came and saw me and threatened me. You said take no notice and go on as we were.'

'Nobody spied on you. You made that up when you realized, sober, what you'd said in your cups. And it was a poor reward for my pandering to you.'

'Pandering to me?'

He fixed his eyes on some point behind me, over my shoulder, and said in a wooden way which told that he was repeating something said before, 'You wanted to keep your hand in – on the smith work – and I was silly enough to let you shoe a pony now and then. For practice, against the time you hoped to get back into the craft. Ain't that right? Out of charity I did it.'

I saw his plump red face, the eyes avoiding mine, the lips moving, spilling out the lies; and then the red mist came down and blotted it out. I could feel, beforehand, the supreme pleasure of smashing my knuckles through the mist and on to that well-padded jaw. But this time I held my hand. Hit him and short-handed or not he would give Kate her quittance, and what she earned was, at this moment, all there was between us and starvation.

Whirling about at the back of my mind was the thought that free men can suffer humiliation deeper and more hurtful than any a serf can ever know. In order that Kate and Stephen and Robin should eat tomorrow – for myself I did not care, I never wanted to eat again – I must accept this lie. I could see exactly what had happened; the Guild Alderman had held a solemn conclave; Webster, a member of the Woolman's Guild, had offended the Smiths by using me, a non-member, to do smith work; and the Smith's Guild had committed, not a fault, but a breach in manners, by spying upon Webster. So there had been a meeting of all the Aldermen, intent only upon smoothing the whole thing over. Webster had lied about employing me and Armstrong had denied the spying. No matter what it took of lies and falsity to do it, the firm unbroken face which the Guilds as a whole presented to the world outside must remain uncracked. Throw lies, throw a living man's body into the breach and then seal it over with cakes and ales and renewed vows of brotherhood and fair dealing.

And I, for the sake of a loaf of bread, dared not speak.

Jesus Christ! I said to myself, if only a miracle could happen and I could deal with them all as they have dealt with me, with joy would I rub their faces in the dirt!

I knew I was like a child, beaten by his father, thinking, *When I grow up!* But there was this difference. The child will surely grow.

I went out on the hunt for work. The town was growing in size and business was flourishing, but work was hard to find. Out in the country more and more acres of arable land were being turned into sheep runs, and one man could tend the sheep where twenty had been needed to plough and sow and reap. Those put out of work came flooding into the towns, so that there were three men for every job. A good deal of the work going forward was building, and with my stiff leg and built-up shoe I did not look a likely digger, or a climber of ladders. I was passed over again and again.

Soon, alongside Dummy and Peg-Leg, I was waiting at the town gates every morning, ready to fight for any despicable little job that might be going, to hold horses or walk hounds while their owners went into the Abbey to visit the shrine, to carry baggage, to lead the way to inns. Sometimes, standing there amongst the riff-raff I would think how far I had fallen, a smith, a craftsman who had served his time. By comparison my father's life, bond as he was, had had dignity and purpose. I'd run a long way and borne a great deal and got nowhere.

Now and again, having done a job and taken the meagre pay, I would go into the country and buy apples or plums or eggs on some day that was not market-day, and come back and hawk them through the streets. The walking tried me and I grew lopsided, since the easiest way was to hitch the whole right-hand side of my body when I swung that leg forward. Dummy's brood, on the rare occasions when they were sufficiently full fed to feel sportive, took to imitating me behind my back, as they did Peg-Leg.

I never passed on to Kate the word that our very hut was threatened, but some time during that summer the old midwife and layer-out, Agnes, came back from making a baker named Barnaby ready for his grave with news which seemed to excite her. She said that Barnaby had left all his money for the building of some almshouses and that as soon as they were standing everybody in Squatters Row was to move into them. It was strange to hear how that drunken old slattern, who lived under a piece of torn sail-cloth, spoke of having a house again, as though that was the one thing she wanted. But nothing came of it. The Barnaby houses were for eight widows whose husbands had been Guild members.

'And there goes my last hope,' Agnes said, and went out and got herself most enviably drunk.

Dummy's wife said, 'They are only one up and one down, they'd be no good to my lot. Laying heel to head we go from here to there.' She indicated the space between two buttresses.

So Squatters Row went on just as before and that summer we had a new kind of visitor. The pilgrims brought their own parasites, bear leaders, tumblers, dancers and singers, but this was something different, a travelling Friar, poorly dressed in a grey hood and gown of the coarsest stuff, and with his feet bare in the dust. At night he slept with the rest of us outcasts, between the buttresses, by day he went about preaching. He'd follow a performing bear or some other entertainer and wait until a crowd had gathered, and then he would call in a very powerful voice, 'Brothers! I bring you good news.' His news was the Fatherhood of God, the brotherhood of man. The more frivolous, or the rough in the crowd, would jeer and pelt him, but he would stand his ground and sooner or later he would speak against the Abbey and the monks. He would say that it was wrong for professional religious to be great landlords; he decried all pomp and ceremony; he said that Christ only once in his life rode, and that on the back of a humble ass; how then could Abbots and Bishops, Christ's representatives on earth, go mounted and robed like temporal princes?

I do not doubt that he was honest and sincere. I suspect that his decrying of rank and power, his praise of humility and poverty were, in a manner, like the clapper, or the whistle by which other people gained the crowd's attention. For afterwards would come the real sermon, urging the virtues of charity and mercy, chastity and honesty, with many a text and story from the Bible to illustrate his point.

Moving around as I did, working or searching for work, I heard him often. Kate, shut away in the woolshed had no such chance, so over supper I would tell her something of what he had said, or how he had been pelted.

One evening she fell thoughtful and after a time said, 'He is a stranger and sounds good of heart. Could he *marry* us?'

'I don't know. If he has taken priest's orders, yes. But all monks are not priests, maybe all friars are not.'

'You could ask him. Go now.'

'Oh, not out there, with so many listening who think us married already.'

'No. Get him out of earshot if you can. I know, bring him here, ask him to sup with us.'

'But we've eaten,' I said, looking at the bare platter.

'I should think my breakfast tomorrow, aye and every morning I have left to live, a small price for such a favour.'

'So should I, of course. Of course,' I said, and ran out into the night.

Squatters Row was fully occupied and the Friar had taken one of the least favourable places, mid-way between two buttresses, with no corner to huddle into. He was eating a slice of rye bread and when I proffered my invitation to supper he said, 'That is kind of you. I have enough here. Perhaps tomorrow…if you can afford it.'

'Oh yes,' I said. 'Truth to tell my…my wife and I,' I had to say that, for there were ears all about, 'my wife and I wanted to ask you something…a favour. Would you come indoors with me? It is very near.'

'Of course,' he said and heaved himself to his feet.

Inside the hut I closed the door, which hung awry from two hinges of leather which I had made, and wedged it close. In the faint light of the dying fire we all looked into one another's faces for a moment, none of us speaking. The Friar broke silence, looking at the children in their bed by the inner wall.

'They are sick?' he asked gently.

'No, Father, asleep, I hope,' Kate said. 'My…this man and I have a confession to make and a favour to ask. We have lived as man and wife for four years now, but we were never married…'

'And now you wish to be?'

'Yes,' I said, 'but not openly.' I told him – not everything, but all he needed to know – of our circumstances: how we had intended to marry and been prevented through no fault of our own, and had come to the town as man and wife and then dared not betray our state.

'You have been living in sin; you know that?'

'We know. And we have suffered for it.'

'And during this time you have performed your religious duties, always with this sin unconfessed and unabsolved?'

'Yes.' He looked so grave that the consciousness of sin did come upon me. I must confess that in the rough and tumble of daily living the matter had troubled me very little; I had only thought of it, occasionally, as having been a mistake, the cause and reason for some of our misfortunes.

'But you are free to marry? And during this time you have been faithful to one another?'

Kate said, 'Always, Father.' And I said, 'Unswervingly.' And that was true. I had never even looked with desire upon any woman save Kate and not for lack of temptation. During my pack-whacking days the chances had been plentiful.

'This can be mended then,' the Friar said. 'Tomorrow you will both fast all day. At about this time in the evening I will come to you and you may make your confessions and in that state of grace, you shall be wed. We will then break fast together.'

We thanked him heartily and he went quietly away.

Next evening we fed the children and put them to bed early. Kate scrubbed the rough board which was our table top, and set out upon it the meat pie she had bought in Cooks Row, a fresh loaf and a dish of red-cheeked apples. She was in high good spirits, calling this our wedding feast, and regretting that we had no wedding garments.

'Like the man in the Bible story,' I said.

'But he was sent away. That can't happen to us.'

We had left the door open and made up the fire with dry sticks which gave light but little heat; and in the light I looked at her with new, searching eyes, making compare with the girl who had entered the hall with me at Rede and roused an old man's lust. Hard work and poverty and misery had aged her by five times the four years that had gone by since then; her face was thin and lined, her hair rough and lustreless as hay. I thought how lightly the years would have touched her had she gone to Abhurst, and I remembered again those silly words, 'My pretty one, you shall be safe with me.'

'It's the Guilds that have ruined us,' I burst out suddenly. 'They threw me out to rot and when I refused to rot they broke my leg. Kate, I never meant it to be this way, I meant to take care of you and cherish you.'

'And so you have,' she said, and came over and put her arm about my neck and kissed me. 'Few men are so careful about fetching water and carrying the heavy loads. Who else would have walked with me to work every day, to spare me? You say what *you* meant. *I* meant never to say a sharp word to you, and Heaven knows I've said many. But from tonight I start afresh.'

I pulled her close. I felt tenderly towards her though there was no desire in me.

'Few women,' I said, 'would have been so patient and worked so hard. Who else would have kept food on the table and washed and mended and made a home as you have?'

These were not romantic speeches, but they were sincere and more suited to our state than any flowery words could be. And I was angry that immediately afterwards my empty belly gave a loud rumble.

'I'm hungry too,' Kate said. 'All day I've been too much excited to notice, but now I am hungry and he is late.'

Presently we were asking one another whether the Friar could have forgotten us and reminding ourselves that he had spoken of breaking fast together; if he intended to fast with us, surely his own emptiness would make him think of us.

Kate began to fidget, going to the door to peer out and complaining that it was too dark to see.

'Go and see if you can find him,' she said. I walked the length of the wall. I could not see the Friar anywhere.

I went home again, and we waited.

It was after Curfew, so we dared not replenish the fire and sitting in the dark the time stretched out endlessly, but at last it was eleven o'clock; we heard the bell tolling the hour.

'He isn't coming,' Kate said.

'Something must have happened to him.' I remembered how some of the rough people had jeered and pelted him. I remembered, too, that many of the things he had said about monasteries and the conduct of the monks was offensive enough to make the Abbot take action against him.

'Have you seen him at all today?' Kate asked.

'No, I've been off the streets all day today. I offered to guide some pilgrims to the Angel Inn and while I was there I got a job sawing wood. I'm going there again tomorrow.'

'He promised to come,' Kate said, and the old complaining note was there in her voice again. 'I really thought that at last we...'

I realized that marriage meant much more to her than it did to me; a woman who lives out of wedlock with a man is called a whore; there is no such damaging term for the man. I made a great effort to comfort her. First I said, fumbling about in the gloom for the knife and the meat pie, 'Let's have our supper. Everything looks worse when your belly is empty.' And then, between the mouthfuls I said what were, perhaps, the first fanciful words I had ever said.

'Kate,' I began, 'when Brother Sebastian took the broomstick off my leg and found that the bone had healed up short he said he would pray for a miracle. We went together to St Egbert's shrine and prayed there. Nothing happened to the bone in my leg. I didn't expect anything, so I wasn't disappointed; he was. But a few hours afterwards he thought about thickening the sole on my shoe and when he told me about it he called that the miracle. You see…the thing you ask for comes, but not in the shape that you think. We thought that tonight the Friar would come and marry us, but he didn't. Kate, really, if we could only understand it we *were* married, that night by the river under the hawthorn tree…and tonight we were, in a fashion married again when you said I'd been good about fetching water and I said you'd been good about mending and making a home. Try not to fret about the words that haven't been said over us. We are, in very truth, married.'

'The Friar himself said that we had lived in sin.'

'Dummy and his wife were properly married, I've heard her boast of it to Loose Liz. Look how they live! Worse than animals. They make the beast with two backs and as soon as a child comes of it he beats her black and blue. Their crooked child takes dole at the Alms Gate, and Dummy meets her on the way home and eats his fill without a thought for his wife's hunger. Kate, in all the time I was a pack-whacker I never ate a mouthful of what I was given until I was back here and sharing with you. When the Friar asked us had we been faithful to one another, we could both say yes, and truly. How could any ceremony make us more married than we are?'

She did not answer immediately; but after a moment she said, 'All that is true; but there is another side to it. The Friar said we were living in sin and that every time we went to Mass with that sin unconfessed and unabsolved we were sinning anew. And our being faithful to one another can't help them being bastards.' Even in the dark I could see her arm fling out towards the bed where the children lay. 'Nothing but ill luck ever since we've been here, and now nothing but ill luck to look forward to.'

I pitied the misery that sounded in her voice, but it made me impatient, too. It may be true that misery loves company, but it finds its comfort in a different misery, not in a reflection of its own.

'I did my best and there's nothing more to do. Let's sleep and forget it,' I said.

XI

That summer had been unusually wet and wet it continued over harvest, so that some of the poor thin crop was lost in the gathering, the sheaves standing mouldering in the fields. It was clear that bread would be scarce throughout the coming winter. Part of the blame for what happened next can be laid on the fear and ill temper which this prospect roused in the hearts of all but the very rich. But something must also be blamed upon the Friar who had appeared in our midst, sown his seed of discord and vanished; and a great deal of blame must be laid upon the Abbey, in particular the Cellarer who dealt with many things affecting the good or ill will between the monks and the townsfolk.

There were two rights which the Abbey held and which I had never, during my years in Baildon, seen exercised. One was the right to *all* the dung dropped within the town boundaries; that is not merely in the streets and market, but in stables and smithies and cowsheds and pigsties. This did not mean that all the dung went on to the Abbey lands, but it did mean that anyone who wanted to use his own manure on his own land or garden must buy it back, *in situ*, from the Abbey Cellarer. That this right had fallen into abeyance I knew from my years in the smithy. Master Armstrong had derived a small but steady income from the sale of dung dropped by horses waiting to be shod.

The other right was to demand that all corn within the area of ten miles should be ground at the Abbey Mill which stood a little way out of town on the south side, at Flaxham St Giles. That this right had not been exercised for many years was proved by the existence of another mill, on the north of the town, which was now being worked by the son of the man who had started it. Two easygoing Cellarers had followed one another in office.

Now, in this year of poor harvest, a new one was appointed, a young man, energetic and avaricious. One of his first acts was to have cried through the town the announcement that in future the Abbey Mill must be used for all corn grinding, and that the rights to the town's dung would be strictly enforced. Next day the Abbey servants, with a flat cart, went about the town, assessing every dung-heap, and what was not paid for there and then was loaded on to the cart and taken away. The Cellarer himself, riding a grey mule, went out to the north mill and curtly informed the young miller that he was welcome to grind any corn brought to him from any place more than ten miles distant from Baildon market place, but no other. That meant ruin to the miller, and two days later he drowned himself in his own mill stream. The Church refused him burial and he went to a suicide's grave at the cross-roads.

This story rang through the town, adding to the ill feeling which the enforcement of the old rules had brought about.

Worse followed; for as soon as the monopoly of milling was assured, the charge for milling was raised. It had been one-fourteenth, that is a pound of flour for every stone of corn ground, henceforth it would be two pounds – one-seventh. This was bad for everybody, since it put up the price of bread.

Everywhere now people were speaking against the Abbey and the monks and it was curious to hear, mixed with the straight-forward grumbling voiced in their own simple words, the echo of the Friar's accusations. Even those who had listened to him least had picked up, from those who had given him their attention, some phrases which sounded foreign on their tongues: 'appearance of sanctity', 'abuse of privilege', 'temporal power', 'private lechery'. Many of them hardly knew what the words meant, but they did know that they were speaking against the Abbey and the monks, and whipping up the ill feeling.

Nothing might have come of it, but in early November the Abbey officers arrested a man known as John Noggs who kept a little ale-house just inside the west gate of the town. He had set up and been working a small hand mill and his customers had been seen to arrive with sacks of corn and to depart carrying sacks of flour. The power to turn the stone was supplied by two simple-minded boys and if it ground one hundredweight of corn in a full day's work that was its limit. Still the new Cellarer was a man rather to take account of the breaking of a rule than of the damage done by the breaking. He was also a man to judge the customers of the illicit mill equally guilty with the miller. Within the next few days several more arrests were made. One of those accused of cheating the Abbey of its rightful dues was a respectable solid townsman who owned a cook shop, and one was a poor old woman who had gleaned diligently all through the harvest and taken her gleanings to be ground where the charge was lighter; the others I knew nothing of.

Immediately all the ill feeling came, like a festering boil, to a head. The whole town was now united against the Abbey. Over most matters it was difficult to get the comfortably off to join with the poor, or the merely poor to join with the destitute, and there was a severance, always, between those within and those without the Guilds. Now the arrest of the pastry-cook, who was a Guildsman, was an affront to them all, the fate of the inn-keeper-turned-miller was of concern to the middle sort, and the very poor were all agog in sympathizing with the old woman. The sullen grumbling changed to a more active, though still vague feeling that 'something should be done'.

At this moment there popped up a very ancient fellow, half blind and more than half rambling in his wits, who could remember back to when he was a little boy, when on a somewhat similar occasion the townsfolk had all joined together and shown 'them' that even 'they' couldn't have everything their own way. The squabble then had concerned the taking of eels from the river – another Abbey right – and when the townspeople had done considerable damage to the Bell Tower and the Main Gate, the rules had been modified. The old grandfather, after years of obscurity, suddenly found himself the centre of attention. The little house of his granddaughter with whom he lived was always thronged with people anxious to hear his tale of what had happened seventy years ago. He conveniently forgot, or left out of his tale, anything which the townsfolk would not find agreeable and the effect was to make them feel that they were a pack of powerful wolves who, for many years, had allowed themselves to be bullied by a few bleating old sheep and who had only to show their teeth to turn the tables. Very soon, before the arrested people could be brought before the Abbey Court, an attack on the Abbey was being planned.

I heard all about it. I was always moving about the town, here and there, in search of work. I was hungry and poor, one of the oppressed whose bread would be dear, whose feelings would veer towards the old gleaning woman. By the simple process of listening and saying nothing I learned a great deal. Sometime in November, at the dark of the moon, the Abbey was to be attacked. The monks would then be in bed and sound asleep; they retired soon after Compline, which was at seven in the winter, and slept until midnight, when they were roused for Matins. It was not badly planned. The postern gate in the great Main Gateway was to be forced by means of a battering ram, and then a body of apprentices, armed with the bows and arrows with which they practised on Saturday afternoons, was to march in and demand the release of the prisoners. The aldermen of the Guilds, dressed in their livery, and unarmed, but under guard of another group of apprentices and journeymen, were then to go and negotiate with the Abbot, or the Prior, and get the charge for milling reduced again to one-fourteenth and the claim on the dung waived. All this under threat of real violence, letting the riff-raff run wild through the Abbey, and firing timbers and thatch. This, according to the old grandfather, was how the townspeople had conducted their business seventy years ago, and they had won what they asked for. Why shouldn't it happen again?

Now it is true that an ordinary poor man like me can go through a lifetime without once testing his loyalty to anything save his own belly and his own family. In the main he cannot even be said to be loyal to his own kind, since at any moment he is prepared to snatch a job or a crust from another man exactly like himself; I had done it many a time by the town gateway. But it is equally true that some extraordinary circumstance may arise and the most simple man must ask himself the question – where do I stand in this matter? And the answer is there, clear and certain, as soon as the question is asked.

Such a testing point I had now reached and there was no doubt at all in my mind that I was with the monks. I had lived in the town for over four years and the only kindness that I had received from anybody had come from within those Abbey walls. Brother Justinius was mean, the increase in the milling charge made my bread dear, but those facts looked small when placed beside the alms Kate had received in both her pregnancies, the fair, just way in which the Trimble Charity had been administered, the careful attention I had been given in the Infirmary, and the way Brother Sebastian had devised and Brother Anthony had carried out the scheme to make me less crippled.

I owed the Abbey a good deal. And I hated the Guilds, their Aldermen, their journeymen and their rules.

At the same time I will not pretend I was ruled either by gratitude or hatred. Expediency played its part. The old grandfather remembered only that the townspeople had gained their point about the eels; the fact remained that after seventy years the Abbey still governed the town; and even if the townsfolk had won back their right to go eel-fishing, the Abbey had retained every right that mattered. It seemed to me that I should do myself no harm by trying to get into favour with those who would surely get the better of the dispute in the long run. I might even contrive to put in a word for my little threatened house. If I warned the monks in time they would be grateful and then I could say, 'Please don't demolish my neat thatched hut with the rest of Squatters Row.'

I was obliged to settle all these things in my mind rather quickly when it came to the point. After all the weeks of grumbling and plotting, the decision to make the attack on the twelfth of November was only settled on the evening of the eleventh. On the morning of the twelfth I was helping a man to slaughter a pig; we had its throat cut and its guts out when the man's neighbour looked over the wall and passed the news. I stood for a moment with my filthy hands hanging idle and the scent of blood in my nostrils and ran through all the arguments again. The townsfolk who had never shown me any kindness at all, or the Abbey which had given me alms and mended my leg? The townsfolk who would never do me any good, or the Abbey which might grant me the right to go on living in my hut?

I made up my mind, and striking my leg in a gesture of sudden comprehension I exclaimed, 'Holy Mother, my shoe! The monk Anthony is the only one who knows how to mend it. If trouble is brewing I should get it done today.'

The man I was helping gave a loud yelp of laughter and smote me on the back. 'Thass the way,' he exclaimed, 'take the honey before you smoke out the hive. Get what you can out of the rogues. They'll hev more than shoes to mend tomorrow, I'll warrant.'

I limped along to the Alms Gate and stood at the end of the little crowd who were drawing their dole. Brother Justinius was on duty, for which I was a little sorry; but when my turn came at last, I took off my shoe and leaning against the hatch said, 'Brother Justinius, I have some information which is of importance to the Abbey.'

I spoke softly, for there were some who, having snatched their dole, were eating it then and there.

The monk had his wits about him. Taking the shoe, he said in a loud, scolding voice, 'What, again! I declare you wear out more shoes than a tinker's ass! You'd think Brother Anthony had nothing else to do. Wait there.'

He slammed down the hatch.

I curled my bare foot round the shin of my other leg and leaned against the wall. One by one those who were wolfing down their food finished it and wandered away; all but one, a stranger to me, his hand wrapped in a filthy, bloodied clout.

'Keep you waiting,' he said, coming close to me. 'Keep you waiting like you was a dog, for the bits they scrape off their plates.' He cleared his throat and spat out his rancour.

'I must wait,' I said. 'Only the monk can mend my shoe.'

'That may be. But if they was the kind brothers to everybody like they make out to be, wouldn't they say, "Come in. Sit you down", not "Wait there". Same with food. Why, once I heard a Friar preach; telling about our Lord Jesus Christ...' He crossed himself piously. 'He fed five thousand once, and He said, "Sit down on the grass", He said, "and be comfortable". And He didn't hev no hatches and waiting about till the hour struck. Fish He give them, too, and when their bellies wouldn't hold another bite He filled baskets for them to take away. Maybe you never heard that tale.'

'I've heard all the tales,' I said shortly, wishing he would take himself off.

'I'm a stranger here. I s'pose you don't know a place where I could lay, cheap, for the night.'

'As it happens, I do.' I directed him to the loft where Kate and I had lived during our first weeks in the town. I praised it, saying it was so good, so cheap that if he wanted to get a bed he should hurry. As I talked he began to unwind the rag from his hand. Under it flesh and bone were whole and sound.

'The monk will return in a minute. If you want to eat here tomorrow...' I said warningly.

He winked at me and hurried off. All poor men took it for granted that they were in league together, I thought. *I* was the one exception.

As soon as he had gone, Brother Justinius opened not the hatch but the whole door.

'Come in,' he said.

The room was small and square with wide wooden shelves on the walls to left and right of the door. There were the remains of the loaves, and the big bowls of pease-porridge, cooked and allowed to set firm and then cut into sections. Someone in the crowd must have claimed Trimble too, for there was a joint of beef, glazed and brown without, pink and juicy within, which even at that nervous moment brought the water gushing into my mouth. I was meat-hungry. The thought struck me that had I stayed until that pig was dismembered I should have been given a couple of trotters, or even maybe a hock.

'Now,' Brother Justinius said briskly, 'what is it that you have to tell?'

Tell him, I thought, and he would push me out, go to his immediate superior and say, 'A man at the Alms Gate just told me...' How much would that profit me?

'It is for the ear of my Lord Abbot alone.'

He looked at me. Kate went round my head and those of the boys every month with a pair of borrowed shears and my time to be shorn was about due. Where I was not patched I was ragged, filthy from my last dirty job, and wearing but one shoe. A likely visitor for the Abbot!

'Who sent you?'

'Nobody. My own conscience compelled me.'

He gave me a cold cynical look and said, 'Oh, come along. What is it you have to say?'

'It is of importance. I can only speak of it to my Lord Abbot.'

He said to me with great seriousness, 'Do you know what you ask?'

And I said to him with equal seriousness, 'I know what I have to tell.'

I could see him debating with himself whether or not to open the door and push me out. Finally he snapped out the one word, 'Come.'

He opened a door in the wall opposite the hatch and set off at a great pace along a stone passage, so cold, with the stored up chill of many sunless years, that my teeth began to chatter. After what seemed to my bare limping foot a long walk, he stopped and threw open a door, saying in exactly the voice he had used before, 'Wait here.'

The room was warm, with a good fire on the hearth and settles on either side. I went and warmed myself, slowly turning round like a roast on a spit, then I sat down. Something about the way I had been received, and this long waiting, started a doubt in my mind. Might it not have been wiser to stay with my own kind, outside these walls, thrown myself wholeheartedly into their plot, perhaps distinguished myself by boldness in the assault, so that they would say – This man must be admitted to the Guild forthwith; he is worthy to be a journeyman.

Well, it was too late now.

The door opened and another monk entered. I jumped up, forgetting my bare foot, lurched and had to catch at the settle to save myself.

'I trust you are not drunk.'

The voice was no more friendly than Brother Justinius', but it was different, cool, distant, very faintly amused. The face, narrow within the cowl's shadow, matched it, thin sharply curved nose, arched brows above bright intelligent eyes. There was nothing about his garb to mark him from any other monk but I knew at once that I was in the presence of someone important.

'I am sober,' I said. 'I am lame without my shoe.'

'And you have some tale to tell. What is it?'

'Are you my Lord Abbot?'

'No. But you must make do with me. I am the Prior.'

It took all my courage to say again, 'It is a matter of importance. It should be for my lord's ear alone.'

'I *am* his ear. Come now, I am waiting.'

I gave in and told him all that I knew. Except that his eyes narrowed a little as he listened, I might have been telling him that the weather was cold. When I had done, he asked one question.

'Why have you turned traitor to your fellows?' His tone was curious rather than accusing or malicious, yet it shamed me.

'I bear them a grudge for several wrongs they have done me. I was well treated in the Abbey Infirmary when my leg was broken. And I hope for a reward.'

His glance brightened.

'I see. Well, rest assured that if your tale is true you will be *well* rewarded.'

'It *is* true. Why should I come and tell…'

'I have no time for that now. Wait here.'

He went away, swiftly and silently. Soon the door opened again and Brother Justinius entered. Behind him were two men, servants, one of whom carried my shoe.

'Brother Anthony says that the upper hardly justifies a new sole, but it will last a little time. Put it on. Then these will show you the way.'

He left us and, when my shoe was on, one of the men said, 'This way' and went ahead; the other fell in behind me. I suspected nothing. The two men might be on their way to town on some business, they might even have homes there and be about to return to them. I did notice that we were not going along the cold passage that led to the Alms Gate, but there was nothing strange about that either. The Abbey had many entrances and the Alms Gate, so far as I knew, was only used for its special purpose. Once, we emerged into the daylight and crossed a paved courtyard and I noticed that even out-of-doors the short winter light was waning. The next passage into which we plunged was almost dark. The man ahead of me stopped suddenly and threw open a door and, instead of going through the opening himself, stepped aside and waited. The man behind me gave me a slight push and I went through the doorway, not into the twilit street as I expected, but into the pitch dark, full of a stench which even I, accustomed to the Town Ditch, found sickening. Before I could turn, the door behind me slammed to with a horrid, final sound.

XII

Stupid bewilderment was, for a long time, the only thing I could feel. Why do this to me?

Afterwards came terror. I had heard – as who had not? – of the deep dungeons under great castles where men were thrown and forgotten, left to starve to death or be eaten by rats or go mad and beat their brains out against the walls. Those dungeons had a Norman name, *oubliettes*, sinister indeed. Somehow I had never dreamed that an Abbey would have such a place. Even when Jack Noggs and the others had been dragged off and imprisoned, I had imagined them in a less comfortable infirmary. Now I knew. I was in even worse case than they were, for they were accused of an offence, they would be brought to trial. I might very well just disappear and never be heard of again. Nobody outside these walls knew where I was.

Sweat of fear streamed over my body and dried cold as I thought about Kate and the children. I had never supported them, but there had never been a day when I had not somehow managed to contribute something to the household, even if it were only a bundle of firewood; and I had kept the hut standing and moderately weatherproof. Apart from that most material consideration, there was Kate's anxiety to worry over. Our first fond love had worn away, like the nap from a woollen garment, but below the fabric of unity was still strong; if she had failed to come home one evening I should have been distraught; I credited her with full as much concern for me.

I should have said that it was impossible to find any spot in Baildon out of the sound of the Abbey bells, but here the silence was as complete as the darkness. The cold had driven me to burrow into the heap of stinking straw and I lay there for hours wishing with all my heart that I had kept clear of this business, imagining Kate going home and waiting and wondering, waiting and worrying. For a long time misery kept me from feeling hungry, but as the slow hours dragged by the gnawing began in my vitals. I was schooled to the feeling of not having had enough to eat, it was almost a constant state with me since my accident, but this was the painful urgent need to eat *something*, anything, the need that will drive a man to beg or steal. Presently, useless as

I knew it to be, I was beating with my hands on the door and shouting.

Nobody noticed, probably nobody heard me. I remained alone with my fears and my hunger and the deadly cold which bit deeper as my hunger increased. In the end I was driven back to the straw again and, comforted by the warmth, fell into a state which was neither sleeping nor waking. Sometimes I was almost asleep, my miseries of mind and body became a little blurred and, behind my shut lids, scenes from my past drifted by, small and very clear. Then I would be jerked back to the straw and the hunger and the terror.

Once, thus jerked back, I had a new thought. I was going to die, and I was afraid to die. Keeping alive had been such a struggle that I had spared little thought for the state of my immortal soul; even the Friar's words about attending Mass while in a state of sin had soon been, if not forgotten, pushed aside. Kate and I could not suddenly absent ourselves, and we could not be married openly without putting the brand of bastardy on the children, so we had gone on as before and I had not worried about it until now. Now not only that great sin but dozens of small ones must be remembered in torment. The lies I had told, one way and another! All out of necessity, one might say, but each one a handing over of my soul to the Devil, the Father of Lies. I had more than once stolen things in the market – and never given the matter another thought. It hadn't seemed sinful then, merely common sense: two eggs slipped from a basketful while the owner turned her back meant a meal for Stephen and Robin; I'd taken the nails that held my hut together from Armstrong's stock – we made nails in slack hours at the forge and I had taken five from a chest containing hundreds. Such petty pilfering I had not even confessed when I might have done, they had weighed so lightly on my conscience. Now they loomed enormous, and presently, thinking of death and the Judgment I reached the point where even my running from Rede assumed the character of a sin. I was Lord Bowdegrave's property and I had removed myself...

Some remaining crumb of sanity became active then and I thought – How ridiculous! How can a man steal himself? And I laughed. The sound frightened me. I clapped my hand over my mouth. Mad, mad! Locked up in the dark, starving to death, and going mad. The next step was to beat my head against the wall and add self-destruction to my other sins.

I was at the door again, beating on it and screaming, not this time saying I was hungry, starving to death, this time begging for a priest, beseeching them not to let me die with all my sins unconfessed and unabsolved.

As before nobody came.

Beating on the door and shouting had been too much for me in my weak state; sweat poured off me again, my heart thudded so hard that it struck sparks from my eyeballs. Without knowing that I had fallen, I found myself on the floor. Then the cold struck again and I crawled back into the straw, turned weakly warm, almost drifted into sleep again, and then was jerked back.

This time it was hope which tugged me. God was merciful. Jesus Christ, in His earthly life, had been poor. Mary the Mother knew how one felt about one's children and their hunger. I could pray for pity and understanding and forgiveness.

So I knelt on the damp stone floor and prayed, passionately. I mentioned every sin I could remember, even my running away from Rede which I could see now *was* a sin, in that it was evidence of my discontent with the condition to which it had pleased God to let me be born.

I prayed for hours. I prayed until the sweat ran down my face and dropped on to the floor and as it ran I began again, 'Sweet Jesus Christ who in Gethsemane...' For He, too, knew the sweat of agony.

Then I swooned, or slept. From kneeling on the floor I was lying in the straw which had, all at once, lost its stench. I was waiting for something, something of which I had been given warning, a pleasant and comforting thing.

What did I expect? Some voice in the silence, something luminous in the dark?

When it came it was merely a thought in my head. I *had* no soul. Serfs had no souls. They were treated like animals and they were animals. The pretence that we were immortal, with Hell to fear and Heaven to hope for, was simply a trick to make us well behaved.

How simple and how sensible, I thought. No master, no steward, however watchful, could keep an eye on us all the time; it is therefore greatly to their advantage to teach us, 'Thou shalt not steal' and make us believe that thieves go to Hell.

Priests pretend too; it keeps the churches full and Peter's Pence rolling in. That must be true because monks are religious men and if they believed that I had a soul they would never dare leave me to die here with my sins unshriven.

Strange as it sounds, the thought that I had no soul was the most comfortable notion that I had ever had. It removed the fear of Hell; it lifted all responsibility. I had lived as an animal and I should die like one. Like an old horse or a dog, past all use and a waste to feed any more. All this fuss about marriage, I thought. We coupled like dogs who don't expect to be chanted over; and as for those eggs...who calls it sin when a starving cat sneaks off with a fish head?

Freed from the fear of Hell, I curled up in the straw and made ready to die.

Everything rocked a little, the darkness lifted, the walls melted away and I was lying on the grass under the little crooked hawthorn tree, freshly green and white, just breaking into blossom. I could smell it, cool and full of summer promise.

'You,' I cried. And all at once I understood everything. Nothing to do with priests or sins or being forgiven, nothing to do with anything there are any words for. Just the beauty of the tree and my acceptance of it, promise and fulfilment all in one. And what there are no words for.

Now I could die.

All nonsense, of course.

The voices reached me first.

'Complete misunderstanding. "Hold him safe," I said. The order was perfectly clear.'

'A gross mistake indeed; but that can wait. Brother Sebastian...'

'Hold the light a little closer.'

Hot tallow dripped on my cheek; I opened my eyes and closed them again, the light struck so painfully.

'Why, this is the man Martin whose leg I mended. Give me the cup.'

Something wet on my lips turned to fire in my mouth.

'Come, rouse yourself, man!'

'...to reach such a state in little over twenty-four hours.'

'Probably he was fasting when he was thrown in. Come, drink properly, wake up and drink. You waste more than you take.'

The cool voice, which I recognized as the Prior's, said, 'This noxious air, as much as the fast, is responsible for his state. Unless we move soon we shall all be insensible.'

I made a great effort and mustered my voice.

'Why?' I cried. 'Why did you leave me to die? I came to bring you warning.'

'Drink,' said Brother Sebastian, pressing the cup to my mouth again.

'Everything shall be explained presently,' said the Prior. 'Get him out of here, give him food. Then clean him and dress him anew. When he is ready, bring him to the Abbot's Parlour.'

Whatever it was they had given me to drink had gone to my head, so that my ears rang, and when at last they heaved me to my feet the floor seemed soft and yielding and a long way away. Brother Sebastian, carrying the candle, moved ahead, murmuring gentle encouragements. One of the men who ordinarily collected the market dues helped me along.

In a small warm room they sat me down and brought a basin and towel so that I could clean my hands before I ate. They served me barley broth, a roast capon, dried figs. Gradually my head cleared and my spirits rose. They seemed, after all, well disposed towards me. I had done them a service, been ill-used…I began to think about reward, began framing in my mind the plea for my little hut. Surely now that would not seem much to ask.

'Now, Martin,' said Brother Sebastian, 'having restored the inner man, let us attend to the outer. That dungeon reek clings hard.'

He led me to the laundry, where stone slabs, hollowed into basins, ran the length of one wall, and a great fire burned, with huge iron cauldrons swinging above. Hot water, tempered with cold, was poured into one of the basins. Brother Sebastian handed me a square of strong lye soap.

'I should get right in and wash all over, hair as well, if I were you. Our Abbot has a fastidious nose. Clothes will be brought you. I must get back to my duties. Fare you well.'

The clothes, brought by a servant as I towelled myself, were such as I had never dreamed to wear, a rich man's clothes. Soft woollen shift, clinging close and warm from neck to knee and down the arms to the elbows, a fine linen shirt, hose and tunic of smooth grey cloth. The touch of them against my freshly-scoured skin gave me a sense of well-being, of bodily ease that I had never known before. I had known its shadow once or twice, back at Rede when I was very young and a few of us boys had stripped and plunged into the river on a very warm sunny day, but we had come out and donned our creased, dirty clothes.

I remember thinking that the clothes themselves were a kind of reward and that the shift was big enough for Kate to cut up and shape into warm garments for Stephen and Robin.

I was stooping to put on my old worn shoes when the door opened and there was a young monk, with a pink, girlish face and his sleeves rolled over his elbows. He had a pair of shoes in his hand.

'Made hurriedly and from memory. We trust they will fit.'

They fitted much better than the old ones.

'Then...if you will come with me...'

We went along passages, up and down steps, and at last came out into the open, where immediately I smelled the sour harsh scent of slow burning wood, like that which fills a room where a log has rolled off the hearth. I stopped and sniffed and said, 'Did they get in then, after all?' If so, all my effort had been wasted and there would be no reward.

'Nobody got in,' he said gently. 'We were prepared and the main gate was reinforced. They tried to batter it down, and failed, so they set it afire. We welcomed its destruction, it was never worthy of its place. The new one is to be made from cedar wood from the groves of Lebanon.' His voice took on a dreamy ecstatic note. 'Cedars are long lived trees. It may even be that St Egbert's new Gate may be made from a tree which cast its shade over Our Lord.'

'But you said you were prepared.'

'Oh yes. Our Abbot has fifty knights to call upon; there was time to reach two of them, and their menies. But our rule forbids us to strike the first blow. Once the Gate was burned and the attackers were inside...then the archers and pikemen went into action.'

'And drove them off?'

'Very easily I believe.'

Most cheerful news. 'We were prepared,' he said. 'Time to reach two of them and their menies.' All thanks to me!

We were walking along a path, grey paved, between two green lawns which ended in a laurel hedge through which the path went on. Behind the fence was a low stone building, made of dressed flint and owning a high, arched doorway, flanked by several windows in each side. The windows were glassed and just caught the last rays of the sinking sun.

At the doorway the monk halted.

'The Prior awaits you in the ante-room,' he said.

I went in, blinking in the sudden light of a huge leaping fire and three or four candlestands. There was a long table in the centre of the room and at it a monk sat writing. The Prior stood at his elbow, reading every word he wrote. He gave me a brief glance of recognition, looked down again and said, 'That will do well. Seal it.'

The scribing monk took a bar of sealing wax, held it to a candle, dropped a great blob on the bottom of the parchment and the Prior took up a gold seal and stamped it down. Then he rolled the parchment into a tube and said to me, 'There you are. Smelling sweeter, I trust. Follow me.'

He opened a door at the back of the room and I followed him.

It was like walking into an oven, but the little figure seated in a chair close to the fire was all shrouded in fur, a great shawl of it lay across his shoulders, and another covered his legs. A woollen hood such as peasants wear in the fields in winter was pulled low over his ears and brow. His face was as brown and wrinkled as a walnut and his lips a thin blue line. He looked a hundred years old. Only his eyes were lively.

The Prior went close to him and said in a high, penetrating voice, 'My Lord Abbot, here is the man, Martin, whom you wished to see.'

Turning back to me he said, 'The Abbot is very deaf. Speak loudly or not at all.'

In a high, thin monotone the Abbot said, 'Ah yes, yes indeed. We owe you a great deal. I wished to thank you. Also I wished to hear why it was that you sided with us rather than with your fellows.'

I said, in my loudest voice, 'They refused me admission to the Guild.'

He gave me an odd little smile and looked over my shoulder.

'What does he say?'

'He says that the townsfolk refused to admit him to the Guild.'

'Ah, those Guilds. Most regrettable! Becoming so arbitrary. I'm not quite sure how far the Guild were involved in last night's affair...' He looked inquiringly at the Prior. 'However. The Guild refused to admit you, so you turned against the Guild. And very fortunate for us that you did. Quite right of course in *any* circumstance.' He nodded and smiled at me approvingly and I thought that now was my chance.

'I had another reason, my lord,' I said loudly.

Once again the Prior was obliged to repeat what I had said.

'Indeed. And what was that?'

I turned helplessly to the Prior who said, with a sly smile, 'Now you see the truth of what I said. I *am* my lord's ear. Very well, tell me and I will speak for you.'

'They speak of clearing Squatters Row. I built a little hut there. I know I had no right to build, but I didn't know at the time. It is the only home I have and it is not unsightly. I wondered...I mean I thought that if the information I brought you served your purpose, you might perhaps overlook...might allow my little hut to remain.'

This stumbling speech the Prior compressed into two clear sentences. I watched the old man's face and saw with dismay that the request found no favour with him.

'The Cellarer tells me that the spot is a disgrace, a mere rubbish heap thrown up against our walls. It does not offend my eyes or nose, I never go abroad now. But we have visitors. What do *they* think when they see human beings living like pigs within arms' reach of the most splendid shrine in Christendom? The Cellarer tells me that nobody entering by the East Gate can fail to see the place – and smell it.'

It was, once again, a verdict against which there was no appeal. Forbidden to be a priest, I thought; forbidden to be married; forbidden to be a journeyman; and now, forbidden to remain in my hut.

'You have the parchment?' the old man asked the Prior.

'Signed and sealed, my lord.'

'You see, we had thought of rewarding you by giving you what all poor men seem most to desire – a piece of land. Perhaps you know it – just outside the town on the south – the Old Vineyard they call it. The blight persists there and I understand that we already have as much acreage under plough as we can handle. So it is yours, in perpetuity, in return for a red rose on the last day of June each year – a formality which shouldn't cause you any inconvenience. Give him his copyhold.'

The Prior pushed the rolled-up parchment into my hand.

I tried to shout my thanks. Whether he heard or not I could not know, but the Abbot nodded and smiled again. Then he said, 'On the other hand, it is poor gratitude which gives with one hand and takes away with the other. Also they tell me that the land is full of stumps, which must be cleared before it can yield any crop. What will you eat while you labour, and where will you live? I think,' he said, looking past me at the Prior, 'we should give him some money, too.'

'As you wish.'

'Give him fifty marks.'

'My lord! Fifty marks is the scutage for the three Flaxhams in one year.'

'Sir Alain and Sir Godfrey reached us, with their men, did they not? If that rabble had made an entry, it would have cost us fifty marks many times over. Fifty marks is no more than his due. Give it to him.'

The Prior pulled aside a piece of tapestry hanging on the wall and opened the door behind it, went through and closed the door carefully behind him.

I said, 'My lord, I know not in what words to thank you.'

The Abbot said, 'It is useless to speak to me. For some reason known only to God I am deaf to all voices but *his*.' He looked towards the door. 'Very occasionally he thinks that gives him the right to dictate to me.' He smiled and nodded his head.

101

I thought that if I could not speak I could act my gratitude, so I dropped to my knees, took the old man's thin cold hand and kissed it. He withdrew it hastily and patted my shoulder.

'Don't let the aspect lead you to think that you can grow vines on that field. Six years ago the blight struck there and though we rooted out every stump and ploughed it over and laid it fallow for a year and then planted strong new stock, still the blight remained. I went out to see for myself I remember – one of my last rides. It was a sad sight – a very sad sight. Ah...'

The Prior returned, carefully closing the door again and drawing the tapestry over it. He carried a linen bag tied at the neck. He said to me, in the cool, amused voice which showed that he had recovered his composure, 'My Lord Abbot must set high store on the people of Baildon. Our Lord Himself was betrayed for only thirty pieces. You have all this – and the Potter's Field as well!'

He could have said sharper things and caused me no twinge.

'Please,' I said, 'tell him how very grateful I am. All my life I have been so very poor...and lately lame as well. All that I have tried has been of no avail. Now I can begin again. I am so very thank...' I choked and tears came into my eyes.

The Abbot gave me one of his bright shrewd glances.

'You would be wise – for your own sake – to conceal the source of your money.'

I nodded to show that I understood and the movement brought two tears spilling over.

'We are grateful to you,' he said. 'Go in peace.'

The Prior came to the door with me.

'The East Gate is nearest for you. Besides the Great Gate is closed.'

The clerk, without being bidden, rose from the table and led the way. On this journey I saw several groups of pikemen and archers as well as a few men in armour, but they, like everything else, were just the background of a dream to me.

It was almost dusk. I intended to go to Webster's and fetch Kate and the children home, for the last time. I would put my arms about her and say – 'Don't ask questions now. I will tell you everything when we are home, but, sweetheart, we are *rich!*' We would walk slowly down Cooks Row, that street which we so often avoided because of the sight and scent of food so far out of our reach, and we would buy everything we fancied. When we were home I would make a fire, not sparing the wood because in future we could have as much wood as we wanted. Over supper I would tell her the story and speak of what I planned. Dear Kate, she should never lift a finger outside her own house again.

Something sloughed off my soul, like the scab from an old sore, and all at once I was able to look beyond that happy supper table. Kate and I could go to bed together, properly, again. Another child would be welcome now. In every way we would start anew.

I reached Webster's gate just as one of the wool-pickers, a bent old woman with screwed up, half-blind eyes, was coming out. She stopped by me and said, 'Kate ain't bin to work today. Master's rare and vexed.'

I turned and began to run as quickly as I could in my new shoes, towards Squatters Row.

Interval

I

THE MAN WITH the bear came into Baildon just before dusk. November days are short. They are cold, too, and the man, heavily muffled, thickset and clumsy, might, in outline, almost have been another bear, forced to stay upright. As though to prove his claim to be human, he talked to himself as he walked. Very often children, keeping at a safe distance, would call after him, 'Talk to yourself, talk to the Devil.'

He was telling himself that leading a dancing bear was all right in the summer, but misery in winter. He said there ought to be a place where bears could be left at the end of September and collected at the beginning of April, well fed and kept in training. There was no such place. He reminded himself that even when a bear leader had money for a lodging for himself and could find a place that had a stable where the bear could sleep, nine times out of ten they wouldn't have you in – horses didn't like the bear smell.

Every time he reminded himself of this, and felt the bitter wind, he looked at the bear with hatred and dragged viciously at the chain. Every time he did so the bear looked at him with a curiously similar expression. In their imposed physical likeness to one another, in the flashes of hatred, and in their dependence each upon the other for the basic necessities of living, they were like an old married couple.

The man's name was Tom, and he was known on the roads as Pert Tom; the bear, neutered at the beginning of his training, was called Owd Muscovy.

As Tom had suspected, there was no lodging for man *and* bear; he took the rebuffs philosophically. It was some years since he had been in Baildon, but he remembered it well and knew of a fairly snug place in which to spend the night, a place where several people lived between the buttresses of the Abbey wall, and made their little fires and were willing – for a small consideration – to allow a stranger to warm himself and cook a bite of food. On his last visit there had been a woman, living behind a screen of tarred canvas, who – again for a consideration – had been willing to grant other favours. That, he remembered, must have been all of five years ago; probably she'd moved on, and in any case she would have aged. Still, in November a man couldn't be too particular.

When he reached the place it was very much as he remembered it, except that in one corner, between the wall and the buttress, someone had built a tidy little hut, with a thatch to its roof and a hole for a chimney, the hole carefully plastered round with clay to keep the straw from catching alight. Pert Tom looked at the place speculatively. If the owner of the place was good hearted he might find shelter for the night after all. At the moment the place was deserted and he wandered on, found two campers whom he remembered from his last visit – a very old woman and a deaf-and-dumb man and his wife, whose family had increased considerably – but the woman who had slept behind a piece of canvas and been willing to share her bed with him was not – to his disappointment – there.

'They laid on to her so hard last time she went to be whipped,' the dumb man's wife explained, 'that she mended her ways. She went off into the country to work in a dairy.'

'What a cruel waste,' Pert Tom said.

He began his preparations for the night, settling down in the corner opposite the little hut. He hobbled the bear by fixing the chain around one fore leg and one back, removed its iron muzzle and gave it its supper. Always, wherever he was, he fed the bear first and when, as sometimes happened, there was only food for one, it was the bear which supped and he who hungered. There was no sentiment concerned, he was capable of using the bear brutally, but to keep it in good fettle was simply common sense. When the beast had devoured its bread and honey, he slipped back its muzzle and went to sit by the dumb man's fire. But he kept his eye on the hut and in the very last of the light saw a small woman, a girl almost, with two young children, enter it and close the door. He waited a little while, then, muttering that he was going to turn in, he went to the corner where the bear was asleep, lay down beside it and waited again. He could see by the light that came through the ill-joined timbers of the hut that the young woman had got the fire going. At what he thought the right time he rose, went softly across the space and knocked on the door. Kate opened it. Against the smoky red fire glow he saw the halo of her pale hair and missed the lines of worry and disappointment on her face. In his smoothest, most wheedling tone he said, 'I wondered if you could oblige me with a drop of hot water. I gotta pinch o' ginger in my pack. With hot water and honey that make a rare warming drink. Ever tried it?'

'No,' she said flatly. 'I can let you have some water if you've got a crock.'

He was trained to take in as much as possible at a glance. One sweep of his eyes informed him that although, having a roof over her head, Kate might be said to be better off than he was himself, she was yet pitifully poor. The two children were eating bowls of water gruel, the very cheapest form of food, and they were eating it hungrily. But he noticed too that a mattress, made of sacking through which the straw was bursting, lay against the back wall, taking up, indeed, more than a half of the floor space. Better than lying on the bare ground in the open.

'I've got a bowl.' In a moment he was back with it; he brought also his pinch of ginger and his pot of honey.

'I thought maybe the lil' dears 'd fancy a spoonful of the honey in their gruel,' he said.

She was ashamed that even a stranger, begging at her door, should have seen how poor the children's supper was.

'You are kind; but they've finished now.'

'Honey,' Stephen said.

'Be quiet. Now, if you'll give me your bowl...' She took it, poured into it the small amount of hot water left over from the making of the gruel and handed it back to him. Outlined against the hearth her figure looked slim and shapely – too thin, but he wasn't fussy.

'I brung the ginger,' Pert Tom said, coaxingly. 'If you never tasted it, you should. Go down right warm, like a fire in your belly.'

'I believe you. I've no time to try. I have a lot to do and my husband will be home any minute.'

She spoke the last words in a very clear, significant way.

'Well,' he said in a deflated tone. 'Thanks for the water.'

He returned to his corner, drank his warming brew, choking a little, put his pack under his head and, cuddling close to Owd Muscovy for warmth, began to drift towards sleep as easily as an animal. Once, just before sleep took him, he was not-unhappily aware of his woman-hunger, a mistake to drink the ginger, he thought, it was well known to heat the blood; if he'd known the woman was waiting for her husband and would refuse her share of the precious stuff he'd have saved it for a more promising occasion. Then he was asleep.

The bear, stirring restlessly and grunting, roused him. He doubled his fist, thumped the heaving bulk beside him and growled, 'Lay down!' The bear, ordinarily – and with good cause – extremely obedient, continued to stir and grumble and presently Pert Tom was wide awake and aware that something was, if not wrong exactly, out of the ordinary. There was a distant noise which roused a confused memory of his soldiering days; and overhead the sky, without star or moon, was curiously light with a pinkish-yellow pulsing glow.

'You're right. Something's afoot,' Tom said to the bear, and got to his feet, shivering in the brittle cold of the night. The confused noise sorted itself out into the sound of men shouting, some heavy thumping and – was it possible? – the twang of bow-strings. Nearer, and quite distinct, came the sound of movement from the hut in the other corner. The pulsing light leaped again in the sky and he could see the woman in the doorway.

There was something intimate about the two of them being wakeful at this hour of the night and he forgave her for her earlier unfriendliness. He ambled over and said, 'Wha's going on?'

'They're fighting.' He could hear that she had been crying. 'And Martin must have gone and got mixed in it. He isn't home.' She gave a sharp sob. 'I never thought they'd do it,' she said, a wild note creeping into her voice. 'And I never thought he'd have so little sense…If he's hurt…Oh, if only I knew!'

The sky lightened and darkened and the distant noise increased.

' 'Sno use me going to look. I don't know your Martin.'

'I know that. I want to go myself.'

'Then why don't you?'

'The children. If I take them and he's hurt then I've got both hands full and couldn't help. And if I leave them and they woke…with all this noise and nobody…The others have all gone to watch. They ran past minutes ago.' She leaned forward and put a hand on his arm. 'Would you watch them for me, just five minutes while I go and look or ask…Somebody must have seen him.'

'I don't mind,' he said, without enthusiasm.

'Oh, thank you! If the little one wakes, put his thumb in his mouth, but the big one, say Mother won't be a minute.'

She was gone, running like a deer.

'So, after all, I'm *in*,' Pert Tom said to himself, ducking his head and entering the low dark hut. He remembered, from his single searching glance, the position of the hearthstone and the fact that at one side of it lay a heap of dried twigs and on the other some more solid pieces of wood. He took out his flint and tinder and soon had the fire alight. He squatted on his heels, warming his hands and the inner sides of his thighs. As the light strengthened he looked about him again. The two children lay against the wall, foot to foot, wrapped in a piece of woollen cloth. The unoccupied portion of the mattress, with another cloth crumpled across it, looked comfortable and inviting. He threw two pieces of wood on to the fire and went and lay down. He teased himself pleasantly with the idea of the woman lying here beside him, and dozed a little, losing all consciousness of time.

He roused when Kate came back.

She was no longer crying. The scene outside the Abbey Gate had shocked her into calmness; she had been obliged to stare into the face of dead man after dead man in her search for Martin, fourteen in all, some horribly mutilated by arrows. She had not found him, nor anyone who had seen him lately, but a woman had told her that some of the men of the town had been inside the Abbey when the archers took them by surprise. She felt certain that Martin was there, dead; and mingled with her grief was a deep resentment that he should not only have joined the rabble in their stupid quarrel, but been in the fore-front of the attack. When she thought of him lying dead she was ashamed of that feeling, but it was there just the same. Torn by two such conflicting emotions and denied the relief of tears, she had fallen into a stunned, somnambulistic state in which she was conscious of a single purpose – she must get home to the children. The sight of Pert Tom sprawled on the bed did not surprise her, although she had forgotten him, and when she had thought of the children had visualized them as being alone. She was past feeling anything so trivial as surprise; in a world where Martin was dead, anything might happen.

Tom propped himself on one elbow and waited for her to speak. After a minute he said, 'You didn't find him?'

Such a stupid question merited no answer. She sat down on one of the two stools and stared at the fire and presently said, '*Why* did he have to join them? They'd treated him as badly as they could. He was a good smith...' As she spoke those words the tears almost came, for she saw Martin as he had been on that evening at Rede, striding back, full of youth and power, from his work at Ancaster and coming to her rescue. A hard bitterness dried the tears. 'A *good* smith,' she repeated, 'but they wouldn't let him into their Guild. And then they broke his leg and lost him his job. He didn't have to side with *them*.'

'How d'you know that he did?'

'If he didn't where, *is* he? Never once since he lost his job has he been away for the night. And I know what he was doing today. Helping with a pig-killing, just over the Ditch. And I know what happened...' She lifted her head so that the firelight shone in her eyes and on her lips, 'He thought he'd get back in with them, show them what he was made of. The fool!' Grief and fury came together in the last word.

So far as Pert Tom was concerned she might have been speaking in a foreign tongue. Lust was lively now and he saw every hope of gratification. He got to his feet and laid a heavy hand on Kate's clenched in her lap.

'Like ice,' he said. 'I'm gonna get my ginger and we'll put the pot on and hev a nice hot drink. Pull you together better'n anything.'

She said nothing; when he returned she was sitting as he left her, staring into the fire. He was putting water into the pot and the pot in the heart of the flames when she said, as though continuing a conversation, 'We never even said goodbye.' Then there was another long pause before she spoke again.

'It was all on account of me that he came here and was so wretched. He'd have been better off at Rede. He said so. No, I said that. I used to say a lot of things I didn't mean.'

The water boiled and Tom made his brew, using the last of the ginger and stirring in the honey with a liberal hand.

'Here. You get that down. You'll feel better in no time.'

'As though I could,' she said, speaking directly to him for the first time. 'Nothing could make me feel better except the sight of Martin coming in that door.'

'Drink it and try.'

She thought that in his dull un-understanding way he was trying to be kind, so she lifted the bowl and sipped and coughed.

'Go down so nice and warm, don't it?' He swilled his own with gusto.

Spices were so expensive that only the rich could afford to buy them for their flavour; to develop a market among the poorer people the merchants had craftily spread the rumour of their aphrodisiac virtues. Pert Tom, because he was ready for Kate and warmed by his ginger, all too easily believed that the sip or two she had taken would render her complacent.

'Don't let it get cold,' he urged her. She lifted the bowl and drank its contents in that same sleep-walking fashion. He waited another minute then he said, 'Don't fret. There's as good fish in the sea as ever came out.'

'What do you mean?'

'This,' he said; and took hold of her, his purpose quite plain.

She woke then and remembered that her first feeling towards him had been one of distrust. He was big and hot and heavy; he reeked of bear; it was like being mauled by a bear. He had his face at her breast – in dreadful parody of a nursing child – and she could feel the heat of his breath through her clothes. She pushed, but he only pulled her closer. She wanted to scream but knew it would be useless, there was no one to hear except the children. She went limp in his hold and let him pull her down on to the bed. Then she said, 'Wait,' and made the first motion of unfastening her dress. Just as he'd expected, Pert Tom told himself. Then her hand moved, quick as a slithering snake, and she had snatched a piece of burning wood from the fire and was on her feet, standing over him, threatening him with it.

'Get out!' she said.

He jumped up and stood hesitant, face to face with her in the tiny room. He had only to get hold of her arm and twist it...But she jabbed at him with the flaming branch; the heat scorched his face and singed his beard. He backed to the door which opened outwards and was unlatched. With the opening of the door under the pressure of his body a draught of cold air came swooping in; the flaming tip of the branch flared more fiercely and a piece of it dropped off and on to the edge of the straw stuffed mattress which broke eagerly into flame.

Kate did scream then and tried to stamp on the new flame, but in a second her skirt was blazing. She threw the branch towards the hearth and stooped, smacking ineffectually at her skirt. Then she grabbed at the children, calling them by name, shaking Stephen awake and trying to lift Robin. They woke and shrank, screaming, nearer to the wall, away from the blazing edge of the mattress, the blazing of Kate's skirt.

'Help!' she screamed to Tom. 'Help!'

It had all happened so quickly that he was still pressing his hands to his smouldering beard. But he had his wits about him. Save her, help her out and what would be the result? Trouble. People were always ready to believe the worst of any stranger. She'd tell how the fire started and the least that would happen would be that he'd go to the lock-up; and nobody would care for Owd Muscovy. You could lose a good bear that way. Better let the bitch burn.

He put out his hand and pushed the door shut. It took another movement of air with it so that the flames leaped up with a hollow roar. Before he could have counted ten, before he dared withdraw his hand from the door, the inner side of the low thatch was alight.

He stepped back then to a safe distance. There was a moment when the woman and both the children were screaming together, then the thatch fell in on them, throwing out showers of sparks and little clots of burning straw. The screams stopped. There was a smell of burning flesh and then, after a minute, mingling with it, the stink of smouldering fur.

'Owd Muscovy!' cried Tom, and ran to the corner where the hobbled bear was plunging about, alight in a dozen places.

'Lay still. Lay! Down! Down! Down!' said Tom, beating at the thick greasy fur, tearing off bits of burning straw. He was not even conscious of the pain in his hands he was so intent. The first lesson a bear leader learned was that it did not pay to have too shabby or openly-intimidated a bear; people liked to think that the bear was much stronger than any man and that but for the muzzle and the chain would tear its leader to pieces.

'Holy St Ursula,' Tom moaned. 'You'll look like the moths hev been at you.'

Even when his pelt was out of danger the bear, in whose early training fire had played a part, was nervous and shivering. Tom would have calmed him with an untimely offering of bread and honey, then remembered that he had taken the honey into the hut. All wasted and the ginger too!

'And all over what?' he asked himself. 'Slice off a cut cake that'd never've been missed. Silly bitch! What got into her?'

He looked back at the hut then. The poor flimsy timbers of its front and side wall had fallen inwards over the whole and had almost burned themselves out.

'Need never hev happened,' he said. 'Could hev been as nice as nice.'

In a mood of self-pity, and with no twinge of conscience, he again settled down beside the bear and slept so soundly that he did not hear the other residents of Squatters Row return from their sight-seeing.

With morning light shining on the ruin, the dumb man's wife and Old Agnes found the destruction of one small hut of far more interest and moment than the burning of the great Abbey Gate which they had seen during the night. They asked the inevitable question, 'How did it happen?' and Tom had his tale ready. He had waked to find the hut blazing and had done his best to save whoever was inside. He had his blistered hands, his scorched face and raggedly singed beard to show. Nobody for a second doubted the truth of his story. Dummy's wife managed, without exactly saying it in so many words, to imply that such an accident could have been expected: if you couldn't have a proper house the only thing to do was to make your fire in the open, as she had done all these years. The accident, in fact, was the result of trying to set yourself up above your neighbours. Old Agnes, remembering that Kate and Martin had dealt more fairly with her over the Trimble than her clients ordinarily did, said that perhaps it was a mercy in disguise – if Martin were really dead; it was a hard world for widows and orphans.

Pert Tom was praised for his attempted rescue and sympathized with for having wandered into Baildon just at this time. Nobody would be in the mood to be amused by a bear's tricks today. The town was in mourning, some said nineteen men dead and many more injured. And all for nothing.

Tom believed that trade would be bad and soon after breakfast was on his way towards the North Gate of the town when he saw a new detachment of soldiers marching in. They moved with the dogged, flat motion of men who have marched through the night, so it was likely that they had come from a distance. The fighting seemed to be over and they wouldn't be marched back without a rest. Soldiers were good customers, easily amused and very open-handed. He turned himself about and followed them back into the centre of the town.

The Market Square was scattered with the litter – some of it curiously irrelevant – that was left by street fighting. There were the spent arrows, the burned-out torches, the thrown-down clubs and sticks which might be expected, but there were also bits of clothing, part of a wheel, a cooking pot, some grey wool on a spindle. Patches of blood showed where men had fallen dead or injured, but all the bodies save one had been removed. An old woman and a boy of about ten were struggling with the corpse of a heavy man, the old woman crying and hysterically admonishing the boy. 'Hold his legs higher. Higher. You're letting his bum drag on the ground.'

Pert Tom remembered how, after the Battle of Radscot-Bridge, he had come across a dead man with a ring on his finger. It was that ring which had enabled him to buy Owd Muscovy, a two-year-old, fully trained. He went carefully over this battleground and saw nothing worth salvaging except the spindle which he put in his pack.

Inside the great stone archway the burned edges of the gate hung jaggedly. Two monks, their faces expressionless, as though every morning they measured up burned gateways, were using a yardstick. Soldiers stood on guard all along the front of the Abbey, and inside Tom caught a glimpse of archers, pikemen, a man or two in armour. The soldiers he had followed had disappeared through the gateway, but soon others came out in groups of three or four and made off up Cooks Row towards the ale-houses. He followed and was soon giving thanks to St Ursula that he had decided to stay in the town. The bear's tricks were well received, especially his imitation of a pikeman's drill with a little cane for a pike, and by two o'clock in the afternoon Pert Tom had collected as much as was needed to live luxuriously by his standards for the next four days, which was as far as he ever looked ahead. He found an inn not yet discovered by the soldiers and therefore spared the sudden inflation of prices, and took a leisurely dinner of boiled beef and dumplings, apple pie and ale. Before he left, he had his wooden bottle filled with ale, and on his way back down Cooks Row he did some pleasant shopping: a meat pie and five pickled onions for himself, a pot of honey, apples, bread for Owd Muscovy, half a pig's head for the wife of the deaf-and-dumb man whose fire he hoped to share again.

For the town this might be a day of mourning, but for Squatters Row, never in any real sense part of the town, it was a jubilant occasion. Old Agnes had laid out six that day and had four more to do tomorrow.

'Of course I could've done the lot today but it don't do to hurry. If you make it look easy they grudge your pay.' She had bought bacon and ale for her supper, and was sharing Dummy's fire because she was too busy to make her own. Dummy had spent the day grave digging and brought home a pig's trotter for each member of his family and ale for himself.

Just at dusk Peg-Leg arrived, begging to be told what had happened. He had been out of town for three days visiting a niece who lived in the country and had a tender conscience. Every now and then, when he grew tired of the food doled out at the Alms Gate, he would pay her a visit; she would feed him, mend his rags, call him 'Uncle Jacob' and restore his self-esteem. Sometimes her patience and his good behaviour would last four, five days, a week; but sooner or later he would offend her and she would reprimand him, and he would return to Baildon, laden with the provisions which it eased her sense of responsibility to provide. On this evening, after an unusually brief visit, he was carrying a piece of pork, a dozen eggs, some flat oat-cakes sticky with honey, and a little sack of walnuts. He was easily drawn into the group and the tit-for-tat bargaining, promising a share of his pork when it was cooked in return for a piece of pig's head this evening, swopping some eggs for a mug of Old Agnes' ale and sharing out the walnuts amongst the children.

The air of festivity mounted until one child was bold enough to ask Pert Tom to put the bear through his tricks. Tom was not going to break an infallible rule for dwellers in Squatters Row.

'Owd Muscovy, he've earned his rest today. Tell you what I will do, though. I'll play you a tune on my whistle.'

He played a merry tune and the children began to hop and skip in time to it. Peg-Leg said, with a trace of wistfulness, 'Nice to be young, and sound of wind and limb. I was a rare one at a hornpipe once on a time.'

'Young!' cried Old Agnes scornfully. 'I can shake a leg with the best. Aye, and after a full day's work, too.'

Gathering up her skirts and exposing skinny legs like knotted twigs and huge flat feet, she began to caper, calling to Tom to play faster, to play louder. Dummy's wife sprang up to join her and their antics made even the deaf-and-dumb man laugh; he rocked from side to side, making a hoarse wheezy sound, like a pair of bellows whose leather sides had cracked.

It was into this merry scene that Martin walked.

He saw first the black ruin of what had been his home. Breath and heart-beat stopped; then reason took control. A few yards away was the leaping fire, a crowd about it, laughing and dancing to music. They wouldn't be doing that if Kate and the children had been...No. The neighbours were celebrating a near escape, Kate and the children were there...beyond the fire.

He walked towards it and Old Agnes, spinning round, saw him, stopped dead, let her skirt fall, and stared. In a second they were all staring and silent; on the defensive, like cattle in a field when a strange dog enters. And he could now see beyond the fire. No Kate, no child of his.

'Holy Mother of God!' Old Agnes said, 'we thought you was dead, too.'

'Dead.' He repeated the word. 'Too? D'you mean...' The rest of the question could not be spoken; his jaw jerked convulsively.

Old Agnes moved towards him and took him by the arm. She was suddenly sober and aware of how callous their behaviour must seem to him.

'Flared up in the night, your place did. But we thought you was dead too...She...Kate was running round, hunting for you and crying. And with all gone together there didn't seem much to grieve about.'

He said, 'Burned,' but the shaking of his jaw mangled the word so that it emerged in a moan of anguish.

Agnes tightened her hold on his arm.

'Come and sit down, lad. Come to the fire and take a sup of ale. It'll ease you.'

He pushed her off and took a few staggering steps back to the buttress which had been one wall of his home, and was now blackened by the flames which had destroyed it. He leaned his head against the cold stone and so stood.

He might have known. It was all part of his life's pattern; every small mitigation of misery had been immediately followed by some new misfortune. An hour ago he had been given the means to make his family safe and comfortable forever, so by some Devil's logic it was inevitable that now he should have no family.

He thought – She never had anything! And the tears came scalding into his throat and stayed there.

Back by the fire, where the silence continued, though the eating had been resumed, Old Agnes eyed Martin uneasily, and presently made her second imaginative leap in the day.

'Go and tell him you *tried*,' she said to Pert Tom. 'Tell him you did your best to save them. Show him your hands. It'll make him feel better to think somebody tried. Coming on us all playing the fool and making merry...Go on!'

Pert Tom rose and ambled over and stood beside Martin and said, 'I did my best. Tried to save 'em. Burnt meself. Look.'

Martin neither looked nor answered, but he put out his hand and laid it on Tom's shoulder. The bear-man could feel the ague-like shudder that ran through the other man's body, and although he felt no guilt in the matter, something of Martin's deep misery was communicated to him.

'Once,' he said, 'a man that knew a lot about things, towd me burning to death worn't as bad as it sound. Talking about holy martyrs, he was. He said the smoke sorta choked you and deadened your senses afore the fire took howd. Reckon thass true, too. They on'y screamed once.'

Through the knot of pain in his throat, Martin said, 'Pray God that's true.' He used the expression from habit, out of earnestness.

118

There was no God, or such things could never happen. How *had* it happened?

He forced out the question, adding, 'She was always...so careful. I'd put in a good hearthstone, and clay round the smoke hole.'

'I dunno. I woke up to find it all ablaze. Like I said, I tried, but that was too far gone, then. Burn meself. Look.' Once again he held out his hands. Some of the blisters had broken, through hauling the bear's chain all day. All Martin could see was Kate, young and pretty, just as she was when she had come to join him under Tuck's Oak. But he managed to say, 'I'm deep in your debt for that much. Leave me alone now.'

Tom went back to the fire.

'He hev took it to heart,' he said to Old Agnes. 'Pity. I know more'n one man'd think hiself well rid of his wife.'

'They was different from most,' said the old woman, thinking again of the Trimble.

The fire burned low; presently every one save Agnes had left it. She took a good drink of her ale to give her heart and then filled the mug again and went to where Martin stood.

'Here,' she said, 'you drink this. I've had my losses too, and I know what I'm saying. Ale'll ease you.'

He made no move to take the mug, and she went on, 'I been with death all my life, Martin, and folks in sorrow. Them that come out of it best take what comfort they can get and turn their minds to other things, even if thass only squabbling over the pickings. You can't bring Kate back, nor go to her till your time come. So you must bear up and comfort yourself.'

'She never had anything; nothing but worry and misery and toil. And all my fault.'

'Don't talk so daft,' the old woman said sharply. 'You couldn't help being poor. I never saw a man more ready to turn his hand to anything. I never saw a better husband neither. I've said that a dozen times, seeing you so careful about fetching the water and the firewood and all. Come on now, lad, don't add to your own load.' She held the mug to him again. He took it, gulped down the contents and handed it back. 'Now leave me,' he said.

'You come and lay down,' she insisted. 'You can lay under my rag.'

He said, 'No,' and flung himself down by the black ruin, the grave of all his love. The old woman sat down beside him, took his head in her skinny dirty claws and eased it into her lap. Her kindness, or the ale – it was a long time since he had drunk anything but water – loosened something in him. Tears came, and with them words, such a flow of words as he was never to loose again. Everything he said was self-reproachful, all concerned with the ruin he had made of Kate's life, how he had promised that she should be safe with him and then robbed her of the only safety possible in this unjust world. Old Agnes hardly listened. She stroked his head and at intervals muttered a soothing word or two. 'You couldn't help that, lad.' 'Aye, I know, I've been through it myself, long ago.' 'Ah, that's the way it is when you're poor.' And once she said, 'Dying young's no real hardship. Plucked off the bough, clean and sound. If you hang on you rot. I've seen 'em, Martin, riddled with rot, stinking like corpses, but still alive. Kate and your little ones are safe from that, they're safe from everything now. We're the ones anything could happen to. We're in worse case.'

II

Pert Tom had been born into an age and a community as devoutly mystical, as thoroughly religious as any in the history of mankind. As a baby he had been baptized, as a child put through his Catechism. As an apprentice the only holidays he had known, the only landmarks in the year's toil, had been the festivals of the Church and the Saints' days. As a soldier even his oaths had been religious, since without belief there can be no blasphemy; and as a bear leader he had never spent a whole day without passing through a town where a new church was building, or mingling with a group of pilgrims on their way to or from some shrine, or hearing a Friar preach, some convent bell ringing.

Of it all he had absorbed and retained only one thing, as primitive and as personal as a savage's devotion to his household idol. Pert Tom believed in St Ursula. That same fellow soldier who had given him the information about the painlessness of death by burning had told him that St Ursula was the patron saint of bears and bear leaders – an excusable piece of misinformation based upon the likeness of the Saint's name to the generic Ursus, meaning bear. When a dead man's ring provided Tom with the price of Owd Muscovy, he had thanked St Ursula and adopted her as his personal Deity. The Holy Trinity and the rest of the Saints seemed, like most respectable people, to be against him and his fellow vagrants, but St Ursula, whom he visualized as a stout, comfortable, vulgar, tolerant old woman, was firmly on his side. When a cunning idea slid into his head, it came direct from her; any trick he played had her nudging connivance; any luck that came his way was her work. She did not, like the rest of them, set a poor man any impossible standard of virtue. She made no demands. She entirely understood that he had meant Kate no harm and that it had been necessary to lie about the burns on his hands and face. Proof of her understanding and partnership was there, concrete, indisputable. Look how he had been rewarded!

By April of the next year Pert Tom had some vague conception of just how full and rich his reward was to be, and it occurred to him for the first time that he should make a gesture of recognition towards this Saint who had been so overwhelmingly generous to him. So when, with the spring, the fresh tide of pilgrims and tumblers and minstrels and vagrants came pouring into Baildon, he began to look out for an image seller, and before long found one.

The image seller was of grave, almost priestly mien. He carried a tray of meticulously fashioned, beautifully coloured little images and a box of holy relics. He wore a hat with cockle-shells which indicated – in his case falsely – that he had made the pilgrimage to the Holy Land, and his box contained, amongst other things, a sliver of wood, purporting to be a piece of the true Cross, two thorns from Christ's crown of mockery, and a two-inch square of St Veronica's handkerchief. Most of the figures on the tray were of the Virgin, the rest were of female Saints after whom girl children were named. What parent, having named a daughter Agnes, could resist buying for her an image of the Saint, with the lamb at her feet?

All the figures were made and fired and coloured at a pottery in Wattisfield, where clay had been dug and worked in Roman times, and they were all made by one old man, who, though he worked quickly enough to keep four salesmen on the road from April to September as well as supplying two settled dealers, one in Norwich and one in Walsingham, never turned out anything shoddy or slapdash. True, the colours of the Saints' garments were a little gaudy, customers liked them that way, but the tiny faces were virginal and saintly, pearly-pale and wearing one of two expressions, gently smiling or gently sorrowful.

On this bright April morning, Pert Tom, now a gentleman of leisure, with money in his pocket, halted and looked over the image seller's stock. He would know his Saint when he saw her, buxom, red-faced, her interest identified by a bear, or perhaps a goad, spiked collar or muzzle. There was no St Ursula; the old man at Wattisfield knew his business: little girls in that district were named Catherine, Ethelred, Winifred, Edith, Agnes, Elizabeth.

'You ain't got what I want,' Tom said reproachfully.

'And who was you wanting?'

'St Ursula.'

'Here y'are.' He proffered a St Ethelreda with her daisy emblem.

'That ain't my St Ursula. She'd hev a bear.'

'A what?'

'A bear. Growler. Got a bit of flesh on her bones too.'

'Oh! That one! Sold the last a day or two back. Great demand. Bring you good health, good luck. Tell you what, I'll bring one on my next round. I'll be back here for the Lammas Fair. You live here?'

He must ask that, for an unpopular outlandish Saint, with a *bear*, would be quite unsaleable, and Pert Tom, though he had now been settled for five months and looked like being settled for the rest of his life, still had a vagrant look, something of the roadster about him.

'I live here. All right. I'll look out for you Lammas time.'

There must be some special interest, something extra behind such choosiness, and it might be open to exploitation.

'Of course, if you *liked* and was prepared to pay for it, I could hev her made with a bit of genuine relic to it – strand of her own real hair or something. Only that'd cost you, naturally.'

'How much?'

'Two shillings,' said the image seller tentatively, ready to abate the price should this odd customer flinch.

'I could manage that. But I want her *proper*, bear and all. Not one of them poor peaked looking things.'

'You should mind your tongue, remembering who these are. And if you want the hair then you'll have to pay half down.'

Tom paid, calling upon St Ursula as he did so, to witness how heart-felt was his gratitude that he should take such a risk.

Weeks after, on the morning of the Lammas Fair, he took delivery of his order with loud complaints.

The old man in Wattisfield, who was a dedicated artist, had disliked being given definite orders; he had protested that, though he knew more about the Saints than any bishop alive, he had never heard of a St Ursula who had dealings with bears. There was only one St Ursula, a virgin, who with eleven hundred other virgins had been martyred at a place called Cologne by some people called Huns. A virgin saint. And virgin saints were all slender, pearly-pale, yellow haired, gently smiling or gently

123

grave. He'd been making them for years and he *knew*. 'Flesh on her bones', the very thought was a heresy.

'But master, I told him two shillings and he paid one down. I promised him real hair.'

Even the artist agreed that such a customer merited some consideration. But when it came to the point he could not bring himself to sacrifice his artistic integrity to the extent of making a Saint as buxom as a washerwoman. He made a solid looking brown bear to crouch at the hem of the blue robe and the inclusion of a flaxen curl cut from the head of his youngest granddaughter cost him no twinge of conscience at all. If people were such fools as to believe that their silver could buy hair from the head of a woman dead and buried for hundreds of years, they deserved to be cheated. What could not be cheated, or ever would be, was his own standard of workmanship.

'Poor starved-looking thing! But for the bear I shouldn't've known her,' said Tom, handing over his money grudgingly.

Still, there it was, he had bought the best that money could buy and St Ursula, who had understood so much, would understand that the false representation was not his fault.

He carried the little image home and set it on a shelf in the room that was his, the first room that he had ever been able to call his own.

'Set you there,' he said, 'and enjoy all you was so kind as to give me.'

He thought of how, in the next dark winter, when the snow fell and the mud lay thick in the roads, the flames would leap on the hearthstone and the howling wind would drop back baffled by the thick walls and the stout shutters, by the heavy door and deep thatch of the house that was already known as the Old Vine.

No member of any Guild had laid a finger on the house. Martin had planned it and done much of the work, the rest had been done by unemployables like Peg-Leg and Dummy. The monks' Old Vineyard lay outside the town walls where the Guild rules did not hold.

It was a small house, two tiny rooms and a kitchen, but there was as much sound timber in it as in many three times the size. The walls were made of oaken posts, planted at eighteen-inch intervals. Smaller beams were set aslant, joining the bottom of the one post to the top of the next, and the triangles thus formed were divided again, horizontally. The spaces were filled in with laths and the whole plastered over, once on the inside and twice on the outside. A brick chimney in the centre carried the smoke from both rooms and from the kitchen hearth.

'We'll have our own fire,' Martin had said, already aware that although he had bonded himself for life to the bear leader his enforced constant company would be intolerable. All that he had, all that he intended to have in the future, he was prepared to share with Tom, who had tried to save Kate, and with Old Agnes, who had tried to ease his hour of misery, but his fire and his bed he must have to himself.

The little house stood at the lowest edge of the vineyard, close to the road, and adjoining it, sharing a wall with Martin's own room, was the new smithy, into which, during the next summer season, much of Armstrong's and Smithson's trade was to be diverted. Once the house and smithy were up, Martin's gang of cripples and misfits, who would work for any pittance and the certainty of one good meal a day, set to work upon a stable block, built of clod and wattle.

Pert Tom could see the reason for the house and for the forge where Martin was going to earn a living for them both, but the stables puzzled him.

'What d'you want them for?'

'I shall offer stabling, like smith work, at a price those in town can't match. To begin with that is. Later I shall have horses of my own.'

'And what d'you aim to do with them?'

'You'll see.'

It was not a satisfactory answer, but one with which Tom must be content. To press a question was useless, although on that

November morning when Martin had talked in stony-faced calm
with Tom, one of his reasons for offering to take him into
partnership was that he needed his company.

'There's not a man in this town that I can ever bring myself to
talk to, except in the way of business, and that the least I can; and
living that fashion a man could be struck with the dumb
madness.'

The other reason he had given was that he needed Tom's
partnership as a screen for his own sudden possession of money.

'I've got it and I didn't steal it. More than that I can't tell you.
Nobody could know what you've earned, or saved over the years.
It'd look natural enough for you to settle down, build a house and
a smithy for me to work in, so that your old age would be taken
care of. You could have come into Baildon with some such
scheme in mind.'

His real, his secret reason, the wish to share with Tom all that
he should have shared with Kate, he never mentioned to anyone.
Nor did he ever put into words his grudge against the town.
When, at the beginning of the second summer season, a
deputation of the Smiths' Guild waited upon him and offered
him full membership, even some seniority, admission at once as a
master man, if he would cease under-cutting prices, he gave no
sign of the bitter, ironic amusement the proposal roused.

'I cannot see how that would work to my advantage,' he said.

And this time, though the damage he was doing them was far
more serious than that he had done by shoeing Master Webster's
pack ponies, they hesitated about taking revenge by violence. For
this there were two reasons. He had his gang of riff-raff, the poor
without a craft, the disabled, reinforced by tougher elements, an
old soldier or two, one of Peg-Leg's ship-mates, a half-crazy
priest who had been unfrocked. They owned an almost feudal
allegiance to Martin, who allowed them to build another, more
solid Squatters Row at the back of his stables, who paid them
when there was work to be done and fed them between times.
And there was also a strong feeling throughout the town that Pert

Tom and Martin, in becoming – as it seemed – tenants of a piece of Abbey land, had moved into the shadow of the protection of that august authority. It was an authority with which, at the moment, the townspeople had no wish to try another throw. After their failure in the previous November, the Abbey seemed to delight in grinding their faces; even the rule concerning the eel-fishing had now been revived and was strictly enforced. The town as a whole had been laid under an obligation to pay a large part of the cost of the new gate and was groaning under the imposition. Not until many years had passed, and a King set an example, would the people of Baildon defy their Abbot again.

The suspicion that the Abbey looked with favour upon Pert Tom and Martin, who had taken a piece of unprofitable land off its hands, was confirmed by the story of an amazingly out-of-character behaviour upon the part of the new Cellarer. It concerned a horse, a young, strong horse, newly broken, and brought to Martin's forge to be shod for the first time. Its owner, an oldish peasant, was sitting on a bench waiting, when he clapped his hand to his chest, gave a loud groan and collapsed. He was dead when he was picked up. It was evening when his eldest son came to remove the body, and before he left he said to Martin, slyly, 'Now they'll come round to pick the heriot, and they allust take the best beast. The horse is the best my father had. Would you let it bide – just till the dues are paid?'

Martin looked the young man in the face.

'Ask me to stable your horse and I agree. I make part of my living by stabling horses.'

He had no intention of involving himself, though he would have agreed that the heriot was a peculiarly heartless exaction, for it meant that when a villein's family lost its bread-winner it also lost – to its manorial lord – the most valuable of its possessions.

'Then will you stable my horse until I fetch it and pay what I owe? They'll take the cow for heriot – and she's dry in two teats.'

Nine or ten days later, the Cellarer rode up on his mule and beckoned Martin from the forge.

'We understand,' he said, 'that you have in your stable a horse which is, by heriot right, Abbey property.'

So the peasant was an Abbey tenant and had underestimated the thoroughness of the system.

'There are several horses in the stable,' Martin said.

'This one is young, freshly broken. Its owner died here, suddenly.'

'I know the one. I'll fetch it.'

'No.' The Cellarer held up a plump hand. 'In this case, because there was some dispute about the heriot – they offered a cow, fit only for beef – the Abbot himself took an interest. He said that if the horse was with you it should remain. He has asked from time to time about the Old Vineyard and was interested to hear that you had laid the rest of the field down to barley. He thought the animal would be useful to you.'

Every word of this singular conversation was audible to the men waiting on the bench outside the forge and was duly reported in the town. What, men asked themselves, was so virtuous about growing barley? And why had such a valuable present been made to Martin, with no mention of Pert Tom who was understood to be the tenant of the land? When all the questions had been asked, and all the speculations made, and the gossip finished, one thing remained in the memory – the Abbot took an interest in the Old Vineyard. Martin in his upward spiral towards success met, therefore, much less opposition than he might have done.

PART TWO

Old Agnes' Tale

I

I NEVER KNEW my age by yearly reckoning, but a woman's life
has milestones of its own, and by their measure I was an old
woman, and had been for years, when Martin took me to live
with him in the house at Old Vine and made me free with all that
he had.

Before that, for more years than I can number, I'd lived in
Squatters Row, amongst – save for a very few – the scum of the
earth. For that I had only myself to blame, in the main. I'd had
one knock as a young woman and never pulled myself up again.
My family were decent country people, and my mother taught
me her midwife's trade. When I married I got a good steady man,
one of Sir Stephen Fennel's game wardens out at Ockley where
we had a tidy snug house on the edge of Layer Wood. We'd been
married two years, and I'd just started a baby, when he died of
a fever and the house was wanted for the man that took over
his job.

What with the grief and the baby coming and all, I didn't act
sensible; I went running round like a hen with its head off, trying
to find – not a job, as I should have done – but some little place
to put my bits and pieces. That took some doing, and before I'd

managed it, along came the bailiff and two men and put my furniture out. I never forgot that day; it was October and pouring wet, and there was my goose-feather bed that my mother had made, the chest my granny had left me, the chair my own father had sat down to die in, and all my other things, set out in the rain and the wind. I was like somebody crazy and stood there crying and howling.

After a bit, one of the men came back and said he'd give a shilling for the lot. I took his shilling, got a ride in a wagon to Baildon and went straight to an ale-house and got drunk. Whether it was that or the jolting in the wagon, I lost the baby the next day; and after that there didn't seem anything to bother for, except to earn enough to keep me in ale. I never tried for a steady job, or to try to get myself a house again. Whenever I even thought about houses I thought of the one I'd had, and how I'd kept it clean, and aired the bed in the sun and polished the chest and the chairs with beeswax. And yet I was a home-keeping body. All those years I never heard of a pig-killing without my fingers itching to do the salting and make the brawn and the sausages; I never smelt bread baking without wishing I'd had a hand in it. I hated the way I lived and the riff-raff all round me; but all I ever did was get drunk and forget it. When Martin took his knock, which was so much like mine, the first thing I did was to offer him some ale and a chance to forget.

One knock didn't down him though, and the day came when he looked for me and said Pert Tom the bear man and he were setting up in business together and had a house nearly built, and they wanted me to go and look after it for them.

I said, 'I don't know. I reckon it's too late by many a year. I've lost all my housekeeping skills. And you've lived alongside me long enough to know my weakness for ale.'

'I don't ask for skill. All we want is food on the table and a stitch put in now and again. And you're welcome to all the ale you can drink, and to anything else you want.'

'You want somebody younger.'

'I want you,' he said. So I said I'd try.

I hardly knew myself. I found there wasn't a thing I'd forgotten. After all those years, living hand to mouth, I could still do things just as I'd seen my mother do them, and been taught by her to do them. Even her wonderful lardy cake I could make as though I'd been doing it all my days. I made a little garden and grew herbs and peas and beans and bushes of lavender and rosemary. As for the ale, now that I was happy I could take a pot and be content with that, just like anybody else.

It was like being born again, and it was all due to Martin who'd taken me out of the gutter. I'd always liked him; he'd been very generous over the Trimble; and now, what with the liking, and feeling sorry for him and admiring the way he worked and schemed, I came to love him. He seemed like my own, the son I never had.

I had three happy, busy years. Then one morning I noticed that my ankles were swelling. That was how Death first put his finger on my mother. Later would come the blue lips, the shortness of breath. Then I'd be useless. And what would happen to Martin?

There were, I knew, dozens of women who would come and keep house for him and Tom; but there is a difference between keeping house and looking after. I kept house for Tom, I looked after Martin.

If Pert Tom came home soaking wet – as rarely happened, for he could pick his time for going abroad – I'd say to him, 'Look at the mess you've brought in!' and let him sit down wet or dry as he chose. If Martin came in wet, and would have gone to his room to get busy with his tally sticks or some such, I would say, 'Oh no you don't. You put off your wet things and on with these dry ones, and drink this hot broth before you so much as sit down.'

Once – the winter he started his wool-buying, and should have gone to Kersey, and had a heavy cold – I took away every stitch of clothing he had, so he had to stay in bed.

I looked ahead and I could even see the new woman making more fuss of Pert Tom than of Martin. For one thing Pert Tom was supposed to be the one with the money, and he was cheerful and joking, while Martin was glum, on the sour side, all wrapped up in whatever he was doing, no matter what it was; Martin worked as some men drink or gamble.

To me and to Tom he was civil enough, so long as we didn't take liberties; even Tom held him in some awe. To speak to him on such a private business was taking a liberty, perhaps; still, I did it.

I asked him, 'Did you ever give a thought to marrying again?'

He gave me one of those black looks of his. They'd come over him since Kate's death. Before that, I'd seen him look miserable or hungry, dog-tired or angry, but this was something different; there was a sort of power to that look, so that it was as bad as having another man curse you.

'It'd put some purpose to all this work and getting gear together,' I went on. 'You'll end a rich man, with no one to take after you.'

'I'll leave a fund to pay nosy old women to mind their own business.'

'I know I'm old, and maybe I'm nosy, but I would like to see you settled. The past is over and done with. A new wife in your bed and a new boy in a cradle and...'

He gave me another, even blacker look, one that cut clean through me, turned on his heel and went out. I never mustered the courage to speak of it again.

Still, there are more ways of catching a coney than running after it shouting. I put my wits to work.

I didn't know any respectable young women, and none ever came to the house. There had been a time, when Martin first looked like being successful, when the townsfolk would have been friendly – they even invited him to join a Guild, after all; but he would have none of that. He never went into anybody's house, and no one visited us. So where to start my matchmaking?

There was Peg-Leg. He was the black sheep of a very respectable family and had a niece, out at Clevely, married to a yeoman farmer that owned his fifty acres; she must have been a very decent sort of woman too, for riff-raff as Peg-Leg had become she never cut him off. I talked to him frankly, telling him what I was looking out for.

He laughed at first.

'Do the man want a wife he'd find one hisself. He get about, don't he, he must see dozens. He've lived alone three year now, and I reckon he must like it.'

'He's never given the matter a thought, being too busy, first with the Forge and the stabling and now with all this wool. There's a difference between going out to find yourself a wife and seeing a neat pretty girl doing the jobs about the house, waiting on you and listening when you talk. If we could find the right girl it'd come over him bit by bit, without any thinking.'

'Well, maybe. I'll hev a talk with Winnie about it next time I go over.'

But I hadn't got endless time; I couldn't wait.

'I'll tell you what I'll do, Peg-Leg; I'll give you the money to buy yourself a ride, and to take your niece a present.'

'Where'd you get it from?'

'The housekeeping. I handle all.' I was proud of that.

'All right then. Only don't set your heart on it too much. You know the saying about the horse and water.'

A day or two later he set off for Clevely and he must have been on his very best behaviour, for he stayed ten days, and when he came back he was as pleased as if he'd thought of the whole idea himself.

His niece's husband had a sister named Jennie, eighteen years old and, said Peg-Leg, as pretty as a hedge rose as well as being skilled in the house. Peg-Leg had explained the situation, and the girl and her family were willing. So I said to Martin that the work was getting a bit much for me and that Peg-Leg had a niece who would come and help me.

'Where'd she sleep?'

'With me. There's room.' My bed was in a kind of alcove in the kitchen; the chimney stuck out, and there was just room for a bed between it and the wall.

'Not much room. If that was shored up stronger...' he said, pointing up to a kind of wide shelf that ran across one end of the kitchen, and was used to store cheese and bacon and onions – all of which we used a lot of, feeding so many men their dinners.

'All right. Maybe that would be best. Thank you,' I said.

So presently Jennie came; and she was as pretty as a hedge rose, and almost as quiet. Asked a flat question she'd say 'Yes' or 'No' as the case might be; and passed the salt she'd say 'Thank you'. For a sensible young man with the itch in his blood that would have been enough; but being so quiet and shy made her seem younger than she was, while Martin was years older than his age. Across the gap he only gave her the kind of attention he'd have given a child.

There was a Fair while she was with us, and I made an effort and went into town and bought her a head-dress, the prettiest I ever saw, made of stuff so thin it was like cobwebs on a frosty morning, all draped over two pointed horns. I'd make her look older, I thought, and it couldn't help but be noticed. It would have made any girl prink and toss her head and flutter her eyelashes and *be* noticed; but Jennie wore it as though it were a woollen hood to keep out the cold.

After six weeks I knew it was hopeless and sent her home. Then Peg-Leg said there *was* another girl he knew, a cousin of Jennie's, not so pretty, rather older, but lively. He'd seen her at his niece's too, and she was enough to make a cat laugh at times.

Her name was Kate. I said we must change that, and she was agreeable – she liked being called Kitty. Her skin was sallow and her hair the colour of mud, but she was cheerful and amusing, and every bit as good in the house as Jennie. Even Martin smiled at her sometimes, with the smile which came rarely nowadays and always looked as though it hurt him somewhere deep inside.

However, after a bit he began to make excuses not to sit down at table with us; he'd say he was busy and would have a piece in his hand. I got tired of having Peg-Leg sidle up to the door and ask how things were going, when nothing was going at all; and also I didn't trust Pert Tom; all the little airs and graces, the jokes and the glances that were wasted on Martin, found a ready mark with the bear man, so in the end I thought it'd save trouble if Kitty went home too.

Tom, who was sharp enough in his way, had seen what I was up to.

'You daft owd besom,' he said. 'Don't you know when you're well off? If Martin got married his wife'd look round your greasy pans and show you the door.'

'That wouldn't matter to me,' I said, thinking of my legs and the way the swelling was creeping up. 'I want to leave him with somebody before I die.'

'I'm here, ain't I?'

'Fine help you are. You'd watch him work himself to death and never do a hand's turn.'

'You can't say that. Didn't I take Owd Muscovy and my whistle, and go round gathering the crowd and yelling my lungs out about the cheap smith work and stabling to be found at the Owd Vine?'

'So you did. Three summers back. Just to get him more work than three men should've tackled!'

There was no love lost between Pert Tom and me. For one thing, after that first night I never believed that he burnt himself trying to save Martin's wife and children. I noticed next morning that the bear was burnt too; and it certainly hadn't tried to save anybody. Tom said it to boast and be admired, and it had paid him well. It seems that he'd saved a bit of money, not a lot, but enough to start a business with, and he wanted somebody to start up with that was capable of earning him a comfortable living for the rest of his life. Martin was just the man. It amused me, though, to see that despite it being Pert Tom's money, Martin all along had stayed top-dog, mainly on account of those black looks of his. Even while Martin was working from dawn to dusk in the Forge and Tom was just idling about, Tom was never master. And later, when Martin went into the wool trade and had smiths working for him in the Forge, and began to call himself with two names, Martin Reed, and was being called Master, the bear man stayed plain Pert Tom.

Well, all I could do, having tried my hand at match-making and being acquainted with no other respectable young women, was to pray; and since by that time I couldn't get to church, the best I could do was to steal into Pert Tom's room now and again and painfully go down on my knees before the Virgin that he had there, calling her St Ursula. I knew better; her cloak was true Mary blue, and she had the face of the Holy Mother. The bear was just there to show that even a savage beast could be tame in Her presence. At least, that is how I thought and believed while I was doing my praying that somehow or other Martin should find him a good steady wife and that he could be fond of. Later on, when I saw what we got, I changed my mind, and I reckon Tom was right: that was St Ursula and I'd annoyed her by calling her out of her name.

We got to June again, and Martin was riding about, buying up fleeces. He'd been away two days and nights and was coming home for supper. I'd got fowl on the spit, peas in the pot, fresh baked bread, and a dish of little strawberries I'd bought from a hawker. Pert Tom was fidgeting about, wanting to begin, saying Martin had changed his mind and wouldn't be back that night; and I said I wouldn't cut the fowl and let the good juice run, just for him. It was well on into dusk, and I'd lighted the candles, when we heard the horse come in at the back and trot to the stable. Then we heard Martin, walking slowly.

'He's met with a mishap, or he's ill,' I said; and I shuffled over to the door and opened it just as he got there. He'd got his arm round what I thought was a child and was helping her along. They were both smeared with mud and dripping with water.

'Oh what is it? What happened?' I asked, the foolish way you do when surprised.

'Let's get in,' he said. I pushed a stool close to the fire and he set her down. Her long black hair reached to the edge of the stool, and water dripped from it to the hearthstone.

'I'll see to her,' I said. 'You go and put on some dry things. Tom, brighten the fire and mull some ale.' It wasn't a cold night, fortunately, but the girl's teeth were chattering and Martin was all goose-pimples.

I threw a blanket from my bed over the girl and stripped her – no hard task, she had on only a bodice and a skirt, such stuff and colours as no decent woman would wear. The bodice was made of red silk, frayed and worn web-thin in places; the skirt was all striped with different colours and had holes in it you could put your hand through. My work as midwife and layer-out made me knowledgeable about bodies, but I never, in all my time, saw a woman quite like this one. She was so thin, but not wasted thin, sinewy rather, square in the shoulder and narrow in the flank, more like a boy, and yet very dainty. And her legs, in proportion to her body, were the longest I ever saw.

I had a queer fancy, when I'd got her stripped and was rubbing her down, that this was the kind of body angels had perhaps, under the long robes, a body not tied down to any one sex.

At the same time I had a great dislike for touching her. I couldn't think why – for except for the river mud she was clean, cleaner than most folk I've had to handle. But she had the effect on me that mice have on some people, or cats, or harmless frogs. In the first instant, faced with a drenched woman I'd snatched the blanket from my bed, but once it had been over her, touching her here and there, I knew I couldn't sleep with it again until it had been washed and hung in the air several times. I put my second shift on her – I was so well provided for these days I had three, just like a bride, and my best dress I gave her, too, knowing that I should never like them again. Shoes I couldn't lend her, mine were too big, and there was no need. I doubt if she'd ever worn shoes in her life; her feet were as hard as horn and so high arched she could have stood on a good-sized pullet's egg without crushing it.

Martin came back into the kitchen, dressed dry and with his hair standing on end where he had rubbed it.

'All right now?'

'I am – thanks to you – very well.'

Her voice wasn't like a woman's, either; it was deep, like a low note on a fiddle, and she certainly wasn't from our part of the country.

Pert Tom poured out the hot, spicy-smelling ale and the girl took her cup without saying 'Thank you,' and sat hugging it to her chest and staring into the fire. Martin took his and sat at his own place at the table.

'Well, what happened?' Tom asked. 'Why was you both so wet?'

They seemed each to wait to let the other answer, and both spoke together when they did speak.

'I fell...' the girl began, just as Martin said, 'I fished...' He stopped and allowed her to finish.

She lifted one long thin hand and laid it to her flat wet hair.

'I am doing my hair, making the water my looking glass, and I fall in.'

'And you fished her out?' Tom said to Martin.

'That's so. Is supper ready?'

'And waiting,' I said. 'Pull that stool in.'

'You are inviting me?'

'You're welcome to your supper and a bed,' Martin said.

'Is very kind.'

'Where did you fall in the water?' Tom asked.

'Some place,' the girl said.

'Flaxham St Giles, by the mill,' Martin put in.

'Where's your home?'

She hunched her small square shoulders. 'Anywhere. Everywhere. I am on the roads and I make my living...Oh!' She dropped her knife and turned to Martin and said in the most heart-broken way, 'My tambourine. I have lost my tambourine.'

'Don't fret about that. We'll see about it in the morning. And if the worst comes to the worst, we'll get you a new one.'

'Is very kind.'

Pert Tom, who had travelled the roads himself, began to ask her questions about this person and that – a stilt-walker, a tumbler called Boneless, a man who swallowed knives. Sometimes she would say, 'Yes, I know him,' or 'He was at York last summer,' but when he pressed for details her answers were vague and unsatisfactory.

'Mostly I am alone. It is better so,' she said.

'And if you'd just escaped drowning by a hairsbreadth, Tom, probably some things would slip your memory,' Martin said.

'Now somebody once towd me that when you drowned you see your whole life spread out like a picture. I allust wondered if that was true. Is it?' Tom asked.

'I do not know. I saw only a hawthorn tree. So pretty, green and white in the sun. I think to myself – Is Heaven, after all. Then here I am, being slapped in the face, very wet and cold. Sir,' she turned to Martin, 'I do not wish you to think me ungrateful, but I was...Oh well, it is over now.'

When she said that, Martin looked at her with a sudden, sharp interest, such a look as I'd never seen him turn on anyone, not even his Kate. You'd look that way, maybe, if you were in foreign parts across the sea and suddenly heard somebody speak in your own tongue.

He stopped eating and seemed as though he was going to say something, but he didn't; the habit of easy talk had gone from him in these last years.

I thought over the words again, and couldn't find anything in them. This was June, the hawthorns would be in flower, and most likely the last thing she saw when she fell in the water was just such a green and white tree. And if it wasn't the words she said, it must have been her looks that suddenly made him come to life that way. So then I took another look at her.

I know that men and women see things differently, and I know that I was already against her, but even so, she had no beauty, no prettiness. Her face was too thin, all mouth and eyes, and the eyes not set in right. Or at least it looked so. It looked as though her cheeks had been pushed up, leaving hollows where flesh should have been and a heap of flesh up under the eyes, shoving them out of shape. Her skin was all over alike, the colour of porridge. Her mouth, I grant, was as red as a berry. I looked at this face and I remembered what I'd seen of the almost breastless, un-female body, and I shuddered as I sat there,

Pert Tom, as soon as he had supped, got up and went off for what he called his 'last breath of air'. That meant Dummy's daughter, not the crooked one, the younger, with the red hair, a very forward little wench, bound for a bad end.

Martin sat on at the table, and again looked as though he was going to say something, and finally did.

'Agnes will look after you. Good night,' was what he got out. Then he went to his room and we two were left.

I didn't want her to help me clear the table. I knew that if she lifted the loaf and put it in the crock I should not want to eat another slice of it. I didn't want her to touch anything; and that puzzled me – life had long ago knocked any fancifulness out of me. But there it was. I said,

'The bed's up there,' and I pointed. 'And the privy is outside, sharp to the left.'

She went out and came in again and climbed the little ladder. I noticed that her toes curled round the staves, like fingers, and that seemed so unnatural that it gave me a shuddering grue once more. Her wet clothes lay on the floor; she'd never thought to hang them out to dry. I did that, because I didn't want her to have the excuse for waiting for them in the morning. For a little while they smelt of wet stuff drying, and then they smelt of wild thyme.

The scent reminded me of the sheep run at Horringer where I had lived as a girl.

In the morning she came down and picked up her clothes and in a minute was down again, wearing them.

'A comb,' she said. 'Could you lend me? That I lost too.'

I had a comb, a good one, not a snaggy toothed wooden one, a fine bone comb that Martin had bought for me one day when a pedlar came to the door. I handed it to her unwillingly, thinking – Another thing spoilt, I shall never really like it again. She ran it through her hair which had dried out, black and glossy as a blackbird's wing, but almost as flat as when it was wet. She didn't plait it or knot it, just left it hanging, and that, for some reason, annoyed me, as well as seeing her with my comb, so I said, 'That skirt of yours isn't decent. Why don't you mend it?'

'I cannot sew.'

'Rubbish. Any woman with hands and eyes can sew. What can you do?'

'I can play my tambourine. And I can cook a hedgehog.'

'A hedgehog! That's no meat for Christians.'

She made no answer, but went and stood by the door, looking out at the morning. I stirred the porridge, set out the bread and drew the breakfast ale. Martin came in from the yard and stood by her in the doorway.

'Did you sleep well?' he asked her.

'Oh yes. Is so long since I sleep in a bed.'

He came in and stood by the board and I put the porridge bowl before him. He always took his breakfast standing. She stayed by the door. After a spoonful or two he said, 'Have you had your breakfast?'

She turned around and, leaning against the door post, laughed. 'Once a day is for eating – with people like me.' She smacked her flat stomach with her hand. 'Get into bad habits and expect to be fed all the time. No!'

Martin, whose very smile had grown into something painful, actually laughed.

'One indulgence couldn't hurt. Still, please yourself. Now, where do I look for this tambourine? Where exactly did you…fall into the water?'

She squinted up her eyes so that they looked more misshapen than ever.

'The name of the place? I do not know. There is a bridge.'

'Stone or wood?'

'Stone. Two archers.'

'Up river from Flaxham. That'd be Marly?'

'Perhaps. After the bridge is a place for dipping water and there is my tambourine.'

I knew that on this day Martin had planned to go to Hedingham, and that was nowhere near Flaxham or Marly way. Wasting his time, I thought.

'Most like it has been picked up by now,' I said.

'I do not think anybody will do that,' she said.

'I'll go and have a look. And if I can't find it, you shall have a new one.'

'It belonged to my mother and I have just bought it new ribbons.'

When he had gone I said to her, 'Would it have hurt you to say "Thank you"? Here's a busy man going out of his way, promising you new if he can't find your old – and that is most unlikely. And you can't even thank him!'

The bulges under her eyes lifted, squeezing her eyes as she smiled.

'You should know. You are a woman. If you thank a man, he thinks you are in debt to him and so he looks for payment.'

'Not him,' I said. 'He's the kindest and best-hearted…This whole place is built up on his good heart, lame folks and daft ones and people in trouble or disgrace, people nobody else wanted.' I thought of Dummy and Peg-Leg and Peter Priest, and a dozen more. Me too.

She said, 'People nobody else will want, they are very cheap.'

Something in my head went 'Snap' like an over-blown bladder. The shocking part of it was that just for a second I thought – That is *true!* Just as he made that tidy little hut in Squatters Row, out of nothing, out of stuff other people would chuck away or overlook, so he's made all this out of human rubbish. Even Pert Tom's savings had been *used*, and Pert Tom so handled that he daren't bring his baggage into the house.

But that only lasted a second; it was like some of the things you see when you're very drunk; they seem very real and you're scared. Then they're gone. And that was gone.

I said, 'I suppose you will have to wait to see if he finds your tambourine; and if you want to eat midday there'll be food here, but I'd thank you to get out of my kitchen.'

She went off and I began on my day's work, which was preserving gooseberries. Our young bushes were in full fruit that year, and some of Dummy's children had gathered them and picked off the tops and tails. I scalded the jars and packed them in close, got the cloths soaking in the mutton fat for the covers, and more mutton fat melted to pour over. Then Pert Tom, who was a slug abed in the mornings, came ambling in for his breakfast.

'Where's Martin's drowned cat?' he asked.

'Out. I'm busy. I didn't want her hanging round me.'

'I reckon you'd better get used to it. I've missed my mark if he don't take up and marry her.'

'Marry her. Rubbish!' But another over-blown bladder had gone 'Snap' in my head.

'You ask yerself. Take the way he looked at her, promised her a new tambourine if hers was lost – and him so mean he didn't even hev a pair of gloves till you give him a pair for Christmas. You couldn't've missed *that*. If you ask me, she's cut to his measure, all skin and bone and grief, somebody to feel sorry for, just like his other one.'

I dished him out the heated-up porridge.

'You knew Kate, then?'

'Kate?'

'His wife.'

'This porridge is burnt, tastes awful. Kate, was that her name? I saw her, yes. I saw her go into the hut – like I say, all skin and bone and grief. And now he've got hisself just such another, after waiting so long.' He laughed and pushed his porringer away. 'Still, maybe she can cook.'

'She can,' I said tartly. 'She can cook a hedgehog.'

'A hedgehog? That ain't Christian food,' he said, exactly as I had done. 'Thass real Romany.'

'And what's that?'

'Oh, foreign. Out of Pharaoh's Egypt some say. There's one or two on the roads, but decent people don't hev nowt to do with them. They're heathen. They don't even lay together like other people, they do it cutting their thumbs and letting the blood mix.'

'The tales you tell!'

'I only pass on what I hear tell myself. And of course if she is Romany I shall miss my mark 'cause she couldn't marry him. They ain't allowed to stay in one place more'n a moon month; if they do they die.'

He finished his breakfast and went off, it being Wednesday, to idle away his time looking round the market and sitting in one ale-house after another, listening to and spreading gossip. He didn't come in for dinner, nor did the girl, so I fed those men who were on wages-and-dinner terms, finished my gooseberries and sat down to rest myself before starting supper. I'd hardly set down before Pert Tom came in, full of ale and something else: I could see before he opened his mouth that he had a fine tit-bit to tell me.

He looked round the kitchen and up in the loft.

'Is she about?'

'No. You can see for yourself.'

He pulled a stool near me.

'Now you listen to this. Know what we've got in the house now? A witch, no less!'

144

'Rubbish,' I said, partly because his tales were so far-fetched and partly because, like almost every other old woman who was poor and looked a bit wild, I'd had the word 'Witch' flung at me in my time. Nevertheless, when he brought out the word I thought – That's it! That accounts for the way I feel about her, not wanting her to handle my things, not wanting to touch her.

'Rubbish away. Only tell me this, where'd Martin say he found her?'

'Flaxham. By the mill.'

'Right. And what lay up-river from Flaxham? Maybe you don't know.'

'As it happens I do. A place called Marly.'

'Right again. Well, Tuesday morning, yestiddy that is, a Marly man heard his dog barking early in the morning; he look out and what do he see but a young woman with long black hair, raiding his hens' nest. He see her take two eggs, one she stuck in the front of her dress, the other she kept in her hand. Jest as he was he run out and ask for his eggs back. She say – Take it, and give him the one in her hand. He say she've got another, she say she h'ain't, and he say all the time he can see it bulging out inside her bodice. So he go to take it, as who wouldn't? And she say to him, "Don't you put your hand on me," she say, "if you do you'll be very sorry." But he don't take no notice, he take the egg instead. And then what happen?'

'His arm dropped off at the shoulder.'

'You're a funny owd crone, ain't you? No, what happen is that he go out to the hay field and afore he've been there a quarter hour somebody unhandy with a sickle cut off two fingers for him. Now thass no good saying "Rubbish", the man that towd me had jest brought the poor man to the Abbey Infirmary; they'd stopped the bleeding with hot tar but he was swelling up cruel. Only, here's the point to this tale. Everybody in Marly turned out to chase the witch and by the bridge they found her. They tied her skirt round her knees and chucked her in to see do she sink or swim. And she swum! Straight down river towards Flaxham, this chap say, sailing like a swan. Now do you believe me?'

I did. It all fitted in, even to her saying that nobody would have picked up her tambourine from the river bank. Of course not. Nobody would want to touch her gear; just as, in my unknowing way, I hadn't wanted to touch anything she'd handled.

'Yes. For once I do,' I said. 'We must tell Martin.'

'I can't wait to see his face. Fancy him swallowing that yarn about using the water for a looking – '

He broke off and turned his head sharply and looked towards the door. I saw his colour change and he crossed himself, openly. I turned too, and there she was, leaning against the doorpost and holding something in her hands. I slipped one thumb over the other in the shape of the Cross, under cover of the table.

She said, 'To wagging tongues things sometimes happen, too.' As she spoke she walked in and laid what she held on the table. It looked like a ball of clay, about the size of your head, loosely covered with dock leaves.

I've seen some frightened people, but seldom anybody worse scared than Pert Tom. He jumped up and blurted out, stammering and blinking, 'I shan't say anything. I shan't mention it,' and he hurried into his room, where, I knew, he would ask his St Ursula to protect him.

The girl said to me, 'You cross your thumbs, but you will tell Martin what you hear?'

'If my tongue still wags, yes. I'm so old that what happens to me doesn't matter any more.'

She leaned against the edge of the table and folded her arms.

'Is all nonsense, of course. Alone, on the road, as I am most times, a woman must take care. The tale is a lie. Partly. Was Monday evening, not Tuesday morning; and there was no egg. You understand me. No egg. Me, looking for sleeping place, and the man, like all men. You should know, once a man has his hand, *here*, who is safe? So his fingers are chopped. Every day, some place, fingers are chopped.' She leaned sideways, still with her arms folded, and laughed. 'If I could say a thing and make it *be*, I am not wasting my time chopping fingers. No. I would say, Let me dance like my mother! Oh, if that could be!' She sat up straight again and threw back her head and for a moment, in the stuffy kitchen, it seemed as though the wind blew on her face.

I was old, and since I had come to live at the Old Vine I'd had a quiet life, nothing much to think about except whether to serve beef or mutton. So now, with so much, all at once, all strange and different, I was confused. Later, I thought, later, in the quiet of my bed, I'll think it all over. Just for the moment I wanted something real and firm to seize upon. And there was this bundle on the table.

'What is that?'

'Is a hedgehog. Is not food for Christians you say, so I will show you.'

'Oh no. You're cooking no hedgehogs here. Not in my pots.'

'He is needing no pot. He has his own. See.' She picked up the bundle and stripped off the dock leaves. 'We bury him, so, in the hot ash and he makes his own pot. When he is ready we crack him and his prickles all come away with the pot.'

She buried the thing at the fire's edge, pushed it inwards a little and pulled a log over it. As she straightened up, Martin, back much earlier than usual, walked in, holding the tambourine.

'Here you are,' he said.

She swooped forward and took it from him, the bells jingled and jangled, the ribbons, red and yellow and blue, green and purple and pink, just like the stripes of her ragged skirt, fluttered and shook.

'Oh,' she said, 'is so *so* kind! My tambourine.' She drummed on it lightly with the fingers. 'Not spoilt. I was afraid, out on the grass...Is good. Now, after supper, I will dance for you.'

Pert Tom had to be called to supper, and came out like a dog with a bad conscience. Ordinarily after market day he would chatter on, and Martin would grunt and show little interest until Tom told of some mishap that had befallen some Baildon man, and then he would look up and grunt in another tone. But tonight Tom was silent, every now and again looking at the girl and if he happened to catch her eye, shake his head a little and make a secret face, trying to reassure her that his tongue would never wag. Presently Martin said, 'What's the matter, Tom? No gossip going round today?'

'Not a thing. Not a thing,' Tom said and bent over his food. He was eating what I had cooked, but Martin was eating the hedgehog.

She'd cracked off the clay and I admit that the meat left inside looked clean enough and smelt very tasty; but I couldn't bring myself to try it, and Tom was too scared. Martin said, 'I will. Come to think of it, if nobody had ever tried anything new there'd be precious little to eat.'

As he ate he praised it and I tried not to mind or be jealous. After all, I longed and prayed that something would happen to make him shake off the dead past and come alive again, and if it took a wild thing out of the woods with a tambourine and a hedgehog to do it, who was I to complain? I could only hope that she would rouse him, make him feel that there was something left in life besides hard work and making money, and then go off and leave him to take up with a decent woman.

All through supper she sat looking at the tambourine and now and again touching it. As soon as the meal was over she jumped up and asked Tom and Martin to move the table. They began to push it towards the hearth, but she said, 'No, no. The other way. Is better the light behind me.'

When the space was cleared and we were gathered at the other end, she walked down towards the fire, keeping close to the wall and sidling along. Then she stood still, like a cat about to make a spring. And then, with a shake of the tambourine and a little hoarse cry, she leaped out into the centre of the space and began to dance.

I've seen many dancing girls in my day. In the old times, in Squatters Row, in a good summer I've known as many as four be there all at once, and late at night they'd dance, not for pay, but to outdo each other. Some were good and some were bad, but the best of them *was* only a girl dancing when all was said and done. This was something different. Dancing she really could cast a spell. What but magic could make that ragged gaudy old skirt shake out into blurred soft colours like a rainbow or the sunlight on the spray over a weir? How else could she move so that it was all movement, a bird in flight, a deer leaping, a tree swaying in the wind? The music was magic too, for a tambourine has but two sounds, the thrum on the skin and the jingle of the bells; in her hands it made real music in which there was the rush of the wind, the birds' calling, even the solemn chant of the Church.

As long as it lasted you could only sit and stare and wonder. Even I, an old woman, with all my fires quenched, could feel again the stir and the ache, not in the flesh, or for it, but for something more: that something which, when you are young, you think lies round the next corner, and, when you are old, you know you missed because it never could be there. Here, just for once, in the homely kitchen, against the light of the dying fire, it all was held out for us.

When she stopped, it was like waking from a dream in which you are warm and full-fed, to find yourself cold and hungry again. We all three let out our breath in a great sigh.

She went and stood by the wall, breathing quickly and lightly. Then I could move my eyes. And just for once I saw Martin's stern thin face and Pert Tom's fat stupid one wearing the same look of naked lust.

The girl spoke first.

'You like?' She lowered the hand which held the tambourine and it gave a little tinkle, like the echo of the question. She dropped against the wall, hunching her shoulders.

'By my mother I dance like a pig. When my mother danced, when she ceased, men wept with the pain of it.'

Pert Tom got up and blundered out of the house, leaving the door open; the cool air, faintly scented with hay, flowed in.

149

All very well for him, I thought; he can go and find his red-haired baggage; Martin has his empty room, with tally sticks for company.

But Martin stood up and said, 'You know, you've never told us your name.'

'Is Magda.'

'Magda.' He repeated the name which was as strange as everything else about her, as though it pleased him. He said, 'We could do with a breath of air, too.' He went towards the door and it seemed to me that he moved more lightly, more freely, leaning less to his limp than usual. She followed him, I thought unwillingly.

II

That evening they weren't out an hour, all told. I was just in bed when they came in quietly, said goodnight and went to their separate beds. I thought to myself – Well, that's over; he's had his will of her and proved to himself that he can so far forget Kate as to go with another woman and now if she'll just take herself off, everything will be all right.

In the morning, quite early, she did go off, with her tambourine; but she was back, just before supper.

'So you've come back,' I said.

'You think I will not?' She squinted her eyes at me. 'Martin, he is the master here, is it not? He says I am welcome. Tonight I shall dance again.'

'Dancing! That's all you think about.'

'Yes and yes and yes. I have danced today. Look.' She held out her long hand and showed me some coins in its palm. 'I am not needing it, no supper to pay for. You can have it.' She walked up to me and tried to put the money in my hand. I backed as though she had offered me something red-hot.

'I don't want your money. Save it and buy yourself a shift!'

She surprised me by giving one of the deepest, heaviest sighs I ever heard a human being give, though I'd heard the like from donkeys, already overladen, when something else was added to their load.

'A shift, a petticoat and shoes. And every night the certain supper and the bed. It is much.'

'What are you talking about?'

'Things to *have*. Me, I have wanted only to *be*.'

'Be what?'

'Such good dancer as my mother.'

I said, almost against my will, 'I fail to see how she could have been better than you were last night. I've seen a lot of dancers in my time but I never saw anybody dance like you.'

Something lit up in her face; she flung herself at me and would have hugged me, but again I backed away, this time almost into the fire.

'Don't,' I said.

'You are not liking to be touched. Me too, but with men only.'

'Then you go the wrong way about,' I said. 'Any man watching you dance is bound to want to get his hands on you.'

'But I am not dancing for men to desire me. I am not dancing to be paid. Enough for supper, and new ribbons for my tambourine sometimes. And now a new comb.'

'Then why do you do it?'

'Because...' she paused, smiled, shook her head. 'There is no because. To dance I am born, so I dance.'

'To me that sounds daft.'

'Must everything be because? There is a poppy, very red, beside the road for just one day. Because? Is a red poppy. No good for eating. You pluck him, he falls to pieces. Is enough for a poppy just to be a red poppy. And so with me.'

I couldn't find an answer except – Poppies aren't people and people aren't poppies – and that, because it sounded quite as daft as anything she had said, I wouldn't say.

That evening I didn't stay to see her dance. I went and had a little gossip with Peg-Leg. We spoke of this and that, and of the girl who'd come into the house, and I mentioned what Pert Tom had said about Martin being likely to marry her.

'He might at that,' Peg-Leg said. 'Once I sailed with a man that had a monkey; he was more set on that monkey than most men are on their wives. Then it died and his heart broke. A month or two after, we sailed into Tangier, where there was plenty of monkeys, cheap. I said to him, "Why'n't you get yourself a new monkey?" He turned white as a sheet and he said, "I'll never have another monkey as long as I live". But...' Peg-Leg paused and wagged a finger at me. 'We went into Naples and there on the quay was a cat, terrible looking, bones sticking out and mangy all over. He took to that and within a week was as fond of it as he had been of his monkey. See? We did no good with Jennie and Kitty; they was decent, home-keeping little bodies, they just called Kate to mind. This, by all accounts, is quite another pair of shoes.'

'What do you know of her, barring what I've told you?'

'I seen her,' he said simply. 'And I was told she was dancing and prancing and shaking a tambourine in the Market Place today. Can you see Kate doing that?'

'I wouldn't mind,' I said, 'if I thought she'd make him happy.'

'I don't reckon,' Peg-Leg said slowly, 'that men look to women to make them *happy*. Martin had Kate and they got on better than most, but when they wouldn't have him in the Guild, and then, later on, you remember when he broke his leg and Webster sacked him – you couldn't say he was *happy*, could you? Holy Mother, he was miserable as sin.' He broke off and rapped his wooden leg with his knuckles. 'Meaning no offence, Agnes, you having been a woman once, women set theirselves a bit too high. Could somebody come along to me and ask which would I rather, the Queen of Sheba in my bed, or my leg back and be at sea again, I know which I'd say.'

'Ah, that is because you're old.'

'Old! God's blood, how old do you think I am? I'm forty. I'd just turned twenty-four when I was beached.'

I'd always thought of him as being an old man.

'Don't you go fretting yourself over Martin,' he said. 'He's got his business. All he needs now is a boy to bring up in the trade, and he can as easy get that out of a slut as out of a mim little wench that couldn't say boo to a goose.'

That at least was true, and I felt my heart lighten a bit.

'Maybe I'd better start fretting about myself for a change,' I said. 'Peg-Leg, if Martin should marry her, I couldn't stay in the house. The other night she brought in a hedgehog and I said she wasn't cooking it in *my* pots. They'll be *her* pots. Everything will be hers, to use and handle. I couldn't bear it. Could I come and turn in with you for a bit?'

'I reckon so.' He looked round the snug little hut. 'Since I took up work again I've let my mending go.' Like all sailors he'd been handy with a needle. 'You could stitch me up. And it'd be nice to find the fire going when I got home. You'd have to bring your own bed.'

So I found myself a hole to run to if the moment of need should come.

It came, three or four days later, when Martin said to me, in his abrupt way, 'I'm going to marry Magda.'

'I hope you'll be happy,' I said; and I meant it. 'There's one thing you should know, Martin – or maybe she told you…'

'What?'

'They say she's a witch and was being swum that day you found her.'

'I knew that. As soon as I'd choked the water out of her I cut the cord. I'd seen one swum before.'

'And you don't mind?'

'I don't care what she is. She's the only woman…Who told you it was being said?'

'Pert Tom.'

'You can tell him to keep his mouth shut.'

'Oh, she did that, threatened to make his tongue drop out or something.'

Martin laughed. I thought to myself, Peg-Leg can say what he likes, a woman can make a man happy or miserable: already Martin is a different man.

'There's one other thing. I told you some time back this was all getting too much for me. You remember? I think now would be the time for me to go. When's the wedding to be?'

'This day three weeks.'

'Well now, there's Dummy's Mary. She's crooked, but she's as strong as a donkey for all that, and she often hangs around watching me work and helping a bit. If I got her in and showed her how things should be...Then there'd be a new mistress and a new maid and that is the best way.'

'Maybe. Where'd you go?'

'I should go and look after Peg-Leg.'

'I always meant you to end your days by my fire, with your feet under my table, Agnes. But then I never thought...'

'But for you, Peg-Leg wouldn't have a roof or a fire, so it come to much the same thing.'

'In a way, I suppose. And we'd send your food across.'

Stuff she'd have clawed over.

'I'd sooner manage on my own.'

'Please yourself. You can have what money you want.'

'That's kind. And any day I feel up to it, I'll go in the shed and pick wool for a spell to help earn...'

He gave me a very black look and said, 'If you think that's easy!' He swung on his heel and limped away. I thought for a moment that he had seen through my excuse for leaving and was annoyed, yet he hadn't been earlier when I said I was going. It took me a moment or two to realize that Kate had picked wool at Webster's, and this was no moment to remind him of her.

Pert Tom had his excuse for getting out all ready to his hand. All these years he'd held on to his bear and been fairly regular about feeding it and putting it through its tricks. Once, when he was grumbling about what the animal cost to keep, I asked him why he didn't sell it.

'Easy come, easy go,' he said, 'and maybe one of these days Martin'll bite off more than he can chew. First he hev a forge, then hev a row of stables, then hev a wool business. Grant he've been lucky, but build a thing too high and it'll topple over. If it do, then out on the road we go, Owd Muscovy and me, and no worse off than we was.'

'Except that you'd have lost your savings.' We'd been given to understand that it was Pert Tom's money that had started the business in the first place.

Pert Tom laughed. 'Ah yes, them savings! Well, they wasn't all that much, and I've had years of soft living. And shall do, till Martin overreach hisself.'

'If you think he's overreaching himself you should warn him. You're supposed to be his partner.'

'I hate wasting me breath,' he said. But he had held on to the bear; and when he heard about the marriage being so near he said to Martin, 'I allus promised meself one more summer on the road and if I don't go soon I shall be too owd. And you'll like the place to yourselves to start off with.'

To me he said, 'I give it a month, but a month alongside her is more'n I can manage. Half the time I'm frit of her and the other half I'm itching arter her and I don't know which is worst.'

'What'll you do if it lasts more than a month?'

'It can't. I towd you, they can't stay in one place more'n a month without sickening. I shall be back in five-six weeks, according to the weather, and you'll see, she'll be gone.'

'Daft talk,' I said. 'In five-six weeks she may be three weeks gone in another fashion. I surely hope so.'

He didn't even stay for the wedding, so he missed the feast Martin gave to everybody on the place. He had an ox roasted in the yard and there was all the ale we could drink and plenty over.

Even Martin who'd never, in all the time I'd known him, taken a drop too much, was tipsy as soon as anyone.

Magda, for the wedding, had a dress, very costly, of crimson silk so dark it was almost black, she had shoes on her feet and her hair knotted up and fastened with a pair of silver pins. That way, she looked ordinary and decent, her skin very sallow between the dark of the dress and the dark of her hair; and she had none of a bride's happiness. She looked so downcast that I wondered if the shoes were causing her pain.

We put them to bed in proper style and I myself put the salt and the handful of barley at the four corners, to make sure that they would be fruitful.

Peg-Leg was easy-going and I was comfortable enough with him, but for me everything seemed out of joint. I missed seeing Martin and seeing to him, feeling as mothers do when their sons marry and move away. I got into the habit of waiting about the yard just to catch a glimpse of him, judging from the way he looked and the way he walked whether things were going well. One morning, not long after they were married, he came out of the house and went towards the stables whistling, and I could have cried with joy. Immediately after, I could have cried with rage at myself for letting such a daft fancy put me out of the house and out of his life. One day there'd be a baby there, his baby, and I should have no part in it. I was like a woman who, hungry as she may be, can't go to her own bread crock because a spider is sitting beside it.

Dummy's Mary was so grateful to me for getting her the job and training her to it, that she was like a dog; she often used to come round to have a bit of a gossip and ask my advice on this and that. She told me that the mistress did nothing in the house at all, still ate only once a day and spent hours in Tom's empty room, playing the tambourine and dancing, all by herself. Martin had put his foot down about her dancing in the town and threatened, if she disobeyed him, to take away her tambourine.

'He should stop her dancing altogether,' I said, when Mary told me this, 'rattling her insides about that fashion, how can she hope to breed.'

Another time, a little later, Mary reported that the mistress had a cough, which she said was because she was indoors so much.

'She's not hobbled or chained,' I said. 'She could do a bit in the garden. The lavender isn't even cut this year yet, and the pea haulms yellowing where they stand. And couldn't she walk into market, like any other housewife?'

The year moved on and it was Michaelmas. Pert Tom had been away longer than he'd planned, because, I suppose, the good weather had lasted. I looked forward to his coming home, partly because I wondered what he would do, and partly because I wanted to tease him about being so know-all about Romanys and their not being able to stay anywhere more than a month.

October was two days old when, one afternoon, coming out of the wool shed, where I'd been picking (which is hard work and made me think of Kate who used to do it all day long and with two children to mind), I saw Tom just shoving his bear into its shed.

'So you're back,' I said.

'So I am, fancy you noticing,' he said sourly and kicked the bear to move it over.

'And she's still there. Using your room to dance in, so I hear.'

'If I want me room back I shall hev it. Remember how I got this?' He turned his face, so that the scar the burn had left on his cheek showed up in the light.

'You'd not speak of that and remind him, just when he's begun to be happy again!'

'Why not? He was the one said we was to live together the rest of our lives. He was the one said no women in the house when I wanted to bed Joan in comfort. I'll remind him all right. I'll remind him of a lot of things.'

I drew a bow in the dark.

'While you're about it, remind him how your old bear was burnt, too, helping with the brave rescue.'

'What do you know about that?'

'More than you think. A lot more than you think.'

Where exactly I'd hit him I couldn't see, but somewhere, for though he scowled he said, 'I don't want to go dragging up owd things. Nor I don't want to go back on the roads. I've got soft and I'm too owd to lay out after Michaelmas. Where're you living?'

'With Peg-Leg – and a right tight fit it is.'

'Well, I shall see what Martin hev to say. Not that I hanker to be under the same roof with her, but this is my home, arter all.'

So off he went and that very evening, when Peg-Leg came home he told me that he and several other men had been taken off their different jobs and set to build again.

'Starting tomorrow, digging holes for the posts. A rare fine big room this is to be, too; twenty feet by twenty and ten high. He talk of putting in a window, glassed.'

'Just for Pert Tom?'

'No. For Mistress Reed. He had a special word for it. Ah, I got it, a solar he called it.'

I tried to imagine such a large room and couldn't see where it be on such a little house, not without blocking up a door or a window of what was there already. Unless he built it on the forge side.

'Is he aiming to move the forge then?'

'No. The other side.'

'That'd block the way the ponies come in from the road to the yard.'

'They're leaving that just as it is and building across the other side of it.'

'Then there'll be two separate houses.'

'No. Martin reckoned to roof over the way the ponies go in and leave that as a passage way. Then folks can get from the kitchen door to the...the solar, just stepping across the passage.'

For the next six or seven weeks I used to go along every day and watch the work going forward. Apart from the big houses at Horringer where my father was shepherd and Ockley where my husband was game warden – so of course I never was in them, only saw them from outside – I never had seen such building. Even the floor was solid oak, every plank about eighteen inches wide and laid as level as a table. And they put in a window, like Peg-Leg said, not flat in the wall, but bowed out, right over the garden I'd made, so it only just missed my lavender bush. It was all made up of little panes of glass, greenish, about as big as the palm of my hand. All that, just for a woman to dance in!

I now had another spy inside the house, as it were. Pert Tom, who had often enough grumbled about my cooking, more to annoy me than because he had any cause, would come slouching round once or twice a week, and without actually asking, would say something smelt tasty, and complain of Mary's cooking, and I'd give him a piece of whatever was going and he'd sit down and talk. He seemed to have lost most of his fear of Magda and to get along with her very well, 'what little I see of her,' he said. 'I never hang around when she takes that tambourine in hand, because thass the only time she's anyway tempting.' He spoke as though, apart from her dancing and her lack of interest in the kitchen, Magda was ordinary enough and life in the house pretty smooth-running.

Once, a little before Christmas, he spoke of her having a cough and brewing up a cure for it; it smelt terrible, he said.

Then, even nearer Christmas, Mary came along one evening and begged me to go in and make the plum pudding.

'All them costly things,' she said. 'If owt went wrong and they was wasted, that would be a pity. T'ain't like spoiling a pot of porridge, is it?'

I said, craftily, 'I'll come and help you, if we can do it some time when the mistress isn't about – then you can take the credit for it, you see. You wouldn't want her to know, would you?'

'She's in the solar every afternoon now.'

'All right then. Now mind this...' I told her that she was to scrub the table, wash the bowl, the spoon and the big iron pot, and scald the pudding cloth. 'Never mind if they are all clean; it's a kind of magic rule: for making plum pudding everything must be washed afresh.'

Even if I hadn't had this hatred of handling anything after those long thin hands had been on it, that would have been a wise order. Nothing in the kitchen was as I left it, everything was greasy and smeared and in the wrong place. I scolded Mary – not too much, for she had been brought up like a pig and only had three weeks' training, but I scolded myself most harshly for running away on account of a fancy. I should have stayed, I told myself. I'd come back, I told myself all the time I was chopping the suet; I'd humble myself to Martin, tell him I wasn't comfortable with Peg-Leg and beg him to take me back. I'd force myself to get over this stupid feeling; if Pert Tom could live in the house with her, so could I.

We had the flour and the suet and the eggs and the fine fat raisins all ready.

'We want a pinch of spice,' I said to Mary. 'Where do *you* keep the spice box? I always had it on the shelf here.'

'I think it's in the cupboard.'

'God bless you girl, don't you *know*?' I exclaimed, and glared at her as she went to the cupboard.

Inside it was all of a jumble, in which she ferreted about like a blind woman, while I clucked my tongue, making the most of my impatience. She reached up to the top shelf and, as she did so, a little bunch of dried-up herbage fell out; she grabbed at it and missed it and it dropped near me. I picked it up, smelt it, and said sharply, 'Mary! Leave hunting that spice box and come here. What is this?'

And I thought – Jesus have mercy, if a poor ugly crooked girl like that can get into trouble! I kept my eye hard on her but she neither blushed nor blenched.

'That? Oh, thass Mistress' stuff for her cough.'

'Her cough! But this…How often does she take it?'

'I don't rightly know. From time to time she'll pour water on and drink it when it's soaked.'

'I see. Best put it back. Then if you look behind that crock of mouldy dripping, you'll find your spice box.'

She brought it to me, saying with a false little smile, like a dog in disgrace wagging its tail too fast, 'You do hev good eyes, Agnes.'

'Too good,' I said.

We went on making the pudding, but my mind was on other things: the feeling that I must come back here and set things right for Martin's sake; the memory of that bunch of dried stuff with the faded flowers that had been pink and pale rounded leaves with their pointed ends.

I was on my feet, the better to give the mixture the good sturdy whack that it needed, and saying, 'Like this, see. Smack it about as though you were beating a bed,' and just about to hand the spoon to Mary, when the kitchen door opened and Magda walked in. First I was thankful that I was on my feet so I didn't have to stand up to acknowledge she was mistress, and second all my determination to come back and see Martin comfortable just ran away like water down a gutter.

She said, 'Hullo Agnes' as carelessly as though she'd seen me the day before. No surprise, no interest that I should be there, in her greasy untidy kitchen, making her plum pudding for Christmas. I just gave her a nod of my head and turned to Mary.

'Now to do the thing properly,' I said, 'we have to have a chunk of wood, borrowed from a friend, to lay on the fire to start boiling. Go along to Peg-Leg's – there's nobody there, but you must knock on the door and say, "Can I borrow a log to cook my plum pudding?" You'll find some logs there; choose the biggest and bring it back.'

Mary went off. I'd made the thing up on the spur of the moment, but it fitted, I thought, Christmas being the friendly season.

Magda was going towards Martin's room, now their bedroom, but I stopped her.

'I want to ask you something.'

She turned back and said, 'Yes.' And at that moment the fright came on me. All those months ago, when Pert Tom had said she was a witch and I'd crossed my thumbs and thought that was why I didn't want any doing with her, I hadn't been really frightened. That is true. She'd threatened the tongue that wagged about how she got in the river, yet I had told Martin. I'd never been really scared. Now, all of a sudden I was. My breath seemed to catch. Still I said it.

'That stuff you take for your cough, every now and then. Do you know what that is?'

'Is a wildflower. Good for the cough.'

She'd turned back and now stood so that the table was between us and we faced each other as though we were fighting a duel or playing some gambling game.

'I never heard it was good for coughs. It has another virtue...' Then I thought – That slipped out because you get used to speaking of the virtues of herbs; in this case it has no virtue. It'd be a virtue if she was a maid betrayed, or the down-burdened mother of a huge family. I shouldn't have said 'virtue'. And of course I shouldn't, because she just said, 'So? Is nice to know!' and went sauntering into the bedroom.

I was so angry that I couldn't breathe. My heart came jumping up into my throat, beating like a hammer, bells rang in my ears and for a moment I couldn't see except for sparks all shimmering against blackness.

I sat down and wrestled with my breath. I would breathe, pull it in, hold it, let it out. I could hear myself making a noise like a blacksmith's bellows.

Then there was Mary, so quick for all she was lop-sided, back, lugging a great log.

'What do we do next, Agnes?'

And I managed to tell her, calmly, how to put the pudding into the cloth, leaving plenty of room for it to swell. And she did it. All the time there was no sound from the inner room.

It was growing dark.

'One more thing, Mary,' I said. 'Take the scissors and cut about an inch off the lavender bush. That has to boil in the water.'

As soon as she had gone I took the bunch of penny royal from the cupboard and dropped it into the heart of the fire.

III

I thought the matter over, by night as well as by day, for what remained of the time till Christmas. I felt it was my duty to tell Martin what his wife was up to, and yet I dreaded to upset him. I didn't want to make *too* much of it. There again, I thought, if I'd had any pluck at all I should have been in the house, and seeing him often, able to drop a hint. However, my chance came, for the Christmas was to be a real merry one of the old-fashioned sort. Martin had a pig killed and roasted whole and we all had our Christmas dinner on the big wool floor which had been three-quarters cleared. As at the wedding there was ale for everybody, and we sang all the old Christmas songs about the Three Wise Men and the Star of Bethlehem, and about The Holly and The Ivy.

Peg-Leg, like all sailors, was handy with his knife and could whittle any shape you asked, and I'd asked him to do a baby, and a donkey and a cow about the size so that a small salt-box could be a manger for them. I put a wisp of straw in the box, laid the baby on it, put the donkey on one side and the cow on the other, and set them all on a board to decorate the table at the end where Martin sat. I'd praised Peg-Leg's whittling and left it at that, and then, on the Christmas morning, when we stood together watching the pig turning on the spit over the fire in the forge, I did another bit of flattering.

'Peg-Leg,' I said, 'somebody ought to thank Martin for all this and you're the one. If it's left to Peter Priest it'll be all long worth and no heart to it, and Pert Tom'll be stuttering drunk before the time comes. You're the one.'

'Aye,' he said, 'I reckon I could stand up and say thanks for us all.'

'And best wishes. I tell you what, Peg-Leg, say that while you're about it you'll wish that next year there'll be another baby at the table. That'll draw everybody's attention to yours.'

'And thass a good wish, too,' he said.

So all I had to do was to wait till Peg-Leg stood up and clapped his hands for silence and started to speak. Then I went and got as near Martin as I could, a little behind, so my mouth was close to his ear, and when Peg-Leg said about the baby I muttered to myself, as any old woman of my age is entitled to do, 'And so there would be, if she didn't keep swilling down that cough mixture!'

He heard, I saw him jump. He said, 'What was that?' pretty sharp. 'What was what?'

'What did you say?'

'Did I speak? I reckon I was talking to myself,' I said, and wandered off.

I really did think to myself that that hint was dropped as well as ever a hint was. And it was noticed. It wasn't long after Christmas, the real cold weather was just beginning, when Dummy's Mary came along with some tale about the Master coming into the kitchen just as the Mistress was brewing her medicine and taking it and pouring it out at the back door.

'Thass all froze now, as hard and smooth as glass,' she ended.

'Take a shovelful of ashes and put over it then, for Holy Mary's sake,' I said. 'We don't want anybody breaking a leg.'

After that I just sat back and waited. The cold weather ended, the days pulled out, morning and evening, a few birds began to sing and even fly about with bits of straw in their bills, and it was spring again.

I stood one morning, where I usually did, and watched Martin mount and ride off somewhere. I remembered thinking that badly as Mary managed in one way, she kept him fed and tidy-looking. He did look just as usual. I stood there for a bit, enjoying the air, and along came Pert Tom to give Owd Muscovy his breakfast.

'Well,' he said, 'if you left on account of her, you can move back. Reckon I was right after all. She's up and quit!'

I had another of those turns when I couldn't breathe or see; I had to lean against the wall to keep myself from falling. He was saying something, but the ringing in my ears was so loud I couldn't hear what it was. I did my careful breathing, in, hold it, out, for a time or two, and at last I could speak.

'What do you mean, up and quit. When, why?'

'I was telling you. You gone deaf? She took off yesterday morning and ain't been seen since. I reckon I miscalculated. That must be a *year*, not a month, they can't stay in one place.'

'Oh, stop that jabber! What about Martin? How's he taking it? Was he off just now, looking for her?'

'Not him. He's off to Lavenham. Know what he said, last night, when he come in and found her gone? He said, "Well, you can't keep a lark in a cage, leave alone make a broody hen of it!" Then he set down and et his supper. If you ask me he've had a bellyful of her and is as glad to see her gone as I am. You'll come back now, eh, Agnes, and cook us some decent grub?'

My mind was elsewhere but my tongue answered him.

'You always used to grumble about my cooking.'

'That was afore I tried Mary's!'

'I'll see. Most like she'll come back. She's like you, born to the road; this first spell of fine weather set her foot itching.'

Maybe that was the way Martin looked at it. Maybe that was why he had eaten his supper and been so unconcerned.

But that wasn't true. He must have known she had gone for good, for that evening Mary came along, her eyes popping, to tell me that the Master, the minute he was home from Lavenham, had told her to take everything that belonged to the Mistress and put it on the fire in the Forge.

'There was that lovely dress she had for the wedding, and the tawny woollen she had for the cold weather, and her shoes and everything, even the pins for her hair. And there was Tim, standing by with the bellows, and the flames shooting up; you never see such flames, Agnes.'

Oddly enough, I didn't picture the flames; I just saw her, going off in the old red bodice and striped skirt, carrying her tambourine, and her hair hanging. 'There is no because. To dance I am born, so I dance.' I thought of that. And I thought of Martin's remark about the lark and the cage. That showed understanding, and was a comfort to me, because a blow that you can understand never hurts so much as one which puzzles you. I also thought of Peg-Leg's words about women overrating themselves; this very morning Martin had gone off about his business in Lavenham. He'd survived a worse knock, he'd survive this. Some decent food and a clean bright kitchen, if they didn't help, wouldn't hurt.

I said, 'So now there's no mistress in the house. It was bad enough when there was. I shall come along tomorrow morning, Mary, my girl, and put you through your paces.'

She looked pleased.

So there we were, in well under a year, back just where we were. My only regret was that there was no baby. Nor would be now. Martin grown even more silent, never thought about anything but work and business.

The big fine room across the passage was never used. I went in now and again to let in the air and watch Mary wipe away the dust. It was a sad room. I'd go in and think what a waste, his building this just for her to dance in; and I'd end by thinking I could see her dancing.

Amongst us her name was never mentioned and for all the mark she had left on the place she might never have come at all.

IV

That was the summer when Martin began to speak of buying a ship of his own to carry his wool overseas. It wasn't until well on into November, however, that he heard of a likely vessel for sale and rode off down to Bywater to view it. It was bad travelling weather, and hardly light all day long, so the trip would take four days at least, and his last words to me were not to worry if he was away longer.

I took the opportunity to make brawn, and on the third night turned one out of its mould to see what it was like. We had it for supper, and very good it was. When Mary went to set what was left away for next day, I said, 'Look, you were a good girl and worked hard on that brawn, you can take that piece along to your mother and show her what a clever girl you are.'

Pert Tom and I drew up to the fire. He was a bit mopish just then because Dummy's Joan had taken up with one of the young smiths in the Forge and he hadn't yet found himself another hussy. Looking at him across the hearth, I thought he wouldn't find it so easy this time, and the next harder still, until in the end he'd just be that figure of fun – an old lecher.

We spoke about this and that, and mentioned Martin and the ship, wondering if he'd struck the deal.

'If he don't this time, he will the next. He'll get whatever he's set his mind on. And arter the ship he'll be hankering for a sheep run, so that from hoof to loom ain't nobody making a penny 'cept him.'

'Well, what's wrong with that?'

'Did I say owt was wrong? You take me up so sharp. I shall go to my bed.'

He went off, peevishly, and I shut my eyes and dropped into a little cat-nap, the way old folks do. It was the door opening and a rush of cold air coming in that woke me. Waking that way neither your eyes nor your wits work well for a minute, and when I looked towards the door and saw a bent-over woman's figure with a bit of grey woollen over the head and upper part of it, I *saw* Mary, and I spoke to her, pretty gruff, 'Don't stand there, letting in the cold.' I was glad to see that though she'd run off just as she was, she'd had the sense to borrow a bit of wrapping to come home with.

Then, before my eyes, the hunched-over figure straightened out and it wasn't Mary, it was Magda. It was Martin's wife, come back. She straightened herself and at the same moment reached out her arm and pulled the door shut. The bit of grey stuff fell back off her head and showed the short stiff spikes of her clipped hair, and the thin face, always hollowed, now like a skull covered with skin, and the queer-shaped eyes sunk back in dark circles.

She stood there, leaning back against the door-post, just as she had leaned that sunny morning and laughed and slapped her flat belly and said that to eat more than once a day was to get into a bad habit. She looked, now, as though she hadn't eaten once a week.

I had no scrap of pity. Only anger that she should have gone off on a spring morning and dared to come back, with the belly-cramp of hunger on her, as soon as winter set in. I was so glad that he wasn't there, with that soft heart of his, under the hard shell, and I was thinking of things to say, harsh enough, scornful enough to drive her away, when she said, 'Martin. He is not here?'

That brought the worth into my mouth.

'No, he isn't. But if he was, he'd say what I do. Be off. You went away of your own accord and hurt him sore. He's done with you. You aren't wanted here. Be off. Back where you came from.'

She laughed; at least, her lips curled back from the teeth that now seemed to be too many in her mouth, and a sound, like laughter, but with pain in it, came out of her.

'You mistake. I am not come to beg; I come to bring something.'

'Your love and loyalty in return for a full belly! He saved you from drowning and what thanks did he get? He's away. He'll be away for a week. Nobody here cares about you. Go on, Get out.'

It was November and in November nobody has food to give away. I knew the signs. In twenty-four hours, without food and shelter she would be dead. It was cold outside and she was starving. I wondered whether, breathless and clumsy as I was, I had the strength to throw her out. As I was wondering she bent over again, put her hand on her knees and braced herself, with a shudder, and the grey woollen, very slowly, slid down, down to the floor.

Then I saw; then I knew.

There is something almost uncanny about having plied a craft for many years; there can come a time when the plying of that craft can become all that matters. You are nothing, you cease to be, except as the tool with which the job is done. You don't even *think*. I didn't think then – This is Martin's child, that he wanted and I wanted. I didn't think – This is the woman whose touch, for me, would have made a bit of bread uneatable.

There was no thinking. There was a woman, in labour, pretty far gone in labour, two good strong pains in four minutes, and there was Agnes, the midwife who could ply her craft drunk or sober.

I wasn't even the swollen-legged old shuffler that lately I had been. I was across the kitchen and I had her by the arm and on to my own bed in the blink of an eye.

'When did you start?' I asked, as I'd asked a hundred times before.

'This morning. Early. In Sudbury. I think this baby will be born in a ditch. Like me.'

'Twenty miles. You walked twenty miles? Like this.'

'Is good to walk, I understand. Good, eh? How bad then is bad? Aagh.'

I remembered, without the least distaste, that lean sinewy body. And I said, with far more truth than I had ever said the words before, 'You'll have no bother.' Then I remembered that hollow, starving look. I turned aside and pulled the pot of broth into the heat. It was part of the liquid in which the trotters and cheek bones for the brawn had boiled, good and strengthening. It was warm already and it began to bubble. I poured some into a cup and gave it to her.

As she sipped, I, Agnes the midwife, did what she always did, talked, tried to keep their minds off, tried to make out that this that was happening wasn't the end of the world.

'What happened to your hair?'

'Is sold. My tambourine also. Like this I cannot dance.'

Another pain gripped her, and the cup wobbled in her hand. I steadied it.

'Why did you leave it so late?'

'To come? Oh, many reasons. Is all a disaster. I go from here to find the wise woman. She is in York, and when I am come to York she is in Chester. And so it goes on. Then too late, or she is not wise enough.'

I swear that it was Agnes the midwife, not Agnes, Martin's friend, who asked the next question.

'You tried to get rid of the baby?' It mattered, it meant upside down, feet first, sideways on.

'But of course. To a dancer a baby is ruin. Always I am hearing from my mother how good she is, until I come to ruin her. Aagh!'

She writhed and bit her lip. I took the cup from her; turned away, laid out my scissors and twine. You never made any show of them, but they had to be handy.

'So you've come from Chester?'

'From Chester. And not easy. My hair is sold, and my tambourine. I am to beg and to beg is slow. Too many people will say, "You wish to eat, you shall work." So here I wash clothes and here I beat flax and here I cut nettles and so goes the time. But I am coming. Then, one day, I steal. Bread. And I am not quick.' Something that started out to be a smile turned into a grimace. She waited, drew breath, and went on, 'Are most kind, these people. For stealing bread is whipping or to stand in the pillory, but these are not suited to my condition. So I am locked in prison forty days. But still they are kind and they say poor baby to be born in such place and I am let to go.' She turned her head from side to side on my pillow and I saw the sweat spring out on lip and brow. Not long now. I took a cloth and wiped her face, as gently as I ever wiped any woman's. At the next twinge she muttered some words in a language I did not know.

'We're nearly there,' I said, 'it'll all be over in a minute or two.'

At that moment Mary came in and stood goggling. I told her to get out fresh candles, 'and the pepperpot' I added in a lower voice. I didn't expect any trouble, but it was as well to be prepared. I then sent her to her bed. I'd always hated to be watched at work.

A little time – more than I'd thought – went by. Magda was plucky; she bit her lip; she muttered the strange words; she moaned. Once she screamed.

'That's right,' I said, 'don't bottle it up. Scream all you want to.'

I had forgotten Pert Tom, who, the next minute, opened his door a cautious crack and asked, 'What's going on?' He held his door ready to slam it to at once. (In the morning he said he thought maybe thieves had broken in and were clouting me; and I said, 'If so, you were ready with another brave rescue, weren't you?')

'Nothing for you to worry with,' I told him. 'Go back in and shut the door.'

The next pang was weaker, and the next weaker still. She was young and sinewy, but she hadn't been looked after well and had come to the job exhausted and weak with hunger. Dallying at this point could be fatal. So I took the pepperpot, shook some into my palm and held it under her nose. She gave a mighty sneeze and it was done.

The moment I had Martin's son by the heels, Agnes the midwife, spry, knowledgeable, intent only on the job, cleared off and left me.

First I had a good look at the baby. If Magda's own brew or the wise woman's muck had marked or marred him, I knew what to do; I wasn't having Martin saddled with something crippled or wrong in the head. So far as I could see, though, he was perfect, thin but healthy, and his first cry was real lusty. Then I paid particular attention to his face. There is a moment – and any midwife will bear me out on this – just one moment, when all the newly born bear the stamp of the man who made them. They may lose it and never have it again, but they all, boy and girl alike, come into the world looking like their father will look when he is an old man. Magda's baby was Martin at sixty, bald and wrinkled. Happiness flowed into my heart. Here it was, the boy he wanted, the boy I had wanted for him.

I knew that what I should do was to call Mary down, hand the child to her and busy myself with the mother. I thought about it, knowing exactly what Agnes the midwife would do. I knew *I* couldn't do it. That old, shuddering loathing was back on me now: her precious load delivered, she had become once more the woman from whose lightest touch I had shrunk. But that was not all. I had no need to touch her. I could have called Mary and told her what to do.

The truth was, I wanted her to die. I thought how happy we could be now. What life was left to me I could devote to bringing up the baby. But not if she stayed. And she would. She spoke of a baby being ruin to a dancer. Besides, any woman, however wild, is settled by motherhood. Martin would be so pleased with the child that there'd be no question of forgiving her wandering off, it would just be forgotten; she'd be reinstated, more than ever mistress of the house, and I should be back with Peg-Leg.

Oh, I know that women do die in childbed, every day, every night, but not without a fight, not until every measure has been tried. Agnes the midwife had had many a hand-to-hand fight with death, and knew all the tricks.

I, I did nothing. I sat down with the child on my lap and saw to him, while behind me on the bed the Romany blood, the witch's blood, the woman's lifeblood soaked away.

●

Interval

OF MARTIN'S VENTURES the Baildon people had said, 'Ah, the bigger you blow a bladder, the louder the bang', and 'The higher a kite flies the farther it has to come down'. As year followed year they waited for him to overreach himself, for the bladder to burst, the kite to fall. Nobody but Martin himself knew how often their ghoulish hopes had come near to being fulfilled. And he himself could not have said what it was that drove him, time and again, to take another risk, exchanging a certain, comfortable security for a touch-and-go chance. He just knew he must go on and on.

Most of his ventures had an element of makeshift about them.

He went into the yard one morning, beckoned to Peg-Leg, who was in the stables, and asked brusquely, 'What sort of sailor are you? Could you take a ship from Bywater to Calais, or Amsterdam?'

'If she was sound, I could sail a ship to Constantinople and back.'

'The one I have my eye on is old, but she's sound. How d'you know that you could?'

'It weren't my head that clumsy barber-surgeon cut off, you know,' Peg-Leg said in an offended voice. 'I'd done eleven years with the best sailing man ever breathed, devil in seaboots though he was. And what you've learned at the rope's end you tend to remember.'

'If I buy this ship, with all I've got tied up there,' he nodded towards the wool shed, 'I couldn't, straightaway, offer a hired captain enough to keep him honest. I've been over, I've seen all their tricks. Good wool marketed at half price, cash in their pockets and written off washed over-board or some such. One deal like that, just now, could be ruin. But a couple of honest trips, Peg-Leg, would see me clear, and after that you should have a share, a good share, one in forty of the whole cargo.'

'You mean *me* be Captain?'

'What d'you think I'm talking about?'

'Mother of God, I'd do it for nothing. I'd pay you to let me – if I had the wherewithal. I trudged, soon's I got this wooden leg fixed, I trudged from Bywater to Hull...Dunwich, Lowestoft, Yarmouth, Lynn, all the way to Hull. I begged for any job, just to be at sea again. Always the same answer – we can get plenty chaps with two sound legs.'

If Martin remembered the time when he had been in a similar case, he gave no sign.

'It'd mean staying sober.'

'I'm sober afloat. Sailors ashore...well, they make up for lost time. And beached like I was, in my prime. What other comfort was there? Look at old Agnes.'

'Agnes?'

'Yes. Rolling drunk every time she had the money. Can't you remember? She steadied up as soon as she had a kitchen. I could steady up if I had a ship. You say you got your eye on one. How's she named?'

'*Mermaid.*'

Peg-Leg rubbed his nose. 'I knew one by that name once, but that's a common name. Where do she lay?'

'Down at Bywater.'

'Then s'pose we went down there...is she manned?'

'More or less. The man that owned her was master; he's sick, he wants to sell, but the crew is ready to sign on with whoever buys her.'

'They would be, ready and anxious. Then s'pose we go and go aboard and you tell me where you want to steer for and I'll land you there.'

'Yes,' Martin said, 'I think you will, Peg-Leg.'

'I got a name,' Peg-Leg said. 'And it's Bowyer. Jacob Bowyer.' He turned away to prop the pitch-fork he had been holding against the stable wall. 'Captain Bowyer,' he said softly to himself, 'Captain Boywer of the *Mermaid*.'

The next sudden promotion from common yard hand to a post of responsibility was made when Richard was six years old, and concerned the unfrocked priest who had joined Martin's gang of workmen when the house was being built and the land cleared, and who had stayed on and had lately been working as a pack-whacker. He had a hut in the new Squatters Row behind the stables; it was set a little apart from the others, and he lived alone, aloof of manner, surly of temper.

One evening Martin surprised him by inviting him into the house and taking him into his own room, where upon the table a piece of virgin parchment, two newly cut quills and an inkhorn were laid out.

'I take it you can write, Peter,' Martin said.

'It's not a thing one forgets entirely.'

'Sit down then.' Peter did so and picked up one quill, rejected it, took the other and said, 'Who cut this? He was no scribe!'

'Cut it to suit yourself,' said Martin, handing him a knife. Although he had cut the quills himself, the criticism pleased him.

'What do you want me to write?'

'This. This is a deed of grant, made to one Martin and the heirs of his body, in perpetuity, of all the property and messuage known as...' He paused, and the pen caught up with him. Peter Priest looked up and asked, 'What is this? A forgery?'

Still unoffended, Martin said, 'No. A test.'

He rose and went to the heavy chest that stood beside his bed and took out another parchment, one with a dangling seal. He took Peter's writing, and scowling heavily, compared the two.

'There is a fault,' he said at last. 'You have spelt my name with an "e".'

'E or I, both are correct. It is a matter of opinion, not a fault,' Peter Priest remarked coldly.

'Otherwise it is well done. How is your reckoning?'

'By tally or mentally?'

'In your head, the answer then written down.'

'In Roman figuring or Arabic?'

'Both!'

'Try me.'

Martin went to his bed and from there dictated four problems in arithmetic, laying out, behind the priest's back, the answers as he made them by tally.

'Read me your makings.'

All but one of the answers fitted, and in that one, when they reworked it, the error was Martin's.

By this time the possible purpose of the test had occurred to Peter Priest; the accounts and records of the business had outrun Martin's ability to deal with them; so he, Peter Priest, was to be taken off the road and installed as clerk. The prospect was pleasing; how infinitely preferable to sit indoors, plying his real craft once more, instead of being on the roads in all weathers, handling greasy bales of wools, urging – sometimes having to pull for sheer force – pack ponies through the mire.

'You see,' Martin said, 'my way is slow and cumbersome, and can be wrong. That is why...'

He came round the table and sat down, facing Peter.

Why, Peter wondered, is he so cursed slow stating his business?

Martin was slow, partly because any but the briefest speech now came hard to him, partly because speaking of Richard brought the child to mind, and roused, as his actual presence did,

177

many conflicting emotions. He delighted in the boy and loved him dearly, but he was an ever-present reminder, not of Magda, but of the two other little boys, especially Stephen. To be troubled by this, not to enjoy his fatherhood to the full, was, he knew, absurd, but he had felt from the beginning, from the day when he had come home and found the baby there, that in some way Richard was an usurper. For a long time even to watch the child being fed, and then later, feeding himself, had been both a pleasure and a pain. Stephen, his first born, had lived on water gruel, on stale bread thinly smeared with fat, and had spent his days on the stinking wool floor, and finally died because his father was trying to save the miserable hut which was all the home he had. Richard fed on the fat of the land, enjoyed old Agnes' whole doting attention. Stephen had been a very good, quiet little boy; Richard was naughty and wilful. The whole thing was in such sharp contrast that comparisons forced themselves upon Martin many times every day.

At the same time, simply because he felt this way, he also felt guilt. It wasn't Richard's fault that he had been born after the tide of luck had turned. So, each time that the affection which should have streamed out, full and free, towards the new child, suffered the inevitable check and recession, Martin would, by some act of indulgence, endeavour to make up to the boy. He could deny him nothing; he could never punish him, lest into the punishment should go some of his unjust resentment because Richard was Richard, not Stephen.

It had all mattered less, been more easily smoothed over, while old Agnes lived. Doubtless, in her time, Richard had been naughty, ungovernable, wild, but she had never complained; she had acted as a buffer, explaining, excusing, saying, 'He is very young. He will learn', saying, 'For myself I like a lad to show a bit of spirit.' Once, jerked out of silence by her ridiculous attempt to defend some particularly prankish behaviour, Martin had snapped out, 'Stephen was never like that.'

And Agnes had made – for Martin – the most terrible answer possible.

'Ah, there's the difference between the colt fed corn and the colt fed grass. You can't expect them to act the same.'

Agnes had died when Richard was four, and within a week Dummy's Mary was crying and saying she couldn't manage the housework and Richard; he didn't come when she called him and when she picked him up he kicked her. The answer to that had been a strong, active young woman named Nancy, whose sole duty was to see to the child. She had had one of her own, illegitimate, which had died at the age of two. Martin, engaging her, had cherished the secret hope that her heart might share, with his, the defence of memory, that she might be a little less doting and lenient than Old Agnes, who had never had a child of her own. If Nancy arrived thus armed, she was disarmed almost immediately. Richard was a remarkably handsome little boy, so charming when allowed his way, so disagreeable when crossed, that anyone crossing him was almost bound to feel that the change of mood was in some way his or her fault, not the child's. In a very short time Nancy, too, was enslaved. And so had happened the stupid, inexcusable incident with the bear.

Richard was almost six, and ever since he could toddle he had seen Uncle Tom go to the shed where Owd Muscovy lived, open the door and place food within the bear's reach. The muzzle, no longer needed, hung on a peg in the wall, and the chain, attached to the bear's collar at one end, was hooked at the other over a strong nail driven slantwise into the wall of the shed.

Pert Tom, after that one summer on the road during Magda's brief rule as mistress of Old Vine, had grown slack and old. Dummy's Joan's leaving him had, as Agnes expected, been a turning point in his life. It, or rather the difficulty he had found in replacing the young hussy, had loosened his mainspring. But he had kept his bear. And when Richard was five, at Christmas

179

time, he had actually brought Owd Muscovy out on to the wool floor and put him through his tricks.

Richard watched entranced.

'Uncle Tom, let me blow the whistle and make the bear dance.'

'He wouldn't do it for you,' said Pert Tom, who was the only person who ever treated Richard as an ordinary human being, an equal.

'Why not?'

'You ain't his master.'

'Let me try'

'Get outa the way,' said Tom.

Shortly after that Christmas, Richard began asking Martin for a whistle, and Martin remembered another little boy who had never asked for anything, had his pang of guilt, and provided the whistle.

The thing in itself was enough for Richard for a long time. He blew and a shrill level noise emerged. By accident he put a finger over one of the holes and a different noise resulted. Bit by bit, untaught, by a process of trial and error, he learned to play a tune, one of those sung in the woolshed at Christmas, 'The Holly and the Ivy'. Once he could do that he plagued Uncle Tom to teach him *his* tunes. Tom said, 'One day' and 'Some time' and 'Don't bother me now', but in the end he succumbed and, after an hour or two with the child, said to Martin, 'He've got a true ear, and come to the point he's teachable. He'd got *Gathering Pescods* and *Granny's Bonnet* in nearly no time at all. If I'd had him on the road, with Owd Muscovy, I'd have made a fortune.'

The two tunes were all Richard wanted to learn. He played them over and over until he was sure and, when he was, he set out to test them on Owd Muscovy.

The shed was never locked for the simple reason that no one except Pert Tom was ever likely to open it. Except for that one Christmas outing the door had never opened save when the bear was fed or the shed cleaned, and when Richard opened it the bear ambled forward, expecting to be fed. Richard pushed past and went to where the extreme end of the chain was hooked over the slanting nail. Even on tip-toe he could not reach it, so he turned back, and exerting all his strength, pressed the hook which held the other end of the chain to a ring in the bear's collar. The chain fell free, into the soiled straw on the floor, and Richard realized that now he had no means of leading the animal up to the kitchen door as he intended, to cry, 'Come and watch, Uncle Tom,' and demonstrate his disproof of the old man's statement, 'He wouldn't do it for you'. But he was undismayed; so long as the bear stayed on all fours – which he would do until the whistle sounded – his collar was within reach of Richard's hand; he could be hauled along by the collar.

Owd Muscovy had never before, since his remote forgotten cub days, been free of both chain and muzzle at the same time. Without them he felt, not liberated, but strangely vulnerable. Children he knew and hated, they tweaked and pinched and poked. Against them Pert Tom was his defence, and now here he was, stripped of his appurtenances, at close quarters with a child, and no Pert Tom in sight. When Richard attempted to take his collar, he backed away nervously but with a warning growl, and when Richard hung on, tugging determinedly, it was nervousness rather than vice that made him bite. His teeth closed on the child's forearm, and through the sound woollen stuff of his sleeve inflicted only two incised wounds. But the blood sprang, and the yell which Richard let out was a yell of pain as well as wrath. He loosed his hold on the bear's collar and ran to find Nancy. Owd Muscovy made no move to pursue him, nor, though the door stood open, did he immediately leave the shed; he emerged a little later, just as one of the pack teams was coming into the yard. The ponies, though weary, were capable of being thrown into a stampede; one of the pack-whackers was caught between a frightened pony and a wall and had his ribs crushed and added his cries to the general pandemonium. Dummy's eldest boy was in the loft, pushing hay over the edge of it into the mangers, ready for the incoming team; he heard the shouts and the cries –

'The Bear!' 'The Bear's on the rampage!' – and with a heroism never given its rightful due, jumped into the manger, fork in hand, jumped from the manger to the stable floor and ran out into the yard, where Owd Muscovy, by this time in a state of panic, had risen on to his hind legs and was doing his dance in an attempt to placate. Dummy's Jack charged, and drove the pitchfork home into the hairy chest thus exposed; one prong must have penetrated to the heart, for within a few minutes Owd Muscovy was dead.

If Richard could have controlled his temper and his tongue he would have emerged blameless, a victim of the escaped bear, like the clawed pack pony and the man with the crushed ribs; but, his wound smeared with tar and his pain deadened by a dose of laudanum, he was furious to hear that Owd Muscovy was dead.

'Now he'll never dance for me. And me going to all the trouble to learn the right tunes.'

Pert Tom, inconsolable at the loss of his bear, which he had hated, exploited, cherished and loved, all at once, said,

'You! Thass it. You let him out, you little hellion!'

Martin said, 'Tom. Mind your tongue!'

'Bugger my tongue! You let him out, didn't you? You opened the shed door.'

'Bugger my tongue,' said Richard, enjoying the sound of a new, attractive phrase. 'I wanted him to dance for me, but he bit me instead.'

'There you are,' said Pert Tom. 'Straight from his own mouth. He opened that door. So Owd Muscovy, the one thing I ever owned, is dead, just a lump of stinking carrion. Go on, sit there making your Goddamn faces at me. Look what you've got, a great flourishing business, ships on the sea and who knows what. Where'd it all come from? Something so dark and dishonest you never could say where. Had to pretend it was my savings. My bitch had to be bedded here and there, out on the hard ground mostly, yours gets a wedding and is called Mistress, and finely she served you. But you get this...' he flung his hand in Richard's direction, 'and he go and let out my bear. So he's dead, my Owd Muscovy.'

'Nancy, take Richard to bed,' Martin said.

'I don't want to go to bed.'

'You see,' said Pert Tom. 'Thass like the Bible say – If these things be done in the green leaf, what shall be done in the dry? You see how he hev the upper hand of everybody here. You mind what his mother was. You're making a fine rod for your own back and I only hope I live to see it beat you.'

And so, in the end, Martin had realized that Richard must be tamed. And so, here he was, having put Peter Priest through his paces, saying, 'What I want is for you to teach my boy.'

Peter Priest's vision of a quiet, clerkly life vanished, leaving behind it a sense of loss so sharp that it hurt.

He said sourly, 'I couldn't teach him. Nobody could. To teach a child you must be his master.'

'That,' said Martin, 'is what you would be.'

'And the first time I punished, or even chided him, he would run to you, wailing, and you would turn yourself inside out to make things right for him.' He rose from his seat. 'Thank you, no! Three hundred days a year in this part of the country the wind blows from the east, but I would rather walk into the teeth of it, running the ponies who can be beaten if needs be.'

'Richard can be beaten – if needs be, but not over the head.'

'Beaten! The young master of the Old Vine?'

'How else could he learn?'

'How else indeed? Well, well. Even you, in the end, come to the end of your indulgence and hand over! What do you wish him to learn?'

'To read what is written and write what can be read. To reckon, as you now did, in his head, and write down his reckonings in figures Roman or Arabic.' Without intending it his voice, as he said those words, took on a sardonic note.

'You see,' said Peter Priest, 'already you are against me. And what the parent is against, how shall the children learn? The figuring, Roman or Arabic, are not terms of mockery, as you in your ignorance make them sound. I can slave out my guts teaching him, and you, with a few mocking words over the supper dish can undo all I have taught him. I will stick to the ponies. You send him to school. From school he can't come running to cry and show his stripes.'

Martin said, with a black look, 'Sit down. Stick to the ponies, you say. Whose? Not mine. I can go to the town gates tomorrow morning and find a dozen pack-whackers. And, maybe not tomorrow morning, but some morning, not so faraway I can find Richard a teacher. You have your choice, teach him, or take your foot in your hand and leave the Old Vine. *If* you teach him, I promise that so long as you do not hit him over the head, what you do will be right with me.'

'Why so shrewd about hitting over the head?'

'Once, long ago, when I was young, I had some lessons. And to be hit on the head made me more stupid.'

'What would you pay me?'

'Twice your present wage. And you would live in the house, in comfort. I planned to build two rooms above the solar.' He remembered the way in which Peter had asked about the figuring and added, solemnly, 'Meanwhile you would have time to renew your learning and get the dirt out of your hands. Also you should have some garment more suited to your new position.'

Peter Priest gave him a look of unadulterated hatred and said, 'That could be seen to.'

From that day onwards Peter Priest did no manual work at all; he would not even help with the building of the new rooms above the solar or the stairway that led up to them. He told Martin, arrogantly, that he would need books, and to buy books cost money; Martin asked how much he required, and Peter named a sum which made Martin gasp.

'By that reckoning a book costs as much as a pack pony.'

'Why not? Ponies breed their young. A new book may mean a year's hard work for a scribe.'

'The priest who once taught me carried his learning in his head,' Martin protested, less from meanness than from his dislike of Peter Priest's tone.

'And he taught you so well that when it comes to passing on what you learned you hire another man to do it for you.'

'Buy what you need,' Martin said.

On the day when lessons were to start he was careful to be absent; he would be away four days, he said. Nancy had her instructions and at the given time called Richard in from the yard, smoothed his hair with her hand, gave him a handful of currants and told him to go up the new stairs to Peter Priest's room.

'What for?'

'You'll see when you get there, my poor lamb.'

Munching the currants and licking his fingers, Richard marched up the stairs. The door of Peter's room stood open, and just by the window was a table spread with unfamiliar objects. Peter had sent for him to show him something, just as the men about the yard would call and say, 'Master Richard, look, I've found a young owl', or 'Master Richard, Peg's dropped her foal, like to see it?'

Richard walked over to the table without noticing that behind him Peter closed the door and shot the top bolt.

'What's this?' he demanded.

'Don't touch anything. Come here and wash your hands. And in future always come to me with clean hands.'

Richard looked at the bowl of water.

'Nancy washed me this morning.'

'Nancy washed me this morning,' repeated Peter in a cruel mockery of the childish treble voice. 'A great boy almost seven years old. Wash your hands and dry them thoroughly.'

'I shan't. I didn't come here to wash!' He swung round and made for the door.

'You come here to take lessons. And the very first lesson is unquestioning obedience.'

'Open this door!' yelled Richard, having found the door bolted and the bolt just out of reach. 'Peter, do you hear me. *Open this door!*'

Peter Priest walked up behind him, encircled him with his left arm, hoisted him from his feet and brought his right hand down on the little backside thus exposed, once, twice, thrice, with a will.

'That,' he said calmly, 'is for saying "shan't" to me.'

Richard roared from pain and insult.

'Stop that. Stop it at once,' said Peter Priest, and shook him until from sheer breathlessness, he hushed the noise.

'Now come here and sit down.' He pushed the boy towards the table and down into a chair. Richard jumped up at once.

'I don't want to. I'm going to Nancy. She's making me some gingerbread men and I...'

'You will have no gingerbread men, nor any other goody until you know your letters, so you'd better listen carefully.'

When he could repeat all the letters of the alphabet without prompting, and recognize ten of them without hesitation, Peter Priest said, 'That will do for today,' and opened the door and let him go.

For today! There would never be another day like this! Never again would he enter old Peter Priest's horrible room.

Next morning, well before lesson time, he went towards the stables, intending to take his pony and be miles away before Nancy could even wonder where he was.

Peter was waiting for him in the dim stable.

'I anticipated some such trick,' he said, and took Richard, not by the hand, or the arm, but by the ear. It really hurt, and pulling away, jumping about and trying to kick at Peter's shins only made it hurt worse.

Upstairs in the hated room, Peter Priest said, 'I am now going to beat you for putting me to so much bother. You will have six stripes today. Tomorrow, if you repeat this idiotic performance, it will be eight and the next day ten.'

He laid on the stripes dispassionately, enough to hurt, not hard enough to cause injury, and then, putting aside the little cane, asked in a conversational tone, 'I wonder how much you remember of yesterday's lesson. Let us see.'

Richard, snuffling, said, 'You just *wait* till my father comes home!'

'We will wait. Meanwhile let us see how much you remember.'

When Martin rode into the yard Richard was waiting for him, and he was hardly out of the saddle before the tale of woe began. The child had already witnessed the collapse of one small world. Mary and Nancy, though they petted him and spoke pityingly, had put up no real defence against Peter, and Peter had managed, at every, turn to out-wit him. Even when he had rushed straight out the house before breakfast and hidden himself at the very back of the woolshed, Peter had found him – and that was ten strokes with the cane. The one thing that had sustained him was the certainty that when his father came home and heard of all this mistreatment, he would take full vengeance.

His father actually asked only one question, 'Were you beaten over the head?'

'Why, no. He beat me here,' said Richard, rubbing his sore seat.

'Then,' said Martin, 'he was only doing what I told him.'

Quite slowly – because this could not be taken in all at once – the rest of the world began to quiver and crumble.

'You mean you *told* old Peter Priest to beat me, and lock me in and not let me have any gingerbread?'

Martin looked at the angry, handsome little face. Going on for seven years old; and if Stephen had lived to that age no doubt he'd have been picking wool alongside Kate and never have known what gingerbread tasted of.

Stiffened by that thought, he said, 'Yes. He only did those things because you were naughty and disobedient, and would not learn.'

So, there lay the world in ruin.

Slowly Richard said, 'But I did learn. I know my alphabet, backwards and forwards, and when Peter draws the letters I can name them. Tomorrow I am going to draw them, too.'

Martin's mind had done its familiar *volte face*, remember Stephen, feel guilty, pet Richard.

'There's my good boy,' he said heartily. 'And now come and see what I've brought you.'

Never again, as long as he was in the schoolroom, did Richard give Peter Priest cause for anything but the mildest verbal rebuke. This fact Peter attributed – not without reason – to his own first firm handling. Richard became a good scholar, a little too studious indeed for Martin's liking.

Youthful resilience survived the shock of those four horrible days, but deep down the damage remained. The spoilt, arrogant little boy grew into a youth more than averagely handsome, talented, charming, a little too eager to please, more than a little lacking in self-confidence. The lack was not obvious and did not show itself in any physical way of slouch or stutter. Transmitting Martin's orders, his voice had the almost genuine ring of authority. He knew the business thoroughly and before he was twenty had made several visits to the wool-buying centres of the Low Countries. Yet even Martin could never deceive himself into thinking that the boy's heart was in the business. It was difficult to say where it did lie: with his books and his lute, perhaps.

The solar was furnished and in use now. Richard spent his evenings there and Martin tried to, but somehow he could never settle there for long; he'd get up and make some excuse for going into the yard or into the office, or even to bed. And as he retreated he would sometimes think that Richard's lute – playing in the big room sounded lonely. What the boy needed, of course, was a wife.

Not – and this thought always followed hard on the other – not a Baildon girl, Martin hoped; there were, after all, plenty of other places to choose from; and he would devise a trip for Richard, to Colchester, to Kelvedon, overseas again. And when the boy came home Martin's 'Well, how did things go?' held an interest not entirely concerned with the business that had been the reason for the journey. Richard never had anything except business to report upon.

Presently he was twenty-four, and sometime during the following spring Martin spoke the words outright.

'Don't you think it's time you thought about getting married?'

Then, though neither of them saw it, the flaw in his confidence showed itself. Richard smiled his charming, rather secret smile and said, 'I think I shall never marry. You see, I know the girl I want, and her parents would never allow her to marry me.'

Everything tough and aggressive in the elder man rose to that challenge.

'We'll see about that,' he said. 'Who is she?'

PART THREE

Anne Blanchefleur's Tale

I

ON THE MORNING when the whole course of my life changed, Mother and I were in our hall, busily contriving to make a new dress for me out of one of her old ones. In its day, it had been a fine garment, but its day was long past. There were many threadbare places and the colours had faded. Our task was made the more difficult by the fact that, at sixteen, I already topped Mother by half a head.

'But there is a hem,' Mother said, with her eternal optimism. 'We'll let it down and hang it in the sun and it'll fade all over alike, I have no doubt.'

The hem came down, showing the stuff in its original colours, green and crimson, in a sprawling, all-over pattern. Elsewhere the green had rusted, the crimson had faded, until they were almost alike.

Mother saw me look glumly at it and said, 'So long as you are tidy, the *shabbier* you are the better. Your Aunt Astallon will take pity on you, I trust, and buy you a new gown.'

Only by biting my lip hard could I hold back the sharp retort, words no girl should speak to her mother, especially one so kind and indulgent as mine. My Aunt Astallon was as likely to give me a new gown as she was to jump in the river, or walk out barefoot in the snow. But my mother had lived in hope – and hope alone – for so long that she could no longer distinguish between the likely and the unlikely. My father, though less resolutely cheerful, was well-nigh as feckless, and the wonder was, not that we should have fallen so low, as that we should, somehow, have managed as well as we did.

While I bit my lip and scowled, we heard a horseman ride into the yard. Minsham Old Hall, as our place was called, was very old, built for defence, not for living in, and the only windows were set high in the walls and narrow. Mother had to hop on a stool to look out.

'I declare,' she said, 'it's Martin Reed again! What can he be wanting now?'

'The same as last time – his money,' I said; and I intended no joke. Mother laughed however.

'Poor silly man,' she said; and hopped down and picked up the dress and gave it a shake.

Master Reed was the man who owned the sheep run near us. Once all the acres had gone with the Old Hall, but they had been sold away, years before we went to live in the house. Our few acres and Master Reed's sheep run were quite separate, and to reach his part and his shepherd's hut he had no need to come into our yard. For a long time after we moved into the house he was just a name to us, and then one day he had come, walking quickly for all that he limped, and asked Mother if she would, as a favour, heat a tar bucket for him. The shepherd he had then was ill or idle or runaway – I never bothered to hear the whole of it – and he'd come out to find several of his sheep fly-blown. He'd found the tar-bucket in the fence, which was nearer our house than to the shepherd's hut, and had run to ask Mother to lend him her fire for ten minutes.

Mother, of course, had been obliging, and while the tar warmed and he stirred it, she had stood by him talking about sheep. Mother could talk about almost everything, she'd had such a crowded life, moving about from place to place and always taking interest. She'd learned quite a lot about sheep when she was staying with her Uncle Bowdegrave at Abhurst in Kent, where the sheep were quite different from those in Suffolk, she said.

Stirring away at his tar, Master Reed shot her a look and said, 'That's right, ma'am; shorter legs and blunter heads.'

Then, his tar melted, he picked up his bucket and hurried away with the briefest of thanks.

But about three days later, when I was alone in the house, my father and mother having been asked to dine with the Fennels at Ockley, Master Reed came to our door and handed in a bundle of cloth, very fine, blue in colour. He said, and I remembered the exact words to tell Mother, 'I don't like to be in debt. I borrowed your fire the other day. I hope this will be accepted as payment.'

There was someone with him, sitting astride one horse and holding the other. I gave him no heed. To Master Reed I said, 'But I am sure my mother would not wish for payment for so small a thing.'

But he pushed the blue cloth towards me and I remembered that my brother Godfrey – at that moment milking the cow – was being fitted out to go to our cousin Fortescue. So I made my curtsey and said, 'I thank you kindly, and so will my mother, though there was no need.' But, handling the good cloth, I thought it would make a fine cloak for Godfrey. I had already started my round of visits to great houses and rich relatives and knew how important clothes could be.

The blue cloth made Godfrey a cloak, but three years later when he must cease to be a page and become a squire, he needed another and more expensive outfit. And it was then that it occurred to my parents to ask Master Reed for a loan.

In fairness to my father I must say that when he borrowed he did have expectations. (Expectations have been our downfall.) Father's Uncle Dawnay was, at that moment, on his death-bed, and so far as we knew Father was his only kin. However, Uncle

Dawnay, who had been a jovial sinner all his life, became frightened on his death-bed and willed everything he had to a Chantry, where Masses are being said for his soul to this day. (Mother, when she heard the sad news, said, 'But I'd have prayed for him, night and day without ceasing, if he'd left the money to us!' Then she'd laughed and added, 'Of course I shouldn't, I should have been too busy spending it!')

Our debt to Master Reed was never paid, and on the May morning when he rode into our yard it was over three years old.

Our windows were not glazed – and never would be – so presently we could hear my father's hearty, booming voice greeting the woolmaster, and Master Reed's gruff tones. We could hear the two voices, but not the words. Mother listened for a moment, her head on one side, then she said happily, 'They don't *sound* cross. We'd better try this on. An empty dress hangs longer than a full one.'

I put on the dress and she walked all round me, looking at it critically.

'Oh dear, you need every inch of the hem down. We shall have to face up the inside. What with, I wonder? Something the same weight or it won't hang right.' Then, to cheer herself, 'We could *dag* the sleeves, Anne. Dagging is very fashionable, and it would cut away some of that worn edge.'

You would have thought that the remaking of that old gown was the only thing in the world that mattered. With the woolman in the yard, demanding his just due.

Presently we heard the horse trot away and after a minute Father came in. He had his favourite hawk, Jess, on his wrist and he stroked her as he went towards her perch, transferred her on to it and fastened the chain. Then he pulled off his glove and stood slapping it against his leg and looking at me as though he had never seen me before. I imagined it was the effect of the dress and hoped that perhaps it was not as ill-becoming as I had feared. Then he said, 'I want a word with your mother.'

I gathered up the long dress and went to the stairs. They ran up alongside the wall and were made of stone and had no hand rail. At the top was a gallery, with the floor so rotted that you had to mind where you trod, and behind the gallery one big room had been partitioned into three. I couldn't hurry, and before I reached the room which I shared with my sister Isabel I heard Father say, 'That fellow Reed has just made me an amazing proposition.' I was curious to know what it was, so I just stepped out of sight, leaving the door wide, and listened. '...wants Anne for his son, Richard. He's prepared to make a substantial settlement and cancel the debt.'

Mother gave a sort of yelp; there is no other word for it. She sounded just like a dog that has had its paw trodden on.

'The saucy upstart! I trust you sent him off with a flea in his ear.'

'Why, no. I said I'd think it over. Talk it over with you.' She must have scowled, for he asked, in a surprised way, 'You mislike the idea?'

'Mislike? Mislike? He must be mad to have thought of it. And you must be mad to have carried it to me. We've come low, Mary pity us! But not so low as that.' Her words began to come out jerkily and I knew she was throwing her arms about as she did when excited. 'Look where you will, through the length and breadth of the land, and you won't find a girl with better blood in her veins. On both sides. Blanchefleur, Bowdegrave, Astallon, Dawnay, Fortescue. And, don't forget my grandmother of Ramsey, Royal Saxon. *And* you'd put my daughter to bed with the woolmaster's son. You should be ashamed.'

'I didn't bed them. I only said I'd think it over.'

'These jumped-up merchants with their new money, they think they can buy anything. If you wish to please me, Blanchefleur, get on your horse and ride after him and tell him my daughter is not for sale.'

'I should never catch him,' Father said, truthfully. 'Besides, perhaps Anne – '

'You are crazed,' Mother said. 'Since when have wenches ordered their affairs or been asked for an opinion? Up and after him. Tell him to buy his great silly son a wife where he buys his fleeces. My daughter is not for sale.'

She had fallen in love with that phrase.

'The man spoke modestly and not in huckstering fashion. He said he knew the difference in their estates. I don't think he was in full favour...but the boy saw Anne once and fell in love.'

'Fell in love,' Mother repeated with great scorn. 'The wool merchants now must fall in love – aping their betters. What next? They'll be riding in tourneys, I suppose.'

'Wool merchants have been knighted – '

'That's enough,' Mother said. 'Will you ride after him and give him his answer or must I?'

'You never even heard his offer,' Father said. But the words were a requiem for something dead and done with, not a renewal of live argument. In a minute he would be on his old horse, and though it might be supper time before he reached Baildon, when he got there he would give the answer that Mother sent.

I rushed out on to the gallery and cried, 'Wait.'

They stared up at me. I went halfway down the stairs and stopped. Standing high made me feel bolder.

'He sets some value on me, which is more than anyone else does,' I said.

'I should box your ears,' Mother said. 'Listening in corners! And what do you know about values? You have never had a chance. You're only just sixteen – '

'And I've been on offer for *years*. Who is her father? Good! Who was her mother? Good again! *What is her dower?* How many times have I been passed over for some snippet with teeth like a rabbit's and two good manors? I'm sick of it. And another Aunt saying I spoke when I should have been silent, or looked up when I should have looked down. Blaming me for what I can't help.'

Every one of the shames and humiliations I had suffered in four years came back, as burning and hurtful as in the moment when they happened. Rage made me feel as though I were drunken.

'It is the same with Godfrey,' I declared. 'Why wasn't he knighted when he'd served his three years? For one reason only. A knight needs equipment and you couldn't, and Uncle Fortescue wouldn't, lay out the cost. He'll spend his life polishing other men's mail and waiting, just as you would have me wait, for something that never comes. And I will wait no more, I will marry the woolman's son.'

'I will box your ears. You are out of your mind. That a daughter of mine – '

'Yes,' I said. I could feel the sneer curl my mouth as I thrust out one foot and held it clear of the stair. 'Saxon royal blood in my veins! And what on my feet?'

It was a little unjust. For my last visit – to my Aunt Bowdegrave – I had been provided with shoes, but I had outgrown them and passed them on to Isabel. For my forthcoming visit to Aunt Astallon I have no doubt Mother would have procured me some shoes, somehow, from somewhere, but at the moment I had a peasant's footwear, a roughly shaped wooden sole with cloth nailed around it and tied in a bundle round the ankle.

'They are only makeshift,' Mother said.

'Our whole lives are makeshift, and pretence, and believing what isn't true.'

As soon as I said that I was smitten with compunction. With their faces tilted up towards me and wearing such shocked helpless expressions, my parents looked like two children – who had been playing happily that they kept house, and a grown-up had come along and kicked over their make-believe furniture and said that the game was silly and unreal.

Father shifted his eyes and looked at Mother, waiting for her to strike, as it were, the next note in the tune. Every time I came back home – my eye made sharp by absence – I noticed that her ascendancy had increased; his movement, speech and impulses were all slowing down, she was just as quick and positive and vehement as ever. This morning though, for once, she was at a loss, and looked as though she might cry. Upset by that, Father lashed himself into a rage and shouted at me.

'You're over-ripe, my girl; that's what ails you. You're ready for a roll in the hay with the pig-man.' Whether he intended to or not, he had forestalled Mother's tears. She rounded on him.

'Pig-man indeed. What a thing to say to your own daughter. Didn't her Aunt Bowdegrave complain of her prudery? And quite right too. A maid should be modest.'

I said, 'I shall marry the woolman's son, who has made me an honest offer, or I shall go to the one aunt I have not yet visited – my aunt at Ramsey – and be a nun.'

I then turned on the stair and made to go up, but I had forgotten the long gown, caught my foot in it and fell to my knees.

From the hall below, Mother wailed, 'Saints have mercy! Nothing is more unlucky than to fall upstairs.'

Where, I wonder, did that superstition have its origin? I can see that to spill salt, or to break a looking glass, is in itself a misfortune, since both are valuable, and the glass at least hard to replace. But to fall upstairs...

Anyway, I had more important matters to think about. I had held over my parents the only threat that a girl could hold; from any other decision they could beat me off, by argument or force if needs be, but once a girl had declared her intention of taking the veil they would be hardy parents indeed who tried to stop her. My great fear, when I came to think things over, was that my parents might take me at my word, steadfastly refuse to let me get married and so force me into the Convent. Little as I liked my present way of life, I should like that of a religious less, especially at Ramsey, where my aunt, the Abbess, was very strict in keeping to the rules of the order. I had seen her once, at a wedding, and even on such an occasion when most nuns disregarded all the rules, she held to her habit, wore no jewels, ate sparingly. To be a nun at Ramsey was to be a nun indeed.

I began to wish I have never spoken those rash words; yet, when, some hour later, Mother climbed the stairs and came and sat on my bed and asked did I really mean what I had said, I replied with a firmness that astonished myself.

'Yes. The woolman's son is the only one who has ever made me a serious offer of marriage; I suspect he is the only one who ever will. Unless I take it, I shall go to Ramsey.'

'In which case,' she said, pulling a sorry face, 'we should see you seldom or never. Baildon is within reach, even with such poor horses as we can afford.'

I said nothing.

'Anne, to please me, try once more. Go to your Aunt Astallon – it will be different this time; her own girls are married and gone. She could give you more mind. And you're prettier, you grow prettier every day. You have everything, except a dower. You'll make a good match yet.'

I stayed silent. And at last she said, 'Oh, if only things had been different…'

Upon that I almost broke down, thinking what her life had been. My father was the youngest son of a youngest son of a great family; he had, therefore, connections, ambitions and military obligations without anything to support or forward them. His one hope was to have married an heiress; instead he married my mother who was, if anything, even more highly connected, but one of several daughters and but modestly dowered. For years, however, the insecurity of his position had not been evident; he was a good man in the lists in time of peace, a good soldier in time of war. Trailing his family after him, as a kite drags its tail, he had moved from castle to castle, from great manor to great manor, riding in tourneys, supporting this lord and that in their petty squabbles, making war on the Scots, and on the Welsh, cheerful good company always, Sir Godfrey Blanchefleur, most admirable knight errant. Mother had borne seven children and four had died before she had a bed to call her own. We had all been born in different places, grand, high-sounding places, Beauclaire, Abhurst, Rivington, even Windsor, but Godfrey was thirteen, I was nine and Isabel was three before we had a settled home, and that came about by accident.

Father was unhorsed in a tournament at Winchester, and fell on his head, denting his helmet so that it could not be removed in the usual way. They say that he was unhurt, rose unaided and walked from the tourney ground to a forge where an unhandy smith, in hammering off the helm, damaged his skull. He lay like the dead for four days and when he finally rose from his bed his days as a fighting man were done. His left arm and leg, though whole and uninjured, had lost power, were weak and heavy; and he was slow, even in his speech.

He was no whit less cheerful, quite confident that somebody would arrange something for him. And somebody did. One of my mother's Bowdegrave cousins owned Mincham Old Hall and the few poor acres that had been left when the rest were sold for a sheep run. The house had stood empty for some time and was so old-fashioned and comfortless that nobody wanted it.

The sad thing was that there was just enough land to have supported us, had it been properly handled; and my brother Godfrey, most sternly sensible always, would have *tried*. The life we had led, flitting from place to place, had aged him; he belonged nowhere and had found his own company, often with working people who, at thirteen, are men. He would have looked after cows and pigs and tilled the few acres. But no! He must follow the pattern, go to be a page, then a squire and finally a knight. I have no doubt that his life had been as full of humiliation as mine.

I had started my round at the age of twelve, going from cousin to aunt, from aunt to cousin-by-marriage, to learn manners, to learn dancing, to learn to play the lute, to learn to embroider. One day, one of my powerful rich relatives was supposed to take a rich young man by the ear and say, 'Marry this girl.' But there was no man so rich that he did not look for a bride with a dowry. And also there was, at that time, a curious dying-out in the old families, so that in many of them there were no sons, only daughters, who thus became great heiresses. Once, at Beauclaire – I remember this so sharply – there was a little creature, Catherine Montsorrel, so ugly, so misshapen that I pitied her. But somewhere near Chester a man could get on a good horse and ride for three days around the boundaries of one of her properties, and out by the Welsh marches another man, on another good horse, could ride for six days. So she got married from Beauclaire and I did not. My failure was, in a way, the failure of the relative with whom I had stayed, and of course excuses must be made. I was sent home with the report that I had two fatal defects, a sharp tongue and a prim manner.

I will say for my mother that she never took these things seriously as most women would. Many another girl sent home with such a character would have been scolded, beaten, had the shame of her failure rubbed into her every day.

So now, looking back all in a moment over Mother's life, and mine, so far, I felt kindly and weak towards her.

'If things had been different they would have *been* different,' I said. 'But they are as they are. This man Reed is well-to-do and we owe him money. He would cancel the debt. That in itself is a thing to consider.'

Mother clenched her little fist – she had beautiful, delicate hands which no amount of work could spoil – and beat upon the bed.

'You are not,' she said fiercely, 'to think of that. I said to your father...but for the debt he would never have dared...You don't know the world, Anne. Poor we have been, but you have never been brought face to face – I mean to talk to, to be with – any man who hadn't...who wasn't...' She broke off, threw her hands about. 'Chivalry,' she said, snatching at the word like a drowning man at the straw in the proverb. 'To know what good manners are

– even if he doesn't always exercise them – that is the mark of a gentleman.'

'Uncle Fortescue once dragged my aunt upstairs by the hair of her head, in the sight of all, and broke the jaw of the young squire who protested,' I said, quietly, as though speaking to myself. Mother blushed her quick bright blush.

'There was reason for that.'

'Unmannerly just the same.'

'That may be. But,' said Mother, wagging a finger at me, 'I'll warrant that none in that hall knew *why*, his real reason I mean. And there is just the difference. He might pull her hair, but he did not besmirch her name as a common man in a rage would have done.'

'I shall be careful,' I said, getting back to the point, 'to behave in such a manner as to give my common man, as you call him, no occasion either to pull my hair or besmirch my name.'

'Marriage lasts a long time,' said Mother drily. 'Suppose you never grow to like him; or tire of him, and he of you. Then where would you turn? To some blabbermouth apprentice who would boast when he was pot-valiant? Oh,' she said, jumping from the bed and beginning to wave her arms. 'These are not things to say to a young maid, yet they must be said. In a proper household such things are understood, arranged, there is constant change, comings and goings, blind eyes turned, allowances made.'

'And ladies dragged upstairs by their hair.'

Mother, like a skilled fencer, ceased her pressure at that point, and attacked from another angle.

'I can't see you as a nun at Ramsey. You may expect no favour from your aunt; if anything she will be harder on you than on the others, out of her wish to be fair. You love your comforts, and are greedy, and vain. You have no vocation, which alone could make such a life bearable.'

She had put into words what I had been thinking, and inwardly I wavered. But I said, 'Add to my failings that I am proud. I cannot go to my Aunt Astallon again, and be looked over and passed by; and have them say, "Let me see, how old are you now?" and have them nod and pull their mouths down. At least at Ramsey I should have no cause for shame.'

'There's another thing,' said Mother, flitting like a butterfly. 'Think how it will sound, to send to all the family and say that you are to marry the son of a woolman. Is that not shaming?'

'Not in the same way. Besides, why should they be told? Except when one of us is being foisted off on them, they forget that we exist. We might starve to death for all they care. They're afraid to visit us for fear their hearts should be wrung. Aunt Astallon went to Walsingham, missing us by four miles; did she turn aside? No, she rode on and lodged at Sudbury. Uncle Bowdegrave visits Rushbrooke every year; when did he ever give a sign of being within riding distance?'

These were truths, facts, which my parents had steadily refused to recognize. Now, confronted with them, Mother seemed to shrink a little.

'Anne,' she said, 'you're very hard.'

But it wasn't true. Seeing my point pierce her last defence I was filled with pity and weakness. I really longed to cry out that I had not meant what I said, that I would go to my Aunt Astallon and try once more. But something held back the words. I was sick of pretending.

'I shall tell your father that you are set in your mind,' Mother said.

Father, always three-quarters in favour of the match, rode off to Baildon to tell Master Reed his offer was being considered, but that before any conclusion was reached, Mother wished to inspect the young man. Master Reed invited them both to supper. So the hem of the green and crimson gown had to be stitched back into the place and the seams let out instead of taken in. Wearing it, and a very wide wired headveil, she went off to Baildon and came back in a very curious state of mind.

I asked her the one question which troubled me most.

'Is he surly, like his father?'

Mother lifted off the head-dress and ran her hands through her hair.

'He's not in the least like his father.' To me that was pleasant news, but she said it regretfully.

My father fumbled in his pouch and brought out a little lump of pink, under-cooked meat and offered it to Jess on her stand.

'If you married that boy you'd have a very comfortable home,' he said.

'If?' I asked.

Mother said sharply, 'My mind is not yet decided. And when it is I shall take my time telling them so. *I'm* not one to fall on my face at the sight of a few silver cups, a glass window and a great tapestry that still smells of the loom.'

'It was well meant,' Father said. 'They wanted us to see that...' He cast a look about our comfortless hall and grinned. 'Four main dishes, then gooseberries in a glazed coffer, and a syllabub that you could have turned upside down without spilling, it was so well whipped.'

'I was ashamed of *you*,' said Mother, 'pocketing a piece as though you feared to be hungry on the way home!'

'I told the boy – what's his name, Richard – that it was for my hawk. He was knowledgeable, though he has never handled a bird. Said he had read a book.'

'What did *you* think of him, Father?'

'A modest, amiable young man. And if he was some poor knight's son that had gone into the wine trade, your mother would think so too.'

I suspected that they had argued all the way home.

'There's a difference between trading in wine and handling dirty old fleeces,' Mother said.

'But the man was at pains to point out that the boy never soiled his hands...'

'That I can well believe!' It was plain to me that something had happened to upset her and bring her to the brink of deciding against the match after all.

Presently Father went outside and I signed to Isabel to go to bed, which she did reluctantly. As soon as we were alone, Mother got up and went over to the livery cupboard and began banging about in it. Our livery cupboard was never well provided at any time, and she couldn't be hungry, having come straight from a supper of four main courses, pie and syllabub, so I could only guess that she wanted to keep her back to me. But why? After a minute I could bear it no more.

'You didn't like Richard Reed?'

'There's nothing about him to like or dislike. Truly, Anne, I'd be more at ease if you were...if it was a question of marrying the father, old as he is.'

'Why?'

'He's a man. There's something about him. You could see that he was being civil, for the boy's sake; he wanted us to take to the idea and know you'd be...well looked after. But in his heart, he didn't care; he thinks he's doing *us* a favour!' This, which she should have mentioned with irritated scorn, she brought out as though it were admirable. 'The boy's grown up in his shadow, pampered, made much of, never had to shift for himself. You'd have the upper hand of him in no time.'

I thought, what an astonishing thing to say – in that *complaining* manner!

'Would that be so bad?'

She flung something into the cupboard and turned round.

'Yes. No woman can be happy with a man she can master.'

I suppose what I thought showed plain on my face.

'Ah, but we weren't always this way,' she cried. 'Not this way at all. Why, I've sat amongst the other women and looked down as Blanchefleur rode by and he'd look up and I'd go hot and cold and almost choke with pride because I belonged to him and he was the strongest, boldest...' She gave a little shiver and hugged herself with her arms. 'You were nearly born on the road. We were at Rivington and he said, "I'm off to Beauclaire in the morning." Just like that, and I knew I'd be in the straw next day

204

or the one after, and I knew that if I let him go alone there were plenty at Beauclaire that would be glad to see him ride in by himself. So I said, "I'm coming too." And he said, "D'you think you'll hold together so far?" And I said, "I shall hold together so long as I have to." And I did. And he liked me the better for it. That was the time Lady Warwick threw him her glove – but he wore mine for all to see.'

There was something – even after all those years – so triumphant in her voice that it made me feel as I sometimes did when trumpets blew. She spoke of what I understood; I had so often sat in the humble back seats of the Ladies' Gallery and watched the knights ride by, saluting the ladies who threw them favours. I'd dreamed of one day having a knight of my own...

I put that thought away.

'Richard has been under his father's thumb,' I said. 'You shouldn't judge from one visit.'

'It isn't in any way what I want for you, or what you should have. Anne, if you'll try once more, I'll persuade your father to sell Jess, and you shall have a brand new gown.'

'I will marry Richard Reed and have two new gowns.'

How long these arguments and this indecision would have lasted I do not know. My Uncle Bowdegrave, staying at Rushbrooke, helped to clinch the matter by, for once, remembering his poor relatives and sending us a haunch of venison.

Mother looked at it calculatingly and said, 'Now, if we were proceeding with this business, we could ask the Reeds to supper. It won't keep, so we must make up our minds.'

'You know mine,' I said.

'And mine.' That was Father, speaking quite firmly.

'Well, only the Virgin knows when next I shall have meat in the house for five people. I think you're being a stubborn, hasty, foolish girl and I only hope you won't live to regret it.'

So she capitulated and Richard and I met.

II

Within a few minutes of our meeting I was certain that Mother's slighting remarks about Richard were due to prejudice, and, perhaps, a little to jealousy. He was such a very handsome young man, and so elegant, with a charming smile and the nicest manners in the world. I think my heart went out to him at once, just as I thought that if only he'd had breeding *how* Mother would have praised him, and said I was lucky. And what is breeding after all? Largely a matter of money and land and staying in one place long enough to establish a name and a family; or pleasing the King and getting some honour conferred on you. I'll warrant that if Richard could have gone to Westminster, calling himself by some Norman French name, and played his lute, he would have pleased the King so much that he would have been knighted straight away.

Old Master Reed was lame of one leg and had grown crooked as well as solid with the years; his face was weathered and deeply lined, he looked as though he had been too busy all his life to take much pleasure in anything. Beside his father, Richard looked like a young larch side by side with a gnarled old oak.

The supper party was much easier and merrier than I had expected, largely, I think, because Father, when Mother was worrying about having only the one dish, had said, 'There are times when wine counts for more than food.'

'This is one of them – and we have no wine.'

'I'll ride over to Ockley and borrow some.'

'Don't say for what reason. Nothing is settled yet.'

Sir Stephen Fennel, bless his heart, gave Father some good Rhenish, which made everyone cheerful and unembarrassed; even Mother so far relented as to behave as if Richard were a very eligible suitor who must be charmed. After supper she bade me fetch my lute and play a little. A little is what I played, just as I danced a little, played Nobbin a little, embroidered a little. I had no ear and no talent, but I had mastered four or five pleasing little tunes.

While I played, Richard watched me, and I could see that he loved me. I remembered something I had forgotten – Father saying some words about Richard having seen me and would look at no other girl. That had a smack of romance to it, like a minstrel's tales, and as I played I looked back at him under my lashes. Presently he rose and crossed the hall and sat down by my feet, and at the end of my last tune took the lute from me and said, 'Allow me now to play for you, Mistress Anne.'

I had never, anywhere, heard anyone play like that. It wasn't just music, it was something more, like being under a spell, so that when it ended you sighed and your spirit settled back into your body again, a little painfully. You could have loved him just for the way he played the lute.

He ended his special music and gave us back our souls and then said, 'Now the tune that everyone knows. Will you sing?'

He struck up 'The Pleasant Month of May' and we all began to sing. Under cover of it, Richard said to me, 'I saw you once. I thought you were the most lovely lady in the world. Will they let you marry me?'

'They must. They shall. Or I will be a nun.'

Afterwards, when more of the wine was being served with some little saffron cakes, Mother came to me and said, 'Well. Are you still of the same mind? The old man is pestering your father for an answer.'

I could hardly speak for the fullness of my heart. I had made my choice in a blind rage against the way the world had used me, and I had picked this jewel.

After that it was settled, and Mother began seizing every opportunity to send messages to every branch of the family. I could imagine, in all those distant places, relatives of all degrees putting their heads together and agreeing that at last my parents had come to their senses and done something suitable to their estate. In their relief they all sent me gifts of great generosity. Ironically, Mother's remark about my Aunt Astallon giving me a new gown proved to be prophecy, for she sent me enough of the best French velvet for a wedding dress; that inclined me to think that she had been dreading my next visit almost as much as I did. With the gifts came excuses for not making the journeys to bring the families to the wedding, and that was just as well; but the Fortescue cousin, in whose household my brother Godfrey languished, gave him permission to ride home – hoping no doubt that the woolchandler had a daughter. When Godfrey did arrive he was leading a pretty grey palfrey, my present from that branch of the family.

The Reeds had no relatives at all, and Master Reed, talking over the wedding with Mother, said that he wanted nobody from Baildon at his son's wedding. But he professed himself willing to provide a feast, so the few guests we had – mainly friends of Father's, who came to see what the poor fellow could find to spread on his board – were vastly and pleasantly surprised.

Martin wore mulberry-coloured velvet, the tunic edged with fur, and the one thing that marred my day was to hear two old men, hawking friends of Father's, muttering about it.

'In my young days nobody less than a knight could wear miniver; and if he tried to, it was ripped off and sold for the benefit of the poor.'

'Times change.'

'So they do, and not for the better.'

I hated them for thinking the old days, when someone like Richard mustn't wear miniver fur even if he could afford it, were better than these more enlightened times.

After the feasting was done, Richard, his father and I rode to Baildon. I was thankful that owing to our circumstances there could be no public bedding. During my various visits to my relatives I had assisted at these grossly indecent rites, and I knew that I should find them agonizingly embarrassing. Yet, when we reached the house which I had never yet seen, and stood uneasily in a small solar, most elegantly furnished, and drank a last stoup of wine from the silver cups which Mother had mentioned, I realized that the public bedding ceremony does serve a purpose. The lewd talk, the thrusting of fertility emblems upon the bride, all the jokes and the laughter and the ducking away from those who try to undress the newly married couple, help to break down the reserve between them, and once they are in bed, with the curtains closed, half the work is done.

If even Master Reed had been a little drunken and hearty and slapped Richard on the back and said, as I have heard fathers say, 'Well boy – to your work!' that would have helped. But he only looked at us, rather sadly, I thought, and raised his cup and said, 'I wish you happy.' And when he had drunk his wine he went away; and we were two strangers, left alone. Then Richard said, as though I were a visitor who had come a great distance, 'I expect you are tired. Come.'

He did take my hand, however, as we climbed the stairs, and still holding it he led me into a room far more comfortable than any I had ever slept in, for even at Beauclaire, being young and a poor relation, I had always shared one of the worst rooms. He pulled on my hand a little, so that we stood close, and he put his face to mine. We were cheek to cheek.

'You belong to me. I never dreamed it could happen.' There was a kind of exultation in his voice, but awe as well. I realized that he was as nervous as I was myself.

'I belong to you and you belong to me,' I said. 'Are you happy?'

'So happy that I am frightened.'

I thought that a strange thing to say, but very touching, too. I put up my hand and pressed it against the other side of his head, forcing our faces closer.

'There is nothing to be frightened about. And if there were, it is I who should be frightened.' I said that rallyingly.

He said, almost in a whisper, 'I would never do anything to hurt you. Never.'

Was it, I wonder, the fear of hurting me that made him fail? He loved me, I loved him, we were both sound and young...But it was no good.

It was an odd circumstance that I, who at Minsham had been so clear-sighted, so contemptuous of all pretence, should change my nature with my name, and whole-heartedly begin to play a game of make-believe. I had not realized that I was so truly the daughter of my parents; here was I, pretending that all was well, pretending that I was a properly married woman, just as Mother always pretended that some day something would happen to restore our fortunes, and Father pretended he was a landed gentleman. I discovered another thing about myself, too: I was hotly passionate. There were times when I felt that out of my own eagerness I could *make* it happen. This time! This time! I would think. Now! Now! Poor Richard, groaning and sweating, as puzzled as I was myself, would eventually fall asleep, and then I would cry, softly, secretly, and rather ashamed. I would accuse myself of being ungrateful, too; for apart from this one thing my new life was wonderful, better than I had ever imagined life could be.

The sheer comfort we enjoyed was a lasting joy and an amazement. People might laugh and sneer about merchants and their new money; they knew how to live, how to build and how to furnish. There was more warmth and softness at the Old Vine than in Abhurst, Beauclaire and Rivington rolled into one. As for Minsham Old Hall, I was soon wondering how I had endured the stone floor, the unglazed windows, the draughts that stirred your hair even as you sat by the hearth.

The Old Vine was really two houses, divided by a wide cobbled passage which was entered by a doorway, big enough and high enough, when it was fully open, to allow a pack pony, loaded, to trot in. On the right of this passage was that part of the house which Master Reed had built first and lived in when he was starting his business. Richard took me over it and showed me how it had been. His father had had one room, his Uncle Tom the other, and there had been a kitchen for cooking and that was all. After some years, rooms had been built above all these apartments. One of them had been the room in which Richard had learned his lessons, he said.

Because I loved him, everything about him, back to when he was very young, was interesting to me, and when he pointed to the door and told me that, I was interested to see the room.

'The servants sleep there now. You don't want to look in there,' he said.

'I think you hated your lessons,' I said, teasingly.

'No. After a week I liked my lessons, but I hated my master. Sometimes even now, I dream – '

'Oh, so do I. My Aunt Bowdegrave, teaching me to dance, and saying I had two left feet and would never find a husband...' I cut that off sharply and said, 'I was ten years old.' Something that I could never find a name for had made me withhold from Richard all the story of my humiliating youth. I wanted him to desire me, so I must always seem to have been desired. 'Little she knew!' I said gaily.

'In those days I used to sleep here,' Richard said, moving to the other door. 'When Father made the office downstairs, Uncle Tom moved up. He's not my real uncle, but I still call him that. He was Father's partner once. He's bedridden now and a bit...' He tapped his head and made a face. 'But if you like to see him...'

'I want to see everything.'

Richard opened the door and said, 'Uncle Tom. I've brought you a visitor.'

The old man in the bed must once have been big and stout; he had shrunken and the flesh hung on his bones in heavy folds. There was a musty, old-man smell in the room, and, added to it, another, even less pleasant, which, as I moved towards the bed, I knew came from a great, badly-cured bear skin which lay across the foot of the bed.

Uncle Tom's eyes were bleary and his stare vague at first, but when I was near enough, something quickened in them and he grinned. I'd seen his like before, hobbling old dotards until they catch you behind the screen or in a lonely passage.

'A pretty one, too. Cure for sore eyes, you are, little mistress.'

'Thank you,' I said, and smiled and for fun bobbed him a curtsey.

'Aye, and better still, saucy.'

'Anne is my wife,' Richard said, a trifle stiffly I thought.

'Your wife, eh?' That seemed to take a little while to sink in. Then he said, 'You're lucky Dick; allust hev bin. Right from the first. Like your Dad. Well…' He looked me up and down and I had a sudden, disconcerting certainty that he knew about us. This going over the house took place on my second or third day there, and the thing was, naturally, still raw and tender, in the forefront of my mind. 'See you do right by her,' Uncle Tom said. 'Make the most of your chance while you can. You shrivel and dry up afore you know where you are.'

Richard took hold of my elbow and said, 'Come along.'

That was the old part of the house.

On the other side of the central passage the rooms were larger and higher. There was the solar, with the window which looked out into a garden, with a plot for herbs, and some fruit trees and roses. Behind the solar was a dining hall, where, every day, at dinner and supper, we and several of the workmen and apprentices sat down together. Except that it lacked a dais it was like the hall of a great house. Richard, his father and I sat at a solid oak table which was never moved; the rest had trestles and boards which could be set up or taken down according to the number of places required. The food served here was good and plentiful and to me, delicious; but there were always other dishes, cakes, fruits and sweetmeats, in the livery cupboard of the solar.

Above the solar and dining hall were the bedrooms of the family.

Across the yard were stables and lofts, the shed where wool was stored, the 'floors' where the fleeces were picked over. There was a smithy, a cow byre, a pigsty and a hen roost, a round house

for pigeons and a pond. Thirty years ago, Richard said, when his
father had started, there had been nothing at all, just a field full
of old vine stumps. It seemed to me a lot to have built up and set
working in thirty years, but that was not all; Master Reed had
two ships on the sea, a warehouse in Amsterdam, and, of course,
the sheep run at Minsham. He would have been justified in being
very proud of his achievement, but I never saw him give any sign
of being so. Except that he loved Richard, was kind to me, and
apparently faithful to his old partner, he showed very few signs of
any emotions; he was never angry, he never laughed, he never
seemed to be in a hurry and he was never ill. Richard said that he
was a strict, but just employer. It took me a little time to learn
that his settled scowl, and silence and sombre looks were not due
to ill-humour, and to the end I was always disproportionately
pleased if I could coax a smile from him. I often felt a little sorry
for him; he worked so hard, every day, from dawn to dusk, just,
it seemed, for the sake of working; rather like an old horse at a
mill wheel or a well, which will go round and round, plodding at
the same pace, whether it is being driven or not.

You might have imagined that a man who set such high store
by work would have been a hard task-master to his son. Nothing
was farther from the truth. Mother had said that Richard was
under his father's thumb, but it was a most gentle, kindly thumb.
'Leave that to me, boy,' or 'I'll see to it,' were words constantly
on his lips.

All through that first autumn of my married life, Richard and
I just frivoled the time away. We took long rides, went to Bywater
– where I saw the sea for the first time – and to Walsingham, and
Colchester, Lavenham, Melford, Sudbury and Clare. Summer
died slowly that year and in the fine warm weather the roads
were busy with pilgrims and merchants and the people who made
their living by amusing them. These last, the minstrels and
tumblers and jugglers, had a fascination for Richard; he would
watch them for hours, even make a special journey in the hope of
catching up with some particularly pleasing performer again, and

seemed actually to envy them. Once he said, 'Not to be tied to any place...don't you think that would be pleasant? I've often thought that I should like to take my lute and just set out.'

'You play well enough. But it must be a hard life, especially in winter. And not being tied to any place means not belonging anywhere. I know. I spent my childhood moving from place to place. I hated it. I always had to leave something behind.' I told him how, once, at Rivington, I had almost tamed a wild cat out of the woods; he was so pretty, striped tawny and grey, with tawny eyes. We must have stayed there for some time, because I had got him to the point where he would come when I called – if I waited long enough – and take meat from my hand, though he never would let me stroke him. At another place I had made a little garden; I'd planted gilly flower seeds and meant to make some gilly-flower water and scent myself all over. We moved on when the little green plants were two inches high.

'Poor Anne,' Richard said. 'You've always wanted to settle. I've always wanted to get away.'

'From what?'

'Ah. That I can't tell you. It's something that comes over me. I sit at the table sometimes and think here we are and here we shall be next year and next and next and I feel as though I were stifling. Then I think – If only I could take my lute and go, gather a crowd and play and *play*.'

For a moment he looked unlike himself, wild, altered, as though the wind were blowing through him, as though he could hear the music he dreamed of making. I felt left out, left behind.

'It's silly. I should hate it really, sleeping in a ditch or under a haystack.'

'And rough company. And not enough to eat.'

One place where we rode often was, of course, Minsham. Mother, on my first visit, had contented herself with asking was all well with me, and I told her everything was wonderfully well. The second and third time she asked no questions, but on the fourth – I remember it well, it was in October, and Richard had gone out to join Father and Isabel in beating the walnut tree – Mother said, 'You've not quickened yet?'

'Two months…no three…Three months is not long.'

'No,' she said, 'No'; but her voice said the opposite. 'But you should lose no time. You know what they say, and truly – For every year over sixteen there's an hour's labour with the first. You were sixteen last February. I bore my first a few weeks after my sixteenth birthday – they say women forget, but I remember it to this day, and I would not have you go through that *and* the extra hour. Get your first with all possible speed – the rest comes easy.'

'It's not a thing I can order.'

'You shouldn't ride so much. We are pleased to see you…But unless compelled no married woman should set foot in stirrup for a year. It's like junket – it will never set if you keep stirring.'

That evening, riding home, I was thoughtful. Once, on one of my visits, I had been present at a birth. One of my Aunt Astallon's attendants had had a clandestine love affair and had, up to the last minute, concealed her state, wearing a heavily pleated houpplard and joking about getting so fat. In the night, in the dormitory where six of us lay, her hour had come upon her, and nine hours later she was delivered. I could hear her screams still. And she was…how old? Getting on. Twenty-five perhaps. Yes, it worked out.

In the night, in the bed I said, 'Are you afraid of hurting me? Is that it? Darling, pain now will spare me later. Hurt me. I want to be hurt.'

But we ended, as we always had, with me comforting him, pretending, pretending. Never mind. Next time. All will be well.

I still rode – though the days drew in; but I made excuses not to ride Minsham way, and I did not have to face Mother again until Christmas, when, at Master Reed's invitation, she and Father and Isabel rode in to keep the Feast with us. They stayed four days, and we had a right merry time and I managed never to be alone with Mother long enough for her to ask me awkward questions. However, my father, who had remembered his first conversation with Richard – about hawks and hawking – had procured for him, as a Christmas gift, a young eyas tiercel which was to be trained, and eventually flown at Minsham.

'A lot of riding for you,' Father said. 'Because if you want him to answer your whistle you must give him his beef as often as possible and whistle as you do it.'

Mother gave me what she no doubt thought was a subtle, sly look, a grimace that would have been noticeable a street's width away. I nodded to show that I understood.

So the new year opened for me with a most embarrassing problem. Richard was riding out to Minsham twice a week, and always expected me, unless the weather was very foul, to go with him. And if I did, Mother would accuse me of stirring the junket. Under the strain of making silly excuses, either to one or the other, I became bad tempered. His lute first, now his hawk, I'd think to myself; he really never wanted a wife at all!

Once that thought had entered my head I never completely got rid of it again. Richard had told me how he had first seen me – at the time when his father brought the blue cloth; how he had fallen in love with me then and dreamed of me ever since. When I heard that story first, I thought it was romantic; now, looking at it in the light of later knowledge, I had a suspicion that perhaps he would have been content to let it *stay* a dream, just as he was content to dream about that other unlikely thing, being a wandering minstrel. He liked the idea of being in love, he liked my company, perhaps (may God forgive me the unkindness of this thought) the knowledge of my better birth and station added to the romantic idea; what he didn't want, and had no need of, was a real flesh and blood woman in his bed.

I rode out with him once during January at the time of the month when even Mother could not complain of my being in the saddle. Then, despite all his pleadings, I made excuses until the next time the moon ruled my blood. That time, as she greeted me, Mother said, 'What, again!'

The ill humour into which this remark threw me was not improved by the tone of her conversation throughout my visit. Had I been eating green apples? Where, I retorted, would I find green apples in February? Don't sit on grass. Lately, I snapped, there had been little temptation to do so.

'You are so irritable,' she said, 'that I wonder if you are not already pregnant and deceiving me. Is that so?'

I was tempted to nod and so end it, but I had no wish to complicate matters even more, so I shook my head. She then went on to tell me two more helpful things. I should steep a pound of red meat in water, let it soak overnight, then squeeze it and drink the juice. And I should borrow a shift or a petticoat from a woman lately brought to bed, wear it without washing it for a month, then return it to her with a present of a new garment, red in colour.

'What an old wives' tale!' I said.

'Old wives are usually mothers and their tales should be heeded,' she replied.

That afternoon, as we rode home, it began to rain, and as soon as we arrived we went up to our room to throw off our wet clothes. Flinging my soaked hood on the floor, I said angrily, 'It'll be a long time before I go to Minsham again!'

'Why, sweetheart? I thought you liked to go.'

Suddenly everything boiled up in me.

'How can you be so stupid and blind,' I shouted at him. Then I began to cry, and mixed up with the sobs and the blubberings it all came out, Mother's questions and admonitions, my evasions and pretences, my suspicions that he wanted a sweetheart but not a wife, everything, everything.

I had flung myself down on the bed, burrowing my face into the pillow, and when I had said *everything* I knew that I had said too much. I lifted my head a little and looked at him. I was frightened. He had the wild look on him and had gone as white as chalk. Now I had thrown away what I had had, a loving and pleasant companion, I thought.

He said, 'I'll show you.'

And there, amongst the wet clothes and the messed bedclothes, in the fading light of the February afternoon, I lost my virginity at last.

III

Now for me no more riding horse-back; no green apples; no sitting on grass; retching and revolted I gulped down pints of red meat juice, and when, early in June, one of the workman's wives in the huts beyond the stables was brought to bed, I borrowed her filthy petticoat and wore it, flea-ridden as it was, and returned it in July with a fine red woolsey cloak. It all availed me nothing; the August moon ruled me, this year as last.

All this was my private concern. Around me things moved on. Master Reed had taken another stride forward, and was building again. His new notion was to bring over some Flemish weavers to ply their craft in Baildon.

The Flemings were, at this time, an unhappy people, subject to this rule and that as the fortune of war decided. Richard had told me how, on one of his visits to the Low Countries, he had seen between three and four hundred people, men, women and children, being herded along the roads, like animals being taken to market. Their ruler of the moment, the Emperor, or the King of France or the Duke of Burgundy – I was never clear on that point – had decided that one town was too full of people and another too empty, so they were arbitrarily chosen and made to move.

With such circumstances prevailing in their home country, Flemings were always willing to take service elsewhere. The best hired mercenaries were always Flemings, 'routiers' they were called. And the best craftsmen, the weavers, were unsettled too. Master Reed, who at set intervals made the voyage in one of his ships and visited his warehouse in Amsterdam, had engaged eight skilled men to come to Baildon and ply their craft.

A new building was reared, running out at an angle from the main house. The upper floor, very stoutly built to sustain the weight and thud of the looms, was to be the weaving shed; below it the weavers, all single young men, were to live. The weaving shed was a unique structure in that its walls were almost all window. The glass was very costly but Master Reed was sure that within four years he would have reimbursed himself. There would be no duty to pay on the home-woven stuff and he reckoned that he could sell it so cheaply that he would undercut everybody else.

'I began,' he said once, 'by doing smith work cheap. Then I offered cheap stabling. And when I went into the wool trade I was still cheap; I gave a little more for the raw fleeces and sold the baled wool for a little less. Now I hope to sell good cloth, *cheap*.'

I think that was the longest speech I ever heard him make.

The building was finished and the Flemings arrived in June – while I was wearing that horrible petticoat and trying to scratch myself without being noticed. And all through July and August Master Reed and Richard were dealing with the problem of language. Master Reed had learned enough to make himself understood in Amsterdam; Richard knew rather more, he had been inland as far as Bruges and being young had a more pliable mind. But the Flemings were difficult; they worked very well and needed little instruction or guidance so long as they were at their looms; trouble began when they took their feet from the treadles. They made straight for the town then, and in the town they were foreigners, everything they did suspect and resented; this they could not, or would not, understand, so fights took place for the most trivial reasons or for no reason at all. They were woman hungry, and since no respectable females would have anything to do with them, they fell into the hands of whores and harpies who cheated and robbed them. It would all have been different and easier had Master Reed been popular in Baildon; but just as he hated all the townspeople, they hated him and took pleasure in dealing him a knock through the foreigners he had imported. Once, they were all inside the town wall when the gates were locked for the night, and then arrested for being vagrants. By the end of August Master Reed was talking of finding someone capable of speaking to them in their own tongue and controlling them.

'Some old routier,' Richard said, 'with a good hard hand. They'd understand that.'

'And where would you find one, except on the road, a broken-down ne'er-do-well?' Master Reed said.

Anxious to be helpful, I said to Richard, 'My father might know of one, or my brother. Mention it next time you are at Minsham.'

He still rode out there two or three times a week and I always sent a present of some kind, with some kind of excuse – we'd killed a pig and were glutted with pork, or this was a cake I'd made myself, or this was one of the first pieces of cloth from the Baildon loom. I did not go myself. Now that all was well between Richard and me, I could send a downright frank message – 'Tell Mother to remember the junket,' I could say. And he could laugh.

Half-way through September he came back from Minsham with two pieces of news. One was that Isabel was to go to stay with Aunt Astallon and the other was that as soon as she had gone Mother was coming to see me; she intended to stay two nights in Baildon at least.

'Is Father coming too?'

'No. Your mother only. She said she had business to do.'

I sighed. What her business might be I could not guess; one thing was sure, she would find time to go into mine. Still, I braced myself. I was no longer playing at being married. Richard and I were *married* and in that assurance I felt I could face her.

She arrived riding the better horse of the two, the one Father usually rode, and when I had greeted her I asked, 'What happened to Mag?'

'I'm going farther afield,' she said, mysteriously. 'I was on my knees the other night, with my rosary in my hands, and the Blessed Virgin herself put a thought into my mind.'

I had a feeling that this concerned me, so I said, with levity, 'That poor old Mag should be put to pasture?'

Dear Mother; she laughed.

'No. That we should go to St Edmundsbury.'

'What for?'

'Anne, you have now been married for more than a year. And you've been a good girl and followed my instructions. The time has come when nothing but a visit to St Petronella can help us.'

'St Petronella. I never heard of her.'

'Nor I, until I consulted the priest. Now there's a thing you never thought to do, I'll warrant.' She looked at me gaily. 'St Petronella is the one for us. And how fortunate that she is so near.'

We had the solar to ourselves; and while Mother refreshed herself she told me all that she had learned from the priest.

St Petronella in her lifetime had been a fish-gutter at Talmont in France, and in a quarrel with a fellow worker had been so slashed about the face that no man could look on her without a shudder. So her longing for children was never gratified and when, after a long and holy life, she died and was beatified, she gave special notice to the prayers of barren women.

About a hundred years before I was born, a Franciscan Friar found his way to St Edmundsbury and was concerned by the number of lepers living in destitution outside the town. He wished to help them, but had no money, nothing but faith and his own resourcefulness. He made a cross of elm wood and carried it, preaching and begging as he went, all the way to Le Mans where he laid it on St Petronella's shrine amongst all the glittering votive- and thanks-offering that covered it. He prayed that some virtue might pass into the wood. Then he carried it back and announced that virtue *had* passed into it. He set it up under an arch of rough stones and it had become a place of pilgrimage for childless women. As long as he lived he used the income of the shrine for the relief of lepers and when he died the Abbey took over the shrine and built a little house for the lepers.

All this Mother told me as she drank some ale and ate cake in the solar. I listened and thanked her for her interest and concern for me. Once I had resented her questions and advice, but now it was different. Nevertheless, when she said, 'We'll go there, together, tomorrow,' I protested.

'What excuse can we give?'

'Why excuse? You can give your real reason.'

'It is a matter that is never mentioned, not even between Richard and me. As for his father...'

'Nonsense! Not to mention a thing is not to say it does not exist. I'll warrant that Richard and his father have watched you with eyes as keen as mine, and been as greatly disappointed.'

'Oh dear,' I said.

'Never mind, we are doing all that we can. And the priest assured me that the Saint had worked some wondrous miracles.'

I announced – brusquely because I was embarrassed – that on the morrow Mother and I intended to ride to St Edmundsbury. Richard put out his hand and squeezed mine, understandingly. Master Reed looked at me sombrely out of his sad eyes and presently, when we chanced to be alone for a moment, said to me, 'Anne, I know the purpose of your journey, and I wish you well. But I...' He hesitated and then said, jerkily, the words coming out of him in a rush, 'Don't count too much upon it. Miracles...' he paused again and looked down at his lame leg and the thick-soled shoe, 'They work in a queer, twisted way,' he said. 'And I can't for the life of me see how what you're wanting could be other than straightforward. And I don't believe they can be that way. Miracles, I mean.' He touched my shoulder and said, 'Perhaps your faith is greater.'

Next morning we set out, Mother and I, with a man to escort us. Richard wanted to come, but that I did not favour, why I could not say. I would not have taken the man but Master Reed insisted; he was shocked to learn that Mother had ridden in from Minsham alone. His view of the open road was the view of the man who transports stuff of value from place to place and must ever be on guard against robbers.

There was no need to inquire the way to the shrine. Long before we reached it we found ourself in the centre of a kind of Fair, a Fair devoted to the exploitation of childless women. It was so shameless that I wonder the Abbey allowed it. There were people selling charms, all guaranteed to bring fecundity; cakes made in the shape of babies; trinkets of bone or wood or stone, even of coral and ivory, all in the shape of babies. There were strings and strings of blue beads – blue being the Virgin's own colour and thus associated with motherhood. There were slatternly women with great broods of children – borrowed or hired, I suspect – lining the road and screaming that they would sell, for a penny, the secret of their fruitfulness. 'Two pence, lady, and I'll put the good wish on you!' 'Threepence, lady, and you shall be in pod by Michaelmas.' I was ashamed and drew my veil close, and even Mother said, 'They overdo it somewhat.'

Monks are cunning. After all that brash huckstering along the road, with the constant demand for pence breeding disbelief until you were ready to think of St Petronella as just another fraud, out to rob you, you rode through a gateway where only petitioners and their attendants were allowed to pass. Inside was a kind of inn; rails to which horses could be hitched, a stone trough full of water, benches and tables where people could refresh themselves. The whole place was shaded by chestnut trees, from which, on this day, the great yellow fans of dead leaves fluttered gently and quietly to the ground.

On the far side of this enclosure was a gate in the wall. Through this the petitioner must go alone. The path beyond was paved and bordered on each side by a green hedge, neatly clipped, very thick and an inch or two taller than a man. The path wound in curves so that at no time could I see more than a step or two ahead. I have never felt more lonely, more isolated from all other human beings. The contrast after the bustle and hurly-burly outside was complete. When I rounded the last curve there was the plain wooden Cross, under the rough stone arch, just as the Franciscan had set it up, more than a hundred years ago.

Offerings to this shrine were always in money – used for the relief of lepers and other purposes – so the shrine was quite bare, without even a flower. It was humble and touching, and in some strange way far more believable and impressive than any other shrine I had ever seen. I went down on my knees and prayed that St Petronella would use her influence, and intercede for me and give me a baby. Here, alone, in the quiet before this simple Cross, I could acknowledge the need which hitherto I had hidden even from myself. I thought about holding a baby in my arms, feeding it at my breast.

We rode home and that evening at supper there was a new face halfway down the first trestle table; and because Mother was staying with us and sat at my usual place, I had a good view of the newcomer.

It is hard for me to describe this man, Denys the Routier, or Denys Rootyer as he came to be called. The most immediately noticeable thing about him was that he had only one eye; over the empty socket on the other side he wore a black leather patch, kept in position by a black string tied at the back of his head. His hair, roughly cut and inclined to be curly, was a pale sandy colour, many shades lighter than his weatherbeaten skin; his one eye was brightly blue.

I was looking at him with interest because he was a stranger, and because of the black patch, when he turned his glance on me and immediately something happened inside me, as though something had given way and all my vitals had slipped. It was not unlike the first onset of sickness and I pressed my hand to my mouth and thought – Holy Mother! The miracle has happened and I have quickened. I looked at my plate, and although the dish was to my liking, specially made in honour of Mother, I knew that I could not take another mouthful.

Richard said, 'The journey was too much for you. Come to bed. When you are rested I will bring you your supper.'

'Fetch some wine; that will revive both our travellers,' Master Reed said. So the wine came and I sat there holding the cup in my hands and turning it about, not daring to drink until my inside settled.

Mother answered questions about the journey.

Presently I said, 'I see we have a new man.'

'Ah yes.' Master Reed turned to Mother and said, 'Please tell Sir Godfrey that I am grateful and obliged to him for his good offices in finding so suitable a man.'

'Oh, did Blanchefleur remember? He grows more and more forgetful these days.' She smiled as though describing a child's vagary. 'Still, he would remember a thing like that better than any simple errand I set him. Which is the new man?' She craned her neck.

'The one with the patch over his eye,' Richard said. 'A good stout fellow, is he not?'

I looked again and saw that everyone else at the board was suddenly diminished. The weavers were always somewhat pale, inclined to fleshiness – that was a mark of their trade – but they were not all weavers at the table. I glanced to right and left; Master Reed looked thick and shapeless, Richard too fine drawn, a pretty boy.

I told myself that it was because the new man wore no collar, his dark, creased neck rose out of a collarless leather jerkin which fitted close to his wide flat shoulders, and so he looked all of a piece, stripped of all non-essentials, ready for action.

Mother was rippling on about routiers; their high reputation for loyalty and courage, despite being mercenaries.

'But that is why,' she explained. 'Nobles and knights are for ever changing their causes for this reason and that, routiers fight for pay and stick with the man who pays them.' She lowered her voice a little. 'You must look to your maids, Master Reed; these old soldiers have a way with women.'

'Not old soldiers only,' he said drily. 'I always choose old serving wenches.'

'Very wise.'

I said, 'I think I shall go to bed now.'

When I had been there a little while, Richard came softly in, bringing more wine and some food.

'Are you asleep?'

'No.'

'Could you eat now?'

'No. I thank you all the same.'

He put the things down and came and sat on the side of the bed.

'What really happened today?'

'Nothing really…' I told him a little more about the way I had felt by the bare, humble little shrine. Then I put my hands on either side of his face and said, 'I love you, I love you, I love. You know that, don't you?'

'Could I ever doubt it? I love you too.'

Words, true words; but I need something more.

'Come in the bed with me, now.'

He came to me eagerly, tenderly. He gave me all that he had. But afterwards, in the dark, I lay alone again, and a voice, within my head, yet distant as a star, asked, 'Is this all?' I closed my mind to it, pushing against it, as one might push a door against an intruder. But it tried again; it asked, 'How would this be, if done with the man with one eye?'

IV

Madness, we know, takes many forms; and this was mine. I never for one instant ceased to love Richard. There never was a moment, mad as I was, when to have saved Richard a pang of toothache I would not gladly have seen Denys the Routier hanged, drawn and quartered. By all that is holy, I swear that that is true. The lust I felt for him was like a poison, swallowed unwittingly, doing its damage, taking possession of the whole sound body.

With Mother gone home I was back at my old place at the table and could see him clearly only when he leaned forward or the man sitting next him leaned back. And after the first few days he was never there for the midday dinner and not to be counted upon at supper time. In no time at all, talking to the Flemings in their own tongue, he had put the fear of God into them, and Master Reed, never one to waste anything, had begun to send him with the pack ponies as a kind of guard. So I never knew, when I entered the dining hall, whether his place would be filled or empty, and every evening, every evening for weeks, I vowed that this time I would not look. But I always did, sooner or later; and if his place was empty a kind of greyness would come over everything, my food would be tasteless...Tomorrow, how many hours? Or perhaps, a long journey, the day after tomorrow...It was like walking down a dark stone passage with a light at the far end. No, not a light, a dancing will-'o-the-wisp. For when the moment came and I looked and there he was, what then?

Oh, then, at some moment during the Meal that one blue eye would look at me, and my inside would turn its now pleasurable somersault; the candlelight would brighten, the fire behind me throw out more heat and I would know a moment of what I can only call timelessness. In that moment all kinds of things would rush together, reminding me of small pleasures I had known in the past and promising me a great pleasure to come – there'd be the cool scent of primroses, the warm scent of roses, the sound of trumpets, the feel of my Aunt Astallon's silk gown, the taste of strawberries, the colours of a sunset – all mixed up in one mad moment, meaning nothing, meaning everything. How can I explain it? It was as though every pleasant thing that I had ever felt in the past was a separate string to a lute, and his glance was the running of a hand over those strings, so that they all cried out together, in no tuneable pattern.

I never spoke to him, never had occasion to go near him, until one morning in the spring. It was March; I remember seeing the daffodils breaking yellow in the garden close, under the apple trees. Richard was riding out to Minsham and I said I would go too. St Petronella had failed me yet again and I had spent the whole winter cooped in the house.

Martin's horse and my palfrey stood awaiting us, and nearby a string of pack-ponies, laden with the new Baildon cloth, were lining up for the first stage of their journey to London. Denys stood with them. He came forward – one of Martin Reed's servants, civil, obliging – and helped me to mount. When he touched me, my bones melted. In the two seconds before I was in the saddle it was all said. 'I am yours, take me,' my flesh said to his; and his said, 'Would that I could.'

'You look so pale,' Martin said, turning his horse beside me. 'Are you sure you should ride?'

'You know that it is only when I am pale with such good reason that I dare face my mother,' I said, crossly. And all the way to Minsham I thought about Denys. We would make a child, I thought, the moment we came together. We could defy the moon, the pale moon with its fluxes...

After that I suppose it was merely a question of awaiting an opportunity.

April passed and May. I had grown thin, which was not becoming to me. One day, looking in the glass, I was horrified to see that after all I had inherited the Blanchefleur nose and would one day look exactly like an aunt I detested. Richard and his father put down my lack of appetite and uncertain temper to disappointment, and were kinder than ever to me which, because it made me feel ashamed, made matters worse.

June was always a busy month, with the new cut fleeces pouring in from miles around, and often Richard would rise early, leaving me to slug abed. One morning he did so, and when I did go down I looked into the office, but he wasn't there, which was nothing unusual. Dinner time came and the oak table was set with two places only.

'Where's Richard?' I asked.

'Gone to Bywater. We had word early this morning that *Sea Maid* had run into another ship and was damaged. He rode down to see what the damage was. He'll be back tomorrow.'

Martin set about his meal and then stopped. 'I'm off myself to Kelvedon this minute. You'll be alone in the new part. Would you like Nancy or Meg to move over?'

'For fear of what?'

'Whatever it is women fear. Ghosties and goblins?' He gave me his painful, rare smile.

'Anything a kitchen wench could save me from I do not fear,' I said.

Yet I had no intention of taking Denys into Richard's bed. I had no intention of doing anything. I did not even go into the hall for supper, to sit there alone, displaying my solitariness. I stayed close in the solar, thinking that he would think that I also had gone away. From the solar I went into the garden.

Every rose had its heart wide open; the langour of a summer evening weighed heavy on every leaf. I walked, lingered, walked on, unable to draw a full breath, my heart was so shaken.

Presently, between the rose bushes, old Nancy came hobbling on her flat feet.

'Mistress,' she began as soon as she saw me, 'There's that Denys Rootyer at the back door. He say Master went off and never give him his orders for tomorrow. He say he ought to talk to you.'

'Oh,' I said, and struggled with my breath. Surely she must notice and wonder. 'No orders were left with me. I know nothing.'

'He seem to hev something in his mind. He just want somebody to say go ahead like. There ain't nobody else but you.'

229

'I'll see him.'

'Out here? Then you should hev a shawl. The dew's falling.'

'Give him the shawl. That will save you a few steps.'

'T'ain't everybody'd be thoughtful of an owd woman's feet,' she said, pleased. 'I give you Good night, Mistress.'

Thinking no evil, thinking only of her bed, she plodded away. And presently, with his light, firm, soldier's tread, carrying my shawl over his arm, Denys came through the roses.

V

There followed some days during which, with a sense of bewilderment, I thought of Mother's words. I'd sit at the table and look at Richard, whom I loved, and then at Denys, whom I did not love, and I knew which of them gave me that feeling of triumph, of pride that had sounded in Mother's voice when she spoke of Father. How I envied her – and any other woman who could have that feeling lawfully, together *with* love. Those were days when I had only to see his great brown hand close on a piece of bread in the trencher to feel its touch on me again and wonder how, through all the years of my life, I could manage with what I had.

Those days were soon over. The July moon was a horned crescent, was a silver-gilt plate, grew gibbous and copper coloured. It drew no response from my blood. To myself I said – I was right; I knew this would happen. To the others I said nothing. I waited until one morning towards the end of August, when as soon as I set foot to the floor, I was deathly sick. Then I said to Richard, 'I think I am with child.' And presently I was sure enough to send a message to my mother.

There was, naturally, great rejoicing. Even Master Reed threw off his melancholy air, and Richard's pride and pleasure cut me to the heart. I had other troubles too. One was shame and one was fear.

Now that the work was done and my womb was filling, all the lust went out of me, and all the madness, and I could see Denys for what he was – a great hunk of man flesh, a common hired soldier to whom I, Anne Blanchefleur, had submitted! There was the shame!

The fear lay in the thought that children tended to look like their parents. Suppose my child were born with that pale sandy hair and only one eye. How could I ever have been so crazy as not to have thought of that?

I studied Richard and his father. At a first glance they were unlike, Richard was much darker, much more lightly built, but the way the hair grew off their foreheads was the same, and they both had crooked little fingers on their left hands. True, Master Reed was lame and Richard had two good straight legs, but there were two schools of thought about such things. Some people held that anything that had happened to a man or woman by accident during his or her lifetime was not passed on to the offspring; other people claimed that anything that happened, even to having been frightened by a mouse, could leave a mark upon the child.

Mother rode in to see me and we had a long talk, all about such mysteries; I encouraged her and then wished I had not. She had a story of a pregnant woman who had longed for strawberries in December and who bore a child with a red strawberry mark on its left cheek.

'Whatever you long for, no matter how silly it sounds, speak out, Anne. Make them get it for you if possible.'

I thought – I wonder how you would look if I told you that the one thing I long for is the assurance that a one-eyed man's child will not be born with one eye.

All this uneasiness of mind took its toll of my body. I think I suffered everything a pregnant woman can. They say that if you are sick at six weeks, at six months you'll be lively. They say that cramps beforehand are a sign of easy labour, you've had so much of your grue. They say that if your legs swell, your face does not.

I broke every one of the rules. I was sick at six weeks, and even sicker at six months; I had cramp; my face swelled to the size of a bladder, and my legs swelled till they were as big as my waist ordinarily was; and in the end I was in labour for two days and three nights.

Before the end I had my story ready. If I gave birth to a child with one eye I was going to say that on the night when Richard and his father were both away, Denys made an excuse to come to me in the garden, and there raped me. Old Nancy would bear me out about the excuse, I was in the garden, innocent as a lamb, and he did make that opportunity to seek me out. Richard and his father would ask one dangerous question – Why had I not complained? To that I had a silly sentimental answer, silly enough to sound true. My father had found Denys for Master Reed and I didn't want him to think that Father had sent him a rogue.

My last sensible thought was of my story and how, if needs be, I must stick to it. Then my agony began; and presently I didn't care if the child were born with one eye or four, if only it would be born. I saw Mother and screamed to her, 'Help me!' and with tears on her face she said, 'You must be brave. You must help yourself. None other can.'

I tried to be brave. I told myself that I was the daughter of one of the boldest knights that ever rode in tourney, and of a woman who had set out to ride from Rivington to Beauclaire, risking being brought to bed in a ditch. But it went on too long. In the end I was screaming like a trapped hare and I went on screaming until I had no voice left and could only make harsh, weak cries. The pain abated and I floated away, and was walking towards St Petronella's shrine, but the solid green hedges were all covered with open-hearted roses, drenching the air with scent. Just before the shrine Richard waited for me, but as I went near he turned into Denys, holding a dark cloak with which he smothered me. I fought against the weight of it and struggled up into the air and light again. The priest was in the room.

I thought – I am dying. I wanted to say – I have a great sin to confess; I have committed adultery. Had we been alone I might have said it, but beyond the circle of the candlelight I saw other people – Mother, another woman, several...Richard will hear about it, I thought, and be hurt, and not revere my memory. No, sooner I would die unshriven and go to Hell.

Hell was the Long Gallery at Abhurst, brightly lighted so that there was no shadow into which one could retire. I stood alone and watched four or five young men crowd about Catherine Montsorrel. My Aunt Bowdegrave came and stood by me, showing her yellow teeth and saying that with my sharp tongue and prim manner I should never find a husband.

From there I slipped into a bottomless pit of darkness and lay there until someone above reached down with a grappling iron and hooked it into my body and hauled me up, screaming and struggling, and with each struggle the iron bit deeper into me; I was being cut in two. When I was severed, what remained fell down upon the bed and the pain was over. I could hear a bustling and a soft clucking of tongues. Then I opened my eyes, and there was Mother, holding a baby, and the midwife with another.

'Twins,' Mother said. 'Boy and girl.'

Twins were freaks; nobody expected them to be quite ordinary; if one, or both, lacked an eye, or even a limb, it would be no wonder. Holy Mother of God, you have dealt with me more gently than I deserve.

'Are they whole?' I whispered.

'Whole? They are beautiful.'

Twins, Mother and the midwife agreed, are ordinarily smaller than other babies, but Walter and Maude were each as large as any single child; from this, and the abundance of hair on each of their heads, Mother deduced that I had carried them over-long and muddled my dates.

'Young women are so careless,' she grumbled. 'You told me March, and if they'd been born when they should, I might not have got to you in time.'

They were not a bit like one another once the red, crumpled new-born look had worn off. They were both born with black hair, but they shed it in the first weeks, and Walter's grew black again, Maude's reddish gold.

'The wrong way about,' Mother said. 'The boy should favour you, and the girl her father. As often happens.'

'To our cost. My Blanchefleur nose! I would sooner have had yours.'

Such trivial, cosy little conversations seemed to underline my sense of safety; as though I had forded a dangerous stream, been almost swept away, but struggled to safety and now could afford to talk about currents, deep waters, lost footholds. I was safe. I was lucky. I now had everything.

In a month I was up and about, fully restored to health, and miracle of miracles, my waist was its normal size. I knew that by my dresses; my nose, now that the flesh was back on my face, took its proper place again, and I knew that I was prettier than ever.

There being two babies to feed, we were forced to engage a wet nurse – a thing not common in households of our degree however rich, and when I proved to be a poor milch cow, while she had enough for four, she took on all that duty, and I was free to enjoy the summer and go riding with Richard again.

It was he who suggested that we should ride to St Petronella's shrine and take a further present to show our gratitude. Something, and to this day I do not know exactly what it was, made me demur.

'I don't think that is customary. Women only go there to ask.'

'Then it's time somebody had manners enough to go and say "Thank you",' he said, smiling.

I smiled too.

'I believe you have never been to St Edmundsbury.'

'That is so. We'll go, shall we?'

'You have to ride through the rowdiest kind of Fair.'

'I shall be with you. And this time you can look down your nose at all the spell-binders. I warrant none of *them* bore two, weighing a full stone between them.'

To settle an argument between Mother and the midwife, Master Reed had carried the babies out and weighed them in the wool scales.

Having no argument, no reason for not riding that way, except a vague and mysterious feeling that it would be wiser not to, I gave way, and we set off on a fine warm morning.

Richard enjoyed himself enormously, especially when we reached the stalls. I was newly puzzled how anyone so gentle and fastidious and dignified should seem so much at ease in such surroundings. He bought gingerbread babies and charms of every kind, and a long string of blue beads which he slipped over my head, tangling it in my veil. Even the shaggy old harridan who so brazenly shouted 'in pod' – only now she had changed her cry to 'in pod by Lammas' – did not disgust him. He gave her fourpence and laughed when she promised us four lusty sons.

'Old fraud,' he said as we moved on, 'none of that gaggle of brats is hers, I'll warrant.'

'Then why encourage her?'

'She must live. There's something about people who try to wring a living out of the world with nothing but a slick tongue or a penny whistle that appeals to me.'

'I know. You might have been born at a Fair, you seem so much at home.'

'Then I could have played my lute.'

'And dreamed of being the only son of a prosperous wool merchant, no doubt.'

'No doubt at all.'

We rode on and entered the enclosure. Richard slipped a gold piece into my hand and I gave it to the monk by the inner gate. I set off briskly down the path, feeling the delight of moving freely and lightly again, and thinking that I had only to kneel and offer a few words of thanksgiving. But as I rounded one curve and then the next, I found myself walking more and more slowly, while the distaste I felt for this apparently simple errand grew until it was terror. The day seemed to darken, and when I looked up at the sky, I saw that a great purple cloud had reared up from the west and engulfed the sun.

I stood still and thought – I don't *have* to go any farther, no one will know. Stand here and count up to hundred, twice, slowly. But that would be cowardly, and later I should despise myself. All my life I had heard a high price set on courage, and cowardice spoken of as rather worse than sin, and when I was a child, with my full share of childish fears, I had always schooled myself to overcome them. Now to be frightened of nothing, that was ridiculous. So I set myself in motion; walked on and reached the shrine which was in all respects just as before.

I went down on my knees and suddenly could think of nothing except the words Master Reed had said to me just before my first visit here. 'Miracles...they work in a queer, twisted way, and I can't for the life of me see how what you're wanting could be other than straightforward.' But I could see, with sudden, clear sight, how my miracle had come about, in, as he said, a queer, twisted way. Doubly twisted. First my madness, and then the fact that neither child bore any mark of its paternity. For let Mother say what she would about weight and crops of hair and muddled dates, I knew.

No doubt St Petronella has been passionately thanked, even if the grateful petitioners did not make a journey to her shrine to do it, but she surely never was thanked so passionately, so much from the heart, as I thanked her in that moment when I understood the extent of her miracle.

I went back to Richard and suggested that we should wait for a little, since that cloud threatened rain. We sat under the chestnut trees and ate and drank, and still the rain held off, and at last he said, 'In summer it often clouds over without a drop falling.' So we set off. When we were on the open road, far from any house, there was a fearful clap of thunder, and the heavens opened and down came the rain, mingled with hailstones as large as the blue beads I was wearing. I suggested sheltering under some trees nearby, but Richard said they were elms, dangerous at any time and doubly so in a storm, so we rode on, soon drenched and then shivering, for the day had turned cold as the hail fell.

Next day Richard was feverish and stayed in bed, hot and cold by turns, and coughing now and then. I made linseed poultices for his chest, and rubbed him well with neats' foot oil, and beat honey and vinegar together for him to swallow, but the cough grew worse, and after the third night, when he had kept all our side of the house, save the babies, awake with it, Master Reed sent for the doctor. He had several remedies to try – one, the nature of which I concealed from Richard – was the liquor in which snails had been boiled, but nothing did any service until one morning he came along with a little horn full of a greenish-grey powder. One pinch of it, as much as one could take between finger and thumb, was to be dropped on top of a cup of warm milk or wine; just the one pinch, and the dose was not to be repeated in less than twelve hours.

'It is,' the doctor said, 'a sovereign remedy, but it is also a powerful poison; taken in quantity, or too often, it could be fatal.'

'I alone will administer it, and I will be very careful.'

That night he slept, and sleep is itself a healer. In the morning his fever was lessened, his skin moist and cool to the touch. During the day the cough returned, but less violently, and so, day by day, he made progress. In most ways he was an easy patient, grateful and cheerful, but being held to the one room irked him; his only complaint was that the walls seemed to be closing in. We pushed the bed close to the window and propped him up so that he could look out and see the sky. And as soon as he was well enough – about three weeks after our unfortunate journey – he came down, leaning on his father's arm, into the solar.

That was a happy day, and as soon as he was settled in the window seat, overlooking the garden, I got out my sewing which

I had neglected lately. I was making Mother a winter cloak, of our own Baildon cloth, the cloth which was to become so famous that men would speak of 'my Baildon breeches', and women say, 'I will wear my Baildon'. The cloth itself was dove grey, there was an interlining of shredded-out lambs' wool, and a lining of red silk, the two last quilted together. It had a hood which could be pulled over the head or thrown back. It was, in fact, such a garment as Mother had never owned. Master Reed, immediately after our marriage, had done a generous thing – hired, for some absurdly high price, several of the acres which went with the house, to add to his sheep run – but none of the extra money found its way into Mother's wardrobe. Isabel went out into the world better equipped, and Mag, the old horse, had been replaced.

I was stitching away, when Richard said, 'That is for your mother's birthday, isn't it?'

'Yes. The day after tomorrow, and I still have this much of the lining to fix, and then the hood to stitch on.' I held it out and showed him.

'It'll be ready. And I shall be ready to ride out and take it.'

'I should no more dream of letting you ride out to Minsham the day after tomorrow than I should dream of...well...of throwing myself into the river.'

'But I'm better.'

'You're downstairs today for the first time. A fortnight hence will be time enough to talk about mounting a horse.'

'I want to see Jason.' That was his hawk.

'Then you must want,' I said, stitching away.

'Uncle Tom once warned me that all high-nosed women were masterful and domineering!'

'How strange. Somebody once warned me that all black-haired men were obstinate and unreasonable.'

He laughed and coughed.

'You sound like riding abroad the day after tomorrow.'

'I shall.'

'Then you'll go alone. I will not lend my countenance to such a thing.'

Just then Master Reed entered the solar and Richard appealed to him to decide.

'You would be more than foolish. Just to visit a hawk.'

'But Anne will want to see her mother.'

'So she shall. Clement can ride with her and take out the tar and spend his day helping the shepherd.'

Mother's birthday dawned clear and bright, and Richard woke feeling so much better that I had to repeat my threat that if he rode I would stay at home. His improvement, and the fair morning, sent my spirits soaring.

When I was ready to leave, Master Reed came into the yard with me, carrying a small cask of wine.

'For your mother, with good wishes,' he said, and muttered something about it being a balance for the tar barrel.

There in the yard stood a big brown horse, and my palfrey, and standing between them Denys.

I know my step faltered, for Master Reed said, 'Forgotten something?'

I shook my head, and went forward wondering whether I could, at this last moment, say that I felt ill. A coward's trick, and disappointing for Mother. And perhaps, after all, Denys was only holding the horses; it was Clement – who understood sheep – who was supposed to spend the day at Minsham with the shepherd. I stood, all confused and uncertain, sweat breaking out on my forehead and upper lip and the palms of my hands while the two men slung the wine cask.

There was still time to droop and dwindle and pretend a sudden pain. But I said to myself – Courage, courage.

Master Reed turned to me and said, 'Up you get,' and helped me into the saddle. I rode out through the covered way first and, once out of the gate, drove in my heel. My palfrey had never once been underfed or overburdened, or hard pressed, and during Richard's illness had stood in the stable cramming corn. 'Let's see what you can do today,' I said in its ear.

It did well. The road, heavy from the recent rainy spell, was in our favour; the brown horse was bigger, but Denys weighed all of twelve stone, and there were the two casks.

For eight of the ten miles I stayed ahead, then my beast slackened pace and nothing I could do could make it recover speed. Out of nowhere there came to me the rhyme which Father had said to us, jogging us on his knee.

'This is the way the ladies ride, trippety, trip, trippety, trip. This is the way the farmers ride, bumpitty, thud, bumpitty, thud.' And in the end, I thought, bumpitty thud will always catch up with trippety trip. How I longed for the horse in the end of the rhyme, 'This is the way the gentlemen ride, gallop and trot, gallop and trot.'

Denys came level with me and snatched at my rein.

'Did the brute bolt?' He pulled the rein savagely, so that my palfrey's head was wrenched round and we stood sideways across the road.

'Don't do that. I set the pace. I am anxious to arrive.'

He said, and I shall always remember the curious simplicity and innocence that there was both in his voice and in his eye, 'I wanted to talk to you. It's been a whole year, with never so much as a word.'

I said nothing.

'This was our chance to fix something; to meet; to get together again,' he said, as though explaining something to a stupid child. 'I've been wanting you so badly, I wonder I haven't done something desperate, all these months. I wonder you never tried...'

He had no suspicion of the way I felt. I'd swung my horse about again so that it was facing the right way, and he brought his alongside, and put out his arm to touch me, but the tar barrel prevented him coming close enough.

'Come on, get down,' he said in a thick, amorous voice.

I thought the quickest cut would be best. He had dropped my rein, so I set my palfrey going, and he came level, and I said, 'What happened last June twelvemonth happened because I was mad. It must never happen again.'

'Oh, come! What was so mad about it? And what harm did we do? I'd lay a year's pay you never had it so good – and nor did I! Things being so cursed difficult I tried to put you out of my mind, but I never could. And you'd say the same if you weren't trying to play coy with me. There's no need for that and no time.'

'I mean what I say. It's finished. Over and done with.'

'It'll come back. Women are often that way, after childbed. You'll see. This evening, eh? On our way back.'

'Not then, or any other time,' I said, trying to get another spurt of speed out of my horse.

He seemed genuinely puzzled. 'What's got into you? What've I done? I'm just the same. You were starving for it – oh, I could tell. And I didn't do so badly by you. Two sound brats, with no lung rot.'

Anger flared in me, but I mastered it, and said coolly, 'You flatter yourself.'

'Do I? Bedded for a year with a pretty boy that couldn't father a mouse – a woman like you! Think back to that night on the grass and look what you're missing.' He followed this by a remark of such coarseness and familiarity as was not to be tolerated, even if it were deserved.

'At the next bend we shall be in sight of my father's house,' I said. 'Drop back and ride behind me as a servant should.'

He laughed. 'That's my lady! Like plums, the higher the sweeter, once you can reach them down.' He hit my palfrey a sharp blow and it shot forward.

'That's the way,' he cried, 'let's ride in in style.'

VI

For me the day was ruined. Mother was delighted with the cloak and the wine, pleased to see me and avid to hear the last smallest detail about Walter and Maude, but I had to make a great effort to chat light-heartedly, and a greater one to do justice to the birthday dinner. I had to ride back to Baildon in Denys' company. The irony of the thought that little more than a year ago no prospect would have pleased me more only served to underline the horror of my present situation.

I have never known a day go so fast.

I gave Jason the gobbet of red meat which Richard had sent him and listened absent-mindedly while Father explained that these last three weeks, during which Richard had not ridden out to Minsham at all, would make an excellent excuse for the fact that the young hawk would never accept him as his master.

'I've feared it all along,' he said in his slow, fumbling way. 'Twice a week...and let him be the only one ever to take the rufter off. I thought that might just do it. I was wrong and I was afraid the poor fellow would be disappointed; we can lay the blame now on these three weeks.'

With some vague notion of handicapping Denys on the return journey, I said, 'I can't think why you didn't let Richard have his hawk at the Old Vine in the first place. Shall we take it back with us this afternoon? I think that would please him.'

'But who at the Old Vine understands falconry? That's just it. A tiercel isn't a lap dog, Anne. Maybe I was foolish...but he had shown some slight interest in hawking...I told you, that first time. And your mother thought...'

'Mother thought *what*?'

'That to get out, out of that office, into the air...Oh, I know twice a week isn't much, isn't enough, but it did make an excuse. And as usual, your mother was right, wasn't she. So the hawk wasn't wasted, though I daresay Richard will be a bit jealous that I can now handle his bird. Still, nobody can help being ill.'

'May I carry Jason back with me this afternoon?'

'No. You can't handle him...Isabel now, if it was Isabel, but you never cared for the sport. And you'd have no place – not so much as a perch. An unhandled hawk, especially one half trained like Jason'd go mad, or pine to death. No. When Richard is better, which God send will be soon, he must come out and I'll fool them both. I'll stand close to him and whistle my whistle through *his*. We'll manage.'

Alone with Mother again, I put on the drooping, dwindling look which I would have been wise to have put on in the yard hours before.

'You warned me about riding, but you had it all wrong. It is now that the jolting hurts me.'

She looked concerned. 'I thought you looked very wan when you came in. You had a hard time, you know, and it's not so long. Richard ill too; I daresay you've been up and down stairs and having broken nights.'

'If my bed were aired,' I said, 'I would lie here tonight. Denys could tell them that I was just tired.'

'The bed hasn't been slept in since Isabel went. But I could air it in an hour.'

'Then I'll stay, and gladly.'

Mother threw fresh wood on the fire and began to climb the stairs.

'I'll help you,' I said.

'You'll do nothing of the sort. I can handle that bed. It isn't like those great fat feather bundles you lie on at Baildon.' She laughed. In a few seconds she came out of my old room with the bed – a poor thin thing indeed, folded over into a roll and held in her arms. She came down three stairs, then the inside edge of the roll loosened itself and fell lower than the rest; she stepped into it, as it were, missed her footing, almost righted herself, and could have, had that staircase had a handrail to clutch at, but it hadn't; she clutched at air and fell sideways on to the floor of the hall.

She was up in an instant, before I could get to her.

'Clumsy!' she said, and laughed.

'Are you hurt?'

'Not a bit.' She went to the foot of the stairs where the mattress, now fully unfolded, lay, and picked it up and gave it a shake.

'Trip me, would you?' she said, 'I'll roast you for that!'

We propped it up before the fire and the amount of steam which rose from it proved its need for airing. Minsham Old Hall was very damp always; on the hottest day of summer you could write your name on the dewy moisture of the walls.

For supper we ate the remains of the birthday dinner and drank some more of the wine, and now we were truly merry. Denys had gone, with a black look for me over Mother's shoulder when she gave him his instructions at the door. Tomorrow Father was to ride in with me, and once in the house I should be safe. I'd never ride anywhere again until Richard was fit to ride with me.

Getting up from the supper-table, Mother clapped her hand to her side and gave a little cry.

'I must have caught myself a clout without knowing it. A bruise, no more.' But even her lips had gone white.

She was up in the morning, however, very cheerful, holding herself a mite stiffly and saying that forty-six was a bit old to go turning somersaults.

'I shall ride in myself next Wednesday to see those dear children,' she said, as we parted. 'Meanwhile, wish Richard good health for me and thank Master Reed for the wine.'

I rode back to Baildon thinking that I had managed very well.

Mother's birthday was on Thursday. I went home on Friday. Richard was better, but still taking his meals apart in the solar. I ate my supper with him, in the golden, slanting rays of the sinking sun. Master Reed, who had supped in the hall as usual, came into the room afterwards, looked into our wine cups, saw them full and poured his own. Then he said, 'Anne, Denys the Routier wants a word with you.'

Whether I went red or white I cannot tell; I could only feel my whole face stiffen.

'With me. What about?'

'I don't know. He just asked if he could have a word with you.'

I suppose it was my guilty conscience that made me think his manner a trifle more restrained than usual, his eye just a little suspicious...no...curious.

I turned and hurried, trying not to hurry, out of the solar.

The dining hall, on the eastern side of the house, was already dim and full of shadows. It smelt strongly of rabbit and onion stew, and even in that moment of extremity some part of my mind noted the curious fact that a dish of which one has not partaken always has a stronger odour than one which one has eaten. Richard and I, in the solar, had shared a cold capon.

Old Nancy stood in the doorway between the hall and the kitchen, watching Meg and Jane, helped by the two youngest apprentices, clear the tables. Denys leaned against the door post of the outer door, his back to the hall, looking out into the yard. The presence of four other – five other people gave me confidence. I walked towards him and said, 'You wanted to speak with me.'

He turned quickly, so that in the doorway we faced one another, and he took hold of my hand. The action could not be seen by those inside in the hall because the bulk of my body was in their way. He fumbled with my hand for a second and then had me by the little finger, bending it down, pressing hard. There is no simple, quiet, secret action that can cause more sharp pain. Anyone who doubts this should try it on himself. Pressing ruthlessly on my finger he pulled me over the threshold. At the same time he hissed into my ear, 'Call back and say your palfrey is lame and you are looking to it.'

I leaned back, and only just able to speak for the pain in my finger, said, 'Nancy. Tell Master Richard I have gone out to look at my palfrey. It is lame it seems.'

'Now,' he said, with a little more pressure on my finger, 'come and look just how lame it is.' He dragged me across the yard and to the fence of the pasture. 'A pretty trick you played me yesterday. Now listen. Tomorrow is Saturday. In the afternoon they'll all go to their shooting at the Butts. I don't have to go. I've done my soldiering. I shall wait for you in the wool loft, the far end.'

I said, and I could hear how thin my voice sounded, 'Unless you let go my finger…I can give you no mind…I shall faint.'

He let go then, but he put his arm around me and said, 'You bring it on yourself, you're so tricky. It could have been yesterday, you silly little hussy,' and he pushed his body against me. 'Now it must wait till tomorrow, and I've waited so long…'

'I can't. I can't. Even if I wanted to…my husband, his father…I can't just walk out of the house.'

'Women always have two excuses – church and the dressmaker. Choose which you like, but I'm telling you, you had better come.'

He let me go, and, stooping, tugged up a little tuft of grass with the soil clodded about its roots. He tossed it gently over the fence at my palfrey which was grazing amongst the other horses, a pale shadow amongst the darker ones. It started and moved away, one hoof hardly touching the ground, lame as a tinker's donkey.

'This time I made an excuse. If you fail me tomorrow I shall ask for you again, and again, and every excuse will be shakier than the one before. And I shall talk about you, in alehouses – '

'You'll find yourself in trouble if you boast of rape.'

He laughed, it seemed with real pleasure.

'I always knew a devil lurked behind that angel face of yours, my pretty! Rape indeed. Was your dress torn? Did you run screaming? Did you complain? Besides which, once I've set them all asking questions I shall make myself scarce, leaving you to find the answers.'

Had I been innocent, I suppose that would hardly have been a threat at all. I remembered how my face had felt when Master Reed brought me Denys' message, I remembered the look I thought he had given me. My best weapon, a clear conscience, was snapped in my hand; I was not equipped to fight.

'I'll come,' I said.

'And I'll set your horse to rights.' He rested one hand on a post of the fence and vaulted lightly into the meadow.

I turned away and hurried towards the house. Master Reed stood at the back door, looking out over the yard. I wondered how long he had been there, and whether, at that distance, he could have seen Denys lay hold of me.

'Anything amiss?' he said.

'My horse is very lame. Denys thinks it picked up a stone. He is dealing with it.'

'How handy is he? He might worsen matters. I'd better...' He went, with his lurching yet rapid step, towards the pasture.

That night I hardly slept at all. It was easy enough to say – Come to the wool loft...two excuses...church and the dressmaker. I had never been one of those pious women, forever running to church at odd hours. Because of Master Reed's hatred of Baildon and all its folk, and because, living outside the town boundary, we were free to choose, we went to Mass at the tiny church of Flaxham St Giles, and usually went, the three of us together, to make our Confessions on Saturday, before supper in winter, after it in summer. Richard would think it very strange if I proposed going to church alone on Saturday afternoon. As for my dressmaker – who was a little hunchback – she always came to the house when I needed her; I wasn't even certain of where she lived. She was a relative of one of the pack-whackers and when I had sewing to be done I simply asked him to ask his Aunt Margit to come.

To people who live more grandly, or more poorly, it may sound incredible that a grown woman should find it so difficult to absent herself, without rousing questions, for an hour on a Saturday afternoon. But always, when I wasn't with the children, I was in the solar or the kitchen or the garden, and with Richard just on the move again the whole thing was doubly difficult. If I said I would go and look in on the children, he would say he hadn't seen them lately and would come too; if I said I would see how my palfrey did, ten to one he would say that a stroll in the sun would do him good. All this I had to worry out in the night, and to think that it wasn't just this Saturday…this kind of thing could go on and on.

In the end I pleaded the routine female excuse: I had a headache, I said, due to sleeping badly. That I had slept badly Richard knew was true. I said that after dinner I would go and lie down. Master Reed went into the garden, where some plums on two trees on the south wall should be ready for plucking, and Richard said, 'I shall go and do an hour's work in the office. Father hasn't complained, but the work must be mounting up.'

That was better than I had hoped for; he might have offered to come and sit beside me and dabble my head with a vinegar cloth. I went into the children's room, brooded over them for a little while and then stole out.

The yard was empty and quiet. No work was done at the Old Vine on Saturday afternoons; the young men went to practise their archery at the Butts on the west of the town; those whose age or some infirmity excused them, sought their own amusements. From the huts which we called Squatters Row, at the back of the stables, I could hear voices and the sound of a fiddle.

I felt extremely large and conspicuous as I made my way to the woolshed, hugging the walls of each building I passed. I told myself that I had a perfect right to go out and see how my palfrey did. When I was level with the pasture fence, I did step out of the buildings' shadow and stand, for a moment, staring. Then I cut back, through the two wool-picking sheds, where the sun cut in in golden, dust-filled rays, and then, at the end, up the ladder and into the wool store.

Denys was waiting for me. He took hold of me and kissed and pawed me for a minute or two like a madman. I pushed him away and said, 'Wait. Wait. You want it to be good...You said, after childbed women were...And it is true. I think that is what ails me and I think a little wine would help.' I held out the little leather wine bottle that I had brought.

'You don't need that,' he said.

'Oh, I do, I do. Just give me time.' I loosed the stopper and tilted the bottle to my lips. I said, 'You know what is wrong with me, don't you. I was in labour two days and three nights...A woman has to be pot valiant to risk that again.'

'You're over the worst. The next lot'll be as easy as shelling peas.'

'I'm pot valiant,' I said, wishing to God I were. For, when neither flesh nor spirit is desirous, this is a sorry, sad business. He didn't think so; and anxious to pleasure him, I made as good a pretence of sharing his joy as I could.

When he was spent he lolled back against the soft, greasy fleeces and sighed and smiled. After a minute he said – forestalling me by a count of ten – 'Is any left in that bottle?'

I reached out and lifted and shook it.

'Very little – but you're welcome to what there is. It heartened me.'

'Rubbish. I heartened you. I told you everything would be all right. Didn't I? Didn't I?'

'Yes. And you were right.'

He set the bottle to his lips and drank.

'I must go now,' I said. 'And I must take the bottle. It might be missed.'

'Next Saturday. Here.'

'Next Saturday. Here,' I repeated. He tilted the bottle and then gave it back into my hand. 'I had to force you. You see, I

249

knew what was best for you. You're my beauty, my darling and I don't know how I shall wait the week out. But I will.' He burrowed his head into my breast and clutched at me with his hands. In one moment it would all begin again.

'I must go...or there'll be no next Saturday.' He sighed and set me free.

I climbed down the ladder of the wool loft with the words 'no next Saturday' still sounding inside my head. By the pasture fence I picked up a young apple that I had left there – how long before, half an hour, an hour? How long had the whole thing taken? I called my palfrey and it came, took the apple and slobbered over my hand and sleeve.

I went back into the solar where Master Reed was laying plums on a dish.

'I couldn't sleep, so I went out to see how my horse fared. I gave it an apple,' I said, 'and look what a mess it has made of me. I must go and wash.'

No next Saturday, I thought. There will be no next Saturday.

VII

The next day being Sunday, Denys was not looked for, and when he was found on Monday nobody could tell which day he had died, until one of the weavers said that he remembered seeing him come into the yard late on Saturday, very drunk. This – though it is unpleasant to think that in cases of felony some of the evidence given may be equally false – most admirably served my purpose, since it prevented the possibility, remote indeed, but lively in my mind at least, of anyone connecting Denys' death with my wandering around on the Saturday afternoon.

'He was probably not as sound as he looked,' Master Reed said, and passed on to the matter of replacing him. Until that was done I knew I must be prepared to face hearing Denys' name now and again. I must keep my face smooth and secret, and show enough, but not too much interest. Actually even that was spared me, though I would rather have been tested than excused the way I was. What happened was that within half an hour of the discovery of Denys' body, a hind, bumping and bouncing on Father's best horse, came to tell me that Mother was in bed.

'Very sick,' he said she was, and anxious to see me.

Richard, who now had great faith in the doctor who had relieved his cough by night if not by day, insisted upon sending for him to ride out with me, but I was too anxious to be off. So he was to follow.

Mother was in bed and as I set foot on the gallery I could hear the gasping rattle of her breath. Her brow and nose and chin were bone white, her cheeks dark purple with fever. Her eyes, dim with pain, were open, but she did not know me, even when I took her hot dry hand and spoke her name. Father was in the room, looking almost as ill and half crazed.

'What happened?' I asked him.

'Yesterday, no the day before, no, yesterday, she complained of pain in her side. I looked and it was bruised, very black and swollen. I made a poultice, a linseed poultice, and she said it eased her. Then she sickened and cried for you, but she was sensible then. It is only this morning...'

Suddenly the deep criss-cross wrinkles below his eyes were wet. I envied him being able to cry. My need to cry scorched me. It was my fault that she had her fall, and if she died, I'd have killed her as surely as I had killed...

'The doctor is riding close behind,' I said. 'He's...very clever. He'll do something.'

'I hope to God...' Father said.

Mother went on fighting for breath. Every now and then a gobbet of thick yellow stuff, streaked with blood, bubbled from her mouth, and I wiped it away. Once, just after I had thus cleared her lips, she spoke, in a surprisingly bright, vigorous, *young* voice.

'I can hold together as long as I have to,' she said, and then went back to that broken-winded breathing.

Father gave a sort of groan. 'She said that to me...once before. The bravest...' he said, 'braver than...'

And brought this low by her own daughter, a coward.

I thought of her courage, her unquenchable hopefulness which I had so much despised; I thought of her kindness to me every time I came back to Minsham rejected and in what was tantamount to disgrace. It seemed to me at that moment that the only person on earth whom I truly loved was my mother.

I did not stand idle. All this time I was busy with what might be helpful. Remembering Richard and his cough, I propped her higher, to ease the breathing; I tried to make her drink something hot to wash the thick stuff from her throat; I wiped her face and hands with a cool cloth. Once, when I was doing that, she eyed me and said, 'I'll thank you, my lady, to take back this glove. Blanchefleur has no use for it!'

'Holy Mother of God,' Father cried, and dropped his head against the wall. 'That that should trouble her now!' He banged his grizzled head against the wall several times and then went to the other side of the bed and cried, 'Maude. You know. You must know, there was never any other. Any good tourney man, it was the fashion to pursue him. Whose glove did I carry?'

But Mother had gone back to her fight for breath, and minded neither of us.

Then the doctor arrived.

He looked at the bruise, just below her left breast, and said gravely, 'Most unfortunate, the heart has been bruised; and the heart governs the melancholy humour. And the melancholy humour, left to run its course, can lead to death. However.' He opened his bag and gave me some small objects, the seed cases of some plant, rounded at one end, pointed at the other.

'Make an infusion,' he said. 'Foxglove is a sovereign remedy for the heart.'

But it was difficult to make her drink – as I had already discovered; the battle to breathe was too urgent, too closely pressed; most of the infusion was wasted.

She died just before sunset. The doctor, sadly disappointed by the result of his infusion, had gone; he had other patients waiting, he said, and he had done all he could. He had, at last, given an opiate, so that Mother seemed to sleep, though the battle for breath went on.

Just before sunset she woke, and returned to her senses. In a very weak fluffy voice she said my name.

'Anne.'

'Here I am,' I said. And my heart lifted. She knew me, she wasn't going to die. Some of the infusion, that sovereign heart remedy, had gone down and done its work; or the drugged sleep had helped to mend.

'Take good care of Blanchefleur,' she whispered. Then her eyelids fluttered, the death rattle sounded in her throat, her mouth fell open and she was dead.

I would gladly, and this is true, have lain down there on the floor by her bed and died too. On Saturday afternoon I had deliberately killed a man and been no more troubled than if I had crushed a fly which pestered me. But this was different. Remorse, perhaps the most terrible of all feelings, now had me in its mangling jaws. By accident, by a side blow, I had killed somebody who loved me and whom I loved. There is, and of this I am certain, no more terrible knowledge in the whole world. I should carry it with me until I died, and that seemed too much to face. I flung myself down on the floor beside the bed, and sobbed, in that dry, tearless way which brings no healing, and wished that I could die, just to be rid of the burden of guilt.

People don't – unless they are old and nearly ready for death anyway – die from the wishing. Presently I was aware of Father, sobbing and groaning away on his side of the bed. 'Take good care of Blanchefleur,' they had been her last words to me; and taking care surely meant comforting him now. I got up and went round to him and sat on the bed's edge and lifted his head so that it lay in my lap. I tried to speak comforting words about Mother soon being with the Saints in Heaven, about the great reunion of all families which would one day take place there.

But Father was also deep in this business of self-accusation; and unlike me he could accuse himself aloud. He blamed himself for a multitude of faults, ranging from never have made a proper home or clothing her suitably, to have given her cause for jealousy in the old days. On that score, at least, I could comfort him with what I knew was truth. I told him of the talk we had had before my marriage and of the pride and triumph in her voice as she spoke of his wearing her glove and rejecting the great lady's. As I spoke I remembered that during my time of madness I had looked at Denys' flat archer's shoulders and imagined myself sharing Mother's pride. So even that was spoiled and sullied, and my worth, which made Father feel better, made me feel worse,

I turned at last, for relief, to material things. I had not eaten since breakfast, and most likely Father had not even broken his fast. I slipped downstairs in the dusk – seeing as I did so, Mother's fatal stumble and fall – and looked into the buttery. There was precious little to eat, some bread and three pigeons, ready plucked but uncooked. Another pain stabbed me at the thought that had she felt well yesterday Mother would have cooked those birds. I turned away from them and took up the bread. And then I saw the little cask of wine which Master Reed had sent on Thursday for her birthday. Her birthday!

The wine, I thought, would help down the dry bread; so I drew a jugful, found two cups, cut the bread into slices and set it all on the table in the hall. Then I lighted three candles, one for the table and one for the head and the foot of the bed, and carrying them went up to the room where Father was waiting.

'I will do what is to be done here, after,' I said. 'You come now and make shift to eat a little.'

Moving like a very old man, he dragged out on to the gallery, and at the stairhead looked down and said, 'If I'd been half a man I should have railed in those stairs. I always meant to, but I pretended to be busy with my hawks and other toys.'

'It was an accident. Like your own. If you had not your mishap, you would never have been compelled to live here. Do not blame yourself over-much.'

Rather pity yourself, too, I thought. And that applied to me as well. We may make victims of one another but we are ourselves the victims of Fate, also. I had turned to Denys to seek what I could not find elsewhere.

We made some pretence, at first, of dipping our bread in the wine and eating, but we soon put that aside. We emptied the jug and I took a candle and refilled it. Father drank most and most, quickly benefited. He began, in his slow bumbling way, to talk of the past.

'You say she was proud of me, eh?' be began, and then went on to tell of triumphs here, there and the other places, of doughty champions met and defeated, of noble horses he had ridden, of presents and compliments he had been given; and all so muddled that sometimes it sounded as though it was the horse which had complimented him and the gift which he had unseated. I thought of the body upstairs on the soiled bed and of what I must presently do, and wished that I could sink into a like soft cushion of mind. So I drank some more, and presently was eased. Father's stories ceased and he began to nod. I said, 'Come to bed,' and he was so fuddled that on the gallery be began to walk, of habit, towards his own room. I took him by the arm and turned him gently towards the other door, towards the bed upon which I had spent Thursday night. Then he remembered and whimpered a little.

In Mother's room I did what was to be done, all the more easily for being a little blurred in my mind. Then I set fresh candles and drew up a stool, intending to watch all night; but the wine got the better of me, and in the end I lay down on the floor and slept.

Interval

I

ONE DAY – Lady Blanchefleur having then been in her grave for three months – Martin Reed said to his son, 'Have you noticed the change in Anne?'

'I think her grief is easing – a little,' Richard said carefully, and turning his head away, coughed.

'She drinks too much wine,' Martin said bluntly. 'Last evening, and the one before, she was flown.'

'I know. And a good thing too!' Answering his father's astonished look, he added. 'If she goes to bed with wine in her, she sleeps. Otherwise she wakes, screaming from nightmare, and then cries for hours.'

'About her mother's death?'

'They were very close,' Richard said. 'You and I who never knew a mother's love cannot measure her loss.'

'It is a loss many people sustain without resorting to wine – in such quantity.'

Richard coloured. 'If you grudge so simple a comfort...' he began angrily.

'I grudge nothing. You know that. I just do not care to see a woman the worse for – and reeking of – wine.'

'What you call worse I call better; and as for the reek, it is my bed she shares.'

'I'm not wishing to quarrel,' Martin said, and left the matter there.

Richard himself was puzzled. Once, in the night, sobbing against his shoulder, Anne had said, 'It was my fault. I killed her.' He had dragged out of her the story about a bed to be aired which had caused the fall. He had said, at the end of it, 'I can see how you feel, but you must not blame yourself too shrewdly. The bed was to be aired some day for Isabel. It could have happened then.'

But she had insisted that it was all her fault. Presently, thinking to comfort her, he said that everybody had to die one day. And that was a mistake, for she flung herself from him, and spoke in a wild way about killing and a sin.

'A sin, sweetheart, to wish to spend a night under your father's roof! Come now!'

That night he took a candle and went padding barefoot down the stairs to fetch the wine which seemed to comfort her; and from then on until Martin mentioned the matter, it had been Richard who would fill her cup, twice, three times, from the livery cupboard in the solar. What harm could it do? She never woke bad-tempered or liverish, as those who drank too much sometimes did. The wine eased her grief, just as the grey powder eased his cough in the night. Where was the difference? It was Richard himself who first gave her another and far more potent draught, 'to try'. It was neither French, Spanish nor Rhenish; it came from the Low Countries, where it was called brandewijn. Half a cup of it was as potent as three of any other kind.

One evening, some weeks after Martin's first protest, he came into the solar to bid Richard and Anne good night. It was almost bedtime and Richard had poured the brandewijn into a cup, given it into Anne's hand and then, taking his lute, sat down at her feet on a cushion, playing a gentle, soothing tune. One candle was out, the other nearing its end, the fire sunk to a rose-hued glow. It should have been a pleasant, domestic scene, gratifying to the older man, but by some indefinable degree it missed so being and was something else, so that, even before he smelt the liquor, he was irritated; and when he did scent it, and knew it for what it was, he spoke more sharply than ever before in Anne's experience,

'Brandewijn!' he said, 'That is no drink for a lady.'

She said, 'How would you know?' Just the four words, with the faintest possible stress on the second, but the whole speech so insolent, so full of hurtful meaning, that for a second he was checked. Then he said, 'I should have said for a respectable married woman.'

Richard asked, with a flippancy which annoyed Martin even more, 'Must all pleasure be reserved for the disreputable and the unmarried?'

Anne laughed and reached out her hand and patted Richard's cheek. Trollop! Martin thought suddenly, and then, because that was too harsh a thought, he said, 'Maybe you know best. I'm old-fashioned.'

From him it was a handsome apology for one word, not even spoken aloud.

He stumped up to bed, and shedding his clothes, wondered – for he was a just man – why it had slidden, that condemning word, so easily into his head? In his cool, undemonstrative way he had been fond of his daughter-in-law. Had been? *Was!* She was part of his achievement. A knight's daughter. And never, until this evening, when he had blurted out his rebuke, had she by word or deed laid any stress upon the difference in rank. Provoked, she had retorted, as any woman of spirit would. He bore her no grudge for that. And even had he done, there was no reason, surely, why his resentment should put that word into his mind. And yet…and yet. Even as he accused himself of injustice he recalled something so fleeting that he had sensed it rather than seen it, something so unlikely that he had pushed it away as nonsense and never thought of it again until now. Three months ago, one evening in the summer, he had stood by the back door of the house and looked out over the yard, towards the fence of the pasture. Anne and Denys Rootyer were standing close together, so close that they might have been touching; if they were, they moved apart instantly, just as his eye lighted on them. No, he would never be sure, never admit to himself even, that they had stood closer than needs be. Nor would he admit that there was anything odd in the man's fetching Anne out in the twilight to look at her lame horse; though there again the obvious thing would have been to call a smith.

Why had he remembered it? Why think of it now?

Getting old, and fanciful. Sixty, he thought, and remembered the priest at Rede telling him that at twenty half his life's span had fled. Out in his reckoning there, Martin thought grimly; but for my leg, I'm as good as I ever was, good for another twenty years. Unless I go awry in my wits! For suddenly, out of nowhere, another fantastic fancy had slipped into his brain. In June of last year, he and Richard had both been absent from home at the same time, and he'd offered that one of the maids should come across and sleep on this side of the house. What had she replied? That what a servant could save her from would never hurt her. And the twins had been born on St Joseph's Day, March the nineteenth.

Here, alone in his own bedroom, he felt his face go red and hot, his heart beat so hard that it thudded inside his skull, exactly as though he had been caught out, publicly, in some misdemeanour. *How* was it possible that he should have entertained such a vile, shameful thought long enough to do the reckoning? Where could such a thought have come from, unless direct from the Devil?

He lay down in bed and blew out his candle. When next his business took him to Colchester he would buy Anne some trinket, something pretty and of value, a secret proof of his shame for allowing fantasy a place in his mind, even for a minute.

II

The busy, happy years sped by. With Maude always just one pace ahead, the twins passed through all the fascinating stages of early childhood. When they were six years old, an uninformed observer would have taken them for any brother and sister, the girl the elder by a year.

Richard's cough persisted, a little better in summer weather, a little worse in winter; his cheerfulness, his fixed refusal to regard himself as an invalid screened, even from Martin and Anne, the stark fact that that was what he had become. He had ceased to ride abroad, never for the reason that he was not fit to do so, always because the weather was remarkably inclement, or there was too much work to do in the office, or the errand was something which Martin preferred to do himself. It was Anne who suggested that it was useless for him to ride with her on her regular visits of inspection to Minsham.

'He doesn't know,' she said, speaking of her father, 'whether we go or not. I only go to see that he is being cared for. I shan't stay an hour.'

'I like to come with you. It's such a miserable business.'

Sir Godfrey had sunk into apathy, prematurely senile, dirty, careless, almost witless, firm only on one point: he refused to leave his home.

'It's miserable,' Anne agreed. 'But why should we both suffer? You stay at home and then I shall be happy to return and find you cheerful.'

She appeared to see nothing sinister in his acceptance. And when, one day when Maude was five years old and in boisterous play had all but pushed Richard from his feet, Anne said, 'Maude, play a little less roughly if you please. Such behaviour is not becoming.' The extreme fragility of Richard, which was then for a moment painfully plain, had escaped her.

On her own remorse-ridden grief time had worked its old healing magic and effected an almost complete cure. She no longer needed brandewijn to make her sleep; on Richard's good nights she slept well. Every now and then – often after she had been to Minsham – she would suffer a nightmare and wake, and be comforted by Richard and presently sleep again. But for Maude, Anne would, during the children's first six years of life, have been perfectly happy. As it was, she was like a person who has fallen amongst thistles and afterwards carefully removed every tiny prickle except one, which breaks off and burrows down and cannot be plucked out; it can be ignored most of the time, but is capable, none the less, at any accidental pressure, of causing a sharp pain. There were days when Maude was just a little girl, inclined to be headstrong and venturesome, but easily ruled because she was so affectionate. Then a slanting ray of light would strike the child's head where the babyish fairness was giving way to bronze; or someone would remark Maude's size and strength – by comparison with Walter – and Anne would be most sickeningly reminded. The mystery was that Walter gave the appearance of being Richard's son; he had the dark, slender grace, the delicate structure of bone, the slight air of defencelessness which called out all that was maternal in Anne just as surely as something unnameable in Maude called forth dislike. The sense of guilt was thus kept alive, and occasionally exacerbated by a curious look which would cross Martin's face, usually when Anne allowed her resentment to take the form of an oversharp rebuke to the little girl.

'I shall forbid you to play with the yard children if you bring their manners indoors.'

'How can you be such a hoyden? Look at your hands, your dress. Anyone would think you were a tinker's child.'

Apart from putting in some mild defensive word on the child's behalf Martin never said anything, but he wore that oddly disconcerting look.

Richard had a warm partiality for his daughter, and one night, in bed, at the end of a day in which Maude had incurred her mother's displeasure, said, 'She's exactly like I used to be, at her age.'

'You!' Anne sounded startled. 'You were never like that, I am sure.'

'But I was. I was the naughtiest boy in Suffolk, until Peter Priest took me in hand. Always into mischief. Uncle Tom's bear…did I never tell you?'

As usual he had come to bed first and then, a little later, Anne had brought up the cup of milk, into which the pinch of grey powder was sprinkled, and his voice was blurred by drowsiness as he recounted the tale of his misdoings.

Anne remembered the old man, the stuffy room, the malodorous bearskin on the bed. Pert Tom had died during that time when she was too much engrossed by her prolonged virginity to give the event much heed.

Lulled by the drowsiness of Richard's voice, she too fell asleep as soon as the story was done.

She dreamed that she was in the Ladies' Dorter at Beauclaire, helping to dress Maude, aged about sixteen, for the St Barnabas Tourney. The girl's dress, a crimson and green silk, was beautiful, and her head-dress was a cloud of gauze. Anne looked at her with satisfaction and pride, thinking that with her looks and her clothes and her dower she was the equal of any young lady there. Then, under her eyes, Maude changed and became Denys. The wide archer's shoulders strained against the silk, the tough-looking red hair lifted the head-dress. She said in an appalled whisper, 'You can't go into the *Ladies'* Gallery.' The dreadful creature said, 'I must. You must take me. You can always say that I am your dressmaker!'

She screamed out her protest.

As on a score of similar occasions, Richard stirred and spoke.

'Sweetheart. It's all right. I'm here.' His voice was thick and when he had spoken he coughed.

She said, 'I'm sorry I woke you. Just another horrible dream.'

He did not, as usual, ask should he make a light; nor did he turn in the bed and put his arm about her comfortingly. He made a coughing sound which ended in a choke, and then there was a gentle bubbling.

Jerked from dream horror to real fear she said, 'Richard.'

He did not answer; and it was she who made the light and saw on the pillow the spreading pool of crimson.

III

For a while the shared sorrow brought Martin and Anne closer than they had ever been before; her grief was so intense, so shattering, that his half-doubt – it had never been more than that – vanished in a wave of shame. They could say, over and over again, how blind they must have been, and then, inconsistently, mention things that they had noticed. They could say that they should have been more careful, and follow that statement immediately by giving instances of how careful they had been.

Under this apparent unity of spirit there gaped, however, a great gulf. Martin, who, thirty-five years earlier, had cried over Kate, 'She never had anything!' could now, in an attempt to comfort Anne, say, 'He had a short life, but he enjoyed it all. He never lacked anything; he had you, Anne, and the children. You must think of that. And think too, how much better this way, than after a lingering illness, knowing that death waits.' That was, in truth, his own private dread.

'Oh yes,' she said. 'That last night, he was laughing, telling me how naughty he had been when he was a...' The words 'little boy' would not be spoken. It was unbearable to think of a little boy growing into a man, stricken with lung rot and now dead.

The dreadful remorse, the guilt which had assailed her after her mother's death, was now returned, doubled. She remembered how once, during her madness, she had dared to think that his love for her was a dream, like his dream of being a wandering lute-player. She had lived to prove how wrong that

263

thought was. Only a true, firm love could have helped her through the time after her mother's death.

Over and over again she remembered that the last words he ever spoke to her were words of comfort – because she had waked from a dream which only her guilt had made possible. She tore herself to pieces on the spiked thought that if she had not wakened him he might have stayed asleep, flat, and the lifeblood would have remained in him. So she was doubly guilty, twice over the murderer of those whom she had loved, those who had loved her.

One evening, when Richard had been three weeks in his grave, Anne and Martin were in the solar. He had forced himself to overcome his dislike of the room in order to keep her company. They had said all the old things and she had broken down again and wept bitterly. She ate almost nothing, he knew, and slept hardly at all. Often, waking from his light old man's slumbers, he had heard her walking about, up and down, up and down in her room.

This evening, at last, she sat down and snatched up a piece of sewing, but she did not work as a woman should. The needle stabbed in and out, like a weapon. Then she would pause, stare wild-eyed at the wall, and stab again.

He watched her. Her looks were all gone. She was worn down to the bone and her skin was the colour of parchment. He recalled suddenly the pretty, soft-freshed woman who in this very room had laughed and patted Richard's face with one hand and held a cup of brandewijn in the other.

He got up and limped to the livery cupboard, fumbled about and turned back to her, a cup in either hand.

'Richard,' he said, and stopped because the mention of his son's name, like that, was still a pain. 'Richard told me that when your mother died, Anne...this helped you to sleep. You see, you have the children. You must think of the children.'

She had not, since Richard's death, been able to bear the sight or sound of them.

And from some deep, obscure desire for self-punishment she had, for three long weeks, avoided the palliative which, she knew, stood there waiting in the livery cupboard. She had proved its worth and knew that, once accepted, it could convince her that she was not to blame; that she had done what was best in the circumstances. One drink and she would be thinking of the joy Richard had taken in this proof of his virility; two and she would be making intimate little reckonings, remembering that on the night before he left for Bywater and on the night when he came back, Richard and she had lain together. Only the one night between. And he never knew. I never by word or gesture gave a sign, or swerved from my outward allegiance...

She took the cup and presently the feeble voice of her own reason raised a bold loud echo in the cavern of intoxication, calling that she was not to blame for everything, that circumstances had played a hand in what had happened, that she also was to be pitied a little.

Nothing however, no amount of brandewijn, no amount of reasoning, could make her look on Maude with anything but a carefully controlled loathing. She knew that as long as she lived the sight of her daughter would call to mind that dream, and with it all that came after. It became her fixed and relentless purpose to get the child out of the house.

Several times during the next months she mentioned, casually, the question of Walter's education. Martin was inclined to shuffle the matter off There was plenty of time, he said; such matters needed much consideration. Once Anne said, 'I seem to remember Richard saying that he started his learning when he was six.'

'I had Peter Priest ready to hand at that time,' Martin said. 'Also, Richard, to tell the truth, was more unruly than Walter. Walter can wait a year or so.'

When Anne next mentioned the matter, he said, 'I bear it in mind. I keep my eyes and ears open for a suitable tutor for the boy.'

She said, with a tinge of sharpness, 'If you wait for another unfrocked priest, you may wait until Walter grows a beard.'

'I'm not waiting for that. I'm looking for some clerk who could help me as well. I'm missing Richard sore on that side of the business.'

The ache in his voice prevented her from speaking on the subject again for a long time.

The twins had their seventh birthday, and in the winter following it, on account of a piece of flagrant disobedience, a narrow escape from death which did give Anne ample reason to say, 'That settles it. Walter must go to school.'

'To school?'

'Yes. He needs the company of boys of his own age – and kind. Also he has some talent for music. The Choir School at the Abbey is just the place for him.'

'Maybe,' Martin said a little doubtfully. 'If we could spare him.'

'We should see him often; and they have holidays.' She then spoke the words to which the months-old discussion about Walter's future had been a mere preliminary. 'As for Maude, I think I shall send her to Beauclaire.'

More startled than when she spoke of school for Walter, Martin said, 'Where *you* were so unhappy yourself?'

'I was so poor, so ill-equipped. Still, even so, I learned everything that a gentlewoman should know.'

'And that has been of use to you?'

'I learned how to conduct myself. I feel it my duty to see that my daughter has like advantages.'

He said, 'Maude could be dressed and fitted out. She will have a dower...but she might...suffer in other ways.'

'Some pert jackanapes or spiteful girl saying "Do I smell fleeces?" Is that what you mean?'

He nodded, a little angered by her instant perception.

'I'll tell you straight, Anne; I've no mind to see my good money go where it will be despised because I made it.'

'No one in their senses would despise it. I said a pert jackanapes or a spiteful girl, didn't I?'

'I'm against it.'

'Very well,' she said, more meekly than he had expected. 'Would you be against her going to the nuns at Clevely for a year or two?'

'Not against; but I see no good reason.'

'Don't you? What about Walter? They've always done everything together, in fact in all their pranks Maude is the leader. Don't you think he would be hurt, and justly, if he were sent to school and Maude stayed here to be spoiled?'

'I hadn't thought of it that way. Yes, it might be so. I expect you know best.'

'I'm their mother. So will you see about Walter entering the Choir School?'

'I will. There's no great haste, is there. I could bring the matter up when I go to pay my rent.'

That ended the conversation abruptly. The rent of one red rose to be paid in June had always been a matter of joking with Richard, who had made, and set to a lively ballad tune, a comical song on the subject, all about a year when poor Master Reed could find only a white rose and was obliged to take it to the dyer's.

The twins had their eighth birthday in March, and in June Martin made application for a place in the Choir School for Walter. Dreading the time when he and Anne would find themselves alone in the house, he was delighted to be told that there would be no vacancy until Easter in the following year.

Making her own inquiries, Anne was much displeased to learn that except in the case of girls who had lost both parents and were homeless, Clevely Priory did not open its doors to those under twelve years of age. Riding back from Clevely, she made up her mind that when Walter went into the Choir School, Maude should go to Beauclaire, despite anything Master Reed should say.

PART FOUR

Maude Reed's Tale

I

S O LONG AS my father was alive, I never noticed that my mother disliked me. We paired off naturally – when Walter sat in Mother's lap, I sat on Father's knee; when Mother hugged Walter, Father hugged me – and though, even then, Mother was stricter to me than to Walter, that was easily explained: I was much worse behaved.

Father died when Walter and I were six years old, too young to understand or to know what we had lost. Children are very self-centred: the sorrow in the house brushed against us but was soon forgotten. For a little while Mother seemed to want neither of us; then she changed, and doted on Walter more fondly than ever. It was then that I noticed that she disliked me. She'd sit on the window-seat or the settle and draw Walter to her, put her arm around him, smooth his hair with her fingers and look at him with love. I would run over to join them, never – I was careful about that – never trying to push between them, trying only to take my place by her other side, hoping that she would put her free arm about me. She never did. She would jump up and busy herself, or push me away, telling me to go and wash my hands or comb my hair, or send me to fetch something.

I could make her notice me, but only in a way which did me no good. If I behaved badly enough, she would give her full attention to scolding me; sometimes she beat me. Once, when Walter and I were seven, a very strange thing happened. It was in the winter and the horse-pond had frozen solid, and Walter and I had played on it for several days, old games which seemed new because we were playing them in the middle of the pond. Then one morning our grandfather came in and said there was a thaw and that we were on no account to set foot on the ice that day. However, Walter had left his hobby horse on the ice, and he said to me, 'When the ice melts, my hobby will fall into the water.' He looked at me the way he always did when he wanted me to do something for him. So I went to fetch the hobby horse, and had it in my hand when the ice bent under me; I shot the hobby across the surface towards where Walter stood, and managed, with my two hands, to grip the edge of the hole and keep my head free. I yelled, and Walter, yelling, came towards me, and great cracks ran out under his feet; he went down too, screaming like a pig having its throat cut. Men came running from the wool and weaving sheds and we were pulled out.

Walter was blue in the face and very sick in his stomach; I was merely wet; so Mother beat me. She said I was bigger, girls should have more sense, and I went on to the ice first. I'd never had a beating like that, and I cried, saying I only went to fetch Walter's hobby horse, but that didn't excuse me.

That night I woke to hear somebody crying and to feel a weight on me. I was frightened until I opened my eyes and saw a candle on the chest and Mother kneeling by my bedside with her arms spread out over me. She looked different, though where the change was I couldn't have said; and she smelt different. Ordinarily she smelt sweet from the little bags of lavender and rosemary that hung and lay amongst her clothes. Tonight she smelt of something sharp and sour. She was crying and saying jerky words, calling me poor Maude and saying she was unfair to me, with many other things which made no sense. I thought she meant that she had been unfair to beat me and not Walter. So I struggled up in the bed and put my arms round her neck and said, 'You didn't hurt me.' I would have had a beating every day if it meant that she would put her arms over me and let me hug her. She went on mumbling about being unjust, and I said, 'I forgive you.'

She gave a kind of squeal and pushed me off and jumped up, crying, 'Holy Mother of God. That is all I lacked!' Then she went out of the room, walking in a funny way, bumping against the foot of the bed and against the side of the doorway. She left the candle and until it went out and I was in the dark I lay and wondered what was wrong in saying, 'I forgive you.' Perhaps it was a wrong thing for a child to say to her mother.

That must have been it; for next day she disliked me again.

We had another grandfather who lived in the country at Minsham and was too old, or too ill, to ride, so we had never seen him. He had a servant called Jacob who used to come to the Old Vine every Friday and pick up some provisions and say, 'Much as usual' when asked about his master's health. Mother sometimes rode out to visit her father, but as time went on she made more and more excuses not to do so.

One day however, on a fine summer morning, she said: 'You're eight years old now and able to make a longer ride. We'll go to Minsham today and you can meet your Grandfather Blanchefleur and your Uncle Godfrey who is staying there.'

Walter and I had ponies which were much more like twins than we were, both brown with paler manes and tails. I called mine Browny; Walter, who was much more fanciful than I was, had named his Robin Hood, out of a story Father had told us.

Minsham Old Hall, we found when we reached it, was shaped like a barn, but built of stone, with very narrow window openings, unglazed. It stood in a yard, with no garden near it, just a tumbledown stable and a piece of pasture.

Inside, it was even more desolate, and very cold, despite the sunshine outside and a fire on the wide hearth. In a chair sat an old man with grey hair and a beard, so overgrown that there was nothing else to his face except a loose wet mouth and eyes which had no life in them. I saw Mother brace herself, like she did once when a servant came screaming that there was a mouse in the meal-bag and Mother had to deal with it. She leaned down and kissed the old man, and then said to us,

'This is your Grandfather Blanchefleur.'

Walter made his bow and I my curtsey, as we had been taught. Our grandfather seemed to take no notice of us at all, but he mumbled and I caught the word 'Maude' quite clearly. I thought he meant me, and intending to be as brave as Mother I moved forward, prepared to kiss him. But Mother said, 'It is not you he means. Go play in the yard.'

As we went out she moved to the foot of the stairs and called up, 'Godfrey!'

There was nothing to do, or see, in the yard; but Walter happened to say, 'Grandfather is like Daft Jimmy.' That was a poor witless creature who lived in the row of huts behind the stables at the Old Vine; *his* grandfather had been deaf and dumb we were told, and Walter and I had invented a game in which we pretended to be thus afflicted and bound to make ourselves understood by signs. We played it now, until we were called in to dinner.

We were then introduced to our Uncle Godfrey, who was very handsome and finely dressed.

He greeted us by name, and very kindly, and – the first person ever to do so – seemed to notice me more than Walter.

'So this is Maude.' He looked me over, and smiled and said something about lovely curly hair. 'A real Astallon,' he said. 'Ralph and his golden Eleanor have managed to breed two little fawn-coloured creatures. Isn't it odd?'

Our grandfather's chair had been turned so that he sat at the head of the table. He ate as we had been forbidden to do, sucking

and slobbering at his food and wiping his fingers, now on the
cloth and now on the front of his soiled robe. Walter gave me a
kick under the table and a meaningful look, like when we played
'Dummy'. I kicked him back and made faces, trying to say,
without words – Yes, and wouldn't we be in disgrace if we did it?

Over our heads the talk went to and fro between Mother and
Uncle Godfrey.

He said, 'You hated it so much.'

'I went to Beauclaire with one pair of shoes. When my feet
grew I had to curl up my toes, and they are crooked to this day.
You hated being at Cousin Fortescue's; you wanted to farm here.
Do you remember that? Are you sorry now that you didn't?'

'Not now. You saved me, Anne. You sent me the money so that
I could buy my knight's equipment and I...'

Mother interrupted him.

'And that wasn't easy; it wasn't a cause that either of them
would have understood or sympathized with, let me tell you.
That was my dressmaker's money for two years, and it meant
refurbishing old ones, turning and twisting. I say this to show
that what I ask you isn't so outrageous.'

'I know. I know.' He looked about the cold room with its damp
grey walls and smoke-blackened rafters. 'Here too, you have
taken responsibility, while I, with your good destrier between my
knees, rode in tourneys. Nothing that you asked of me in return
would be too great.'

'You see,' Mother said, 'when I made the suggestion he
rejected it, flat!' She put her hand down on the table. 'For me to
raise it again would...You may find this hard to believe, but they
have a pride of their own, more stubborn and stiff-necked than
ours. When they speak of "my good money" that is the same as
"my good name". I told you what he said. But an invitation, from
you, would allow me to open up the matter again.' She looked at
Walter and me and said, 'If you have finished, you may go back
to play.'

We played until we were called in to make our adieus. As we stood there, my Uncle Godfrey looked at the figure in the chair and said, 'My God, Anne, what a way to end! I can just remember when he won the King's Cup at Windsor. If you ever pray for me, pray that I never stop a half-fatal blow.'

Mother turned the colour of the heaped-up ashes on the hearth. She looked towards the stairs.

'He was all right,' she said. 'Flying his hawks, riding his old horse. Until Mother...' She broke off and shuddered. My uncle took her by the arm and said, 'Poor Anne, you had that too! I was in Poitou. You've borne it all.'

'More than you will ever know. But this one thing. You will do it?'

On the way home she set such a pace that Walter and I on our ponies, and the servant who attended us on his thickset solid horse, had much ado to keep up with her.

Shortly after this visit Walter was told that after Easter in the next year he was going to the Choir School at Baildon. The idea disgusted him; the schoolboys lived monkish lives, slept on hard beds, ate horrible food, washed in cold water.

'I don't want to. Why must I?'

'Because you will be a merchant, with a great business to run. You must learn to read and write and reckon.'

'I don't want to be a merchant,' Walter said. 'I want to be a minstrel...you know, walk about from place to place, playing the lute and singing.'

Mother said, in a way in which I have never in all my life heard anybody say anything, 'You want *what*, Walter?'

Confidently he repeated his statement. She snatched hold of him and kissed him.

'One day you'll know better. You wouldn't like to be poor. And at the Choir School you will learn all about music.'

'Church music,' he said. 'Not the same thing at all. Besides, it isn't fair that I should go to school and Maude should stay at home.'

Mother said, 'Maude is not staying at home. When she is twelve she is going to the nuns at Clevely, but in the meantime she has received a very pleasant invitation. She is going to stay with your Uncle Godfrey, at Beauclaire.'

For a moment, that took the sharpest edge from Walter's dissatisfaction, but he was soon grumbling again. I, he said, should be leading a merry life with ordinary people, while he was shut up with monks. If anyone beat me, I should have Uncle Godfrey to complain to; he would have no one.

When the arrangements were first made, 'after next Easter' sounded a comfortably long time away; but the months sped past. When the details were fixed and Walter learned that I was to ride into Sussex on Browny, while he must leave Robin Hood at the Old Vine, he flung himself screaming on the floor, shouting that it was unfair. My grandfather came to see what the noise was about and said, in an uncertain manner, 'Anne, is it worth it? Perhaps we were hasty. I heard recently of a young clerk who might serve our purpose.'

Mother simply said, 'Walter is jealous because Maude is to take her pony. Imagine his state if she were staying at home!' She took Walter by the arm and jerked him to his feet, speaking more firmly than she usually did to him.

'Straight into bed with you, you naughty boy!'

He was still in bed, being given possets and mixtures to bring down his fever, when I left for Beauclaire.

My grandfather, always a man of few words, gave me a broad gold piece, and kissed me.

'I hope you'll be happy. You mustn't mind too much if you find things different there.'

Mother came into the yard where one of the men, named Jack, was ready, with my little clothes chest fixed behind his saddle. She kissed me, and for a moment I clung to her, hoping even at

275

this last moment for some sign of love. She loosed herself from me in the old familiar way.

At the end of the covered passage which led from our yard to the highway, I turned and looked back. Mother was staring after us and her face was just like Walter's when I had let him win a game. Whatever we played at, I could always beat him if I tried, but now and then I would hold back and lose deliberately. Then he wore a satisfied look, a look that said, 'Well, I managed that!'

I puzzled over it for a long time. Much later, when I learned that Walter never did go to the Choir School, but stayed at home and had his lessons there, I did understand all too well. I saw then exactly what Mother had managed; she had kept the child she loved and got rid of the one she disliked. At the time I could only wonder *why* she looked like that. All the same she had done me, all unwittingly, a good turn. Had she gazed after me with the slightest affection I should have broken down, for I still loved her then. As it was, she sent me on my way exercising my head and not my heart, and that, in many of life's turning points, is an excellent thing.

II

Three days later we approached Beauclaire from the east at the end of a sunny afternoon, so that it stood up against the gold and rose of sunset's first display. I thought to myself – But this is a town, not a house; and my homesickness deepened.

A great castle of grey stone stood in the embrace of a wide moat which was spanned by two bridges, one directly in front of us, at the end of the road which we travelled, and the other to the side, at the right. The second bridge linked the castle, which was very old, with the house, much of which had been built within the last sixty or seventy years. The face which the house turned to the road was very handsome, and large, but – as I was soon to learn – it was only one small part of the whole. It was built of brick at the bottom and above of timber and plaster, the plaster moulded into patterns. There were many windows and all glassed, but I could see no doorway at all.

We clattered over the drawbridge, through a gateway at its far end, and there turned sharply to the right and through a small deserted courtyard, then over the second bridge and into a larger yard full of bustle, several men mounted, and servants running about. We then passed through an archway and into a stable yard, where I thankfully dismounted.

Almost immediately there appeared a solemn-looking man, by his dress neither gentleman nor servant, to whom the man who had been sent to fetch me said, 'I'm back and all's well, Master Sheldon.'

Master Sheldon glanced at me as he might have done at any package or parcel that had been conveyed from one place to another, noted that I was all in one piece, and nodded his satisfaction.

'You made good speed,' he said.

We should have made better had the servant had his way. I had disliked him from the start; he was one of those – a type then new to me – who was intensely servile when they must be, and make up for it by being insolent when they can. It was plain, at the moment of our meeting, that he despised me on account of my youth, and Jack because he was a plain unliveried servant. The new man wore green with the Astallon badge, a falcon, on his breast.

Jack helped me on to my pony, for the last time, and then dived into his pocket, brought out a little handkerchief, edged with pegged lace, and tucked it into my sleeve.

'It's to be hoped you 'on't need it, my little dear, but if you do you'll know where it is.'

He then turned to the Astallon man and said, 'You take good care of our little mistress; she've never been from home afore.'

That remark, and the thought of parting with Jack, thickened my throat again. The Astallon man merely sniffed and looked down his nose in a way that said, plainly, he was taking no orders from servants.

I said, 'Goodbye Jack. I shall see you at Christmas.'

We rode in silence for some time. The man broke it to ask, in a burring voice which made it hard for me to understand his words, 'Is that the best pace you can make?'

I thought I had not heard aright; Browny was, for his size, very speedy and he was trotting his best.

'What did you say?' I asked. He repeated the question.

'Yes, it is. Browny is only a pony, as you can see for yourself.'

'We'll see,' he said, and he lifted his whip and brought it down hard on the pony's rump.

Certainly since the two matched ponies had been given to Walter and me on our fifth birthday, Browny had never been struck like that; Grandfather Reed was soft-hearted towards all his horses and had given us a little homily about treating the ponies properly; and I loved Browny who was, anyway, quite willing to run as hard as he could without being beaten. Now, frightened and hurt, he broke into his little short-stepped rocking gallop for a minute or two, and then slowed down to a trot again.

I had a good enough reason of my own for not wanting him whacked into a gallop; I had been in the saddle a long time and was very sore. I was only accustomed to taking short rides, or – as on our visit to Minsham – a long one with a rest in between. When Browny galloped, I bumped, and it hurt.

When the man came up to strike the pony a second time, I cried, 'Don't do that!' But he did, and we bumped forward as before. It happened twice more and Browny began to blow; so next time, just as he began to slow down, I pulled him to a standstill, clapped my hand to my eye and let out a yell.

'There's a fly in my eye,' I said.

The servant, close behind me, said, 'Damnation!' and then, coming alongside, 'Can't you get it out?'

I made a quick movement and snatched the whip, which he was holding in a slack hand just then, and I pulled the pony round a little so that my hand, with the whip in it, was as far as possible from the servant on the tall horse.

'Give me that whip,' he said between his teeth. I was going to say – Not unless you promise not to hit my pony again! – but what good would a churl's promise be? So I simply said, 'I shan't.'

There then followed, right out in the open road, a most unseemly scuffle. He pulled his horse round and made a grab for the whip, but I was ready and brought it down smartly on his wrist; he cursed and made another snatch, not this time at the whip, but at the top of my arm, which he seized and twisted. I was quite helpless then, and the only way to break his hold was to slip out of the saddle and stand in the road; even so I dangled for a moment, held by his hand, before my weight carried me to the ground.

I was by this time thoroughly frightened; dismounting so hastily and carelessly had rubbed my sore bottom, and my arm had had a cruel twist, so I started to yell. I stood there, holding the whip behind me, my back pressed to Browny's heaving side, and I yelled as if I were being murdered.

'Give me that whip and get back on that pony,' the servant said.

I yelled louder. He was in a rather awkward position; he could lift me back on to the pony, but to do that he must himself dismount, and when he did, I thought – some part of me quite calm for all the fright and pain and the yelling – I would strike his horse, hard, so that it galloped off, and while he chased it I would jump back on Browny and ride in the other direction.

The road was far from being deserted. Two old women were herding along a great gaggle of geese and looked at us with interest, not untinged with amusement, but they were too busy with their charges to stop and ask questions. A man with a panniered donkey, waiting for the geese to pass the place where the horse and the pony narrowed the road, did speak.

'Whassa matter? Hurt yersel'?'

'Mind your own business,' said the Astallon man so fiercely that the man with the donkey quailed, smacked his beast with the flat of his hand and passed on.

'My Lady will hear about this,' the servant said to me.

'Aye, from *me!*' I said, and was straightway frightened again at the thought of some great lady listening to both our tales and believing *him*. So I yelled some more. But I kept my eye on the man and saw that he was going to dismount. I got ready, but just then along came some horsemen, riding fast. The first one cried, 'Make way, make way!' and the Astallon man, instead of dismounting, pulled in a little to the side of the road. The gentleman rode past, his companion followed, but he looked at us, the third gentleman passed. Then the second rider wheeled round and rode back. He was about the age of, and not unlike, my Uncle Godfrey.

'What is all this to do?'

I said, 'Oh sir, please, please help me.'

The Astallon man slipped from the saddle and put his hand to his forelock and began to speak rapidly...a sore task...sent to conduct the little lady...no will for the journey...

I ran forward and took hold of the gentleman's foot in the stirrup.

'It isn't true. It's all lies. I was going willingly till he hit Browny.'

The gentleman said, 'If you would speak one at a time I might make some sense of it.' He leaned forward a little and studied the badge. 'Astallon of Beauclaire?'

'That's right, sir. And sent to conduct...'

'Ladies first,' said the gentleman. 'Now, why do you stand here and make a noise like a hound in full cry?'

I told him in as few words as possible. 'You can see I speak the truth,' I said, and I pointed to the welts that had already risen on Browny's smooth rump.

'All right. Now you be quiet for a moment. You, tell me, was there any particular urgency about this journey?'

'I was told to make it with all possible speed, sir.'

'All possible speed. Well, your master would know that so small a child would not be mounted on a saddle horse. All possible speed, for that pony would be...let me see...three days. I shall pass close by Beauclaire; I'll turn aside and say that if you arrive earlier you have over-driven both pony and rider and should be beaten.'

He turned to me with a smile and said, 'A pleasant journey and a safe arrival, demoiselle. Would you like me to take that whip?'

I said, 'Oh, I do thank you. Thank you. What is your name?'

'My name? Why, what is my name to you?'

'I shall mention it in my prayers every night as long as I live.'

He laughed. 'Then I shall be greatly in your debt. But I hope you will outlive all memory of me by fifty years. My name is John Fitz Arle. And what is yours?'

'Maude Reed.'

'I wish you well. As for you, fellow, mind what I said.'

(I put his name into my prayers that night, and I kept it there, for years and years, by rote and habit, long after I had forgotten what he looked like and everything about him, except that he had stood by me in a moment of great need.)

So I had won, but victory has its price. At inns, one's accommodation and food depends very largely upon one's servant and his care for one's comfort. Jack had seen that I slept and ate well in Colchester, Chelmsford and Brentwood. Now anything would do.

What I didn't know was that in all great establishments all the servants are for ever trying to make their duties profitable. My escort had been given money for the journey; if he could have shortened it by a night – even if Browny had ended broken-winded – the price of a night's lodging for us and our mounts would have gone into his own pocket. This form of cheating was rife at Beauclaire, as it must be, I suppose, in any establishment too large to be sharply looked to by one person. Even over the candles my Lord Astallon was swindled by his house steward, whose duty it was to see that new candles were placed in every sconce and stand every evening. The short ends were one of his perquisites, and since hundreds of candles were used every day, they would have amounted to something. But he was not content. The new candles were put in place and they were lighted; then some minion of the Steward's would run around, replacing them by the stubs of another evening. So the cry, 'Bring fresh candles' was constantly to be heard, together with complaints that candles these days lasted only half the time that they were wont to do.

Even taking three days for the journey, thanks to my behaviour, I think the man made some small profit for himself: I do not think that my Uncle Godfrey, nor my Cousin Astallon, would have wished me to lie in the common sleeping room, with tinkers and drovers; or to dine on boiled goose-grass root three days in succession. Fortunately, as my homesickness and misery grew, my appetite lessened. And as the appetite lessens, so do the spirits. It was a very miserable, quiet little girl who got stiffly down from her pony's back, and saw him led away and thought – There goes my last friend.

The servant indicated that I was to follow him, so on foot we went through another archway and into a court with a well in its centre. An old man was drawing up water in a bucket and tipping it into a barrel which fitted into a frame with two wheel and shafts; a donkey stood between the shafts, and a boy stood by the donkey's head. This vast household used so much water that the old man worked at the well, and the barrel made journeys to and fro, all day long.

One side of this court was enclosed by a wing of the house itself, and here was an entry, a deep, dark porch with an iron-studded door set within it. As a sign of his displeasure with me, the servant halted by this door, instead of taking me in and handing me over.

'In there,' he said, and walked away.

I stepped into the porch, feeling smaller than I had ever done in my life, knowing how dwarfs feel in a world fitted to ordinary people. I stood for a moment gathering my breath and my courage, then I pulled off my glove, and making a fist, knocked on the door. It was, I soon saw, a very thick door, and plenty of noise was being made on its further side. Nobody answered my knock. I beat on the door again and when it stayed closed, turned the great iron handle and pushed.

Immediately inside the door was a kind of small room, the door behind me forming one wall of it, the other three made of finely carved screening through which I could see. Our solar at the Old Vine was reckoned to be a wonderful apartment, unmatched in the whole of Baildon, but this room was three times as large and half as high again. Yet it seemed full, for the young ladies within were all wearing wide-spreading dresses and enormous head-dresses. Four of them sat in a group, with a piece of embroidery spread over their laps, each stitching away at her own portion, and talking and laughing as they worked. One sat alone on a window seat, playing a lute very softly and sweetly. Some others, at the end farthest from the hearth, stood at a table, throwing dice and making loud exclamatory noises; and three stood quite near the door, divided from me by the lacy woodwork of the screen.

I stood in the enclosure, like something in a cage, and looked about, then I pushed against each side in turn and the left side proved to be a swing door. I walked into the room and went near to the three young ladies who were talking. One was telling some tale, making gestures as she did so.

'...so I said, "Oh, *is* that so? Then what about the evening of Holy Cross Day?" Could you have seen her face?'

One of the listeners said, 'Oh, Ella, we swore never to mention that!'

'I was so much provoked. But listen! She then said, "That is what comes of lending one's cloak!" And she tossed her head and turned...God have mercy, where did *you* spring from?'

Tossing her head and imitating the turn she had come face to face with me.

'I came by that door.'

'And what do you want?'

'I've come to live here. My uncle arranged it.'

'Who is your uncle?'

'Sir Godfrey Blanchefleur.'

'Oh. Well, I don't think he is here now...'

Perhaps she would have shown more concern, but one of the other girls tugged at her sleeve.

'Ella, go on! I must skip in just one minute. Lend her cloak, why, she wouldn't lend a pin!'

There was nothing to be hoped for from them, so I went farther into the room and from shyness approached the lady who sat alone, rather than another group.

All I had time to see, or wit to notice then, was that she was pretty, with a beautiful pale unblemished skin and hair so fair that it was almost silver.

I planted myself in front of her and said all in one shaky gulping sentence, 'My name is Maude Reed and my Uncle Sir Godfrey Blanchefleur invited me here, and now he is gone and I don't know what to do and I want to go to the privy very badly indeed!'

'Poor poppet!' she said, and laid the lute aside, jumped up and took my hand and hurried me through a doorway, into a passage, up some steps, down some steps, into another passage and so into a room where stood a row of big square boxes covered with black velvet. She threw open the lid of one of them and showed a gleaming copper pot, sunk in the black velvet of the inner frame.

'There you are,' she said cheerfully.

Urgent as my need was, I waited for her to go. I was unused to the ways of the great. At home there was a privy, with a screen of bushes around it, and there was, of course, the night pot under the bed in case of need, but I had not – at least since I could remember – used either with anyone watching.

While I stood, almost weeping with indecision, the door opened and one of the young ladies who had been dicing hurried in. I knew her by her violet-coloured dress. She threw up her skirt and took the stool next to the one opened for me.

'Holy Virgin,' she said, 'that onion broth! It goes through me like a purge.'

Encouraged, I sat down and did what I wanted.

My friend, so pale and slender, looking so far removed from such gross human needs, lifted her sleeve and held it before her nose.

'Catherine, what a stink! Little one, have you done?'

She took up a bell which stood on the ledge of a niche like an unglazed window set in one of the inner walls, and rang it vigorously.

'Now,' she said, 'if anyone knows about you it will be Dame Margaret and I think she is in the Still Room. We'll find her. So you are Blanchefleur's niece; yes, you have his eyes.'

In the passage we met an old woman carrying a bucket and a jar of sudsy water; she stood aside to let us pass. When the passage widened, the young lady took my hand, asked me to tell her my name again, asked how old I was, was I homesick? Yes, so had she been, she said, when she first came to Beauclaire, but that soon passed; in the Children's Dorter there were several boys and girls, some about my age, and I should enjoy playing with them; and Dame Margery, who governed us, was not too strict, it was said.

I made bold to ask her her name.

'Melusine.' It was one I had never heard before and I repeated it to make sure I had it right.

'Yes, Melusine. I was named for a fairy lady in a French romance.'

'You could be one,' I said. 'I thought just now...' but I could not tell her the thought I had had in the Stool Room.

'What did you think?'

'That you are beautiful.'

She laughed.

'You have the Blanchefleur tongue, too.'

But she sounded pleased.

When we had walked for what seemed to me a long, long way, she stopped and opened a door. It smelt as though the lid had been taken off a spice box. Behind the door was a smallish cosy room, lined with shelves and cupboards, all the shelves full of jars and bottles and boxes. At a solid table in the middle of the room sat a stout, elderly woman with a plain linen head-piece, moving her hands about in a wooden trough, full of some dry-looking, sweet-smelling mixture. Ranged along the table were many bowls, some of silver, some of pottery, pewter and wood.

'What have we here?' she asked, looking up.

'We have Maude Reed, who has come to live here.'

'Why, yes, of course. They were warned at the entrance that she would arrive, today or tomorrow, and should be taken to Dame Margery. What has happened?'

'She came to the Well Yard door, and Dame Margery has taken all the children blackberrying, or so I thought.'

'You thought right – so tomorrow, I shall be busy with the cordials. And this not off my hands yet! Very well, very well. They will be back very soon, it's nearly dark. She can stay with me.'

Melusine smiled and left me. Dame Margaret asked if I were at ease, and if I needed to eat now or could wait until supper.

I said I could wait. So, having tossed the mixture again, she said I could help her to dish it out into the bowls.

It was just the kind of task most useful at the moment; it kept me busy and made me feel a little less lost and unwanted. When she saw that I was careful and neat-handed, she left it all to me. She took a cup and poured some dark rosy-red liquid into it and sat down, leisurely sipping. Between sips she asked me questions. At one point she snapped a finger and thumb and said, 'But of course. Your mother was Anne Blanchefleur. I remember her well.' She looked at me with a new, close interest, up and down, noting my very shoes.

'Reed, you said? And your father is a wool merchant.'

'No. My father is dead. My grandfather is a wool merchant the biggest between London and Lincoln.'

She made a little noise as though clearing her throat.

'Family ties are strong, for all that. Lucky for you you are like your mother – in appearance, I mean.'

'I'm not. My mother is very pretty, and I have red hair.'

'It runs in this family. My Lord Astallon is red as a fox. As for prettiness, one day you may be pretty too if you learn not to glower.'

The door opened and another plain linen head-piece poked around its edge.

'Ha, Margaret! There is no linen, nor towels, laid out for the Merlin Chamber, and my Lord Ashford just arriving.'

'God be my judge!' cried Dame Margaret, jumping up. 'It was tomorrow. I swear my Lady said tomorrow...' She trotted out of the room.

In the moment or so that the door had stood half open, the scent of roasted meat had come in and mingled with the spicy air of the room. I realized that I was, if not actually hungry, very empty. All through the journey my stomach had been full of misery, and the food at the inns, for the last three days, had been very unappetizing. Scratching up the last of the mixture of rose petals and lavender and bergamot heads out of the wooden trough and into the bowls, I began to think about supper. And that made me think of the Old Vine, of the bustle and chatter as the weavers and pack-whackers and smiths came trooping into the dining hall, my grandfather, quiet but kindly, taking his place at the end table, Mother beside him and Walter next to her. My place empty...

Here, at least, I was alone and could snivel a little; so I did, folding my arms on the table's edge and leaning my face on them.

I snivelled until one of the candles went out. The Still Room was on the inner side of the house, with only one small window which looked out on a narrow court, so the candles had been lighted there early. Now one, and then another, guttered away. And I was afraid of the dark. Walter was too; but somehow he had managed to make his fear known, and when, one day, I confessed to Mother an equal dread of darkness she had said, 'Copy cat! Just because Walter has this whim, so must you.' So after that I had made light of it, sheltering behind Walter's need to have a light through all the hours of darkness. Now I was alone in a strange room, and where there had been four candles there were now two, and they were failing.

I went over and opened the door. The passage outside was quite brightly lighted. I walked along it, following my nose which would, I thought, lead me to the food, the scent of which was now powerful. Soon the passage divided; one arm of it, narrow and dimly lighted, ran off to the left, the other, wider, very bright, led towards a set of stairs. I went that way, and at the stairhead found myself in a room which was as much bigger than the one by the Well Yard door as that was compared with the solar at the Old Vine.

It was so magnificent, so unlike anything I had ever seen before, that for a moment I could forget that I was homesick, alone, hungry and forgotten, and just stood staring. Every inch of the walls was covered with tapestry. At home we had one, and that was reckoned a marvel; here one joined on to the next, all the way round the great room. Ours at home was a scene from the Bible, Adam and Eve in the Garden of Eden, their nakedness screened by flowers and bushes, Eve offering Adam the fatal apple, and the Serpent, coiled about a tree-trunk and wearing a human face, watching the triumph of his wiliness. The tapestries in the Long Gallery at Beauclaire were pictures of stories which I had never heard; there was a knight on a great horse driving a lance into the body of a thing all covered with scales like a fish, but with a thick solid tail and claws like a bird and a head more like that of a horse than anything else. The knight wore a red cross on a white background on his breast-plate. Every one of the woven pictures was concerned with knights. In one, a knight lay on the ground, sorely wounded to judge by the blood that oozed over his shoulder from under the edge of his gorget, but he was blowing a great horn, and his enemies made a ring about him, waving their swords, aiming their pikes, while far off, on a distant hill, a gathering of knights seemed to be waiting and listening.

I walked all the way round, looking at the pictures and wishing that there were someone with me who could tell me the stories about them.

At the far end there was another high doorway, and I went through it and found myself in a smaller room, all hung with rose-pink draperies; and beyond that was another passage. There were many doors in it, and I opened them, one by one. Most of them opened on to darkness, and one, just opposite a candle sconce on the passage wall, gave me a fright, for it was full of suits of armour, on their stands, which looked, at first glance, like men. That room smelt of the oil used on the harness, and of the vinegar which was mixed with the wood-ash for polishing the metal.

By this time I could not even smell the food and knew I was lost. But just as I knew this, I opened the door and found myself in the room into which, a lifetime ago, I had walked. There was the screen about the door, the table at which the ladies had diced, the piece of embroidery, and, on the window seat, Melusine's lute, just as she had flung it down. The candles were burning low here, too, but there were so many of them that the light still served. I walked over to the window seat and stood there, thinking that this was her place, and she was the only one who had been kind to me. I touched a string of the lute and it gave a little tuneable twang.

There was a lute at home; it hung by a silk ribbon from a peg in the solar and I had always wanted to handle it; but it had belonged to my father and was sacred. One day, however,

Mother had reached it down and put it into my hands. 'There you are,' she said, 'see what you can do.'

All I could do, to start with, was to make a discordant noise. She sat and watched me, which was not helpful. I had, however, just begun to work it out that when I touched this string, such and such a sound came forth, and when I touched this, another...and in a moment I felt sure I should have made a less distasteful noise, when she jumped up, snatched the lute from me and hung it back on its peg, saying, 'You have no art.'

Now, left alone with a lute, I would have tried all the strings again and endeavoured to remember what I had learned in that one brief handling; but as I reached the window seat where Melusine's lute lay, I could look out of the window and saw that the wall which ran out at right-angles to the Well Yard Room was pierced with windows, all aglow, and as I looked a door opened and a man came out, holding something in his hand which he raised to his mouth and bit upon. So I went through the screen and out by the door and across the Well Yard and in through that opened door.

I was at the lowest end of the dining hall, from which all but a few servants and a table full of pages had gone. At the other end was a low platform, with a table running across it, from side to side of the hall, and that table was edged with crimson velvet, heavily embroidered, a little like an altar cloth. Another vast table ran the whole length of the hall, and at the lower end there were others, set near the wall. Broken meats, half-eaten trenchers of bread soaked in gravy, spilled ale, gnawed bones and apple cores littered the boards. Some men, each with a bucket, were going around sweeping everything from the tables, and behind each man came a boy with a filthy cloth which he drove – swish – across each surface as it was cleared.

The pages were eating heartily and talking and laughing at the same time. One looked up and saw me, nudged his neighbour, who looked and nudged his. They all stared but not one did more, and though some of the servants eyed me they said nothing. I walked along by the long central table, looking for something to eat. When I did – it was a pigeon, all that was left of a dishful, to judge by the bones scattered round – I sat down, pulled the dish towards me and began to eat. It was in that worst state, no longer hot, yet not quite cold, and I should have liked some bread with it; however, it took the edge from my hunger. As I ate I watched the clearing being done and thought how much more carefully we did things at the Old Vine, where the bones were collected separately and put on to the dung-heap where they softened down into manure, and all the soft waste went into the swill pail for the pigs. Nor would my mother, or for that matter Old Nancy, have allowed such filthy cloths as the boys were using anywhere within reach of our tables.

I crammed the last piece into my mouth just as the clearing man reached the place where I sat. I then walked down the hall again and out into the Well Yard and into the room where the ladies had been, hoping to find Melusine. There was no one there and the candles were almost dead.

I have known sharper grief, deeper misery, but never a feeling of more complete wretchedness, of being alone in a hostile world. Dame Margaret had spoken of my having been expected by the main entry; if I only knew where that was, I thought, I might find someone who would know me and tell me where to go. The idea of still being alone and lost, when all the lights were dead and darkness everywhere, filled me with panic.

Often, during the next few days, I looked back on my first evening at Beauclaire and thought how contradictory was its way of life. I truly believe that a homeless person, provided he or she were decently dressed, could have moved about the house, eaten in the hall, slept in a corner and gone unchallenged for a week, a month, maybe forever. Everyone would assume that the stranger belonged to some other department, or to some visitor's train. Yet, side by side with this was the equally true fact, that once you were claimed and recognized, and made part of the establishment, you could never for a moment get out of the place. There was somewhere where you must be, someone you must be with, something you must be doing, from the moment you left your bed until you went back to it.

The household, which to me just then seemed so dreadfully disorganized, was, in fact, very closely and highly organized. All my misery was the result of having been sent to the wrong doorway.

Not daring to stay longer in the empty darkening room, I opened a door, found myself in a passage, and could hear some music and the sound of someone singing. The sounds seemed to come from the top of a flight of steps, so I climbed them and opened the door at the top and knew at once that I had solved one problem: I was no longer alone. The room was crowded with ladies and gentlemen, some ladies seated on benches and chairs with gentlemen around them, but most standing in groups. The music came from the other end of the apartment and most of them were facing it, so had their backs to me.

I went in, like a pup looking for its master, hoping to find either Melusine or Dame Margaret. Here again, as I moved about, people looked at me with a mild curiosity, but nobody asked *why* I was there. I was halfway up the room, at a point from which I could catch glimpses of the lute player, and of a man with a harp and a boy with a wooden frame, the top bar hung with little bells, arranged in order of size, the smallest like a thimble, the largest as big as a cup, when I saw Melusine standing with a very fine young gentleman.

I had been moving diffidently, but at the sight of her I flung myself forward and took her hand.

'What!' she said, 'You again. You should be abed.'

'I know.' I began to blurt out my woes, how Dame Margaret had left me and nobody had called me to supper and how I had been lost.

Faces began to turn in our direction; somebody said, 'Hush!' The music ended with a loud sweep of the player's fingers across all the strings, and, in the vibrating silence immediately following, a sweet, high, languid voice called, 'What *is* all this ado?'

Holding me by the hand, Melusine led me towards where a lady sat on a bench with high, in-curved ends, all gilded. The lady did look, indeed, like a statue of gold; her dress was yellow and so was her hair, and she wore it uncovered, pulled back from a high white forehead, and held in a net of gold, set with yellow stones where the strands crossed. Her face was like a statue's too, carved into an expression of faintly shocked surprise, due to her eyebrows being shaved off and then painted on again, a full inch above their natural place.

Melusine let my hand fall and stepped back a pace and said in a stiff way, 'Madam, this is Maude Reed.'

'Maude Reed,' she repeated the name, just as I had hours ago repeated Melusine's. She turned her head towards a man who stood behind the gilded bench. I remembered Dame Margaret's remark about the red hair. His was very red, quite different from mine. He leaned over and whispered in the lady's ear.

'Of course,' she said, and turning back to me gave me a smile and said, 'You are welcome.'

I knew what to do and I meant to do it, to make her the best curtsey I had ever made, holding my skirt clear on each side and letting my head dip just at the right moment. And I did.

But the truth was that one of my reasons for misery and wanting to find Melusine, was that I needed, once again, to visit the Stool Room; and my inside didn't know that I was making my duty to my mother's kin, Lord and Lady Astallon of Beauclaire; it thought I was attending to its needs. I felt the warm wetness run free, scouring my saddle-chafed thighs.

For ever disgraced, I thought, rising with the shamed blood scorching my face. I cannot stay here. Tomorrow I must go home. And here they will remember me forever – Maude Reed, the girl who made a curtsey and made water at the same time.

There was the little puddle; the moment I moved, it would be seen by all, and though I knew that I must move and that it would be seen, something made me try to defer the evil moment. I was like a person on his way to the tooth-puller's booth, lingering by every other booth that he passed.

'Madam,' I said, 'my mother sent you her loving greetings and her deep gratitude for taking me into your household.'

'Your mother,' she said, and again turned her head. My Lord again leaned forward and whispered into her ear.

'Your mother has trained you very prettily,' said my Lady, turning back to me. 'Now…You will join the Children's Dorter and be governed by Dame Margery, and I trust you will learn well!'

Ignorant as I was, I recognized the tone of dismissal. But I still stood, guarding my shameful secret.

My Lord saved me. He made a sign to the musicians, who broke at once into a merry tune; and a slim young man with red cheeks came from behind the bench and bowed and extended his hand and said, 'Madam, I beg you, dance with me.'

She smiled and stood up; and since she could neither walk through me nor over me, I was bound to step aside.

Now, I thought, they will all see.

But her skirts were long and full and edged with fur. When she had passed there was nothing left to show that I had misbehaved myself. After a moment Melusine came to me and said, 'I will take you to Dame Margery.'

The young gentleman who had stood by her said, 'When did you turn nursemaid? May I be your next charge?'

She said, 'You do not expect to reach second childhood so soon, surely?'

Outside another door, which we reached after a long walk, Melusine halted, put her arm around me and kissed me.

'Our paths may not cross for many a long day,' she said. 'I hope you'll be happy.'

I clung to her for a moment; then she put me gently away, and once we were inside the room, face to face with a dignified, solemn-looking lady, her manner was formal again.

'This is Maude Reed, Dame Margery,' she said. 'By some mistake she came in by the wrong door.'

III

The Children's Dorter at Beauclaire was really an establishment on its own. The actual Dorter was the chamber in which we all slept, boys and girls together, but separated by screens down the centre of the room; when people spoke of the Children's Dorter, however, they meant also the big room in which we worked and played, and took all our meals except the midday dinner, and very occasionally our supper.

There were eight of us at the time when I joined the Dorter. My Astallon cousins had two children of their own, a boy of nine, named Ralph, a girl of six, Constance. There was another girl of eight, who bore about the same relationship to them as I did myself; she was a Fortescue – sent, after the fashion of the time, to be schooled in the house of a cousin, while, in her own home, other girls and boys were being trained; her name was Alison. There were two brothers, aged nine and seven, Henry and William Rancon, whose father had died by my cousin Astallon's side in the French Wars lately ended; and there was an eleven-year-old girl named Helen Beaufort, who was a relative – some believed an illegitimate daughter – of the great Cardinal. There was also a girl named Madge FitzHerbert who was a true half-wit; she understood very little, spoke indistinctly and had protruding brown eyes which did not see very well. I never knew her to manage to thread her needle. She was there because her own mother was dead and her father, when he remarried, did not wish his new wife to see what manner of child he had bred already. He had some position at Court and was in high favour, especially with the Duke of Gloucester, the King's uncle. My cousins had accepted Madge as an inmate of their Children's Dorter in return for some favour which her father was able to do for them. My Lady Astallon had ambitions and was always craving to live in London and take what she called 'her proper place in the world', but her husband preferred to stay at Beauclaire, with only short visits to his other estates, to attend to the management of his affairs and mind no will but his own. I've heard him say that the Duke of Gloucester was 'riding for a fall', that when the tree fell the ivy fell too, and that for himself he would sooner rule his own acres than be just one voice on the Privy Council of the King.

Our days were strictly ordered, but by no means tedious. We girls learned to sew and embroider; not to spin – spinning was at that time out of fashion for the gently reared, and the distaffs lay idle in a corner. We learned to dance, and to play various games without showing chagrin when we lost, or pleasure when we won. Self-control was a virtue highly rated by Dame Margery; she never, for example, minded how much, how often or how viciously we quarrelled, but we were not allowed to smack one another, or scream, or cry. The boys, when they fell out, were allowed to use violence on one another, but not in the house.

'Into the yard and settle it,' Dame Margery would say; and the one who came back defeated had scant sympathy.

'You'll take harder knocks, if you live.'

The boys, when they were ten years old, were removed from her care altogether – 'And I want no one saying, when you get amongst men, that I have brought you up soft.'

We girls, though treated differently, were disciplined too. We must learn to stand still, perfectly upright, without fidgeting or sighing, for long stretches of time on end; we must always eat, without any sign of distaste, anything put before us. We must learn to govern even the working of our bowels.

'Bless you, child,' Dame Margery once said to Helen Beaufort, 'in a few years' time, when you wait upon some great lady and are tiring her hair, will you drop the pins and cry "I must to stool!" You will *not*. Go stand in that corner, place your hands on your head and await my permission to go.'

Unlikely as it sounds, impossible as it seemed to us at the time, her methods did work; bowels and bladders learned that they were not masters to be pandered to, but servants to be obedient.

In many ways we were fortunate in our mistress; she was a countrywoman who after some years in London had come back to the place that she loved, and she liked nothing better than to take us out, riding, or afoot, naming us the wildflowers or the birds, warning us which berries were poisonous, letting us share, in a manner unusual in most households, the seasonal activities of the manor. On the day of my arrival the children had all been blackberrying; later we gathered mushrooms and hazel nuts. When the summer came, we were allowed – the girls demurely sun-bonneted – to toss hay in the meadows, play amongst the stooks in the harvest fields. Once she took us all into the woods, carrying food with us, and let us make a fire and cook, tinker fashion. The meat was bitter with smoke on the outside and red raw within, but somehow it tasted different, and better than a dish similarly spoiled would have seemed eaten indoors.

My appreciation of our Dame did not come all at once. My first weeks at Beauclaire were very wretched. I made mistakes and was punished, I lost myself several times. When the boys teased me, I fell into a rage; when Alison and Helen tried – as they did at first – to show themselves superior to me, I wept. So much that we did seemed to me useless, false and hypocritical, and there was so much else that I did not understand.

This wool merchant business, for example. Alison and Helen seemed to hold it against me that my grandfather was a wool merchant. At least here Helen, who was the older, always gave the lead and Alison followed her.

Once I cried, 'And what's wrong with being a wool merchant?' and in fury took up the scissors and slashed into Helen's embroidery. Dame Margery punished me and I yelled that it was not fair, I hadn't started the dispute.

'And do you expect fairness in this world, Maude? If so you are going to be very sorely disappointed. Better learn now. Go stand in the corner and place your hands on top of your head.'

I could learn, that was one blessing; I wasn't like poor Madge who could make the same mistake three times in one day. Next time Helen twitted me about the wool business I stayed calm. I didn't even look at her, I looked at the wall straight ahead and I said, 'My *father* was in the wool business too. And when I was born he did not call me his *niece!*'

Now for that I should have been whipped. But no! Dame Margery, a little later said, 'I am glad to see that you are learning to stand up for yourself in proper fashion.'

Proper fashion, for young ladies, meant lashing out with hurtful words, not slashing with scissors.

Not long after that, I performed, out of cowardice, an act of bravado which gave the boys a good opinion of me.

Every fine day, after the midday dinner, unless Dame Margery had something planned for us, we were allowed to go and play in what was called the Low Garden. In days long past, when Beauclaire consisted of the castle only, this garden had been the pleasance where, in times of peace at least, the ladies could take the air. Since then new and better gardens had been made near the new house, but they were for the pleasure of grown-up people who did not wish to be disturbed by children's games. The Low Garden was now somewhat neglected, its grass tufty, its bushes overgrown, its walls surrounding it tumbled in some places. There was one stretch of wall still quite sound, however, and one day the boys took a ladder into the garden, climbed by its help to the top of the wall and there strutted about like young cockerels, jeering at us girls who, they claimed, couldn't do what they were doing. They then began a game of taking turns to run the length of the wall and back.

My head for heights had never been put to the test and I couldn't see why William, a month or so younger than I was, could do something which I could not, so in the end I called that it was now my turn; and I climbed the ladder and stood on the wall, which was about twelve inches wide at the top, and which on the garden side dropped ten feet, and on the outer side twice as much. The moment I stood on the wall and looked down I realized the truth of their jeers: this was something no girl could do, or should attempt. I also knew that to stand there, teetering, was the worst thing I could do; only speed could save me. Trying not to look at or think about the drop on either side, I walked briskly to the end of the stretch of wall where it ran into the side of a solid square tower. I turned and pressed my back against the blessed solidity of that tower and knew that I should never have the courage to leave it and set out on the return journey. My head was already spinning and my knees had turned to melted wax. So I did the only thing there was to do; crying, 'I'll wager you daren't do *this!*' I jumped down into the garden. A sharp sickening pain stabbed through my ankle, but Dame Margery's exhortations of self-control bore fruit; I did not cry out, nor did I hobble, though my ankle remained swollen and painful for many days, and will even now, in wet weather, pain me.

Henry Rancon took up the challenge, climbed the wall, ran along and jumped as I had done. William said he couldn't jump because he would jar a tooth that was already giving him trouble, and Ralph Astallon said it was time we went back to the house.

After that, however, whenever they wanted a fourth for any game they chose me rather than Helen, who was older and stronger.

So, bit by bit, I worked myself into place at Beauclaire and before I had thoroughly recovered from my homesickness, Christmas was drawing near. I expected to go home for Christmas, and I cherished a hope of being allowed to stay there. After all, one of the reasons for sending me away had been that it wouldn't be fair for Walter to go and for me to remain, and Walter had remained; and another reason was that I should learn, and I had taken care to learn all I could.

Advent came; the first Sunday in Advent, and then the second, and nothing was said about my going back to Baildon for Christmas. It seemed to me that it might be one of those things overlooked or gone awry – like my arrival – so during that week I said to Dame Margery, 'Madam, I am supposed to go home for Christmas.'

'Are you indeed?'

'No one has spoken of any arrangements yet.'

'Heaven bless you, child, have patience. Your home is how faraway?'

'Five days' ride.'

'Then there is plenty of time.'

Another Sunday came; and I reminded my Dame, and she said, 'Maybe I should make inquiries.'

She must have done so, for next day, at dinner in the hall, my Lady Astallon sent for me and, when I stood close, said, 'This notion about going home for Christmas! What put that into your little head?'

I asked myself, what? When there was talk of Walter going to the Choir School and of me going to Clevely there had been mention of being home for Christmas; but he was now at home and I was here. It was I, bidding Jack farewell at Brentwood, who had said, 'home for Christmas'.

'It was understood, Madam,' I said in a weak voice.

'Not by me. And not I think by your uncle. In any case, travel at this time of the year is undesirable; the inns so uncomfortable and the likelihood of being snowbound...'

She waved an elegant hand in dismissal and I now knew better than to argue.

Next day, on my way out of the Hall after dinner, I was stopped by my Uncle Godfrey. He had, on and off, paid me some attention, for which I was very grateful. He had returned to Beauclaire four or five days after my arrival and had at once sought me out and asked how I fared. Now he said, 'This going back to Baildon for Christmas, Maude, would be very silly.

Christmas here is kept in such style. People come from London to share in the festivities.'

'But I expected to go home.'

'There you are mistaken. Your mother was clear on that point. You stay here until you are twelve.'

'And not go home at all?'

'Running to and fro,' he said, 'vastly expensive and bothersome and unsettling. And all to what purpose?'

'I want to see my mother and Walter and my grandfather.'

Something changed in his face, so that for a moment I feared that I had offended him. Then he took a lock of my hair between his fingers and twisted it, saying slowly, 'You know, child, sooner or later you have to learn to do without people. It's best to learn young.'

'But why? If it is a question of expense, I still have the broad gold piece my grandfather gave me.'

'You'd only make it harder for yourself...'

Where the words, or the thought, came from I do not know, but I heard myself saying, 'My mother doesn't want me at home, does she?'

'She knows that you will do better here. And so for that matter, do I. Who else looks to go home?'

'Alison, Alison Fortescue.'

'Does she so? Well, for your ear alone, in that house Christmas is so meanly celebrated I'll wager she'll wish she'd stayed here. Many's the Christmas I've spent there and, believe me, even the plums in the pudding are counted out, one by one.'

I wanted to shout that it was no matter to me whether there was one plum in the pudding or a thousand. Most of all I wanted to go and cry somewhere, alone, by myself. But the truth was that at Beauclaire there was no place to cry alone; once you were part of it you lived a public life where every sigh or frown or tear was observed and remarked. At this moment, because my uncle had stopped me on my way out of the Hall, there were Constance and Helen, Alison and Madge waiting for me.

I walked slowly to join them, thinking that when I had said that Mother didn't want me home my uncle had not denied it. I remembered then what I had forgotten: the face she had worn as she watched me ride away. Something within me hardened. I thought, Well, if she does not want me, I don't want her. It wasn't true at first, but thinking it over and over made it become true. I still yearned for the smallness and friendliness of the Old Vine, for the kitchen where I was welcomed and given gingerbread men, for the yard full of men like Jack who would call me 'Little Mistress' one minute and 'Maude' the next. But, over that Christmastime, I began to be weaned.

That I had not been expected to go home was made very clear by the arrival, two days before Christmas, of gifts for me. From my grandfather – or so I imagined – another broad gold piece, from my mother a blue velvet hood, lined and bordered with fur. With these gifts was a square of parchment, bordered all down the left side with leaves and berries painted in green and red, and with words written in the remaining space. The letters were very black, except for a few which were gaily coloured.

I held it out to Dame Margery and learned, to my surprise, that she could not read. But she knew what it was.

'It is a Christmas Piece, to bring you good wishes. Carry it down to the Well Yard Room. Most like one of the young ladies can spell it out for you. If not you must ask the Chaplain.'

I was delighted to have a chance to go where I might see Melusine, for whom I still entertained a passion of gratitude and admiration. There was, rightly, a firm barrier fixed between the Children's Dorter and the Well Yard Room and the Ladies' Dorter, and I seldom saw her except at a distance. That morning I found her, and she read me out what Walter had written. It said,

> 'On this, the Birthday of Our Blessed Lord,
> I send Greetings to my Dear
> Sister and wish you Joy and God's

Blessing on you, from your Brother
Walter Reed.'

Melusine read for me three times, so that I could get it by heart.
Then she asked how old was Walter and, when I told her that he
was just my age she said, 'He must be a clever scholar. It is nicely
written and very even.'

The Christmas Piece, bringing home almost as much as
Walter to mind, made me homesick again. The pretty furred
hood seemed a mockery, and when I returned to the Children's
Dorter I gave it to Madge FitzHerbert who had received no gifts
at all.

The Christmas Piece I carried about with me all through the
Twelve Days – which were kept, as my uncle had promised, with
every possible gaiety.

While I was showing it to my Uncle Godfrey I said, 'I would
dearly like to read and write, too.'

'You would *what*?'

I said it again.

'Then you must consult with Dame Margery.'

'She cannot read. I had to ask the Lady Melusine to tell me the
words.'

'She has learning? Perhaps she could teach you. As I said,
consult with your Dame.'

Dame Margery showed more sympathy with my desire than I
had dared to expect.

'You are to be a religious,' she said thoughtfully, 'and some
learning might serve to advance you. I will speak to my Lady.'

The answer, when it came, was typical of Beauclaire, where
the most prodigal extravagance ran side by side with sparing
economy over trivial things. It seeemed a pity for Melusine to
waste her time teaching one child to read; who else would like
to learn? Everyone else showed the utmost horror for the notion; I
went round, pleading with one after another, even poor Madge.
I argued that writing might be the one thing she *could* do, how

could she know till she had tried. But she just giggled. In the end it was Henry Rancon, the least likely of all, who came to my aid. I thought of a good argument to use on him.

'At Easter you will move out of the Children's Dorter,' I said, 'and your life will be changed. So you would have only a few lessons, and meanwhile I would do anything you asked. I would be your liege man.'

Henry was always wanting somebody to be his faithful unquestioning servant and neither of the other boys was obliging,

'All right,' he said. 'I'll have lessons till Easter. Now you kneel down and put your hands between mine and swear to be my faithful liege and obey my every command.'

That I did most gladly; and though Dame Margery said, 'Wonders will never cease,' when Henry professed his desire to learn to read and write, by Candlemas the lessons were arranged.

Tucked away in that same long passage where the suits of armour occupied a whole room, there was a small room in which some earlier Lord Astallon had gathered several books; there was a table, too, and a bench, and a slab of wood out of which sprouted three horns. One held the ink, the other the quills, and the third the sand for drying anything which was needed too hastily to permit the ink to dry itself.

And here, on three afternoons of the week, in the space between our play-time and supper, Henry and I and Melusine met. On the first day, when I thanked her, most eagerly, for agreeing to teach us, she said, 'The saddle is on the other horse, Maude. To escape even for an hour from the everlasting chatter and bickering, to get out of that carp pond, delights me.'

Another time she said that it should be a law that every woman who was not a busy housewife should learn to read.

'If they could find stories in books, they would be less ready to make up tales about those they live amongst. And they would learn that their own small joys and troubles do not fill up the world.'

I learned fast, partly because I wanted to and partly to please Melusine. Henry was content to learn how to write his name. Page after page he filled with 'Henry Rancon, Henry Rancon', then 'Sir Henry Rancon', or 'Henry Rancon, Knight'. He just lived for the moment when he should be a knight; he had the same feeling for my Uncle Godfrey – who was reckoned one of the best knights in England – as I had for Melusine; and I think one thing which resigned him to the tedium of the lessons was that, every now and then, and always unexpectedly, my uncle would look into the Book Room to see what progress I was making. My uncle, unlike most of his kind, spoke of learning with respect, and told Henry he was lucky to be taught.

'I never had the chance,' he said. 'At your age I was never in one place long enough.'

'I could teach you now, Sir Godfrey,' Melusine said.

'I am an old dog, too old for new tricks. But there are old tricks that I could teach *you!*'

'Of that I have no doubt,' she said, and laughed.

IV

It was towards the end of that February month that Henry made one of his demands upon me, in keeping with my vow. There had been some days of continuing snow, during which our afternoon playtime had been spent indoors where tedium had led to squabbling and squabbling to punishment. Rheumy colds had afflicted us too, and my Cousin Ralph was still abed on one side of the screen, and Helen and Madge abed on the other side. Our Dame had her hands full and her temper was short.

On this day, however, the sun shone and the snow was melting fast, and as we came out of the Hall Henry said, 'Come and play Hare and Hounds in the Maze.'

The Maze at Beauclaire was a singular oddity. It was part of the old Low Garden, at least it formed one of its boundaries, but it was said to be older than the garden, older even than the castle. It was an intricate puzzle of narrow paths, crossing and turning back on themselves, bordered by clipped yew hedges as tall as a mounted man. In its very centre stood a block of black stone on a mound of grey ones. There was a story that in the very faraway past, when the people who lived in England were heathen, that stone was worshipped.

I had only penetrated deep into the Maze on one occasion; very soon after my arrival at Beauclaire Helen Beaufort had mentioned, in Dame Margery's hearing, something about the Maze being the haunt of evil spirits, and Dame Margery had said, 'Rubbish. It is just a puzzle, laid out in the days when people could not walk far from the castle walls for fear of enemies, so they made the longest walk, and the most interesting, on the smallest possible space.' And to prove that she believed what she said, she had taken the lot of us, on a sunny autumn afternoon, and we had gone in and lost ourselves, and run this way and that, and shouted, and laughed and in the end come breathless to the black stone in the centre, and Dame Margery had said, 'You see. You have all lost your breath and wearied your legs as though you had run a mile. It is simply an exercise ground.'

'Then what is the stone, Madam?' Helen Beaufort asked.

'To mark the centre, so that people could know that they had arrived.'

'It's a Rune Stone,' Helen said in the stubborn way which she had mastered; not rude or ill-tempered, just a flat, unshakable way of stating something.

'And what might that mean?' Dame Margery asked.

'I don't know. I heard it spoken of as a Rune Stone.'

'Meaning a marker, like a milestone,' said Dame Margery. 'Now, all take different paths and let's see who can be out first.'

That night, in the Children's Dorter, after the light was out, Helen said to me, 'A Rune Stone is not a marker, say what she may. Before I came to Beauclaire, I lived at Greenwich, and one was found there, and the priest had it hacked to pieces; he said it was evil.'

There was no need for Dame Margery to tell us girls not to play in the Maze, we avoided it; but the boys often played a game of Hare and Hounds there, and certainly seemed to suffer no harm.

On this afternoon I said, 'Oh, Henry, it's so cold and so sloppy underfoot.'

'Running will warm you, and you can put on thick shoes. Besides...you promised.'

That was true, so I said meekly, 'Can I be a Hound?' Hounds could run in company, the Hare must go alone.

'You are a Hound; with William. It is my turn to be Hare.'

'I'll get my cloak and my thick shoes.'

'We'll wait for you by the Maze,' he said.

Alison and Madge were waiting for me, and as we went up the stairs I said, 'I am going to play Hare and Hounds with William and Henry in the Maze. You come too.'

'God's teeth,' said Alison, who was fond of using grown-up expressions, 'on a day like this? A cold thaw. I thank you, no!'

When we reached our room, I went and stood before our Dame and said, 'I am going to play with Henry and William.' I hoped that she, like Alison, might think a cold thaw a bad thing to brave. And that would let me out. But she only said that the fresh air would do me good, so long as I kept moving. So I fetched my cloak and looked for my thick shoes, and they had been taken away to be greased. So the bell must be rung and by the time it had been answered and the servant had been despatched for them, and had brought them, the brightness of the day had gone. In the Maze, I thought, it would soon be dusk.

However, I was sworn. So I ran out and joined the boys who were waiting impatiently.

The rules were that the Hare started first, while the Hounds stood still and counted the fingers of both hands twice over. The

Hare, as he ran, also counted twenty and, when he had done, cried, 'Hee, hee, hee, you can't catch me!'

The Hounds then replied, 'Woof, Woof, Woof.'

Henry ran into the Maze and presently made his call. William and I ran in, crying 'Woof'. It was already – for me – unpleasantly nearly dusk between the high hedges, so I stayed close to William; at one place where two paths met he said, 'You take one, I'll go the other way.' But William was not, even in pretence, my liege lord, so I let him run along his path and then I followed. At intervals Henry made the Hare call and we responded. Henry's voice seemed to come from a different direction each time.

Presently William, as he ran, drew away from me. I tried to keep up, and when I couldn't, gasped out a shameless, breathless appeal, 'Wait for me.'

He threw back over his shoulder, 'We're not supposed to stay together; it spoils the game.'

At the next turn I found that I had lost him; one path went left, one right, and, so far as I could see along either, he was not there. This was the moment that I had dreaded ever since Henry had issued his command. I stopped running and stood still. I needn't play any more; I could always say that I had tried to find them and failed. Had I had any sense at all, I thought, I should have fallen behind and turned back minutes ago, before I was far into the Maze.

Just before I turned, I heard Henry's call faraway to the left, and William's answering cry, to the right it seemed. To show that I hadn't given up too easily I cried 'Woof, Woof, Woof,' too, but there was something about the sound of my voice that I didn't like: it sounded lost and frightened, less like a hound than a little bleating lamb.

I turned right about and began to walk, hoping that by going in that direction and keeping on long enough I must emerge at the entry. As I walked I could hear Henry and William calling and counter-calling; once Henry sounded close at hand and I hoped the next turn would reveal him. It did not. Nor the entry. And the dusk was deepening every second. To be alone in the Maze in the dark would be as bad as being in the Long Gallery at midnight on the sixth of November, when a long dead Anne Astallon, whose husband had killed her in a fit of rage, was said to walk, weeping and wringing her hands.

I stood still and shouted, with all my strength, 'Henry! Henry!' There was no answer, and I thought – Of course, he wouldn't answer, he'd think I was cheating in the game. One call, though – if he heard it – he was bound to answer, being my liege lord, as I his man.

'A moi, Rancon! Aide! Aide!'

When that brought no response I knew I was out of earshot. I began to whimper and run any way, without trying to stick to one direction, and presently I found myself at the intersection of four paths and there was the big black stone.

I crossed myself and said, 'God between me and all harm.' I remembered what Dame Margery had said and tried to believe that it was placed there only to mark the centre; but Helen's words were much more powerful. It was still just light enough for me to see the chisel marks on the stone, deep in places, in others worn almost smooth.

I was extremely frightened, but with just sense enough left to know that what I feared was being alone in the dark, and that at such a place and such an hour even the most homely thing – a porridge bowl – could seem sinister. I didn't even know what 'Rune' meant, so what happened next was not due to my imagination.

First I went back away, into the mouth of the path by which I had come; and I found that I couldn't move. It was like one of those horrid nightmares when something pursues you and your feet are too heavy to run. My eyes were fixed on the stone, and I stood as fixed as it was. Then, in it, just level with my eyes, a light appeared, as though a small window had opened, with candles in the room within. The golden glow was faint at first, but it strengthened as I stared; and then out of the lighted square a face looked at me.

I did not, at that time, know what a Cardinal looked like; the nearest I had been to one was when I listened to speculations about Helen's paternity, so I did not know what I was seeing. It was the face of the man that held my attention, not from any remarkable feature, but because his eyes, dark under heavy brows, looked straight at me in a very compelling, forceful way, as though he were using his will to beat mine down. I had no glimmer of a notion what he wanted of me, but I knew that, whatever it was, it was important to me; I knew also that I must not give in. As I thought that, the face disappeared; the square glowed faintly for a moment and was gone.

By this time I was beyond fright. I knew I was about to die. I couldn't draw breath. It was as though an iron hand were clenched round my throat. Fighting against it, just to pull in breath once more took all my strength and I was failing, just about to die, when the most beautiful sound in all the world reached my ears: a human voice, calling in its homely Sussex speech, 'Stay right where you be, little Lady. I'm coming for ye.'

The iron hand fell away and I drew in breath with the sound of a cloth being ripped. I began to shake all over.

'Could ye give us a call for a bit of a guide?'

I tried, but my tongue was dry flannel between my chattering teeth.

'Now, now,' the voice said, a trifle crossly, ''tis no use pretending, or hiding from me. The game's over now. You give us a shout!'

I tried, and had just enough breath to make a small mew, like a kitten.

'Hi there! Can ye hear me?'

I managed to cry, 'Hi!' and then, at the next try, 'I'm by the stone.'

'Stand still then.'

In no time at all he was with me, a little bent gnome of a man, carrying a lantern. He put my fear – I was shaking still – down to the fact that I had been lost.

'That need never worrit you. We watch. We count 'em in and we count 'em out. Come on, now follow me.'

As we walked he told me that once, long ago, when his own father was 'just a little gaffer', some young people had gone into the Maze during the Christmas revels, and all come out but a young lady who was not missed until the next day, and was dead when found.

'I should have died too, if you hadn't found me.'

'Oh no! 'Tisn't freezing tonight. Yon was a hard frost.'

'I should have died of fear.'

'There's naught to be feart of. There's two of us and one is always on the watch.'

'I didn't know that.'

'No. We don't make much of ourselves. People don't like to think they're overlooked.'

I don't think I was any more pious than the next child. I performed my duties and observed the Holy Days of Obligation and the Fast days, but I seldom thought about religion. Now, however, I thought – That is like God, watching our comings and goings, Himself unseen but ready to help in time of need.

From that thought it was only a short step to be wondering whether the face I had seen in the Rune Stone was not really a heavenly vision, and that what the man had been trying to convey to me was not to be frightened. The French girl, Jehan the Maid, had put visions and voices from Heaven in the forefront of everyone's mind. And *she*, I remembered, had been burned for a witch.

Dame Margery, who had not, I think, noticed my absence, because she was so busy with the three sick children, scolded me for giving her needless anxiety, and set me yards of hemming to do for a punishment. Henry and William said I had spoiled the game, they thought I had given up too soon. I said to Henry, 'I gave you the Cry of Extremity and you did not aid me, that cancels all vows.'

I never mentioned my vision to anyone; and perhaps for that reason thought about it the more. Walter and I were born on St Joseph's Day, and I thought it possible that the face I had seen had been that of the Saint. After that, I had a special devotion to St Joseph, and when, around Easter-tide a seller of statues and medallions came round, I broke into one of my gold pieces and bought a medallion of St Joseph and fastened it to one of the cords of my velvet purse.

V

When the next Christmas came round, I did not expect to go home and felt no sorrow about it. The love which I had felt for my mother was now firmly fixed upon Melusine, who was just as pretty, and just as sweet-scented, and who never pushed me away. When Henry moved, with my Cousin Ralph, out of the Children's Dorter at Easter he gave up his lessons, as I had known he would, but, as was the way at Beauclaire, a custom once established went on and on, and it would not surprise me if, in that house, one lady went on opening the Book Room and spending three evenings in it every week, with or without a pupil, until the Wars of the Roses brought all those great houses to ruin.

For ruined they are. I have lived to see things change, and those great rambling houses where three hundred people would sit down to supper every evening, where any traveller of noble rank was welcomed like a brother, where everyone above the rank of knight had his own cook, and bloody battles – sometimes fatal – would be waged in the kitchens over who should use this hearth, this spit, they are gone. The wars between the Red Rose of Lancaster and the White Rose of York are blamed for the change, but I sometimes think they were bound to end, those great establishments, out of their own unwieldiness and waste.

And perhaps because, under all the glitter and splendour, there was something rotten, something that made human beings of small account, and wealth of too much.

Helen Beaufort was older than I, and had already left the Children's Dorter and joined the Ladies'. This had two results for me. Although Helen welcomed the change and thought herself greatly superior to me now, she was lonely at first, and would seize opportunities to talk and tell me bits of gossip which I should not otherwise have heard. And, with her going, I became the eldest in the Dorter, entrusted with certain duties and responsibilities and allowed, in return, certain small privileges. The one I valued most was to be allowed, now and then, to go and read in the Book Room after supper. Whenever I had that permission I would tell Melusine and sometimes she would say that if she could slip away too, she would come and join me.

One evening she *had* managed it and we were sitting close together on the bench, both reading from the same book, which was what I liked to do because it gave an excuse to press close to her. The writing of the book was poor and difficult to read, but the story was so interesting that we read on, taking turns to read a piece.

All at once the door flew open, and when we looked up, startled, it was to see Ella and two other young ladies with expressions of smiling mischief slowly changing to astonishment on their faces.

One of them, Millibrand, said, 'Holy Mother of God! It *is* true. She *reads*.'

Melusine said, 'What did you think I was doing?' Her voice was cool, but her face was red-hot.

'We couldn't believe it,' Philippa said, gazing round the small room. 'There is a Welsh minstrel in the Long Gallery. To miss him, in order to brood over a book that smells of mould...' She turned up her eyes, begging Heaven to witness the unlikelihood.

'To miss him, in order to spy on me, seems even poorer exchange,' Melusine said.

'Ah but – ' Ella began. Millibrand pulled her by the arm.

'We are missing the music. Come along.'

They ran away, laughing and rustling their dresses.

I got up and closed the door which they had left open. As I sat down again, Melusine put her arm around me and gave me a quick hug.

'My good angel!' she said.

'Why?'

'Oh…well, if you had not been here they would have dragged me off with them.'

Now that I was learning something which I enjoyed, and seeing so much of Melusine, and had lost all trace of home-sickness, I was happy at Beauclaire, and my eleventh birthday, bringing with it the thought that the coming summer would be my last, saddened me. I began wondering whether it would be possible for me to stay and in the end join the ladies in the Well Yard Room, instead of being uprooted again and going to Clevely. It was plain to me that I wasn't wanted at home, and, so long as I stayed away, I couldn't see that it mattered to anyone but me where I was. Walter and I had now become competitive about our writing and sent letters to one another twice or three times a year; I would write to him, I thought, early in the summer, perhaps at Whitsun, and ask him to ask Mother if I might remain at Beauclaire. Walter was to me, now, hardly a memory; I had changed so much in these three years, I knew he must have, too; he had become somebody whose writing remained much neater and more stylish than mine, try how I would.

With the summer, life at Beauclaire always became very gay; besides the big Tournament, regularly held on St Barnabas Day, there were several smaller ones, and there were many unplanned entertainments, too; wandering players would come and perform their mysteries, jugglers their tricks, sword-swallowers and fire-eaters their seeming miracles. Most of these delights we children were allowed to share, increasingly so as we grew older. There had at one time been talk of two young children coming into the Dorter, but Dame Margery had argued against it; Constance was now 'getting off her hands' she said, and she herself too old to start all over again. So in that summer of my eleventh year, when even Constance could stay up late without yawning or falling asleep where she sat, we had more fun than ever before.

One day in June – I remember that the garlands and banners from our Tournament were still up – there was a bear-baiting. We children took our places, at the back of the Ladies' Stand. I saw Helen Beaufort sit with the grown-ups, and reminded myself that I had not yet written that letter to Walter. It again seemed unfair, and unnecessary, that next year I should go to Clevely, and should have borne all Dame Margery's training for nothing.

I'd watched bear-baiting before and never been squeamish about it, but on this evening something happened to me. I stopped being Maude Reed, a spectator up in the stands, and entered into the feelings of the bear. I may be wrong, but I think learning to read had had an effect on me. When you read, you must get out of your own skin and into the skin of the people you are reading about; that is the only way to enjoy it.

They'd cut the bear's nose, both to make him savage and to let the dogs smell blood to make them savage, and I began by having a pain in my nose; then, as the fight went on, pains went all over me, particularly low down in my body, where I had never had a pain before, and between my thighs. I sighed and shifted about on the seat, and Dame Margery looked at me reprovingly.

It was a remarkably good bear; dog after dog it dealt with. Now and again, when a dog was clawed or crushed or bitten, my feelings went that way for a moment or two, but in the main I was with the bear, I *was* the bear.

Everybody became excited. The ladies, who must, in all circumstances, remain well-behaved, smiled and clapped their hands and made little murmuring or squeaking sounds; the gentlemen were more noisy, wagering money on whether a dog would 'score' or not, a 'score' meaning a bite which held while one could count up to five; they shouted, and laughed, and yelled the counts aloud, and groaned when a dog they had backed was shaken off too soon.

Presently, even from where we sat, we could smell the blood. Then somebody called, 'Try two dogs at once.' So they did, and the bear dealt with them gallantly and cleverly.

The dogs – some were strays that had been collected and kept for such an occasion, or young hounds which had something wrong with them which made them of no value to their proper sphere – were let loose from one end, of the tourney ground, and presently, from that end, there was a cry.

'Only one dog left, my Lords and Ladies.'

Then it'll soon be over, I thought; and despite all his wounds the bear will have won.

But somebody shouted, 'Blind the bear!' and somebody else called for pepper.

After all that, to have pepper thrown in his eyes.

I knew then that I was going to be sick. I was surprised. The pain in my body hadn't been anything like the belly-ache which often ends in sickness. Nevertheless, I was going to be sick. I pressed my hands over my mouth and made for the stairs which led down from the stand. I was near them, and did not have to push past Dame Margery. I just blundered down and to the back of the stand and then I was sick.

I couldn't go back. Never willingly would I watch a bear-baiting again. I didn't much want to go into the house, either. It would be deserted. Some other entertainment was to follow the baiting; tumblers or mummers were to perform by torchlight. I'd walk about for a little while, I thought, and then, when the poor wretched bear had been taken away, and sand spread over the blood patches, creep back into my place.

From the tourney ground the nearest pleasant place for walking was the old Low Garden, so I went there, not minding being alone there, partly because being alone out of doors was never quite so uncomfortable to me as being alone within walls, and partly because somewhere at the far end of the Low Garden there was the Maze and nearby, keeping his watch, would be one of the old men. I didn't go near the Maze, though, I stayed on a path edged by ancient rose bushes, so long un-clipped that they were almost wild again, but covered with a profusion of flowers, pale pink, striped with deeper colour, and very fragrant. In the mild evening air they shed their scent, and I breathed it in gladly after the reek of blood and terror in the tourney ground.

I walked up and down the path, and every time I turned I could see, at the other side of the overgrown garden, the tall blackish-green hedge which walled in the Maze; and one time, as I turned and looked that way, I saw two figures standing just inside the entry of it. At first my only feeling was of surprise, because I had imagined that everybody was at the bear-baiting. As I looked, wondering who they were, and wondering also why they had avoided the entertainment, whether they had at one time been sickened, too, they moved together and so stood in a long embrace.

By this time, from my reading, from talks with Melusine, from gossiping with Helen and from merely being alive and not stone deaf, I had picked up all there was to know about the relationship between men and women. I knew exactly why this pair had been in the Maze rather than at the baiting and I wondered whether they knew about the constant guard. Then I remembered that the old man had asked me to call out so that he could know my whereabouts, and thought with some relief that that showed that he could not see clean into the Maze, he could only watch the entry.

The man of this pair, whom I did not recognize, broke from the woman's arms and walked briskly away in a direction which would take him to the stable yard. The woman stood still for a moment or two and then took a path which would eventually meet, in a corner, the one upon which I stood. She had hardly taken four steps before I recognized her; it was Melusine. I knew by the way she walked. Recognition had been slow because she was wearing a new dress, scarlet, a colour she never wore, and a narrow, steeple head-dress instead of a wide, horned one.

My first impulse was to run and meet her, then I thought better of it. This had been a secret rendezvous, she might be displeased to know that it had been – at the end – overlooked. So instead of running to meet her where the paths joined, I drew back, and then, when she had passed, followed her. If she went into the house, then I could go into the house too. A little time in her company would be far more delightful to me than the best entertainment in the world.

At the end of the path she turned towards the house, not towards the tourney ground, and I followed her, keeping my distance all the time. I reached the Well Yard and was inside the deep porch when my Uncle Godfrey's voice hailed me.

'The baiting – is it over?'

I told him no, I had come in because I felt slightly unwell. He laid one of his hard hands against my neck, just under the ear, held it there a moment and said, 'No fever.' He smiled and said he hoped I should feel better soon. That emboldened me to ask why he was not at the tourney ground, and he said that he had been watching poultices applied to the leg of his destrier, Tristram, which had suffered a slight injury in the Tournament.

'Will he be better in time for the Dover Meeting?'

'It's to be hoped so,' he said, and we parted. I was inside the Well Yard Room before my mind took notice of the fact that the man who had stood with Melusine just inside the Maze had worn a yellow doublet, and that my uncle was wearing that colour.

I knew by this time that my uncle was a knight without any land or other source of income and that this was an unenviable thing to be. He had, more than once, tried to marry an heiress whose parents or guardians, in their turn, were looking out for a husband with money, and his efforts in this direction were now so bruited abroad that parents or guardians of heiresses looked at him a bit askance. That is what I mean when I say that the whole society of which Beauclaire was a sample was too much concerned with money. My Uncle Godfrey was handsome, kind, good-humoured, and acknowledged to be one of the best knights – some said the very best – in all the South of England. He was a man whom any girl could have been pleased and proud to marry, but he had no money, he could not be seriously considered. On the other hand he was extremely popular with the ladies. In a strange, entirely false, stilted way, it was the fashion, just then, for any married woman who was not positively repulsive in appearance to have a string of adorers who pretended to be in love with her. Perhaps pretended is a harsh word; some of them did, perhaps cherish a hopeless passion; now and again perhaps a lady would slip from virtue, but it was rare; as a general rule the ladies wore their lovers and flaunted them as they wore and flaunted their jewels. Before a Tournament, for example, there was a competition amongst the ladies to count how many knights begged the honour of wearing their favours, just as fierce as the competition presently to be waged in the lists. There was a secret and very subtle game to be played with colours. A knight might ask a lady for a favour, a glove, a scarf, a sleeve to wear in the next event; he might be refused because her favour was already given; he would find out from her body servant what colour of gown she intended to wear, and then he would ride out on the day wearing, somewhere about him, that same colour. In this custom lay the origin of the ladies' hatred for having a gown the same colour as another's. There was another variation of the game, too. The ladies would go to great lengths and show much ingenuity in showing their preferences; my uncle's name being Blanchefleur their task was easy, and at many a Meeting I have seen a dozen women wearing a white flower as a sign that they wished him well and had faith in his prowess. Officially my Uncle Godfrey 'belonged' to my Lady Astallon, he was her kin by marriage, he was part of her husband's household, and she was very beautiful in the manner most admired just then, unreal, inhuman, with her shaved eyebrows and her hair plucked out all about her forehead to make her brow look high and the hair line as even as though it had been painted.

I thought of all this as I went into the Well Yard Room, and found it empty. I went on to the Stool Room; Melusine was not there, but she had been, just before me – I could smell her gilly-flower water fragrance through the faint, stored-up, stink of the place. As I rang the bell I wondered had she gone into the Book Room. But when I reached the door it was locked. I turned back and, at the place where two passages joined, saw two old women; one had the bucket and jug of her occupation, the other carried a mug wrapped in a piece of flannel.

'Traipse, traipse, traipse,' said the stool-emptier, bitterly, 'all day long. And my feet as tender as the bird of your eye.'

'But on the level,' said the other. 'Them stairs are my undoing. And I'll swear there's such a call for ginger, some of 'em must come round twice a month.'

'Who is it this time?'

'The Lady Melusine. It ain't so long since ladies kept quiet about it, and danced the higher and laughed the louder so nobody should know, but *now!* No, we must lay abed and cosset our bellies with hot ginger twice a day.'

'I'd swop with you.'

'And after a week of the stairs you'd be glad to swop back!'

I was close to them now, and I said, 'I'm going up. Shall I take it?'

'Young ladies ain't allowed in the Ladies' Dorter.'

'No one would know. I'd just put it in.'

She looked at me with the suspicion of her kind; nobody ever did anything for nothing.

'Don't you go sipping at it. It's medicine, turn you black in the face if you drunk it without needing it.'

But she handed it over.

I went upstairs slowly and carefully, pondering over why Melusine and my uncle must meet in secret. So far as I could see – quite apart from the fact that they were my two favourite people

– they were well matched. Melusine was not a great heiress, she had a very modest dower, the freeholds of some properties in London, the rent of which was paid punctually four times a year and as punctually expended on new dresses or pieces of finery. Neither she nor my uncle was married, or betrothed to anyone else; her income, added to that he won in prize money, would keep them; she certainly wouldn't need a new dress if she lived to be a hundred.

I had reached the Ladies' Dorter, a room I had never, in all my time at Beauclaire, entered before. It was very large; the walls were painted and all the beds had hangings, some of plain silk, some embroidered with the family emblems of the owner. Great chests stood by the side and at the foot of each bed, and in the centre of the room was a table with several looking-glasses on it. The room smelt of women, of musk, and violet and gilly-flower and lavender, of linen fresh from the washing, of velvet, and under all of human flesh. My not-yet-settled stomach moved uneasily.

Melusine's bed was on the far side of the door; it had plain blue hangings. She had undressed and was lying flat with her bare arms exposed, her hands linked behind her head. She raised herself a little when I entered, and then, seeing me, sat up straight.

'Maude! What are you doing here? You know it is forbidden.'

'Except for two old women we are alone in the house. So I brought your ginger.'

'Why aren't you at the baiting?'

'I was sick.'

'Poor sweet,' she said, instantly sympathetic. 'Look, you drink that posset. There's nothing more comforting to the stomach.'

'I'm better now. It's for you.'

The ends of her lips curved upwards in what was almost, but not quite, a smile; it was a look I knew, and generally accompanied some words of gentle mockery.

'It would be wasted on me. Drink it quickly and then run along. If you are found here...'

'Nobody will come yet. There is an entertainment by torchlight and it isn't nearly dark.'

'Sit here and drink it then. Sit on the bed.' She patted the place and then lay back, linking her hands behind her head again.

'Are you sure you don't want it?'

'That is one thing I am sure of.' So I sat down and began to unwrap the flannel from the mug, saying, 'The servant said that one sip would turn me black in the face.'

'Why did she send you with it?' I explained that I had not been sent, I had offered to carry it.

She accepted – as I realized afterwards – this evidence of my devotion, plumbing its depths by the simple question, 'How did you know it was for me?'

And I said, 'She said so; besides, I saw you come in.'

'You saw me come in?' She was upright in the bed again. 'Where have you been, Maude? *In the Low Garden?*'

I nodded.

'Then you saw us?'

I nodded again, stricken to think how I had given myself away.

She reached out and took hold of my arm; I could feel the heat of her hand through my sleeve.

'That's a secret. It must be kept, Maude, until the end of July. Do you understand? Will you promise?'

'Anything you said was a secret, Melusine, I would keep to myself, even on the rack.'

'My poor dear child, you've never seen a rack! And it isn't so serious. Just till the end of July.'

'And then you will be married?'

She nodded.

'Where will you live?'

'On his manor at Minsham.'

I thought of that cold, bare hall, with the damp dew on the stone walls, the unrailed stairs, the bleak bedchambers above, and of that poor drooling old man, my grandfather Blanchefleur.

'Oh no!' I said. 'Couldn't you stay here?'

She said sharply, 'No!' And then, in an ordinary voice, 'I forgot that you knew Minsham. Tell me about it.'

I described it as well as I could. I also mentioned my grandfather. Melusine looked surprised and said she had never heard of him.

'He may be dead,' I said. 'I last saw him before I came here, and then he was almost dead.'

'The house,' she said, 'it could be made comfortable – if money was spent on it?'

I pictured Minsham furnished with some of the comforts of the Old Vine, some of the elegance of Beauclaire.

'Oh yes.'

'They'll soon be back,' Melusine said, 'you had better go. We'll talk tomorrow. And remember, this is between us.'

I repeated the words which were traditional in the Children's Dorter for the making of any very special promise.

> *Else*
> *May my liver and lights die in me*
> *May Old Scrat fly away with me.*

Melusine laughed and said, 'Oh, the memories that recalls! A most solemn oath.'

I was in my bed and almost asleep when a thought jerked me wide awake again. If my Uncle Godfrey and Melusine were married and went to live at Minsham, perhaps I could go there too. That would be even better than staying at Beauclaire. Thanks be to St Joseph, I thought, that I hadn't written my request to Walter. I wouldn't write now until the end of July, when I could convey the news in any case, and, if I had persuaded Melusine to agree, beg to go to Minsham instead of to Clevely.

She was easily persuaded; she was, I think, genuinely fond of me, and as she said, she would lack company, because my Uncle would be away a great deal. I asked again couldn't she stay at Beauclaire, and I cannot remember whether it was then or another time that she told me what lay behind the secrecy and the need to leave Beauclaire once the truth was out. My Lady Astallon, Melusine said, would be furiously angry.

'But why? Uncle Godfrey is bound to get married some day.'

'She sees no need for it. And if he did she would like to do the choosing for him, somebody he couldn't care for. You see...' she checked herself. 'I shouldn't speak of such things to you, Maude. Here in this room I forget how young you are.'

I would show her, I thought, that young as I was I fully understood the situation.

'He is her lover *in fact*? They bed together?'

'They *did*.'

'Would she have minded his marrying Alys Courtney? There was talk of that, wasn't there?'

'Alys Courtney was very rich. That would have been understandable. She was plain, too. Our marriage will be a very different thing. He loves me, and that my Lady will find hard to accept.'

'I see,' I said; and I did, though not very clearly.

Another time when we were talking – for we now talked far more than we read in the Book Room – I asked her how long she and my Uncle Godfrey had been in love.

'He with me, or I with him? He with me only lately, a year maybe; I with him, oh, years, ever since I moved into the Well Yard Room. The first thing I noticed about you, poppet, was that your eyes were like his.'

I remembered how she had said, 'You have his eyes,' and that simple statement which had pleased me when it was made, because it gave me a feeling of belonging somewhere, now hurt because I loved her and was afraid that all her kindness to me had been on account of that likeness and not for myself.

'A year, eh?' I said, fumbling about amongst the thoughts in my head. 'Then how would you have felt had he married Alys Courtney?'

'How you harp on her! There was nothing in it. My Lady tried to match them, that is true. But Godfrey *loved* me and so nothing came of it.'

That was not the way I had heard it; the failure of the match between my Uncle Godfrey and the Courtney heiress had been reported to me by Helen Beaufort, and she had said that he was willing, eager, the Courtney family reluctant. But then, Helen had a spiteful tongue and would gladly deal me a slap through my Uncle. And Helen, naturally, did not know the truth.

In another of these most exciting conversations I learned why the end of July was so important.

'He'll come riding back from Dover with that great prize in his hand, and then the announcement will be made. In the hall? Is that the way it will be? Oh, I hope I shall be there.'

'Hope that he wins the prize! It will be all that we shall have to live on until my rents come in at Michaelmas. I've been such an improvident, prodigal fool. On Lady Day I had the price of as good a destrier as ever wore harness, and I frittered it away on a new dress and a brooch to go with it, and a ring for *him*. How was I to know that Tristram would take a wound?'

'Tristram. What has the horse to do with it?'

Melusine made her right hand into a fist and ground it in the palm of her left hand.

'This waiting,' she said. 'He must joust at Dover, and he must win. And his horse is unsound. My Lady Astallon has promised to mount him – a Great Horse from Flanders – so well-trained, they say, that if you mounted a sack of flour on him, with a lance fixed, he could unseat his man. Godfrey, with such a horse, could not fail.'

'He won again here,' I said, 'and on Tristram, wounded as he was.'

'He'll win at Dover, a silver cup filled with gold pieces.'

We counted the days to the end of July. I wanted to write my letter to Walter, asking him to ask Mother if I could go and live at Minsham, but of course I must not do that yet, for to do so would betray the secret.

In our counting of the days we reached the place where we could say, 'Only twenty days more.'

VI

Earlier in the summer, in June when the people assembled for our St Barnabas Tourney, some of them had brought rumours that this year the plague was worse than usual in London. Lord Astallon had seized upon this fact gleefully, and said in the Hall, loud enough to be heard from end to end of the High Table, 'There you are! Was I not right to refuse Bowdegrave's invitation to spend the summer in his London house?'

Lady Astallon said discontentedly, 'Your cousin Bowdegrave is now with the King at Windsor, which is full as healthful as this.'

'I doubt it,' said her husband.

And he was right. This year the plague reached Windsor, and amongst its victims were Madge FitzHerbert's father, his wife and the child of their marriage, a boy of five years old. All in a moment Madge changed from being a half-idiot, kept in the Children's Dorter because she was too stupid and ugly to be promoted to the Well Yard Room, into that most covetable piece of property – an heiress.

It was Helen Beaufort, who now knew everything – and who was quite pale and venomous with jealousy – who explained all this to me. Unmarried girls who had great fortunes were always taken into wardship by some man who administered their estates, and arranged a marriage for them, and out of both procedures made some pickings for himself. This was so well known and accepted a rule that the wardship of an heiress would be given away as a reward for service to the King.

'The King,' said Helen, 'is probably at this moment looking around to decide who shall have the privilege of being that ninny's guardian.'

'My cousin Astallon should have it,' I said. 'She has lived under his roof all these years; as far as I can see, nobody else has minded whether she had enough to eat or not, or anything to wear.' It was a fact that any garment more than was strictly necessary which poor Madge possessed had been given to her by me, for I had passed on to her everything my mother had sent me in the way of a present.

'Astallon,' said Helen, 'will never be thought of. He is not near the King, nor has he done him any service.'

'Then it's very unfair.'

'The whole thing is unfair,' said Helen bitterly. 'They'll probably marry her to an Earl.'

'That couldn't happen. She still can't thread a needle for all her riches,' I said.

'If Astallon knew his business,' said Helen in her most adult manner, and probably repeating something she had overheard, 'he'd betroth her quickly to Ralph, or to Henry Rancon, and so keep control for himself.'

Madge's new status, and her future, though a matter of interest to me, was not very near my heart, and as soon as Helen and I parted I half-forgot about it, and went back to thinking about my own future, with Uncle Godfrey and Melusine at Minsham. However, on the evening of the next day I learned that Madge's future was very much my concern, and that Helen's gossiping prophecies had been wrong in only one respect. My cousin Astallon had taken the one way open to him to make use of Madge's fortune for the family good, but he hadn't chosen Ralph or Henry as a husband for the heiress; he had chosen his kinsman, Sir Godfrey Blanchefleur.

Before supper in the Great Hall, in full sight of the whole assembly, up stood the Beauclaire chaplain, silly Madge and my uncle, and the betrothal vows were made. Madge repeated her words in her thick flannelly voice, without any sign of understanding; my uncle pushed a ring on her finger and kissed her on the brow. And all over the Hall people got to their feet and raised their wine cups or their ale mugs and wished the happy couple well.

For a moment or two I was too stunned to think. When I did, my first thought was a thoroughly selfish one. Now I should never go to Minsham! Immediately I thought of Melusine. If I was too stunned and shocked, what, in God's name, was she feeling? I turned my head cautiously and looked along to where she sat. In my heart I saluted her. Men may win honour in battle, and prizes and praise in tourneys, but women have their own kind of courage. You could never have guessed that the scene on the dais meant more to Melusine than to Ella or Philippa or any other of the ladies. She was laughing and raising her cup.

All through the meal – and it was a festive one, with several extra dishes – Melusine's behaviour was so ordinary that in the end it deceived me. I thought to myself that this was just another trick – like getting the Great Horse of Flanders out of Lady Astallon. My uncle had gone through the act of betrothal in order to further some scheme of Lord Astallon's: now, if they sent from Windsor to take Madge into wardship, she need not go, she was betrothed. Then afterwards, when it was all forgotten, the betrothal could be annulled, and my uncle and Melusine be married after all.

That must be it, I thought; and Melusine knew. How else could she laugh and talk as though nothing had happened? I gripped on to this thought because it was the only comfort in my desolation, and soon I came to full belief and felt better.

However, next morning, in the Chapel, the Chaplain called the banns – for the second time, he said. And as soon as we were all back in the Children's Dorter my Lady Astallon came there, a thing rare in the extreme; she brought with her a sewing woman who carried a roll of rich tawny-coloured silk. Madge stood there like an ugly doll while the sewing woman measured her, and my Lady and Dame Margery conversed in voices too low for us to hear. Then the silk was spread out on the table and slashed into by the shears; the sewing woman treated the lovely stuff as though it were the coarsest cheapest homespun. When the gown was cut out, Lady Astallon said something that Alison and Constance and I *did* hear, all too clearly. We were to spend the day sewing the long seams of the skirt, while the ladies in the Well Yard Room did the more skilled work on the bodice, and the sewing woman managed the trickiest part of all, the long, falling sleeves. The wedding was going to be solemnized next day and the dress must be ready.

So it *was* going to happen.

Sewing was the worst occupation for me just then, since it left my whole mind free to brood over my misery, and Melusine's. Presently, I thought – Nothing goes right for me! And all in a moment, the tawny stuff and my needle and thread wavered and blurred; one tear, then another, splashed on to the silk, making dark, star-shaped blotches. Dame Margery, who was watching, quickly thrust her plump white hand between me and the work and made the sign of the Cross.

'Tears on a wedding gown,' she said in a shocked voice, 'the worst possible luck, God and all the Saints guard against it! What ails *you*, Maude Reed, to behave so unseemly?'

I said the first thing that occurred to me.

'This is my morning for lessons; and I do not like to sew.'

'And you dare show me this rebellious spirit, after I have governed you for three years? Shame on you,' she said, and dealt me a clout on the ear. Her hand, for all its plump white velvet look, could deal a shrewd blow. 'Get into the corner and put your hands on your head until you can control yourself.'

She sat down in my place and began to stitch.

In the corner, gazing at the blank wall, I thought about Melusine. I had ceased crying – it is almost impossible to cry with your hands linked above your head – and presently I was able to say, without turning from the corner, 'Madam. I am now controlled.'

'Then you may return to your work.'

'The Lady Melusine,' I said.

'What of her?'

'She will be awaiting me in the Book Room.'

'I doubt that. She will be sewing too.'

'She goes to the Book Room early...'

'Then run along and tell her that you are sewing and she should be. And waste no time. You are to be back by the time I reach here.' She measured off a tiny length of seam.

I held my skirt high and galloped in the most unseemly way to the Book Room, but it was locked. I thought she might have locked herself in, so I knocked on the door and called that it was I, Maude. There was no sound from within. I then turned and ran to the Well Yard Room, which was like running from the Old Vine into Baildon town; only two of the young ladies were there, sewing diligently on the tawny silk. One said that Melusine was in the Book Room, the other said she was in attendance upon Lady Astallon. Just as I was leaving, three others, Ella amongst them, came rustling in, and I asked them if they knew where Melusine was. Nobody knew; and I had already been away much longer than I had been given leave for; so I had no choice but to go back and sew on that hateful tawny silk. I looked forward to the dinner hour; somehow I would make an opportunity to speak to Melusine then, no matter what trouble I brought down on myself.

But Melusine was not in the Hall for dinner; several other young ladies were absent, Helen Beaufort amongst them. Word went round that my Lady had suddenly decided that she had nothing fit to wear for a wedding, and that they were sewing at full speed on a new, wonderful, cloth-of-silver gown.

My Lady having decided to make the wedding properly festive (and from my talk with Melusine I could see that this was, to her, the most welcome match in the world) the Chapel was to be hung with wreaths, the symbol of unity. So first thing in the morning we were all sent out in search of flowers. We children were to confine our search to the Low Garden, which yielded very little: the first flood of flowers was over, the big daisies which grew in the long grass were withering, and the poppies which had taken their place were useless for wreaths as they shed their petals too easily. There were a few roses on the bushes and a few heads of blue bugloss and that was all. Then Alison said she had seen, on the banks of the moat, a great bush of honeysuckle.

'Honeysuckle smells sweet, and it isn't prickly and it weaves well,' she said.

So the four of us – Madge of course was indoors, being washed and made ready – went off to find the bush. Alison had seen it when she went to the bear-baiting, and it certainly was a big, lush-growing bush but it was on the outer bank of the moat and to reach it our shortest way would be across the drawbridge, upon which we were expressly forbidden ever to set foot. William said, 'Who will know? And even if they did, nothing would happen today. It's a *wedding!*'

Alison was in favour of venturing, because the bush was her find, and I didn't care one way or the other, and Constance always did what we did. So we ran across the bridge and set about the bush, pulling off great flowery strands, some of them a yard long. And I thought with what joy I should be gathering flowers and making the wreaths were Melusine to be the bride, and what a sorry mockery it was now.

Then we heard men's voices shouting from the inward end of the bridge, and looked up guiltily, thinking that they were calling us. But they were not. They were looking and pointing down into the water of the moat.

'One of them's dropped something,' William said. 'Look, they're bringing a rope and grapple. Here, you have these...' he pushed all his flowers into my arms, and went scampering off to watch something he hoped would be exciting.

I laid the bundle of leaves and flowers that he had given me aside and went on, dully and methodically gathering more, until I heard Alison, just beside me, let out a kind of hissing breath. I looked at her and saw that she was staring bridge-wards, so I looked that way and saw Melusine brought up from the water.

The hooks had taken her by the middle and she hung in a curve, very gracefully, almost as a girl might hang from a man's arm in a more than ordinarily roisterous dance. At one end of the curve hung her blue-green dress, at the other her silver-gilt hair, both a little darkened by the water and that was all; and, as they pulled her up, the water fell from her hair and from her skirts, in sparkling, sun-touched drops. The thought shot into my head and out again – Even *so*, she is lovely.

Then I began to cry. Clutching the latest-gathered sprays of honeysuckle, and crying wildly, I ran back to the bridge and crossed it. By that time they had laid her flat on the grey stone pavement, and they tried to prevent me going near, but I pushed past and looked down on her. I noticed then, and later took comfort from the fact, that she looked most peacefully happy; her eyes were closed and her lips were almost – not quite – but almost – smiling. My own raucous, gasping sobs seemed an intrusion upon that peacefulness, but I could not stop them.

One of the men took hold of me and told me in a rough, kind voice not to distress myself. Alison came up beside me, and Constance; they stared, shocked, but quiet. 'Come on now,' one of the men said, 'you must go in. Rightly you shouldn't have been there, you know. What's your Dame about this morning?'

Alison and Constance had gathered up all the flowers; they were loaded. Alison said, 'Come along, Maude, we still have the wreaths to make, you know.'

Across the bodice of Melusine's blue-green dress the green slimy strands of water weed lay, soiling, out of place. I laid my strands of honeysuckle over them, thinking, Wedding wreath! and sobbing more and more noisily.

More and more people had come running; there was quite a crowd. Alison said in my ear the most damning of all Dame Margery's rebukes, 'Maude, you are making an exhibition of yourself!'

I knew that, but there was no help for it. I went on crying. One of the men picked me up and carried me into the house.

Dame Margery was kind at first. She petted and patted me and gave me something soothing to drink; then, when I continued to cry, she lost patience, shook me, finally slapped me and forbade me to attend the wedding. So I lay on my bed and wept for Melusine while silly Madge became my aunt-by-marriage.

I knew that crying was useless; all it did was make my head ache more and more; I tried to stop, but I couldn't. Even when every tear was squeezed out of me and I was as dry as sawdust inside, I still went on making the hiccupping noise.

Dame Margery came back from the wedding feast, and finding me still crying, gave me another drink, a poppy-smelling one, which sent me to sleep. But the moment I was awake I was crying again.

They began to treat me – perhaps rightly – as though I had gone out of my wits. I was moved out of the Children's Dorter and lodged in a small room alone. Dame Margery seemed most concerned because I could eat nothing; she was convinced that if I would only *try*, I could do so. Once, she seized my nose and held it until, in order to draw breath, I was forced to open my mouth; instantly she popped in a spoonful of something she had ready at hand. It was a dish of fresh raspberries sprinkled with crushed sugar which was a rare luxury, even at Beauclaire. For me that mouthful had the very taste of misery, and I have never eaten raspberries again, nor indeed any sweet thing at all.

Finally, as though in desperation, they fetched the Chaplain to me.

Remembering that he had taken the betrothal vows and called the banns, and officiated at that farce of a marriage ceremony, I had nothing to say to *him*, and lay on the bed, with my face turned towards the wall, crying and hiccupping, my mind closed to his talk until he said, 'I am surprised. I was given to understand that there was an affection between you and Melusine Talboys.'

'There was,' I said, without realizing that I was speaking at last. 'She was my friend, the one person who was kind to me when I came here, frightened and alone.'

'Then you owe her a debt which you should begin immediately to repay.'

He now had my attention. I cried, 'But she's dead, she's dead. I can never repay her now.'

'Her body is dead. But her soul – and that surely was the source of her kindness to you – is still alive and more in need of help from you, from us all, than ever before. If you had seen her cast herself into the water, would you have stood in a safe place and wrung your hands and wept, or would you have tried to save her?'

'I *would* have saved her.'

The arrogance of that remark he deplored with a small sigh and went on, 'Her state of mind no one can know, therefore no one can say that she died finally impenitent; she *did* die unshriven and her last act on this earth was the sin of self-destruction. She will be long in Purgatory, I fear, poor child. But her time there could be shortened, and her way out of it eased, by you, by your faithful and unremitting prayers. The scales of God's justice are finely balanced, and against the sum of all her sins and her final awful wrongdoing, prayers inspired by love and gratitude would weigh heavy.'

I gave a great gulp and said, 'I will pray.'

'Ah,' he said, in a pouncing, triumphant voice, almost as though he had said, 'I've *got* you!' 'Ah, but are you in a state to pray effectively? This unrestrained grief – as though you were a heathen for whom physical death was the end of all things; this refusal to eat or sleep – as though you too were bent on self-destruction: do these make for a claim to God's ear?' He gave another small sigh. 'You're very young. I will try to put it plainer. Suppose your friend Melusine had deeply offended Lady Astallon and was to be punished, quite rightly, but you wished to plead for some mitigation, would you, do you think, serve any purpose by rushing into the Bower, crying loudly, your clothes in disarray, your whole manner distraught? Answer me.'

'No.'

'Very well, then. If you believe, as you must believe, being a Christian, that Melusine is not that poor dead body, but a living and immortal soul, at this moment suffering the cleansing pains of Purgatory, you will get up from that bed, wash and tidy yourself and eat some plain, nourishing dish. You may have small appetite for it, but our appetites should at all times be under our control. Tell yourself that you eat in order to gain strength because your strength is needed. When you have done these things, come into the Chapel. I shall be waiting for you there.'

Later in my life, when I often heard priests discussed critically and designated 'good' or 'bad', I would remember the Chaplain at Beauclaire. He was, so far as anyone could judge from outward signs, a worldly man, he lived luxuriously, he did Lord Astallon's bidding quite unquestioningly (as in that hasty marriage between my uncle and silly Madge), he was fond of fine clothes, addicted to hunting, not, in fact, a 'good' priest. But, and this I do believe, ordination to the priesthood does convey some power, some authority outside the layman's understanding. And those upon whom that power has been conferred carry it, as a man may carry a lantern. He may keep the horn clean and clear so that the light is always visible, or he may let it grow smoky and smeary so that you might not know that the light was there. It is there, however, and in a moment of emergency it can be produced. So now the Chaplain, without saying anything which was new to me, without even being persuasive in his talk, had altered everything. I no longer saw Melusine as they lifted her from the water, dripping and dead. I saw *her*, as alive and real as she had ever been, suffering the physical pain and the spiritual misery of Purgatory, but knowing that it was only for a season, hopeful, not lost, not despairing.

The effect of this was not only to assuage my sorrow; it altered my whole attitude towards life. I no longer wished to remain at Beauclaire, and as that summer passed into autumn, and the autumn into winter, I began, more firmly every day, to look forward to going to Clevely and joining the nuns. I made no hasty decision about becoming a nun myself; in that mood of religious mysticism which followed my talk with the Chaplain I doubted my own worthiness to take such a decision. When I thought of Clevely I thought of it as a quiet place, with no distractions, where I could spend hours on my knees praying for Melusine without seeming odd or making myself conspicuous. At the age of twelve, having seen only one of the world's many aspects, I was prepared to retire from it.

VII

I left Beauclaire soon after my twelfth birthday. With one exception, nobody seemed sorry to see me go. Madge might have been, but she was gone already, making, with my Uncle Godfrey, a tour of all her estates and hereditaments. The exception to the general indifference was, most startlingly, Henry Rancon, to whom I had hardly spoken a word since he had left the Children's Dorter and become a page.

I had seen him, of course, in the hall and about the courtyards, and I had noticed, in an idle kind of way, that since leaving Dame

Margery's rule his appearance had not improved. He was never very clean and he was often bruised, or scratched, or scarred in some way. He'd grown very rapidly too, and however often he was given a new outfit of the Astallon green, his clothes seemed too small.

On my last afternoon at Beauclaire I was sorting out my possessions and packing what I had decided to take with me in the same little chest which I had brought from the Old Vine. I discarded whatever seemed to me, in my limited knowledge, to be unsuited to life in a nunnery. Nuns, I believed, were vowed to a life of poverty and non-possessiveness, and a girl who went to live with them would need very little.

The other children were in the Low Garden, it being a fine afternoon, and Dame Margery, having seen me employed, took a little nap and then went out to gossip with one of her cronies. When she returned she had Henry Rancon with her. She said, with one of her smiles which were secretive and sly and knowledgeable, 'Maude, Henry wishes to bid you Godspeed. He has remembered some of the mannerliness I beat into him, it seems.'

I had been taught manners, too, so I said, 'That is very kind.'

We stood and looked at one another across the little chest and the pile of discarded clothes. He wore the Astallon green – velvet for pages – and they were supposed to change from their uniform when they went to the stables or out for their exercises, but Henry plainly hadn't bothered; his velvet was rubbed and spotted and he stank of sweat, horse and human. His hair had just been roughly clubbed and should have been washed. He had a long scratch down one cheek and a large scab on his chin.

He said, in a grudging aggrieved way, 'I didn't know that you were leaving until just now, after dinner.'

He spoke as though he should have been informed, and I almost said – What is that to you? But I remembered my manners and said,

'I leave tomorrow.'

'Back to Baildon?'

'Fancy you remembering that! Yes, Baildon, but not to stay. I'm going to the nuns at Clevely.'

'To a nunnery?'

'Yes. I should have gone there in the first place, but they wouldn't have me until I was twelve.'

'You're not going to be a nun?'

I said, and it was true, 'I don't even know that myself. I should like to, but –'

'Don't,' he said. He looked over to where Dame Margery had seated herself in the window, and scowled fiercely. He tried to speak softly but his voice had just broken and he had no note between a gruff growl and a squeak. 'Soon I'll be a squire. With any sort of arms I do well, none better. I'll be a squire, and very soon a knight. Maude, don't, I beg you, decide on being a nun until I'm a knight.' He said all this in a squeak and then suddenly dropped to a deep manly voice. 'You can't be a nun yet, and in four years I swear I'll have my spurs – if I have to break my neck to get them. And ever since we used to play together I've always thought...' He broke off and glared at Dame Margery again, his face going a dark, unbecoming crimson. 'When I'm a knight, I want you for my lady, and you can't be that if you're a nun.'

I laughed, for the first time since Melusine's death.

'If I decide not to be a nun, Henry, somebody else might have the same notion.'

He said furiously, 'But I asked you first!' He tugged at one of his dirty fingers and pulled off a ring; it was of some base metal – lead I should think, from the weight of it – with a zigzag pattern in blue enamel running round it. Even to make it fit his own finger he had been obliged to wad it with a twist of thread, now worn black and greasy.

'Here you are,' he said, groping for my hand and pushing the ring on to my finger, 'I've spoken for you and done it properly, ring and all. You can bear witness to that, Dame.'

Dame Margery laughed.

'It's a bit one-sided, but it'll do for now. Unless Maude cares to say something.' I could tell from the way she spoke that she thought it silly child's play, as I did myself. And then all at once it seemed pathetic that the awkward, blushing boy should be the only one to be serious; and I remembered that it was Henry who had offered to learn to read, so that I could have lessons. I said gently, 'I can't promise anything, Henry. But if you like I'll keep the ring to remember you by.'

'Do that,' he said. 'So then, goodbye, Maude.'

He pushed his head forward and kissed me. Most surprisingly the lips in his rough battered face were as smooth and soft as silk.

Interval

I

THE GIFTS which Anne Reed had, in most cases, fashioned with her own hands and despatched to Maude at Beauclaire, and which had been passed on to Madge FitzHerbert, were not, in fact, such perfunctory and deceptive offerings as the girl imagined. Once Maude was out of sight, the pangs of memory and conscience eased, and Anne could think of, could speak of, 'my daughter' as any woman might.

When Maude's first letter arrived, Anne said, with complacency, to Martin, 'Things have improved since my day; nobody bothered to teach us to write. And you will admit that she sounds happy.'

(The letter had been written in the Book Room, with Melusine sitting nearby.)

It was presently possible for Anne to look back upon her own youth, and with that selective memory common to all whom the years have damaged, to see those early days golden with sunshine, brightened by hope, lively with appreciation of any occasional joy. She was convinced that she, too, could have been happy at

Beauclaire or any other of the places where she had sojourned so miserably, had she not been so wretchedly poor.

As the days went by, she came to think of her daughter as a more fortunate version of herself, just as pretty and graceful, but well shod, elegantly clothed, moving against the background of the Long Gallery, the Great Hall, the Low Garden. One day, she assured herself, when she had persuaded Martin into the provision of a dowry, the elegant, eligible young man of good family, for whom she herself had waited in vain, would pay his court to Maude and all would be well.

Never once did she suspect that her attitude towards the child was that which most people, after the first burst of grief, held towards the dead. Gone away. In safe keeping. Happy now. Anne had never felt that way about her dead, and could not know that she had watched a little girl ride away on a brown pony with the finality with which other people see a coffin lowered into the earth. Anne's dead, Denys, her mother, Richard, were all her victims, to be thought of as little as possible, subjects of the occasional nightmare from which refuge must be sought in the wine-cup.

She had Walter, whom she loved extravagantly, both for himself and for what she could see of Richard in him. Richard's dark hair and eyes, his delicate look, his skill with the lute. Even when, at an early age, Walter declared that he was never going to be a wool merchant, he was going to take his lute and wander the roads and play to admiring crowds, the statement roused in his mother much delight and little concern. Richard had cherished that dream, too. Walter was Richard's son. Upon that certainty she could rest, much of her guilt absolved. As a statement it was not to be taken seriously; he would know better when he was older.

Martin had found him a good tutor, a young man called Nicholas Freeman, who had been trained in the monks' school at Norwich and come very near taking his priest's orders, changed his mind and worked for a time in the office of a leather merchant in Norwich.

At first Anne had attached little importance to him, minding only that he should teach Walter thoroughly and as gently as possible. Walter learned swiftly.

'It will help if I am a scrivener as well,' he explained gravely. 'I can play to please the people and myself, and then if anyone wants a letter written or a copyright made, I can do it and so make sure of my bread.'

To count he refused, absolutely; and, when pressed, twice ran away. He was soon recovered; a small boy carrying a lute was not difficult to trace, and Martin's men knew the roads and were well mounted. He was beaten, sobbed tearlessly, worked himself into a fever and was cossetted, but still refused to learn to count.

'I know all I need to know. I am not going to be a wool merchant.'

Nicholas Freeman, with time on his hands, began to take an active part in the business. Martin's lame leg grew stiffer as he aged and sometimes he found difficulty in mounting his horse. One morning Nicholas asked, 'Would you like me to go for you, sir?'

'You think there is no skill in fleece-buying? They'd sell you anything.'

'My father has a sheep run. I helped him until I was nine. I know all the tricks.'

'Go then. But bring back any maggotty polls and I'll knock their price off your wages.'

The young man laughed.

'With the price of wool as it is, and my wages what they are, that would be to take a quart from a pint pot.'

Anne thought that an impudent answer, but Martin laughed and said,

'I've been doing that all my life, boy.'

Little by little the young man worked his way into Martin's confidence, was allowed more responsibility, was moving, Anne felt, into the place that should be Walter's. On that eagerly-awaited day when Walter should, as she termed it, 'come to his senses', there would be Nicholas Freeman standing between him and his grandfather. Martin seemed to find him easy to talk to, and sometimes as they sat at table she would study them both. The young man wore, for a clerk, a very healthy look, as though his farmyard tan had survived the years in cloister and counting house; in a slightly saturnine way, he was handsome, with bright hazel eyes, brown hair and excellent teeth. Beside him Martin's lined face looked old. Old, she would think, and he never spares himself. Suppose he died, before Walter settled and knew anything of the business; we should depend upon this stranger, and he might cheat us, we are so ignorant.

Spurred by the fear of material loss she began to take interest in the business, listening, asking questions, sometimes venturing a suggestion. Martin, after the initial surprise, took refuge behind the immemorial barrier, 'Nothing for you to bother about, my dear,' 'You wouldn't understand if I did explain,' and 'Leave all that to us'.

With Nicholas she had no better luck; he was a vain young man and had from the first resented her manner towards him; he rebuffed her gleefully, saying, 'Why not discuss this with Master Reed?' and once, 'Master Reed engaged me and it is to him that I render account of my doings.'

The years went by. The twins' twelfth birthday came. Walter showed no sign of change of heart, but so long as he was allowed to go his own way he was amiable and inoffensive. When she thought of Maude, Anne imagined her moving from the Children's Dorter into the Well Yard Room at Beauclaire and taking her place with the young ladies. Upon that thought, Anne braced herself for the tussle with Martin concerning the dowry. If he remained obdurate, she had one other hope: Godfrey, now married to the FitzHerbert heiress, was extremely wealthy; he might do something for Maude; he should do, out of gratitude for what Anne had done for him, long ago.

She had entirely forgotten that she had ever intended to send Maude to the nunnery at Clevely. That had been a move in a secret game, won at the moment when a little girl rode through the archway on a brown pony.

But Maude had remembered that she was to leave Beauclaire when she was twelve; Dame Margery remembered it too, and so did Lady Astallon. And one lovely April morning, on that same brown pony, now too small for her, Maude came riding home.

II

On a sunny morning, about a fortnight after Maude's return, Martin Reed came down to breakfast with some of the pain lines eased from his face. He flexed his lame leg two or three times as he sat in his chair and said, with satisfaction, 'This weather suits me. I shall ride out to the Minsham run today.'

Two years before, the whole of Suffolk had been ravaged by sheep tick fever, and in replenishing his flocks Martin had tried an experiment. He had brought – with great expense and labour – sheep from the Cotswolds, where, in the greater cold of the high hillsides, the animals which flourished were the ones with particularly thick fleeces. He had been resigned to the possibility of the sheep growing lighter wool once they were on pastures less exposed; but that had not happened in their first year. He was anxious now to see for himself what difference a second winter had made.

'Like to come with me, Maude?' he asked.

'Oh yes, I would,' she said, eagerly. Then doubt and uncertainty clouded her face. Since the moment when the Chaplain at Beauclaire had given her a new aim in life, she had made some advances of her own. Self-denial was good, as well as prayer; a thousand small sacrifices of comfort or pleasure might 'count', if offered in the proper spirit against the pains which Melusine was suffering in Purgatory.

Perhaps, she thought, imagining the pleasure of riding out in the sunshine, she should retract that acceptance and go instead to church, kneel until she was dizzy, pray until she was tired. That would 'count'.

But her grandfather's face had brightened and he was already considering which horse she should ride. She hadn't the heart to withdraw. Presently, at Clevely, there would be time and opportunity to make everything right.

So they rode out together, and for some time spoke little and of trivial things. He explained about the sheep from the hills. He said, in a disgruntled way, that he had last year asked Walter to ride out and see them and that Walter had said a sheep was a sheep and no more. Cuckoos were calling from every thicket, and he described to her how, as a boy, birds – nesting at Rede on a precious Good Friday holiday, he had seen a cuckoo throw a blackbird's egg from a nest and settle down to lay her own.

It was talk to interest any child, and over Maude's response there was the patina of Dame Margery's training – not enough to listen and be interested, one must *look* interested, give signs of pleasure, encourage the talker to go on. Unaware of this, Martin simply found his granddaughter most pleasingly responsive; he found himself telling her things that he had never told anyone, things he had once, long, long ago, planned to tell Stephen and Robin when they were old enough to listen to his tales.

Thinking of them, which he seldom did nowadays, made him feel very old. Sixty-six this year. Forty long years had sped since the priest at Rede had told a stalwart young man of twenty that half his life was already sped. A long life, and superficially dull, work and work and work again. Two great sorrows, some success, several disappointments. And now, towards the end of it, here he was, riding alongside his granddaughter and feeling, under natural affection, something more lively stir.

He broke the silence by saying abruptly, 'You didn't mean what you said the other day about going to live with the nuns, did you?'

'Oh yes,' she said, without any hesitation, 'I meant it. I have to.'

'What does that mean? Your mother? That was all some silly idea she got into her head when there was talk of sending Walter to school. She said it would be unfair to send him from home and keep you. But the nuns wouldn't have you then. So she wheedled me into letting you go to Beauclaire. Against my will, I may tell you. And now you're home, and if I have any say in the matter, there you'll stay.'

'I can't go without your permission. They ask five pounds a year for my keep. And I must take a bed and blankets, linen. But I should cost as much at home.'

'Cost!' he said. 'Cost. That is nothing to me. You stay home, Maude, and I'll show how little cost matters. I'll buy you a grey mare. I know where to go – a fellow at Flaxham breeds them and trains them to paces that suit a lady. They have manes and tails like floss silk. You shall have a grey mare, Maude, and silk dresses, and a gold ring, a ring with a blue stone to match your eyes.'

She closed her eyes for a moment and prayed one of the simple, unorthodox prayers which had become almost a habit.

'All this, God! You alone know how badly, at Beauclaire, I wanted a proper mount. The dresses too, and a ring with a sapphire. I'll sacrifice them all for one hour of Melusine's sojourn in Purgatory. Please take it, God. It is mine to give. I could have it, and I refuse it.'

She opened her eyes and said, 'You are very kind. You help more than you know. But I must go to Clevely.'

'Why?'

It is his five pounds, she thought; his money pays for the bed, the blanket and the linen. He has the right to know.

'It is all so sad. I'm afraid that if I speak of it, I shall cry.'

'Your mother,' he said, trying to be helpful. 'You must mind this. Mothers tend to like their sons better than their daughters, and when the pair are twins it shows more. You mustn't mind her, Maude. Let her have Walter. You're my girl.'

'All this, God, too! Please count my grandfather's favour which I am about to forego, against one hour of Melusine's torment.'

She said, 'It has nothing to do with Mother. I know how she feels about me; and it must be very hard for a mother not to like her own daughter.'

'Dear God, that is tolerance. I learned that very hard, could that count too? Just a minute. Because it was *so* hard to learn. Please, of Thy mercy, just a minute.'

'Then *why*? ' Martin asked in a grating and impatient voice, 'why do you say you *must* go and shut yourself away there, when I want you home.'

A long and horrible story. Something which in its entirety she had never had to tell. The Chaplain had known the details.

'When I first arrived at Beauclaire...' she began, and Martin tilted his head sideways, the better to listen. She told him everything. The story ran smoothly at first and then was broken, like a stream which in its course runs over rocks. When she came to the recountal of Melusine's body being taken from the water, she leaned forward over the pommel of her saddle and wept, and Martin, speaking for the first time since the story started, said, 'There, there, say no more, I understand.' And he saw himself with his head pressed against the cold, smoke-blackened stone of the buttress of the Abbey wall, and then, falling prone, nursed in the lap of Old Agnes. To love hard, he thought, that is in our blood. For that reason I struck through the red mist and hit my master; for the same reason I cherished that mountebank, Pert Tom, and Old Agnes. I paid it tribute when I brushed aside, as though it were a cobweb, the almost certain proof that Magda had witchcraft in her; and years later I pandered to Richard over the matter of his love for Anne Blanchefleur.

'But I must say more,' Maude said, wiping her gloved hand across her face, 'because how otherwise can you understand? The Chaplain...'

She told him of the interview with the Chaplain, of her restoration to life and hope, of the task which he had laid upon her.

Martin listened attentively, thinking at first, with deep irritation, that this was all the result of her going to Beauclaire, but presently his mood changed. He realized that when she spoke of Melusine she did so as one would speak of the living, that she had achieved what all Christians should, but rarely do, do, the power to look upon death as an incident, not as the end. He compared this with his own feeling in similar circumstances. Kate, Stephen, Robin, and then Richard, all, to him, irrevocably dead. And God non-existent. Brought face to face with a faith so simple and unquestioning, so urgent that this child was plainly prepared to govern her whole life according to its requirements, he felt a thrill of almost superstitious awe. Not for him to oppose her decision. At the same time something in him rose in protest. When he spoke, he did so slowly and carefully.

'You don't feel that you could pray, and be self-denying and all the rest of it, equally well at home? Nobody would interfere.'

She shook her head.

'You see that would be doing what I want. All the end of time at Beauclaire I did want to go to Clevely. But since I have been back…Days like this,' she said, looking around at the fresh young green of trees and meadows, all a-glimmer in sunshine. 'No, I know what I should do; and I hope that you will give me permission.'

'I'm sorry you stumbled upon heart-break so young,' he said. 'I was older when the blow fell on me. And I had no faith. You have that comfort. And if you're set on Clevely, you must go. Promise me one thing though. Don't think that going there means that you must be a nun.'

'Oh, I'm not nearly good enough for that.'

He ignored that. 'It'll be some time before you have to make such a decision; I may be dead by that time, so I'll say my say now. It means having no husband, Maude. That may not matter; in most cases I think wanting a husband is something that wears off after a time. But it means no child, and that's a different thing. Women, unless there's something very queer about them' – he remembered Magda – 'need children, live through them. I've seen a woman, aye and she was hungry too, give her share of a poor meal to a child who had gobbled down his own. There's all kinds of love, my dear, but none to touch that. I wouldn't wish you to forego it. That poor drowned girl was friend to you, and if you feel she's in Purgatory and your praying and fasting for a couple of years'll help, I've nothing against that. You mustn't make a life job of it.'

I'm a clumsy old fool, he told himself. Maybe I've gone and put the idea into her head. With a return to his gruff manner he said, 'There's Minsham Old Hall. You want to see your Grandfather Blanchefleur?'

'Not today,' she said, averting her eyes, so that she should not see the place about which she and Melusine had held those long, happy conversations, made so many plans. The memory revived her revulsion for money, money and the greed for it which had brought about the whole tragedy. And even her grandfather's kind offer of a grey mare with a mane like silk, of fine dresses and a gold ring – all to do with money. I will have none of it, she thought. Once again she thought kindly of Clevely, where she would be free of it all.

PART FIVE

Nicholas Freeman's Tale

I

WHEN MAUDE REED came home to her grandfather's house in the April of 1447, she was just twelve years old, and I was twenty-three: a full quarter century too young, one would have supposed, to be attracted by a girl of her age. And age was not my only safeguard: I am by nature unsentimental and cynical; I was at the time happily provided with a mistress who suited me; and I had already, in the most practical and coldblooded manner, made up my mind to marry Maude in about four years' time whatever she was like, even if she were the spitting image of her mother, whom I disliked.

Martin Reed himself put the idea into my mind. He was one of the least communicative people I ever had to do with, but even he, when in particularly low spirits, or provoked, would seek some relief in talk. Several times, when Walter had annoyed him, he would speak of Maude, saying that twins were tricky things and the girl had been born with all the sense: saying that since Walter refused to have anything to do with the business, the one hope for it was for Maude to marry some decent, steady man, capable of running it.

Why should not I be that man? I was already, in addition to teaching Walter all he would consent to learn, keeping the accounts, and being trusted, day by day, with more of the practical side. As far as Master Reed could know, I was as steady as Baildon Tower; decent, too, for I had learned by experience: my new mistress lived some distance away, and was safely married. Her husband was a game warden whose duties, most conveniently, took him abroad at a time when I was free of mine. In four years' time, I thought, I should be twenty-seven and ready to settle down; Maude would be sixteen, and unless her grandfather and her mother changed their ways, she would have had little contact with men. The Reeds were singularly friendless people. In Baildon, indeed, Master Reed was hated, though farther afield he was held in respect as an honest man and just.

Not being a fool, I realized that my plan to marry my master's granddaughter was very vague and vulnerable. When I joined the household at the Old Vine, the child was placed with one of Mistress Reed's noble relatives. Mistress Reed was highly connected, and had married the woolmaster's son for money – by the cast of countenance she usually wore, I judged that it had been a bad bargain: she had a very discontented look. She was mightily devoted to her son, and, I thought, to her daughter; she was always stitching away on some fine article of clothing to send to the girl at Beauclaire. And from a few words dropped here and there by Master Reed I gathered that the mother's ambition was that her daughter should marry back into the class to which she herself belonged. But there the matter of dower was paramount, and the old man was obstinate.

'I'm not laying out my good money as bait for some young popinjay,' he told me, once. 'It wasn't by my wish that the girl ever left home. She was a merry little thing and I missed her sore.'

I thought over that statement; Mistress Reed had had her way once; she might succeed again.

There was very little that I could do to influence events, so I did not worry. I made myself as indispensable to my master as I could, was civil to Mistress Reed and patient with Walter and lived comfortably for three years.

Then Maude Reed came home, and I fell in love.

At the time it seemed unaccountable, even to me. Now that I am middle-aged and accustomed to wealth and power I understand my young self better. I am a lover of, a collector of, beautiful things, and to me for a thing to be beautiful it must have a touch of the exotic. Anything that is lovely and unusual either in workmanship or material is to me irresistible; the moment I see it, it makes an immediate impact and appeal, and I am not easy until it is mine.

Maude was Walter's twin, and I had expected her to be like him; it was hardly necessary to make allowance for the difference in sex, for Walter's looks were girlish: he had a slim, seemingly boneless body, soft dark hair and large dark eyes with long lashes.

My first sight of Maude, therefore, gave me a surprise. I looked, looked again, found myself unable to look away from her. And even now, after many years, I find it impossible to say exactly what it was that so charmed me. It was a face that *meant* something. Not pretty. Not young even. Already, at the age of twelve, her beauty was the beauty of the ageless, undamageable skull. It showed in her brow, in her cheek-bones and jaw. Her eyes, which were very blue, were set back in hollows, and below the cheek-bones her face was scooped out, too. Her nose was low between the eyes, and then jutted out, blunt-tipped and wide-nostrilled. The lips of her mouth were long and both flat and full, and on either side lines had already formed, lines of fortitude, or perhaps of humour, a little on the wry side. The hair which was revealed when she threw back her hood was a warm reddish brown, crisp and springy.

For the rest she was somewhat taller than Walter, and, though delicately made, not without bone; thin square shoulders, bony wrists, long, clear-jointed fingers. No breasts yet; and as I stared, wondering at myself and seeking some reason for my interest and for feeling as I did, I suddenly bethought me of the carved and painted angels in the roof of the St Mary Chapel in the Abbey. Her beauty, like theirs, was of angle and plane, not of curve, and, like theirs, it was sexless, and, despite what her grandfather had said about merriment, on the sombre side. I had always had a weakness for small, plump, smiling women.

She was noticeably ill-dressed in a gown that had been lengthened, not very skilfully, and was still too short, especially in the sleeves. Mistress Reed had every reason to start demanding where was this and that garment, recently despatched to Beauclaire. Maude said she had given the things away.

'In Heaven's name, *why?* '

'I had sufficient without them.'

Mistress Reed gave her a look of intense exasperation and then asked, 'What is that you have on your finger?'

'A ring,' the girl said, clipping her other hand over the ornament protectively.

'Show me!'

She held out her hand unwillingly and withdrew it quickly. We had all seen the clumsy, ill-fashioned thing and the dark mark, like a bruise, which the base metal had left on her finger.

'Tawdry rubbish. I should have thought that after three years at Beauclaire you would have known better than to wear such trash. Where did you get it? At a Fair?'

'It is a keepsake; from a friend.'

Mistress Reed, through her delicate, high-bridged nose, gave a sort of snort, and said, 'The things I sent you...good sound things, you gave away!'

'Yes,' Maude said.

They stood eyeing one another like wrestlers, each of whom has once thrown the other, and who now hesitate to try another fall. I saw that I had been wrong in thinking Mistress Reed devoted to both her children; she had no fondness for her daughter. And as Maude stood there, very straight, defiant and yet oddly vulnerable, I was conscious of a wish to take her part, to protect her. It was a feeling quite new to me. But after all, we have, every one of us, a weak point. The most hardened blasphemer has one name he holds holy, and once, in Norwich, I heard a triple murderer on his way to the gallows call to someone in the crowd, 'Look after my owd dog!' Maude Reed was my weak point, the place where ordinary rules no longer held. I began to love her at that moment; but there should be another word for it; there should be several words to cover the widely diverse feelings for which we can only use the one word 'love'. I loved myself; I loved my amiable, cuddlesome Bessie; I loved Maude. Three very different uses of the word.

Maude had been home only a few days before I had an opportunity to serve her, to please her, and to put myself into her favour. She chanced to say that Walter wrote a much better script than she did herself. It was at table, where generally I was content merely to look at her.

'Who taught you?' I asked.

'One of Lady Astallon's ladies.' I saw her eyes change colour, the black centre expanding until the blue was a mere rim. I had noticed before that light-eyed people, however strictly they rule their expressions, betray themselves thus. 'Her name was Melusine,' she said, and looked down.

Now Melusine is an unusual name, the name of a character in a French romance. Just the name, it seemed to me, to slip into the mind of a young girl who, for purposes of concealment, tells an unpremeditated lie. That could be thought over later. I said smoothly, 'Ladies seldom have the advantage of being taught by a cloister-trained clerk. My teacher was a famous penman. If you like, demoiselle, I can show you, in a very short time, how to better your script.'

At my use of the word 'demoiselle' Mistress Reed and Master Reed both looked at me, the former with surprise and a touch of approval, the latter with one eyebrow cocked sardonically. It was a term of courtesy, used only towards young ladies of high birth, and not one to slip easily from the tongue of a clerk.

'That would be very kind,' Maude said gravely. Then she smiled and her whole face was transfigured.

Mistress Reed, who liked me very little, could not forbear saying, to me, 'I should have thought you had enough to do, without taking on any more.'

And to Maude, 'You would be better employed with your needle. You write as well as you will ever need to.'

'Not if I go to Clevely,' Maude said.

For the first time since she had entered the house, her mother looked at her kindly, almost lovingly.

'You wish to go to Clevely?'

Before Maude could answer, Martin Reed brought his hand down on the table in a smack which made the platters jump.

'We'll have no talk of that,' he said. 'You're only just home. There's a whole long summer ahead. You stay here, learn to write, read if you want to, be a bit of company about the place. There's Walter, always on the fidget. I want no more of it.' As though fearing an argument he jumped up and limped away.

'If you wish to go to Clevely you shall,' Mistress Reed said, looking at Maude and then quickly away again in the way she had. 'I shall support you.'

'If you do, you're mad,' Walter said. 'Shut in, doing the same things, seeing the same people day after day. I'd rather be dead.'

'Nobody,' said Mistress Reed, in the soft fond voice which she kept for her son, 'is suggesting that you should go to Clevely, Walter. We're talking about Maude.'

'I came home to go to Clevely,' Maude said. 'It was all arranged, long ago, wasn't it? When I was twelve, they said. I thought it was settled.'

'Of course, of course,' Mistress Reed said hastily. 'There was just the likelihood of your preferring to stay at Beauclaire. So the final negotiations were never...but it will be all right, I am sure.'

I saw then how those lines, so out of place on either side of a young mouth, had been made. The girl knew, as well as I did, that her mother wanted her out of the house. How far that knowledge had influenced her decision to go into a nunnery as a lay boarder – which was all she could be at her age – I did not know, but, with that curious extra sight which infatuation lends, I could see, with painful clarity, that upon this matter of going to Clevely she was in two minds; half of her mind welcomed the idea, the other half rejected it.

I rejected it absolutely. I knew very well that dozens of girls every year went into convents as lay boarders; it was the fashion for girls of good birth to go and spend some time in the company of nuns, most of whom were well-bred, educated, capable of inculcating good manners, a smattering of learning and a shrewd business sense in their charges. Most of the girls emerged, little or none the worse for their cloistered years; a few became novices. Of that few, half – invariably well dowered – went on and took vows. An ordinary girl, going as a lay boarder, would have a likelihood of, say, one in twenty of becoming a professed nun.

But I wanted Maude here, in the Old Vine, here with me, susceptible, malleable. There was something about her, a kind of other-worldliness, that would make her very open to persuasion. I had been schooled by monks; I knew how insidious mere atmosphere could be. I knew also how greedy – not as individuals, but as a community – any professed religious body could be. Maude Reed's dower would be a tempting bait. Especially to Clevely, which was surely the poorest house in all England.

Walter had by this time given up even the pretence of taking lessons from me, so when, at the time arranged, Maude came to the schoolroom, we were alone. I took a clean piece of parchment and across the top of it wrote the alphabet in small letters and in capitals.

'There it is,' I said, 'and the secret is to make each letter sharp and clear, with points rather than sprawling, circular strokes. And with the capitals be sparing, write as though ink were gold – it is with gold that the great penman wrote, you know – not to be wasted. You see, economy, economy and clarity is the result. You try now.'

She was twice as teachable as Walter, though about writing he had been eager and good. In no time at all she had mastered the better style. Presently, looking up, she said in a defensive way, 'You mustn't judge the teacher by the pupil, you know, Master Freeman. Melusine wrote beautifully.'

Anxious to ingratiate myself, I said, 'Of that I am sure.' I then asked, as casually as I could, 'You were fond of your teacher?'

For a moment I thought she was about to cry; but she set her mouth, deepening the lines each side of it, and merely nodded her head.

There sprang into my mind a complete and feasible theory. There had been a writing master at Beauclaire – I could see him, sly, meek and ingratiating – and although he would not dare aspire to the affections of one of the high-born young ladies, the woolmaster's granddaughter would be within his range. Something had happened, discovery, scandal perhaps, and so she had come home, a trifle broken-hearted, and ready, with girlish impetuosity, to fling herself into a nunnery. Or again, he, in his cunning, might have suggested that, it being the safest place where a girl could wait a year or two. Was it his ring that she wore?

The coarse, cheap thing was prominent on her hand as she wrote, and presently I ventured to say, 'I think your ring is very pretty.'

With something of her grandfather's bluntness, she said, 'Oh no. Nobody could think that! But I like it.' Once again she put her other hand over it and held it fast. At the same time her mouth took on such a tender look that I detected, beneath that carved wooden angel exterior, the possibility of great sensuousness. With a quickening of my own blood I thought – He kissed her when he gave her that trinket.

I bore him no ill-will; what has been done once is the more easily done again, even if it is falling in love with one's writing master. She was very young; he was faraway and I was here on the spot.

Then I remembered that she was going to Clevely.

I let her write for a while; then I said, 'You read as well as you write, I imagine.'

'Tolerably well.'

'It is a pity, then, that you will have small chance to practise either art at Clevely. It is a very poor house and the Ladies are few. They work in the fields and the dairy.'

'How do you know that?'

'We buy their few poor polls of wool – or did, until they lost their sheep from the tick fever. I've seen the Ladies, their habits hitched up, working like hinds.'

She said, dreamily, 'I like to read and write; therefore Clevely will be all the more suitable for my purpose.'

'Your purpose?'

'Something I must do.' As she spoke she reached out for the pen-rag and wiped the point of her quill clean; stood it in the stand; rose to her feet, and after a few words of thanks to me for the lesson, walked away, very graceful and dignified.

I felt rebuffed; I tried to feel resentful, too, but the genuine feeling would not be evoked. For the first time in my life in connection with any female I was inclined to self blame. I should not have dared presume, on so slight an acquaintance, to question her.

Master Reed continued obstinate about Clevely. Once, through a half-open door, I heard Mistress Reed ask, in a quiet, cutting tone, 'Is it that you grudge the five pounds a year for her lodging?'

'You know better than that. I'm thinking of her happiness.'

'It is her own choice.'

'Of that I must make sure.'

The weather warmed, and one day Maude and her grandfather went out together. When they returned he had somehow convinced himself that her desire to go to the nuns was genuine. I could see, by his glumness, that he had been convinced against his will; nevertheless, without further protest, the preparations for her leaving began to go forward.

I now began to be concerned, for the first time in my life, for another person's creature comfort. On my wool-buying visits to Clevely I had seen inside the house; the nuns had no Frater even, they ate at a table at one end of the kitchen, which had a floor made of trodden earth and walls of undressed stone, running with dampness. I had not seen the rest of their accommodation, but I imagined that it would be equally comfortless. For a professed nun, vowed to poverty and self-denial, such surroundings might be, ethically, more right than the ease and luxuries that some communities enjoyed; but I hated to think of Maude in such a place.

I was silly enough to make one last effort to dissuade her. It was not planned, would indeed have been impossible to plan, for since the writing lesson which had ended so abruptly there had been no chance and no reason for us to have speech in private.

On this evening, just after supper, I was in the office, doing an extra hour's work. The weather had changed again and for the time of year it was bitterly cold, with a driving rain and a howling wind. Even for the sake of Bessie's embraces I was not prepared to ride three miles out and back again on such a night.

The door opened and I looked up crossly, expecting to see Mistress Reed, who had the annoying habit of coming into the office now and again when she knew her father-in-law was not there. She'd turn things over and ask questions – some of them, I admit, shrewd ones; and sometimes she would make suggestions which I would ignore and then, in my own good time, present as my own.

It was not Mistress Reed, however, it was Maude, who, from the threshold said, 'I thought my grandfather was here.'

'He's gone to bed. In weather like this his leg troubles him.'

'*We* trouble him too. I could see that at supper. So I thought…'

It was true that at the table Walter had once more referred to the time when he would travel the roads, playing his lute. Mistress Reed's expression had changed from discontent to piteousness, and the old man had looked first at Walter, then at Maude, and heaved one of his tremendous sighs. Disappointed in both his grandchildren.

I heard myself saying, without any of the respect or the desire to please that formerly I had used towards her, saying, in fact, quite roughly, 'I'm sorry for your grandfather. Walter is past praying for; he was born with this bee in his bonnet. But the poor old man had hopes of you. Piety can be as selfish as anything else and, if you stayed at home and cheered your grandfather's last years, Almighty God would probably count it more of a virtue than wearing your hands out in the Clevely dairy and your knees on the Chapel Floor.'

She looked at me with wide-eyed astonishment, as well she might. I was astonished at myself.

'I'm not trying to acquire virtue for *myself*. What made you think that?'

Master Reed, who had been in the office before supper, and who felt the cold, had lighted the fire; it had burned down now to a heap of ashes, fitfully glowing pink under a coating of grey. I had got to my feet when Maude opened the door; now I turned and threw two billets of dry wood on to the fire, and then, reaching past her, I closed the door.

'Come in and get warm, it's one of the last chances you'll have,' I said, in that same brusque way. 'I know what I'm talking about. I went to Clevely for their last lot of wool in the month of May and Dame Clarice Gracey, who acts as Treasuress, still had chilblains to the elbow. *In May.* She had her sleeves rolled up while she weighed the wool.'

Maude gave a little shudder, moved her hands together, twisting the ugly ring, and then moved towards the fire and sat down on the settle, holding her hands to the warmth.

'The worse it is, the better. Don't ask me why. There are some things that shouldn't be talked about. It makes them seem...' she paused. 'It makes them seem less real, less important. Can you understand that? I have a reason for going to Clevely. I told it to my grandfather, because I thought he had the right to know, and because I wanted to speak of it...yes...there was that, too. And ever since,' she turned her head from the fire at which she had been staring and looked into my face, 'it hasn't seemed so real or so urgent. I've begun to wonder...' She paused again. 'I believe that you could, if you wanted, talk a thing clean away, make it be nothing.'

I had seated myself on the opposite settle, and now, leaning forward, I said, 'Try. Tell me why you think you must go to Clevely. Maybe then you won't want to go.'

'That is what I fear. Except that...there is this in it, the less I *want* to go, the more it will count if I do.'

'Count? Count against what? Come on,' I said, 'you can tell me. Another fortnight and the Bishop's hands laid on me and I should have been a priest, qualified to hear any confession and advise on any matter. Imagine that! So you see, you can tell me anything.'

Like all women she went off at a tangent. They do it, not deliberately, or because they are incapable of sticking to one line of thought – as any man who has been nagged can bear witness; they do it for the same reason that a partridge, whose nest is in danger, will go limping and flapping away, deluding the intruder into the hope that she can be taken by hand. It is a defensive measure.

'I did not know,' Maude Reed said, 'that you were almost a priest. What stopped you?' She spoke as though I were a runaway horse, grabbed by the reins.

I could hardly tell her what was my chief reason – that I knew myself unable to live celibate and should tire of pretending to be; my other reason was enough.

'I'm a farmer's son, with no family and no wealth to count on. For me, the ladder to promotion was set very steep and lacked several rungs. Besides, I preferred the life of a layman; a priest should have a vocation.'

She nodded, gravely, and her hair changed colour where the firelight caught it.

'I know. Something – just a little thing it was too – happened to me and made me think there was something in the world, after all. But there is a long time before I have to decide about a vocation.'

'You make such a mystery of it all,' I said brusquely, 'talking about a purpose and what will count and other vagaries. You're far too young to take life so seriously. I'll tell you what I think...'

'Yes?' She looked straight into my eyes.

'I think that at Beauclaire you had a bad attack of puppy love and something went wrong with it, so you go jumping into a convent like a scalt cat. It's very silly.'

'I'm not jumping into a convent. I'm only going to live at Clevely for a time, as anyone might do.'

Quite a lively temper, too, I found myself noting with approval. And another defensive tactic.

'I'll hazard a further guess,' I said recklessly. 'Your bit of heart-break at Beauclaire was concerned with your writing teacher – the one you call Melusine.'

Dear me, that brought a result for which I was not prepared. She gave me a wild look and half rose, and then dropped back, laid her arms on the side of the settle, put her head down and began to cry.

I've heard dozens of women cry, with cause and without, and the most I have ever felt was a mild pity if they had what I considered good reason to weep, a testy impatience if I thought otherwise. Maude's tears seemed to come from my throat, her sobs to rend my chest.

I went down on my knees by the settle and put my arm round her and began to talk rubbish, saying that I meant no harm, that a little sentimental attachment was nothing to cry about, that I would sooner lose my right hand – what things people say in the endeavour to be persuasive! – than cause her a moment's pain. I reverted to childishness and referred to myself by the name that no one had used since I went, a boy of nine, to the monk's school at Norwich, 'Tell Nick,' I pleaded, 'tell Nick all about it.'

She did too! Melusine and Uncle Godfrey and Madge FitzHerbert and how everything depended on money, and what an awful world this was. I kept my arm round those thin little shoulders and held her steady, and pulled out my sleeve and wiped her face on it. I hated all the three that she talked about, because they had hurt her. The wench who'd lifted her skirt before the ring was on her finger was dead and beyond ill wishes; I wished a pox on the other two; and on all at the great house who had let such a situation develop, not seen what was afoot, and then, after the end of it, let this child carry her grief all sealed away in loneliness.

Presently, when she had cried herself out, I asked, 'This is what you told your grandfather?'

'Yes. But I must *not* cry. I promised not to cry about it any more.'

'Who made you promise such a daft thing?'

'The chaplain.'

Pox on him, too, I thought; a few good crying bouts and the wound would have begun to heal. She actually said, in a sad way, 'There, now I've told you and it seems even farther away.'

'That is why miseries should be talked over, not bottled up.'

I left her then and put another log on the fire and again sat down opposite.

'Now listen to me,' I began. I raked through my mind for any scrap of comfort to offer her. Heresies I could have gone to the stake for poured from my lips. I told her that there wasn't a word of evidence of the existence of Purgatory in the Bible. That Christ never exhorted anybody to pray for the dead. That the descent into Hell mentioned in the Creed was a man-made myth. 'On the Cross, to the dying thief, Christ said, "*Today* you shall be with me, in Paradise", what could be plainer than that?'

My years of training for priesthood now served me, in reverse as it were; I was persuasive, logical, like a lawyer who can plead this side of a case or that, according to who hires his tongue.

The result was disappointing; she listened, but was not convinced. The point I thought most telling she countered with, 'That man was only a thief; not a suicide.'

'Your friend had been wronged,' I said. And then I paused, remembering that I had wronged at least two women in precisely that same way, and never until this moment had a pang of conscience about it. 'Nobody can judge in these matters. She may have been acting in a spirit of self-abnegation; if she was with child, and had a family who would have shared the disgrace. If you want to make a disputation about it, theft is forbidden in the Commandments, there is no mention of suicide there. And if you care to be strictly logical, Christ Himself was the outstanding suicide of all time; at any moment *He* could have called down an army of angels to rescue Him.'

In my eagerness to comfort her I had gone too far, forgetting that I was talking to a child of twelve. I saw horror dawn and grow in her face and savoured the full irony of having done myself deep damage in her estimation, simply through pity. I stopped speaking.

She said, 'Now I know where I have seen you before. It has bothered me, not being able to *quite* remember. In the Maze at Beauclaire.'

'I never was there.'

'Not you. Your image. In the Rune stone.'

It was my turn to stare. And it was my turn – I who have always been impatient of women who told long tales about their dreams, and sceptical of those who claimed to have had premonitions – to listen to the story of a supernatural experience, which had at least one redeeming feature of being comic. She described the man she had seen in her vision, and whom she claimed to be me, in full Cardinal's wear! Maybe I had missed my mark after all.

'You were trying to convince me of something, just as you were just now. And I knew you were wrong, as I know it now. Though I am sure,' she added with magnanimity, 'you were trying to be kind. And I'm sorry to have made such a show of myself. The first thing we were supposed to learn at Beauclaire was self-control.'

'Of which,' I said, 'as with many another thing, a certain amount is very good, and too much deadly poison. The one thing I wish for you – because it would mean happiness in the end – is that you shouldn't act hastily over this matter. It was a shock, and you've brooded over it in silence, and the whole thing has grown out of all proportion. If you spent, say, just the one summer here, living an ordinary life and trying to keep your grandfather cheerful, I'm quite sure – '

She said, 'You know what they say in Suffolk when temptation offers, "Get you ahind me, Old Scrat!" I must say it to you.' She smiled, with the tear marks still damp on her face. 'I know what I must do, and I am going to do it.'

Master Reed could be stubborn, and Walter was obstinate past all reason, and she was of their blood. But there was something other than obstinacy, there was something almost piteous in her last words to me that evening, 'Besides, even if I wished to defer going it would be awkward; everything is prepared.'

And that was true. Mistress Reed had brought her undoubted capacity for industry and organization to bear upon getting Maude's clothes and household goods ready for Clevely with such effect that when, on St Barnabas' Day, she left the Old Vine for the second time, two pack horses were needed to carry her gear.

II

I had never cared much for Mistress Reed, thinking her cold and proud, admirable only in her devotion to her children, and in that I was but half right. After seeing her with Maude I liked her less and, because she had encouraged the girl to leave home, even hastened her going as far as possible, I began to detest her. Her punishment was on its way, however, and I sometimes wondered how far she had herself helped to fashion it. How could anyone account for Walter Reed, who was, of all the people I have ever known, the most peculiar?

His mother was ordinary enough; she had married beneath her, but when one compared the home from which she came with that to which she had come, that was understandable enough. She had never, I am certain, entertained a thought, or experienced an emotion, uncommon to her kind. She preferred her son to her daughter, but then thousands of women do that, but conceal the fact, perhaps out of deference to their husbands who usually have a fondness for their daughters and govern their sons strictly.

Walter's father, who had died young of the lung rot, was by all accounts ordinary, too. He was musical, and rather better educated than some merchants' sons, but everything that was remembered about him indicated that he had been industrious and businesslike and sensible.

Whence then Walter? How did two such ordinary human people ever breed that changeling child?

He cared for nothing but his music. He accepted his mother's adoration without the reciprocation of even the most tepid affection. He condescended to learn to read and write because those arts would, he thought, be useful to him when he was an itinerant musician. For music he had some talent; he could pick up the words of any song, however long it was, at one hearing, and from a fragment of a tune, hummed or whistled, he could reconstruct the whole. He also made good songs of his own. Mistress Reed, up to a point, encouraged him, often remarking that he had inherited his father's ability – that was how I learned that Richard Reed had been musical. Even when he talked of his future, although one could see that the thought of his leaving home cut her to the heart, she was curiously infirm of mind, saying, Oh there was a long time to go before he could think of that, saying when he was older he would have more sense, saying that his father had talked the same way and settled down to business in the end.

His grandfather's attitude towards the boy was equally uncertain; he was deeply disappointed, as any man who had built a great business out of nothing and then finds his heir scorns and repudiates it, would be justified in being. But never once did he make an open protest or seem to realize that a child could be governed and controlled. In the first three years of my time at Baildon the harshest thing I ever heard him say to Walter about his wild-cat plans was, 'All right, if you go, when the time comes, you go. Don't keep talking about it!' And even that order Walter disobeyed when he felt like it.

Twice in those three years Walter, after some row over his lessons, had run away and been brought back. Excused from learning to count – which in any case he was completely unable to do; he left home at last still counting on his fingers – he settled down until the summer which followed Maude's going to Clevely.

During that summer, in August, the height of the pilgrim season in Baildon, there was an incident, trivial but curious, which I remembered years after, when Walter's fate was decided.

He came in, on that warm, dusty evening, a little late for supper, his face flushed, his eyes fever-bright and his whole manner that of one who moves in a trance. He sat down, and ignoring the food before him, told us that he had been playing his lute in the market-place. Those who had listened had given him cakes and fruit and sweetmeats and a variety of small trinkets. He laid them out on the board; a little image of

St Christopher, a knife with a horn handle, a belt buckle and a money pouch made of plaited straw.

'They had no money to spare,' he said, 'but those who had...look!' He opened the pouch and spilled out six or seven shining farthings. 'They liked it so much that they paid me! They paid me!' he said.

His grandfather looked at the coins as though they had been earned by blood, fraud, prostitution. Mistress Reed looked at them as though they were her death warrant. I simply stared, thinking – Well, if he can earn that much in an hour, he's cleverer than most; a good thatcher working from dawn to dusk earned a penny and a half in the day.

Mistress Reed spoke first. She said, 'Of course they liked your playing, Walter. You play extremely well. I always said so. But you mustn't take all this,' she pointed to the stuff on the table, 'as proof that you can make a living playing the lute. You see, you are very young and rather small, so they think that it is *marvellous* that you should – '

'The Devil take your tongue,' Walter cried. All the blood went out of his face, leaving it the colour that I had only seen before on a corpse. 'That isn't true. They liked it, I tell you. No matter about me. When I sang of the Death of Roland they wept. Great rough men. One man said, "What magic is this. I have not shed a tear since my child died, and what is this Roland to me?" He said that with tears running down his face. And then you say it is because I am small.'

He would have been weeping himself, had he been able, but he never could cry; he could sob and moan, but I never saw him shed a tear.

His mother shrank back as though he had hit her across the face, but his grandfather leaned forward and said in a voice of controlled fury, 'Never, in all my days, have I known a boy speak so insolently to his mother. She spoke for your good and she spoke the truth. So, in the market-place a few fools praised you, and you come home calling on the Devil. You ask pardon this minute, or I'll give you what I should have years ago, a damned good hiding.'

I watched, with great interest. When I first came to the Old Vine the boy's choosiness over what he would and would not learn had been attributed to my failure to manage him. Let them learn.

Walter looked defiantly at his grandfather, but the old man was not to be outfaced. Set in their myriad wrinkles, under the scowl-scarred brow, his grey eyes bore down, unflinching. Walter's stare flickered and wavered. He put out his hands and gathered all the things he had laid out for display, as though they were his defence and consolation. Across them he said, 'I ask your pardon, Madam. But truly it was not because – '

'That will *do!*' Master Reed said.

There was a silence at the table, broken when Walter picked up his little silver coins and passed them lightly from hand to hand. Mistress Reed leaned forward and seemed to be about to speak, but though her lips moved and her throat jerked, no sound came. She lifted her cup and drank, set it down, and then, rather like a woman who has heard evil tidings, put her hand over her mouth and the lower part of her face. Her hands, I noticed for the first time, were like Maud's, very long and thin, the finger joints clearly marked.

I saw Master Reed give her a sidelong glance. I thought that this was where I, one of the company, yet not emotionally concerned, should make some tactful, impersonal remark which would smooth over the awkward moment. Before I could think of one, Master Reed, in a casual way which contrasted sharply with his last manner of speech, said, 'It would serve you right, Walter, if nobody spoke to you for a week. But that would punish your mother more than you. You'd better ask her to say that she forgives you.'

Walter said as meekly as possible, 'Please forgive me, Mother.'

Master Reed then seemed to be affected by madness. He hit the table with his hand and said, more furiously than I had ever heard him speak, even to a pack-whacker who had foundered two horses, 'God's blood! Can't you just for once do what you're told?'

Mistress Reed again moved her lips and tried to protest, but the old man thundered on. 'I said, ask her to say she forgives you. Do it, or I'll break your neck!'

By this time every eye in the dining hall was turned towards our table. Mistress Reed, ever mindful of formalities, moved a hand in a gesture very eloquent and graceful to draw Master Reed's attention to this fact. He shook his head like a horse tormented by flies and kept his eye on Walter, who, after a minute, said, 'Mother, please say that you forgive me.'

The words came from her like liquid from an upturned bottle.

'I do, Walter, I do. I shouldn't have said what I did. Of course they liked your playing.'

'Now mark this,' Master Reed said, 'when you lose your temper and say things like "Devil take your tongue", that is a plain invitation for the same ill wish to fall on you. You be mindful of what you say.'

I admit that, on the face of it, it was no more than any man might say to any child, a mere paraphrase of the old adage about ill wishes coming home to roost; but the way he said it gave it weight and importance. It was almost as though he believed that Walter's angry words had affected his mother's speech; as though the grandfather believed that the boy had a power to ill-wish, and wanted to warn him, privily, against inflicting hurt.

Rubbish, I told myself, superstitious nonsense. The one power which Walter Reed possessed was the one of making people think that he played better than he did. In the main he was secretive about his music, shutting himself away in the solar and playing for hours alone. On these occasions when he would say, rather pompously, 'Now I will play for you,' I always reminded myself that I had been schooled at Norwich where the choir is famous, and had twice heard Blind Hob of Lincoln play for the Leather Merchants' Guild in that same city. But always, before the end,

Walter would have me, and with all judgment suspended I would fall under the spell, too.

During the time immediately after Maude's departure, whenever I heard Walter play I would ask myself whether both these children hadn't been born with a curious power to charm, Walter by his music, Maude by just being. Walter's charm ended when his lute was silent, but Maude's could survive her absence. I thought of her, not always sentimentally, sometimes critically, at almost every moment during the day when my mind was not actually engaged upon some immediate business. I would try to recall her face and succeed only partially, making a picture in my mind of a blur dominated by one over-prominent feature, the way one does when someone tries to describe a person unknown. 'He has a big nose' they say, and you see just a nose. So I would think, in turn, of her blue, deepset eyes, the hollow in her cheek, the turn of her lip or the way her hair grew. Then, at another, unexpected time, I could recall the whole of her, down to the nails on her fingers. I thought of her, at such times, much as a man on short commons would think of some favourite, flavoursome dish. I craved to see her, and when, one day early in December, Martin Reed said, 'I take it Maude will come home for Christmas,' I wanted to jump up and shake him by the hand, slap him on the back, give loud and obvious evidence of my approval.

'I take it Maude will come home for Christmas,' he said.

Mistress Reed said in a doubtful voice, 'I don't know about that. Nobody mentioned it. Would it be allowed?'

Forgetful of my place, I said, 'Of course it would. Who could prevent it? She isn't a novice, or even a schoolchild. She can come home when she wishes.'

'So I should think,' Master Reed said.

'I'm not so sure.' Mistress Reed looked me in the eye and said, 'You were schooled by monks; did you go home for Christmas?'

She'd heard me say – the cunning bitch – that I did not.

'My home was thirty miles from my school, Madam; and in return for my lessons I sang in the Choir. I could not miss the Christmas Masses. The cases are hardly comparable.' I almost added – and it would have been true – Except that my brothers didn't want me home, any more than you want Maude.

'It shouldn't be too difficult to find out,' Master Reed said in his dry way. 'Nicholas can write a letter, which I will sign.'

'But are you sure that it is wise to unsettle her so soon –?'

'Holy Virgin, you talk as though we wanted her there, Anne. She took this whim to go, but if she's outlived it there's nothing I'd like better than to unsettle her. Unsettle, that's fool's talk.'

Mistress Reed said with cold dignity, 'I'm remembering my own childhood, always on the move and longing for some settled place. That was all.'

'Well, if you can't see the difference,' he said angrily, and snatched up his mug, drank from it and set it down with a clang.

Later, in the office, he stamped about, bringing his good leg down heavily.

'I'm the customer, ain't I?' he demanded of me. 'I pay five pounds a year for her to be there when I'd pay four times the amount to keep her at home. You can tell them that if you like. The whole thing was a mistake from beginning to end. She should never have gone to Beauclaire. Beware of women, my boy. You don't have to be in love with one for her to lead you by the nose and you don't notice till too late. Get your things and write. How do you address a Prioress? You should know. Now I'll say what I want to say, and you wrap it up so she'll not think she's dealing with an ignorant old fellow.'

My former visits to the nunnery had been made after the shearing season, when the sun was warm and the fields green; even then I had been struck by the dreariness of the place, set all alone, far from the highway behind a barrier of trees. The House and the Chapel were both shaped like hay-stacks built of dark, dressed flint, the least cheerful of all building materials. They were linked

372

by a kind of cloister, begun in stone and finished in wood; some of the pillars retaining their bark. Immediately in front of the cloister was a little herb garden, at this season bleached and depleted, but as neat as a piece of embroidery. Everything at Clevely was as neat as it was bleak.

The only door in the House opened directly upon the kitchen, and there was no portress here. My old acquaintance, Dame Clarice, answered my knocking, told me that the Prioress was ill in her bed, and without ceremony opened the letter.

'This is for Maude to decide. You may ask her. Let me see, Tuesday. You'll find her in the dairy.' She indicated a door immediately opposite the one at which we stood, and said, 'At the end of the passage.'

I stepped in, aware at once of the smell of a religious house. Ordinary people on their way home from Church shake the incense odour off into the air; professed religious on their short cloistered walk carry it with them to mingle with the scent of boiled onions and stockfish and the porridge that burned, very slightly, in the pan. With this smell of my schooldays in my nose, and my heart jumping because I was, in a moment, going to see Maude again, I walked along the cold dim passage, feeling suddenly young and unsure of myself.

I could hear, before I reached the dairy door, the sound of girlish chatter, once a merry laugh, mingled with the clatter of pans and the swish of a scrubbing brush. Perhaps she was happy here, I thought, and perversely took no joy in the thought.

There were three of them in the cold dairy, all wearing coarse sacking smocks over their clothes, wooden clogs on their feet and linen hoods covering their hair. One was engaged in scrubbing the shelves, one, on her knees, was scrubbing the floor, the other was scouring a bucket. The three faces turned to me with looks of surprise, then the one who was kneeling scrambled to her feet and said, 'Oh, Master Freeman, is anything wrong?'

Even as I assured her, I was thinking to myself – Name of God, yes! Wrong that she, who had never been full-fleshed, should have grown so much thinner; wrong that her hands should be so red and swollen, the nails broken short and grimed from the dirty water. I told her my errand and for one unguarded moment pure pleasure lightened her face, only to go out again like a blown candle. She said in a wooden way, 'I thank my grandfather for so kind a thought; but I had best stay here.'

'He is counting upon your presence. Would you ruin his Christmas, when in the course of nature he can have few more? Remember what I said to you about selfishness.'

'And you remember what I said about Owd Scrat!'

I longed to pick her up in my arms and run with her, out of the place; to shake the obstinacy out of her. I could only use words, and I was choosing, out of my own hurt, the most wounding ones I could muster, when the bucket scourer came to my aid.

'Oh Maude,' she said, 'please go home and bring us back some Christmas fare. Raisins,' she said, in an ecstatic voice.

'Ham,' said the other, and I swear that her teeth shone for a second like a hungry dog's. 'Ham for me, Maude. Please. We'll do your work. You go home and bring us back some goodies.'

'A fine impression we shall make upon Master Freeman,' Maude said. 'He'll think us entirely governed by our appetites.'

I took note of the conventual 'we'. I said, 'You see, demoiselle, at the cost of a very slight sacrifice of your own self-esteem you could mightily please three people – these and your grandfather.'

'Four,' she said. 'I should myself be pleased.'

'Five then, for I also should be…delighted.'

'I should have to ask leave.'

'It is already given. Dame Clarice said that it was for you to decide.'

'The words must have *choked* her,' cried the girl who had asked for ham. She giggled and put her hand to her mouth.

'Not for twelve days, then. Four.'

'Good Maude. Kind Maude. The sooner I shall have my raisins.'

Maude made a gesture of impatience, and moved towards me and the door. We went out together and she pulled the door closed and leaned against it.

'You must not misjudge,' she said. 'They are both orphans and have lived here for four years. We have enough to eat.'

'That I beg leave to doubt. You've grown very thin.'

'We eat with the nuns and they work far harder than we do.'

'You and they, in there, are growing,' I protested.

'Which we shouldn't do if we lacked sufficient nourishment.'

'There's no arguing with you. Shall I fetch you on Christmas Eve?'

'If you have time to spare.' She smiled at me and I saw that her odd little face, which so easily assumed an expression of melancholy, could just as easily shape itself to merriment. Martin had mentioned that she was a merry, hoydenish little girl. I cursed once again the bad management, the ignorance and false values that had brought her to *this*.

Yet there was no denying that six months at Clevely had done a good deal to lighten her misery of spirit. During those four days of Christmas when my eyes, whenever possible, were upon her, as though they could never look their fill, I noticed that the old haunted look of desperate unhappiness had gone, and been replaced by a serenity which had a beauty of its own. Life at Clevely might be harsh and comfortless – some of the things Maude let slip shocked even her mother – but it seemed to be spiritually satisfactory and I, watching every blown straw that betrayed the wind's direction, saw several ominous signs.

Mistress Reed, as before, grumbled about her daughter's clothing. Why was this one dress so much worn, had Maude donned it every day, and why, where were the others? She was little pleased to hear that Jill was wearing one and Avice the other. Even I, doting as I was, detected a certain priggishness in the way Maude said, 'At Clevely we have all things in common.

Except shoes. Feet vary so much. But,' she added as though in extenuation, 'we share the clogs.'

Mistress Reed said, with a tartness which I understood, 'That calls up the three-legged race which children run.'

Maude laughed.

'So it does! I should have said that we wear any clogs which come to hand, or to foot.'

I recalled how teachable she was; in six months she had mastered the art of Christian imperturbability, as one of my teachers had called it.

Then again, at the well-spread table, the question of convent food arose.

'When you go back,' Master Reed said, 'that is if you insist upon going back, I shall send some hams and salt beef, and good wheat flour.'

Maude said, and hate the word, as any man of sense must, there is no other, *demurely*.

'That would be very much appreciated. Dame Winifred Challis, who often has sick poor people in the guest room, is mostly at her wits end to find them tasty dishes.'

'You mean you wouldn't eat what I sent?'

'Oh, no. We all eat from the same dish. Even the Prioress.'

'Going hungry is no virtue,' Master Reed said. 'Thousands of people live their whole lives without knowing the feel of a full belly. You're enjoying what you're eating now, aren't you?'

'Oh, yes. Very much. But to eat like this every day would be gluttony.'

How well I knew it, this prate about the deadly sins! It could have only two effects. Hearing it often enough the young must give in, accept that to enjoy a comfortable bed was sloth, to eat a good meal was gluttony, to think one independent thought was pride, and on and on, until in one day of ordinary living you could commit the whole seven, twice over. (Whoever named them, did so cunningly: murder, which comparatively few people are tempted to, is not among them, anger; which every man must feel, is.) The only other way for the young to take is plain rebellion, bouncing away in the other direction, as I myself had done. Was Maude capable of it? That only time could tell.

In the privacy of the office Master Reed loosed his complaints. 'I've worked very hard, and at times been ruthless to see my family secure and comfortable; now the one I care most for might as well be a scullion. Better. Scullions grow fat on the dripping.' He scowled at me. 'I always thought food was plentiful in such places. They hand it out. When I was first lamed I lived on what was given me at the Abbey Alms Gate.'

'It varies,' I said. 'All religious are supposed to be vowed to poverty. Their interpretation of it varies, and some merely disregard it. I believe Clevely is genuinely poor. They never managed to replace their sheep, and so lost what piteous income their wool brought in.'

His scowl lifted.

'I'll give them some sheep. How many could they look after properly without unduly adding to their labours? Three dozen? Fifty?'

'They had eight, if I remember rightly, before. I don't know how much pasture they have.'

'Ask when you take Maude back. I'll give them what they can take, of my good Cotswolds from Minsham. And I'll buy every handful of wool at top price. That should help them to feed those poor girls a bit better.'

'It wouldn't benefit Maude in any way, sir. The sick poor might fatten. And you'd be putting the gyves on Maude tighter than ever. Once make Maude a supply line between you and Clevely, and next time you see her she'll be in novice garb. I know my monks, and nuns differ from them only in ways that have no effect on greed.'

He said, 'I think you're wrong, Nicholas. Oh, right about the persuasion, possibly, but wrong as to the result. My family is naturally perverse. I believe if they tried to coax her *into* a habit she'd run home and turn Lollard.'

'You say that, because she resisted our persuasions.' I saw one of his eyebrows twitch when I said 'our'. 'Yes, I tried to talk her into waiting, at least. But we were arguing against something that she felt she should do; and we were only using words. They – if they do try to persuade her – will be arguing for what she feels she should do, and words will be the least of it. Inside every community there is an atmosphere, a kind of mental climate which is very difficult to withstand.'

He gave one of his enormous sighs, and said, as he had once said when Walter was under discussion, 'People do what they must, I suppose. But in this case,' he scowled as he sought for the words he needed, 'I never can feel that this is something that was in Maude and must out. It's been brought on from outside. If you knew what drove her to religion, you'd understand what I mean.'

'She told me the whole story, once. And sorry hearing I found it. *One* person had been kind to her in her loneliness, so she fixed on her the whole affection of a young and tender heart. And then the only word of real comfort she was given came from a priest. The result was inevitable.'

There was a pause and I thought he was finished with the subject, but he said, 'I failed her, too, perhaps. I thought of my own griefs – over which by this time, God knows, the grass should have grown. I envied her the certainty of her faith. I said as much. And I was wrong.'

'As to that,' I said, 'I answered her with no faith, only with logic. It was a waste of breath.'

He gave me one of his sharp looks.

'You seem to have a...' I thought by the way his lips shaped he was going to say 'a fondness', he amended it, 'an interest in the girl.'

I said boldly 'I am very fond of her, sir. Who could help it? Her looks are charming, her mind is lively, and even her obstinacy shows a good spirit.'

He was pleased; it showed in the softening of his harsh old face. Then his eyes narrowed, as though he were regarding a bale of wool, assessing its weight and value.

'Her mother,' he said slowly, 'is often somewhat harsh towards her. You notice that?'

'Too often. I am tempted at times to forget my place and speak up in defence.'

'Ah,' he said, as though some question had been asked – not in words – and answered in the same fashion. 'And you are now, how old?'

'Twenty-four.'

'You know the business; you are trustworthy and healthy, as handsome as a man needs to be. And twenty-four. Are your affections or interests engaged elsewhere?'

I told him, No, which was near enough to the truth as mattered.

'Then I'll tell you, Nicholas; if I could wish one wish, it would be that in two years' time, or three, you and Maude would marry. I could die easy then.' I muttered some deprecating words about time being young yet, and being honoured by this proof of his confidence and liking. Never again did the matter come into the open; but the words had been said; and if justification of my action was needed, later on, there it lay.

III

The next two years seem to me, when I look back, to have been as long as any other ten in my life. At Master Reed's insistence Maude came home at fairly frequent intervals, always for Christmas, for the birthday she shared with Walter, and again, either in August or September; between these visits time sagged and dragged.

I had always held that any man who suffered any avoidable trouble or pain was a fool, and after Maude had gone stubbornly back after that first Christmas visit I made great efforts to rid myself of my infatuation.

I tried a change of mistress. My Bessie was as cheerful and cuddlesome as ever and I was fond of her, but I had become increasingly aware of some lack in our relationship. It was a coupling of the flesh only – a business with which I had always hitherto been supremely content but which now seemed to fulfil only half my needs. I had only just determined to do something about this, when an astonishing and unlooked for piece of luck came my way. Mistress Reed's brother, Sir Godfrey Blanchefleur, he who was responsible for all the trouble that had sent Maude to Clevely, came down to visit his mad, moribund old father at Minsham and was shocked by the conditions in which he found him. It chanced that on one of the manors he had gained by his marriage he had found some distant relative of his wife's family, a widow with two young sons, living on sufferance. He spent a little money on making Minsham Old Hall weather-tight and slightly more comfortable and installed this lady, with three good servants, to rule the household.

Clemence Kentwoode, had she possessed the minimum of money or property, or even been childless, would not have remained a widow for a week; she was pretty, witty and amorous. She had the smattering of learning, and the grace of manner, common to her kind, and although, at first, the greater freedom and independence which life at Minsham offered pleased her, she was soon desperately lonely. For me it was an easy conquest, but as soon as the excitement of the advances, and the novelty of the affair, had worn off, there I was, in no better case than before. Worse indeed, having proved the failure of any substitute, however delightful. I was still in love with a child, a sanctimonious, sentimental, stubborn child.

And then, suddenly it seemed, a child no more. It was the birthday visit when she and Walter were fourteen years of age. I went, as had now become customary, to escort her home on the afternoon of the twelfth of March, and the moment I saw her I noticed the change. The sexless, carved-angel look had vanished. Though the Clevely diet and her growth upwards had assured that no flesh should accumulate on her bones, from somewhere Nature had found material enough for little pointed breasts which pressed against the material of her plain grey bodice, pulling it taut. The child had become a woman, the joy-giver, the child-bearer.

For me that was a miserable holiday; she seemed to have turned shy, losing what frank and confident friendliness she had ever felt for me. Nor was I the only one to suffer. Master Reed had bought her, as a birthday present, a fine gold ring with an inset sapphire, a trinket both valuable and beautiful. At the sight of it she burst into tears in which my experienced ear detected unmistakable hysteria and, holding one hand over the ring she had brought from Beauclaire, sobbed out that at Clevely nobody was allowed to wear more than one ring.

Her grandfather, with what I considered admirable restraint, said, 'Well, wear them turn and turn about, then!' She turned, and, sobbing, flung herself upon him, putting her hands about his neck and saying that he had always been so good to her and she did not wish to displease him. He patted her, awkwardly, and said, rather as though soothing a frightened horse, 'There, there. There, there. It's all right. Don't upset yourself. There, there.'

Mistress Reed, with a look of controlled loathing said, 'If this is cloister hysteria, we want none of it here.'

And where, I wondered, in her restricted life, had she heard of 'cloister hysteria', that ease in the shedding of tears which, alongside its opposite, stoic fortitude, is reckoned a virtue by all those communities who must make virtues or sins out of every natural thing. Her words inevitably made me take Maude's part and I said, 'Sudden contrasts are very upsetting. At Clevely she has so little and here she has so much. I remember when I was at Norwich we were all, for some prank which no one would confess to, confined to Dorter and Frater for a week. Then we were let out, and in the grass a single daisy had flowered. We all wept at the sight of it as though we had received news of bereavement.'

'That,' Mistress Reed said with cold dignity, 'is exactly what I mean. Cloister hysteria. We don't want it here.'

Maude pulled herself free of her grandfather's patting hand.

'You mean you don't want *me* here. That is nothing new. You never did. I've known for years that the sight of me affronts you. Everything you've ever given me was a sop to your conscience. I know. And you need not worry about my bringing the cloister here. I shall not come here again. When I go back I shall begin my novitiate.'

Martin Reed banged his hand on the table.

'Enough!' he said. 'That's enough. In all my days I never heard such a to-do over nothing. You, my girl,' he looked at Maude, 'will never be a novice with my consent. Five good pounds a year I paid them for your keep and never in all my dealings have I had worse value for money. That'll stop. Tell them that. If they take you in a veil they take you bare. See how they like that. As for you,' he swung round and faced Mistress Reed, 'all the wench said was true. Out of the house, first to Beauclaire, then to the nunnery. Why, God alone knows.' He reached out and snatched up the ring which had precipitated the scene, and tossed it towards me. 'Take it,' he said, 'give it to your leman. She can sell it and buy one of her boys some bit of gear that'll set him on the road to knighthood.' He spat out the word as though it were an obscenity and rushed on, 'That's been the ruin of us all, pretensions, with nothing behind them, sacrificing decent sober hard-working people and silly little girls who love the first person to speak a kind word and fine gentlemen so fine they'll wed lunatics for the sake of their acres...' He had, on the whole, been coherent up to that point, then he began to mutter and babble.

I jumped up and went to him and took him by the arm.

'Master Reed, you are unwell. Let me help you to your room.'
His weight, greater than I had reckoned for, defied me. I said to
Walter, who throughout the whole business had sat watching,
detached and observant, 'Give me a hand.' He came forward
unwillingly and took the old man's other arm. We got him to bed
and sent for the doctor, who bled him and diagnosed a fit of the
choleric humour. No meat, he said, and no wine for two days,
and we were all to take care not to anger him; he advised, too,
that during the two days of low diet the old man should remain
in bed.

So next morning, speaking as usual, looking pale after his
blooding, Master Reed said, 'Send Maude to me.' My heart,
which had been very low since those words about the novitiate,
rose a little. He looked very pitiable, propped against his pillows,
and she, I knew, was fond of him; maybe he could talk her round.
But I found, when I went in search of her, that she had gone
already, stealing out before breakfast and taking one of the yard
boys with her to bring back her horse.

I began then to think seriously about my future. With Maude in
a nunnery and Master Reed likely, according to the doctor, to fall
down dead any time he was crossed, my prospects were not
promising. It was too late now to begin insinuating myself into
Mistress Reed's favour; in the event of my master's dying I should
be out on my ear smartly.

Up to that time I had been completely honest in my dealings,
which included handling considerable sums of money and
negotiating even larger ones. But from that St Joseph's Day I
began to emulate the Unjust Steward in the Bible story, whom
Our Lord Himself praised for his foresight rather than blamed
for his dishonesty. I was very careful, never taking more in coin,
or making as a false entry more than could, at a pinch, be
regarded as a genuine mistake; and it was all the easier because
after that birthday visit and Maude's running away my master

began to decline, not only in body but in mind and spirit. He began to talk of Maude as though she were dead, and sometimes he would call her Kate, and then catch himself.

I said to him once, 'You mustn't despair too soon. Every novice doesn't take vows by any means.'

'Despair,' he said. 'It isn't that. It's acceptance. It all goes by rule and the rule laid down for me was that Walter the smith's son should never have anything.'

Then he said, 'Did I say Walter the smith's son? My memory plays tricks. I knew him as a boy. It's I who must lose all I gain.'

'Oh come,' I said, 'You've been very successful in business.'

'Yes, I've got a good business.' He said it as though he mocked himself and it.

When the time came round for the five pounds to be sent to Clevely, he sent it meekly; and charged me to tell Maude that she had but to ask for anything more that she needed. That message I was not able to deliver since Maude was either not allowed, or had herself chosen not to see me. Dame Clarice took the money and told me, kindly but firmly, that it was impossible for me to see Maude.

Before I got back to the highway I dismounted and lay in a field full of tall white marguerites. I threw myself from side to side, crushing the flowers, full of misery and self-pity and fury at my own folly. To have let romantic love get hold of me and wreck my happiness, fool, sick-minded fool! Gay Nicholas Freeman, over whom several women had cried, lying in a damp field, perilously near crying himself!

I resolved to throw off this weakness. Goodbye to Maude Reed, I thought, when at last I rose up and brushed the grass and broken petals from my clothes. Being already halfway to Minsham I would go on, and see Clemence and take full pleasure in the thing I had, instead of crying, like a baby, for what was out of reach.

IV

Halfway through the next month, July, any wrong which Mistress Reed had done her daughter, and, through her, Master Reed and me, was repaid ten-fold.

Walter walked into the dining hall for the midday dinner carrying his lute and wearing his best clothes. His mother made some comment upon his attire, and he said, as casually as though he were announcing a visit to church or a nearby fair, 'I'm going to Walsingham. A party sets out this afternoon.'

I knew, and so did his grandfather, that the hour had struck. Mistress Reed, ever blind to what she did not wish to see, spoke for a moment as though he were merely joining a pilgrimage. Did they go mounted or afoot? Were any of the party known to her by name?

His smooth, secret face took on for a moment the bony stubborn look that was his sister's.

'They're tumblers and jugglers, riff-raff. We shall walk, from Walsingham to Lynn and then to Lincoln.'

She could not be blind to that. She turned pale, and with trembling lips began to plead.

'Too young,' she said. 'You're too young, Walter. Wait just a year, one more year. I promise then that you shall go, if you want to, with my blessing.'

'I'm as old as Maude, and she has chosen what she is to be.'

'Girls are always older for their age. Besides, Maude is safe.' She reached out and took him by the wrist. 'Walter, I beg of you. The roads are full of dangers. Thieves,' she said. 'Cut-throats.'

'The poor are safe enough. Thieves only set upon merchants with fat money bags.' He gave Master Reed a saucy, provocative glance.

'Don't be so sure,' his grandfather retorted. 'The only time I was set upon, beaten and left for dead, I was in rags and hadn't a farthing to my name.'

'There are plenty on the road who would kill you for your shoes,' Mistress Reed said. She turned, still holding her son's wrist, and appealed to the old man. 'Forbid it,' she said. 'You are head of the family and he is only a child. Forbid him to go.'

He said harshly, 'What would be the use?'

Walter jerked his wrist free.

'All this fuss,' he said disgustedly. 'It isn't even sudden. I've been saying for years what I would do. And now, I know, is the time.'

As he said the last words he threw back his head, and the fine black hair that was smoothly clubbed about his skull shifted and stirred, as though, in that still place, a free wild wind blew on him.

'You must take some money,' Master Reed said. 'In case of sickness, or other ill fortune. It must be sewn into the lining of your jerkin.'

'You're encouraging him,' said Mistress Reed, beginning to cry. 'I see it...because I let Maude go, you...Walter...yes, I see. I'll fetch her home, I promise. Make Walter stay here and I'll persuade Maude.'

Walter jumped up and grabbed his lute and looked ready to run.

'Wait,' the old man said. 'You must have the money and the names...the names of honest men I know in many towns, who would help in case of trouble. I'd have done as much for her,' he added inconsequently, 'if I had known.'

'Nor is that all,' cried Mistress Reed, checking her tears, 'Walter, wait. I never wholly believed – you see, your father talked the same way and he never...no matter now – I never believed you would go, or so soon. I would have done something about it. Don't waste your music on the greasy, gaping crowd, Walter. Make something of it. Go to Beauclaire or Rivington, or to your Uncle Godfrey at Horsbury where you could be heard by those who could advance you. Music like yours should be played at Westminster or Windsor.'

That was flattery. To do him justice I will say that during the last months his playing had improved, and the spell which he could cast on his hearers now had solid worth behind it. But Westminster and Windsor!

Walter said, 'I would hate that way. To be taken up because this man was my cousin or that one my uncle. Not for me! When I go to Windsor or Westminster it will be as plain Walter Reed, the strolling player. *And I shall go by invitation.*'

Since the day when I heard the fourteen-year-old grandson of a wool merchant speak those words, I have mingled with the great; I have spoken with crowned kings and stood in the presence of St Peter's anointed successor. I have never, anywhere at any time, heard anyone speak so arrogantly.

Mistress Reed, her last card thrown and the game lost, said in a dull voice, 'Come, let me sew in your money.'

'Wait,' Walter said. He looked into the hall, where the weavers and yard men and such pack-whackers as were home for dinner that day had their eyes and ears upon our table, even as they plied their knives and spoons. He climbed on to the bench where he had been sitting and took up his lute.

'I am going away for a little while,' he said in the clear, confident voice of one already used to addressing a mob. 'This is my farewell to you. It is called "A Song At Parting". I made it for this occasion.'

He had based it on one of those old pagan tales which had managed to slip through the close net of censorship which the Church had tried to drop between the stories of the antique world and those of Christendom. In a light, pleasing voice, neither child's nor man's, he sang of the final leave-taking between Orpheus and Eurydice, when, he having broken the condition of her release from Hades, she must turn back into the shadow world.

I suppose everyone within hearing, the stolid Flemish weavers, the rough urchins who swept the stables, the brutal drivers of the pony teams and the maids who came crowding into the doorway to the kitchen had at some time known a parting from someone of whom they were fond. The song spoke direct to the memory. I sat there, thinking of Maude, that tender mouth never to be kissed, that slim, just nubile body doomed to sterile virginity. I felt my own eyes moisten. Mistress Reed broke down and put her face in her hands and sobbed without restraint. Everyone cried except Master Reed, who stared straight ahead of him, God knows at what ghosts.

Walter struck the last note, looked around with satisfaction and jumped down from the bench.

Perhaps his music had touched his own heart. He laid a hand on his mother's shoulder and said, 'I'm not going for good. I shall be back one day.'

Master Reed got heavily to his feet and said, 'I'll go get the money. Show it to nobody, Walter, and don't speak of it. Keep it in case of need.'

V

Walter's departure had two results. Martin Reed now began to speak openly of me as his successor.

'It'll be in your hands,' he said, speaking of the business. 'Even if Walter comes home when he tires of the road, he'll know nothing. I want my daughter-in-law kept in comfort so long as she lives and I've always helped keep her father who'll probably live to be a hundred. Then there's Maude's dower. And I hope you'll get a family of your own. So you'll need to keep busy.'

The third time he spoke to me in this strain I said to him frankly, 'Unless, sir, you make a will and state clearly that it is your wish for me to take charge of the business, all these plans will come to nothing. If you die intestate, Walter is your heir, and his mother, on the spot, will be his regent. Before you are in your grave – God forgive me for mentioning such a thing – I shall have a month's wage and my quittance.'

I spoke the more surely because, since Walter's going, the relationship between Mistress Reed and myself had undergone a great change for the worse; and for a reason which no one would credit.

She had attempted to assuage her melancholy over the loss of her son in a way unusual to women: she took to drink.

Openly, at the supper table, she would drink three or four cups of wine in place of her usual one; and secretly too. I've gone into the solar in an evening and found her there, her hands idle on a piece of embroidery or plain sewing, and the air reeking of brandewijn; I've seen the cup standing on the floor, half, but not quite, hidden by her skirts. I've passed her on the stairs, standing aside where they widened, and turned to allow her to go by, and smelled the same pungent odour, and she just come from her bedroom, early in the day.

She was never noisy or truculent; indeed in her cups she became more agreeable; the lines of her face would lift and soften. One realized for the first time that, if she married young as most girls do and quickened soon after, she could still be just short of thirty. My Clemence was thirty-two. Mistress Reed had always seemed at least ten years older. But drunken, she lost something of her stiff, cool, self-contained look.

One evening, when Walter had been gone a month, I came in late, from Minsham. I had no more reason for secrecy, for over the episode of the ring on that fatal birthday morning Master Reed had betrayed that he knew about my attachment. After that, any errand of supervision of the Minsham sheep run, where the sheep from the Cotswolds still flourished and produced their over-weight in wool, would be undertaken in the afternoon; then I would have supper with Clemence, make love, and ride home.

It was now four months since Maude had gone back to Clevely, without even a goodbye, and my defences were building up. As I rode home I had thought to myself that if I could persuade Martin Reed to put me upon a sure footing, either now, or by will, which would take care of the future, I might do far worse than marry Clemence. She had much the same background as Mistress Reed and would be a match for her, I

thought. And though the two boys were imps straight from hell
– you could almost smell the brimstone on them – one thorough
good beating apiece, which, as their stepfather I should have the
right to administer, would improve their manners if not their
characters. I toyed with this thought, not enthusiastically, but
rather with the resignation of someone making the most he could
of the second-best, all the way home, while on the warm night air
the scent of honeysuckle and meadowsweet lay heavy.

I noticed as I came to the Old Vine that there was a light in the
solar window. Mistress Reed, a bit drunken, had left the candles
burning, I thought. When I'd stabled my horse I would go in and
pinch them out.

When I re-entered the passage which ran clear through the
house, the solar door was open and she was standing just inside.
Her hair, which I had never before seen completely uncovered,
hung loose to her shoulders, very curly and pretty, pale gold. She
wore a blue velvet bed-chamber robe, so ungirded that I could see
her breasts. And they were pretty too. She was very drunk.

I was reminded of my first visit to a house of ill fame. It stood
in a narrow lane, just off Tombland, in Norwich; the girls had
worn exactly that half-revealing, half-concealing garb, and that
same air of deliberate welcome.

'You're very late,' she said.

'Yes, I am. Would you like me to put out the candles for you?'

'No. Not yet. Come and talk to me for a little while.' She put
her hand on my arm and I went into the room with her. She
moved towards the window, which stood wide on the garden.
The lop-sided moon which had lighted me home hung like a
lantern, and the sweet night air, the breath of flowers and green
things growing, came in to mingle with the sharp scent of the
brandewijn.

'I'm so lonely,' she said. 'Years and years and years with nobody
to talk to.'

She sat down on the window seat and would have pulled me
down beside her, but I stiffened myself, and her hand, as I

resisted, slid down from my arm to my hand. She twisted her fingers so that for a moment they were twined with mine and she looked at me with as plain an invitation as any woman ever gave any man.

I thought very rapidly; a dozen thoughts in a breath's space. Ha, I thought, and I had believed that it was too late to work my way in with her. And I thought, how amusing to see the trollop who had lived behind that screen of whalebone and good breeding. And I thought, you are the one who sent Maude to Beauclaire and therefore to Clevely and I will have no truck with you. Other thoughts I had too, of how long she had lived widowed, of things Clemence had murmured in moments of joy, of how it was better to live out your time as a maid than to be widowed, since what you had never had you did not miss. Almost I could be sorry for her. But not quite. Besides, I had just come from Clemence and there was no desire in me. So I pulled my fingers free and said, 'Madam, it is too late now for talk. I am for bed. I advise you to do the same.'

She began to whimper, saying that she could not sleep; that once the brandewijn would assure her slumbers, but now no more.

'In the end there is nothing,' she said. 'Nothing left. Nothing at all.'

I reached over her bowed head and closed the window and latched it. As I did so, she half rose and pressed herself against me. I stepped back and said, 'Madam, you are not quite yourself this evening. Come, take my arm and I will help you upstairs.' I left one candle burning and put out the rest.

Still whimpering, she said, 'I *am* myself. Locked in, all alone with terrible things to remember.' She looked at me with drunken cunning and, with a change of tone, said, 'Ah, you would like to know, wouldn't you? And all I'll tell you is that God has taken away Walter, to punish me. So I'm all alone, and even you won't be kind to me.'

My surprise and mixed feelings had settled down now into simple disgust. I said briskly, 'I am always civil to you, Madam. Even now I am offering you my arm, and to light you upstairs.'

She gave me a beaten look, but she put her hand in the crook of the arm I offered and, moving unsteadily, mounted the stairs. At the door of her own room she paused.

'They come and stand by the bed and look at me,' she said in a complaining, confidential way. 'They never did that before. I'm afraid.' For a second I suspected that this was a cunning trick to get me into her bed-chamber; but almost immediately her manner underwent another sudden change. 'I shan't flinch,' she said. 'The blood of brave men runs in me. Let them do their worst.'

She opened the door and marched in, as though meeting a challenge, and before I could give her the candle, slammed the door in my face.

I went on to my bed thinking about Joseph and Potiphar's wife. As a character I had never much admired him, but now I saw the story from his viewpoint. I only hoped that when she woke, sore-headed and sober in the morning, she would have forgotten the whole episode. But her manner betrayed her. She had never been markedly pleasant to me; now she became even less so, always speaking to me in a cold, contemptuous way and taking trouble to make wounding remarks. She told me that I was going bald very early, and another time said that I was getting fat, unbecoming in a young man; she even hinted that my hose could do with a wash. One would have thought that I was the one who had made an attempt to seduce her.

That was why I spoke frankly to Master Reed of the need to make his will; but like all unlearned and self-made fellows he regarded the making of a will as tantamount to signing his death warrant.

'Yes,' he said, 'I will see about that.' And did nothing.

For a boy who had evinced so little affection for his family while he lived in its bosom, Walter wrote very regularly and at some length. I suspect that some, at least, of his letters were written to advertise his skill and in the hope of drawing custom. He had plainly become one of the great fellowship of the open road and at various times his letters were delivered to the Old Vine by tinkers, minstrels, pilgrims, friars and merchants. Once even, a gay young knight,with two squires in his train and his jousting armour on a packhorse, came jingling along to hand in a letter which Walter had written at Nottingham Castle.

'The boy played with such skill,' he explained, 'that I invited him to come with me to Colchester, where I join my Lord Delahaye, who has a lively appreciation of talent. The young knave made mock of my offer but said that if I went to Colchester I could deliver a letter for him. It has added some miles to my journey, but no matter; I have seen the nest that hatched so sweet a throstle.'

Master Reed and I had just finished supervising the loading of one of the pony trains, and were on our way into the house.

'If you would be pleased to dismount and enter, sir,' Martin said, 'you would be welcome to the best I have to offer.'

'I thank you, but I am already delayed.'

'Run find your mistress,' Master Reed said to me; and to the young knight, 'One moment more, for charity. The boy's mother...it would ease her mind to speak with one who saw him so recently.'

Mistress Reed came running out, and the knight doffed his feathered cap and answered, with civility, the questions she asked about how Walter looked, was he still well shod, and what kind of company he was in. He repeated the story of his offer to introduce Walter to Lord Delahaye and Mistress Reed, already a little mazed with wine, drew herself up with great dignity and said, 'If Walter had wanted advancement in that way, he could have gone to his cousin Astallon at Beauclaire.'

The young knight said, 'Madam, your son will never lack advancement. With his skill and effrontery he should go far.'

If Walter's letters were to be believed, such offers, and some even more dazzling, were an everyday matter to him. His reply was always that to him confinement in a great house, even a palace, would be as irksome as in a small. He seemed more impressed by his smaller triumphs: 'everybody wept', 'some women came and kissed my hand', 'a man gave me his last farthing'.

Mistress Reed kept all the letters in a box of carved wood, spent hours brooding over them and fingering them, and constantly referred to them as proof that Walter was dutiful, that he remembered his home and family with affection and would most surely return.

Once, when she said that, Master Reed said, mildly, but with meaning, 'We trust that he will. And it would be a pity if he found us in less good fettle than he left us.'

That was the most pointed remark he ever made to her in my presence; but then, despite his lack of learning and his gruffness, he was not insensitive. Whether in private he remonstrated with her I do not know. To me, on one occasion, when her insobriety was such as no one could overlook, he said, 'Poor woman. She cannot face grief. When her mother died it was the same, and when Richard died. It is her refuge, as work has been mine.' He thought for a second, sticking out his underlip. 'At least she hurts nobody but herself,' he said. 'By my work I've ruined two men that I know of, and probably others.'

I forgot Mistress Reed. I thought to myself, it is a bad sign when old men who have led successful lives begin to look back and reckon what damage they have done. It is a foreshadowing of the final reckoning which they are preparing to face.

Time went on; the seasons changed. My little secret hoard of coins grew, more swiftly as Martin Reed relaxed, bit by bit, the strictness of his supervision. Physical changes in those one sees several times every day escape one's observation; it was with surprise that one summer evening, coming suddenly upon Mistress Reed in the garden, with the level rays of the westering sun fell upon her, I realized that she had grown fat, and that puckers of loose skin hung like little bags beneath her eyes and under her jaw. She was drunk, as usual; and she was staring so fixedly at a place where the grass grew lush under an apple tree that I thought she had dropped something and was searching for it. She actually pressed one hand against the trunk of the tree for support, and thus balancing, bent over and with the other hand touched the grass.

I was going straight past her, but she heard my step on the path and straightened up, and squeezing her eyes against the light of the sun, said, as though we had been for some time in converse, 'That is the *one* thing that is sure and certain, the one thing you can count on. God punishes every sin.'

'So we are taught,' I agreed, and made to pass on.

'But we don't believe it. That is where we make our mistake. And then it is so subtle. The punishment never comes either from the direction, or in the form, that you expect. Bear that in mind. You plant a sin like a grain of wheat and you think punishment will come up, a full ear of wheat. For that you are prepared. But it isn't wheat that comes up; it's a damask rose, and you pluck it, and the thorns tear your flesh and the scent of it is poison. I know what I'm saying.'

'I have no doubt of that, Madam. Would you like my arm to assist you into the house? Then I must ask you to excuse me.'

I went on into the house, thinking that here we were with another year almost half gone, Midsummer Eve again. And Master Reed still with his will not made, my future still very insecure and Clemence growing a little, a very little, but still noticeably cooler. It was fifteen months since Maude had gone back to begin her novitiate and, though I had done my best to shut her out of my mind, more than once, in the very act with Clemence, I had suddenly thought of her and gone impotent.

That had frightened me; and Clemence, sympathetic the first time, had turned suspicious the second.

Leaving Mistress Reed maudlin under the apple tree, I thought to myself – It hardly needs God to punish us; we somehow contrive to punish ourselves.

VI

The news about Walter took a long time to reach us. A letter written in the April of 1451 arrived from Gloucester in June. It said he was well, and about to set out for Winchester. After that there was silence.

We should hear at Christmas, Master Reed said; yes, Mistress Reed echoed, we should certainly hear at Christmas. But the season came and went without a word. Mistress Reed burrowed more securely into her refuge, and the old man said, whether to comfort himself or her, that the absence of news might be a good sign. Probably in the autumn, faced with the discomforts of another winter, Walter had turned his face for home and therefore did not think to write.

Then, on a blustery March evening, my master and I were in the office when a servant girl, white of face and wide of eye, ran in and said that there was a creature asking for Master Reed at the yard door.

'If you mean a beggar, say so,' Martin said, and prepared to lever himself out of his chair.

'I'll go,' I said, and jumped up.

'If it is a letter or a message from Walter, bring the bearer in. A spoken word tells twice as much,' Master Reed called after me.

The servant girl ran straight back to the kitchen instead of hanging about, as their habit is, to catch a word out of which to make a long story.

When I reached the door I realized that her use of the word 'creature' had a frightful accuracy. There are the natural

396

deformities to which the eye become accustomed, the squints, hare-lips, hunch-backs, mutilations due to accident or battle. But there is another sort, inflicted by unscrupulous showmen upon infant children. They take them when their bones are soft and pliable and shape them, as a gardener shapes a tree that is to be espaliered. Then, if the unfortunate child survives – few do – they have something truly unusual, something out of nature, for a sight of which, in a dim-lighted booth, the sensation seekers will hand over their pence.

This was one such, a striking example of the devilish art. His left arm had been trained to grow behind his head, so that he had two arms, one long and one short, on the same side, and his head appeared to grow from under his arm, like those of a strange people mentioned in some traveller's tale.

In his armpit his head lay sideways, so that to look up he must turn his eyes almost out of their sockets.

'Are you Master Martin Reed?' he asked. His voice was muted.

'I'll take you to him,' I said, sickened beyond being able even to ask his business. With my back to him as he pattered after me towards the office I managed to ask, 'Is it anything concerning Walter Reed?'

'Yes. Yes. Bad news that I hate to tell. But I promised.'

Outside the office door, which I had closed behind me because the wind was raging through the house, I said, 'Wait here a moment.' I went in.

'It is about Walter,' I said, as gently as I could, 'and bad news, he says. And the bearer, sir, is one of those freaks that they show at fairs – a shocking sight.'

He drew a deep breath which lifted and straightened his heavy bowed shoulders.

'Let's know the worst,' he said.

I admitted the poor creature, but did not go in myself. I went and sat on the stairs, near enough to be within call, telling myself that this was, after all, the proper thing to do. I was *not* one of the family, intimately as I lived with them; nevertheless, knowing the real reason for not going into the office, I knew that I was a deserter. Still, I was here if I was wanted. And in a minute, no more, the office door opened and Master Reed, grey-faced, but quite calm, came out, turned towards the kitchen, saw me and stopped. He lifted a warning finger.

'Go and ask them to mull some ale,' he said, almost in a whisper, 'and bring it, and some bread and meat, to the office. Then go and bring down my sheepskin coat. The poor creature's starving and soaked to the skin.'

The stout old cook and the two serving girls were in a huddle by the kitchen fire, sharing a horrified pleasure.

'Is it gone?' asked the girl who had answered the door.

'The master is asking for mulled ale and bread and meat, in the office; and look lively,' I said.

'I ain't taking it in. Opening the door and seeing *that* stand there hev took ten years off my life already.'

'Put the things outside the door of the office, then, and knock. And look sharp,' I said.

As I went out of the kitchen I heard the girl say, 'Use a crock we can smash, Kitty; if I'd to set my lips to cup *that'd* used, it'd turn my stomach.'

I went and fetched the coat, and not wishing to behave like a silly serving wench, went into the room, determined to conceal my aversion. The poor creature knelt, shivering, by the fire. Master Reed still sat at his table. I looked at him questioningly and he said, 'The boy's dead, Nicholas; in bad circumstances.'

I mumbled that I was sorry, which was true, though my feeling was, in the main, pity for him.

He was a remarkable man; there is a great deal of talking – and some writing too – about the beauties of chivalry, of physical courage, hardihood in the face of danger, all of it very far removed in most people's estimation from an old wool merchant whose hand had never closed on a sword hilt; but that evening he was magnificent in his fortitude. He got up and took the coat from me and went over to the grotesque and said, 'Throw off your wet things and hug this about you. You'll soon be warm. Food and drink are coming.' Then, as though resuming the conversation which my entry had interrupted, he said, 'That kind of thing means a lot to women. She may well ask what infirmary. Can we answer?'

'There is a House of White Ladies nearby.'

'We'll tell her that. The best of nursing, the kindest of attention. After all, the boy's father,' he paused and swallowed, 'was in his own bed, he had every care, and a physician, yet he died. She will believe, and feel that no one was to blame.'

The serving girl tapped on the door. She had gone by the time I opened it. I took in the cup and the platter and carried them to the freak, who had wriggled out of his clothes and was wearing the coat as a cape. His own jerkin, I noticed, with a fresh little thrill of distaste, had been made for him; it had no sleeve on one side, two on the other. He snatched at the things I offered, taking the mug in the hand nearest his face, the platter in the other.

Watching his ravenous attack upon the food, Master Reed said, 'There's plenty more. Ask if you want it.' He then gave one of his great sighs and set himself in motion. 'I must break this to his mother. She might insist on seeing you. You know what to say if she does.'

'I know, master. Maybe I should've softened the tale for you. It never entered my head.'

'No, for me the truth was best. And I thank you for bringing it.'

He indicated with a jerk of his head that I was to look after the freak, and went limping away. I pulled a chair into a position from which I could look straight ahead of me without seeing the man, who was still stuffing his mouth like a man filling a sack in a hurry.

'What is the truth?' I asked.

'He died, alongside me in Winchester Gaol. November, December, cruel cold it was, the walls running with water and puddles on the floor. He took a cold and then a cough and it

killed him. Not but what that was a mercy in a way; he'd have
burned, otherwise. They'd got upwards of twenty witnesses and
that was too much to overlook even though he did have friends in
high places and the Bishop himself was inclined to give Walter
the benefit of the doubt. He was so young, too, and had such a
nice way with him, enough to make anybody wonder. But twenty
witnesses and more. No, that was too much. And in broad
daylight too.'

'What had he done?' I asked; though I knew all but the details
of the answer, for I remembered that summer evening, the hasty
angry words, the grandfather's warning.

The man by the fire crammed his mouth and chewed loudly.
'Mind, I wasn't there. I was in the gaol then – for stealing – but
never mind me. I only know what Walter said, and that wasn't
much. Till they took his lute away he used to spend his time
playing; only afterwards, when he was sick and heartbroke, did he
talk. And of course when I was turned loose I heard the talk.
They're talking about it still in Winchester; some feel a bit ill
done by to have missed the burning.'

He chewed again and resumed his tale.

In Winchester there was always a fair on St Luke's day, and
most often it was a summer day crept into autumn, 'St Luke's
little summer' people called it. This year was no exception; the
sun shone clear and bright. There was a man who sold medicine,
guaranteed to cure anything from a winter cough to the stone,
and he gathered his crowd about him by banging on a drum.
Twice during the morning Walter's playing had stolen his crowd
away before he had sold much, and about midday the man had
approached Walter and protested. Walter had moved away, but
the people had followed, and within an hour the medicine seller
had come to him again and suggested a partnership.

'They say – but of course afterwards people will say anything
– they say he offered him a fourth share, Walter to play and
gather the crowd and then break off in the middle of a tune and
let the man cry his wares. And they say that then Walter went

white with rage and said, "Am I to play that you may gull fools? Devil take your pills and potions." Fifty people claim to have heard him say that.'

He broke the tale and I heard him chewing. I also heard, from the other side of the house, some wild, most lamentable crying. I pitied Master Reed from the bottom of my heart.

The story went on. Within five minutes, before, in fact, the medicine seller could get back to his stall, a bullock, running amok from the nearby cattle-market, crashed into it, became entangled, and stamping, rolling, tossing its head, smashed every pill to powder and broke to fragments the thing which had been the medicine maker's greatest pride and treasure: a big flask of Venetian glass, half full of red liquid which he claimed to be the elixir of life – the other half had been, he said, poured into the pills.

'Well,' the freak said in his soft voice, 'that could have been accident, though they counted it uncanny that, except to that one stall, the beast did no damage and was easily taken. In itself that would never have damned him. But next day...'

Next day the medicine man, with nothing to sell and a damage to avenge, took his drum and followed Walter round, banging loudly and out of time, spoiling his music. At first only a few people, who cared neither one way or the other, found this amusing, but presently even those who wanted to hear the proper music gave way and found the situation rather comic, and laughed. Walter stopped playing. He took some coins from his pocket and threw them towards the man with the drum.

'Will that buy your silence?' he asked.

The man scooped up the money and said 'Aye'; then, as Walter began to play again, amended it to 'Aye, for two minutes,' and banged on his drum. The crowd laughed. Walter said, and this was what twenty reliable people were prepared to swear to, 'Then there's no help for it. Let your arm wither.'

'And they say that it did. It fell limp and began to grow small. By evening it was dry and shrivelled as a twig. There it was, and no help for it. One day he was mixing medicine and banging his drum – the next helpless. And twenty people near enough to hear what the boy said. It was hopeless. The Church court had him first and they handed him over to the secular arm, and that meant the townspeople. And how they felt is shown by what happened to the bullock. They claimed that was no ordinary beast, but possessed of the Devil. They burned it alive, and those who hadn't tasted meat in six weeks or seven forebore to touch a shred of it, though it lay there, open to all.'

How much to believe, how much to discount? I sat there and wondered.

At last I said, 'The boy himself; did he think he was guilty?'

'How can I answer that? In the beginning I thought he was a thief, like me. In the end, when they'd taken away his lute, and he was miserable and talked more, he said...Yes, once he said that to feel strongly enough was to have power. I do remember that. I remember because I said that it was not so, because I felt strongly the wish to be shaped like other people; and he said what was done was done. And then he said that he wished...No, he said, "If I had the power they say I have, I'd wish one wish for myself, to be out of this, and free, in the open, with my lute in my hand." And he had half of his wish, for presently he coughed and choked on the blood and died, and they did put his lute in the grave with him. Or so I am told.'

He went on with his supper, and we sat in silence until Master Reed came in, looking like a man who had just been released from the rack. But his most immediate concern was to find a place for the deformed man to sleep. When that was settled, and I ventured to offer a few words of sympathy, he looked at me steadily and said, 'Poor child. With such promise too. But the two things sprang from the same root. And I know it. That made me less firm than I should have been. Poor Walter.' He sighed again. 'Maude should be here,' he said. 'Her mother'll need her, and I need her. I've not been firm enough in the past, but over this I shall be firm. Maude must come home.'

VII

From the way in which Mistress Reed had behaved since Walter's departure, and the wild cries with which she had received the news of his death, I expected the following days to be made hideous by the manifestations of her grief and by her efforts to escape it. I looked ahead and imagined that life at the Old Vine, never very cheerful of late, would become dreary in the extreme. For the first time I began to wonder whether there might not be something unlucky about the house itself, or about the family. I knew I was a long way from being the carefree, cheerful, philandering fellow who had come there to teach Walter his letters. However, I soon shrugged that thought aside as nonsense. I pitied Master Reed, and his daughter-in-law too, but Walter's death had not harmed me; my future indeed looked brighter and more certain. And, I thought to myself, although Walter was buried faraway in Winchester, there would surely be a Requiem Mass for him, and surely Maude would be bound to attend, and perhaps she would feel some pity for her grandfather and decide to come home and gladden his last years. It was a frail hope, but I clung to it.

I kept well away from the house all the morning and at twelve o'clock went in for my dinner. The square family table was unoccupied. The men, assembling at the long tables, were quieter than usual, and the serving girls, running round with bowls of meaty broth, had an air of suppressed excitement. The news about Walter had spread, I thought. The door behind me, the one which led into the main part of the house, opened, and Master Reed, instead of entering, stood in the opening and beckoned me to join him.

'Come here,' he said, and stumped away up the stairs and to the door of Mistress Reed's room. His face wore a strange expression, something only just short of pleasure, as he opened the door and said, 'What do you make of that?'

It was as though he were showing me something which, after long labour he had made, or, after long waiting, had at last achieved.

Mistress Reed sat on the edge of her bed, dressed as far as her petticoat; she held a comb in her hand and was slowly, almost sensuously, passing it through the length of her hair. She acknowledged our presence by the open door by turning her head; there was no interest, no recognition, no expression at all in her face. The lines which discontent, grief and anxiety had graved had all been wiped away, leaving a blank placidity. It was the face of a half-finished statue whose maker has not yet decided whether it shall portray joy or sorrow.

Having once looked our way, she looked away again and resumed her slow combing. Master Reed gently closed the door and said, 'She has been like that all morning. Pray God she stays so.'

'Amen to that,' I said. 'Her father did.'

'Aye. That's the way it takes them. He turned simple when his wife died.' He pondered for a second. 'It's not much of a life, but better than being crazed with grief; and easier for everybody else. I must set one of the wenches to mind her.'

In one way Mistress Reed was more fortunate than her sire; if the materials were put in her lap, or by her side, she would stitch away, contentedly, for hours. She no longer made anything, just worked away on long hems and seams, or did embroidery stitches without any design or pattern. One of the serving girls, glad of the easy task, devoted all her time to her.

On the third or fourth day Master Reed said, 'We need a girl to take Phyllis' place in the kitchen. And who has time to see to that? Not you. Not I. This house lacks a mistress. Maude should come home, now. She must come home.'

'The question is, will she?'

'Properly tackled, I think so. For one thing a house without a mistress is as tempting to any woman worth her salt as a ship without a captain to a sailor. For another, it offers her a chance to do something that would *count* as she calls it. To come home and look after the sick woman who, all these years, was never fair to her, is to return good for evil, surely. Yes, that'll appeal to Maude. I'll go to Clevely tomorrow.'

It rained in the night, and though the morning was fine, a biting wind blew, and the heavy black clouds rushing across the sky threatened more rain or even snow. I was in the weaving shed, settling some petty dispute, when I looked through the wide window and saw Master Reed emerge from the house so muffled in clothes as to be shapeless, and wearing a woollen cap pulled over his ears and brow. Remembering how he had held close to the house all winter, and thinking of the inclement weather, I went down and said unwillingly – because I doubted the outcome of the errand and felt that if it failed he would blame me – 'Let me go, sir.'

'No. You mean kindly, but you don't have enough authority. Today I'm going to have it out. My mind is made up, and when my mind is set I mostly get my way.'

I realized, with a faint start of surprise, that that was true. Mild and quiet as he was, this whole great business with its many aspects ran smoothly under his absolute authority; only within doors, with his family, did anything displeasing to him continue for longer than it took for him to notice it. He had given in to Maude's whim, Walter's waywardness, Mistress Reed's insobriety, not from weakness, but from kindness of heart.

Well, I thought, all power go with you. I helped him into his saddle, and then stared at the evidence of his confidence in himself: another horse, saddled with Maude's own saddle, and wearing a leading rein, was led out. Master Reed took the rein, said 'Come up, then,' and they trotted out of the yard.

When I went in to dinner, one of the maids was thumping about in Maude's room, making it ready.

And faith, we are told, can remove mountains.

While we were at dinner there was a short sharp shower; but immediately after, just as I was leaving the house, the sun came out. I stood for a moment beside a lilac bush which had thrust a branch over the garden fence; it shimmered with buds, wetly green. Somewhere in the depths of the garden a bird was singing with passionate joy, and the golden light lay everywhere like a blessing. I was suddenly certain that Maude would come home that afternoon, and that everything would be well. Anticipation ran, with the tickling thrill of a finger touch, all the way from my thighs to my throat.

Half an hour later it was snowing lightly, and when, in the premature twilight, my master rode home, alone, he was furred all over with white; even his eyebrows bore their little load.

I had imagined, from the length of his absence, that Maude had packed her goods, and that the return journey had been made with laden slowness. But the led horse's saddle was empty except for the snow.

Master Reed replied to my unspoken comment.

'I went on to Minsham and took a look at the sheep. Had to do something to settle my mind.'

He dismounted stiffly, and instead of pushing away my proffered arm, took it and leaned on it heavily.

'It's been a bad day, my boy. And a fine fool I made of myself, as you shall hear.'

I had made a good fire in the office, and a pint of well-spiced ale in a pewter mug waited on the hearth. I'd had the poker in and out of the heart of the fire for the last two hours, and now I pushed it home again. By the time I had helped him to shuffle off his wrappings it was glowing red, and I plunged it into the ale.

'That'll warm you, sir,' I said, handing him the steaming brew.

'It's cooling I need. Feel that if you doubt me.' He reached out his free hand and touched mine. 'You'll understand, if I can bring myself to tell you.'

My curiosity was lively; but the hand he had laid on mine was unnaturally hot and I remembered what the doctor had said about the danger of his being upset. I said as soothingly as possible, 'I can see for myself that you are disappointed. Beyond that you can tell me as much or as little as you like.'

'That's right! Now you begin to talk to me as though I were a baby. That's all I need after the day I've had.'

He sipped his ale and I saw the sweat break out on his forehead. He pulled at the neck of his jerkin, exposing his stringy throat. Another thought struck me.

'Mistress Maude...She is well, I hope.'

'How can I know? I tell you I never even...But I'd best begin at the beginning.'

Clevely had altered; he'd spotted the change as soon as the place came in sight. Upwards of fifty ewes gathered in a field for lambing, with a shepherd and a boy in charge; another man in the house-yard, and not a nun to be seen anywhere. And the old kitchen door was now fenced off and a new one made at the far end of the house, with a deep porch in front of it and a portress to answer the bell. He'd asked for the Prioress, which was mere courtesy, since everyone knew that she was now bedfast; but it was not our old friend Dame Cecily Bracy who came into the cold little room where he was bidden to wait; it was a new nun, young, not more than thirty, who said she was the Prioress, so favouritism must have been at work to set her so high at that age.

He explained the situation and asked to see Maude. The Prioress, in a manner as smooth as cream, commiserated with him of the loss of his grandson and the indisposition of his daughter-in-law, but said that it was impossible for him to see Maude.

'Nicholas,' he said, leaning forward a little, 'when she said that, it was like being hit over the heart. I thought she'd taken the veil without a word to us, and I might never set eyes on her again. Come to my senses just too late, I thought, and for the rest of her days the poor silly child will come and go, eat or fast, sit or stand according to the word of this high-handed, mim-voiced bitch. And that roused my blood. I said even a nun was allowed to see her grandfather; I said she could stand by and hear every word that was spoken; I told her they weren't an enclosed order and if she didn't let me see Maude I'd complain to the Bishop. She wouldn't be ruffled; she said Maude was still a novice, free to see me or anybody else she'd a mind to, but I couldn't talk to her today because she wasn't at Clevely.'

He hadn't believed that. He thought the Prioress quick-witted enough to have guessed what he wanted of Maude; and he thought of his five pounds a year; and he thought that maybe the Prioress had already seen that Maude was in two minds about the matter. So he as good as called her a liar to her face and accused her of not daring to let him talk to his granddaughter.

'So then, Nicholas, she said, "Daren't is a strange word to use to me. What have I to fear? That you remove her from this house? I assure you I could fill her place ten times over and with girls well-dowered." Dowered is a word I hate the sound of. Before she could toddle it was dower, dower, dower. Hearing the word then, on top of all else, maddened me. I said, "Then, if you've nothing to fear, why daren't you let me see her?" And she said, "If you suspect me of hiding her in this house, search it. It is unusual to make a man free of the house, but if it will set your mind at rest, you may have my permission to go anywhere and conduct your search." And I thought to myself, there's been ample time for that woman at the door to carry warning and have the girl hidden somewhere. So I said, "I thank you, Madam. That I will do." And I did.'

He drained the mug and set it aside and began to twist his hands together. He had big hands, calloused and seamed with ingrained dirt which no amount of scouring would ever remove; but they were oddly skilful; he could splice a broken thread on a loom as neatly and delicately as any of the weavers who made the care of their hands an excuse for never handling a tool. Now he moved his hands as if he were trying to wrench out his fingers one by one.

'I went everywhere, not once only, twice, three times, turning back in my tracks in case they had Maude on the move. My boy, if she'd been the size of a bobbin I couldn't have missed her. Dorter, storeroom, chapel, cellar, everywhere. And it all so poor; I swear our bed in Squatters Row was softer and warmer than any in that house; and as for their storeroom, it was pitiable, braxy mutton and weevilly flour such as I wouldn't offer any seaman of mine to eat. And in the end back I was in the little cold room and she waiting for me, saying, "And now will you perhaps accuse me of spiriting the girl away?" Then she said she'd tell me what she would have at first, if I had asked her. According to her, the singing at Clevely is an offence to the ear and an insult to God, so Maude and one other – the only ones that can carry a tune – are sent to Ramsey to learn better and come back and teach the rest.'

'Enough to make any man angry,' I said. 'But why blame yourself? Your suspicion might have been correct. You acted rightly.'

He moved one eyebrow.

'You think so? I felt all in the wrong. And I apologized. She took advantage of that. She talked about Clevely, all the improvements that must be made; how in the past it had not been a nunnery in the real sense of the word, just a place where women lived and worked together and went to chapel when the milking was done or the butter made. She's going to alter all that; and her great need is money. Five pounds a year, she was good enough to say, was generous enough when Maude lodged there and worked to earn her keep, but since then, as I, a businessman, should know, money had lost some value and the noble was worth but six shillings nowadays. She talked to me like a huckster. What did I propose to do for Maude when she took her vows? And there's Maude thinking that all the world outside has gone awry through love of money. And me, that always called a dower a bait for knaves. I'd have done better, Nicholas, to have sent her to Beauclaire with the promise of a dower on a tag about her neck. A knave would at least have seen that the bed he had to share with her was soft and warm.'

'What did you promise?'

'Nothing. I'm not that much of a fool. I tell you, we bargained like a couple of stockfishmongers. I said I wanted Maude to come home and see the state her mother was in, and I wanted one last good talk. Then, I said, if I could be sure that her mind was made up and no hope for it, I'd give a dowry they'd talk about for years. And so I will, but I must be sure first. She said that was fair enough and Maude will come home as soon as she's back from Ramsey.'

'When will that be?'

'Oh, that depends on the singing.' His voice took on a sardonic note and then changed. 'And she did say one other thing; whether to set much store by it or not, I don't know. She said the visit to Ramsey would do Maude good, aside from the music, to let her see a properly conducted house, because that was how Clevely would be in future, and discipline must be accepted meekly. That sounded to me a bit...but there, they have such a way of wrapping things up, half the time they mean something other than you'd think.'

He shuddered suddenly and held out his hands to the fire.

In the morning he woke with a cold, of which he made light; the Minsham shepherd, he said, had a much worse one the day before, and was out in the snow making a lambing pen. Giving this as an excuse for not keeping to his bed, he sneezed through the day, saying after each bout of sneezing, 'There, that cleared it.' He went to bed early with hot brick to his feet and a basin of onion gruel inside him. He'd budged many a cold with such simple remedies.

This one refused to be budged. It resisted even the curative measure of a day in bed, and by the third day had settled on his chest. He drew his breath with a wheeze and a rattle, and spoke with a hoarse croak. But he held that it was nothing but a cold, he'd had many worse. A linseed poultice was what he needed;

surely to goodness somebody in the kitchen could make a linseed plaster.

The cook made it; and also a concoction of honey, vinegar, horehound and cinnamon, upon whose virtues she was prepared to stake her own.

I took upon myself the application of the poultices, since, with Phyllis minding Mistress Reed, they were short-handed in the kitchen. When I put it on hot that evening for the last time and settled him for the night, he seemed easier, and still most resolutely cheerful. But his cough, a rattling, ineffective effort to clear the clogged rheum from his chest, kept me awake most of the night. Three times I made a fresh plaster, plied him with the mixture, warmed a cup of milk.

'I shall get the physician to you in the morning,' I said. He made no protest. Surprised and a little frightened by this, I thought that perhaps I should fetch the priest, too.

I wished that that could have been done in a more casual, less ominous way. But the Old Vine was not a house where the priest was a visitor; we had nothing to do with Baildon, our parish was Flaxham St Giles, and the church, and the priest's house, were three miles away. Sir Andrew, the priest there, was elderly. To send for him was to hint that things were in a bad way.

I might have spared myself these cogitations, for in the grey dawn of the fourth day, when my master roused from an uneasy restless doze, he stared at me for a moment as though he did not recognize me and then said, his voice more hoarse and weak than ever, 'It's beat me, my boy. I want the priest. Make my confession and my will at the same time.'

'Sir Andrew?'

'Yes. Send a good horse…pillion.'

'I will. But you mustn't lose heart, you know. You've got a stubborn cold, and you can't throw it off as you did when you were younger. I'll get the doctor to you, too.'

411

He wheezed out something about a waste of time, and something I didn't quite catch, about a hawthorn tree. Then he coughed and hawked and spoke more clearly for a moment.

'You mustn't fret. I've had my day; and it's a long time since Kate went.'

That name, as much as anything, convinced me that he was dying; dying men look back over their lives, they say, back to their very beginnings. And Kate, whoever she was, must have belonged to his youth; I had never heard anyone mention her, though in the yard there were one or two who claimed to remember his wife, 'a queer body' who'd never settled down in Baildon, but gone to her own people and then come back to have her baby and died when it was born. Her name was not Kate; I'd heard it, once, I think, and it was outlandish.

The thought that Martin, my master, was about to die fell on my mind and clove it in halves, like an axe coming down on a billet of wood. On one side there was all concern for *my* future. He had no heir except a girl in a convent; I understood the business, he trusted me, and liked me. Surely I must be provided for. But he had spoken of giving Maude a dower which would be talked of for years; and if he thought he was dying, it would matter very little to him whether she stayed at Clevely or not. Blood, when the test comes, is thicker than water, and I could well imagine him saying that it was all to go to Maude.

On the other side of my mind there was no material consideration at all. I just realized how much I held him in respect and esteem, how much, whatever happened, I should miss him, quiet, solid and sensible. True I deceived him a little and robbed him a little, sometimes railed at him in my mind for being slow and stubborn and old-fashioned and fussy over details, but I knew his worth; and although his honesty had not made me honest, and his kindness had not made me kind, he had shown me a standard against which I myself, and any other man I ever met, would measure very small.

Having sent for the priest and the doctor and seen the work in the yard begun, I went in and carried up a new poultice and then a piece of clean parchment, the quill and the inkhorn. I looked down at these and thought – Instruments of Fate. A few scratches one way or another and a whole future is settled and sealed. I was tempted to remind him that to leave a fortune to Maude would be to make sure that she stayed in Clevely for life. Without saying much he had limned that new Prioress for me; she would be capable of settling, in the way she wanted it, the shilly-shallying mind of any girl so richly dowered. When it came to the point, however, I found that the words would not be said. Instead of speaking I fluffed up his pillows, and then went and fetched my own to add to his, so that he was propped almost upright, and seemed to find relief so.

'You're very good to me,' he croaked.

'I'll remind you of those words at Lady Day,' I said lightly. I drew my wage then. He saw the joke and smiled. But he said, 'I've seen my last Lady Day.'

A pang ran through me, for him, for myself, for all poor people who must, in the end, face the unknown dark. Kings, nobles, clerks and swineherds, all laid level at last, the songs sung, the good meals eaten, the kisses forgotten and done with. A great hunger for life took me. I decided, all in a moment, that I wouldn't darken another day of my life by hankering for anything; if he doesn't leave me a farthing, I thought, I'll still be alive, and young, capable of enjoying myself.

The priest arrived, red-faced from his ride in the wind, carrying a bag of embroidered linen.

'I am sorry indeed to find you thus,' he began. Master Reed dismissed me with a glance and I went out, closing the door.

The woman who cooked for us all caught me on my way out of the house. What, she asked plaintively, should she do about dinner, and supper moreover; it was four days since anybody had given her an order and she'd managed as best she could, with bits of this and that, but now she was at the end. With the mistress gone silly and the master taken to his bed, whom could she ask but me? 'Thass all very sad, but when they come in, all them great hearty men, they ain't to be put off with sorrowful words and tidbits.'

That, I knew, would be the last thing that he would wish. His attitude towards food was extraordinary; very abstemious himself, he was always careful to see that his table was spread with good food and plentiful. Yet the waste of a crumb worried him. I had often noted this incongruity and concluded that he was a man who, in his time, had gone hungry and knew the value of food.

And now, once again, my severed mind bothered me. By the time dinner was on the table...oh, let us not think of that! Dying can be a long business. They'll come in hungry; and this is one of the days in their lives, in my life; all of us being rushed along by uncheckable time towards the moment when food will concern, will please us no more.

'You say you've been on the makeshift,' I said. 'To put it even, what is the thing they like best?'

'Salt beef and dumplings.' She was beautifully certain about that. 'But that'll mean opening a new cask of beef. You say I am to do that?'

'Yes. Open a new...' I broke off, hearing overhead the imperative banging of the stick which I had placed by Master Reed's bedside so that he could summon attention.

'Cask,' I said, 'and plenty of dumplings.' I took the stairs two at a time.

It was the priest who had done the banging. When I entered, he stood there, the stick in his hand. He gave me a sidelong, curiously shamefaced look and then looked down at the carved knob of the stick.

'My hands,' he said. 'All knotted with old age and stiffness. It's as much as I can do to write my name nowadays.'

And probably, I thought swiftly, as much as he could do at any time. In some places and in some circumstances very little learning was demanded of a man anxious to take orders. And that little, unpractised for thirty or forty years in a country parish, would shrivel to nothing.

Master Reed, coughing and hawking, said, 'You do the scribing, Nicholas.'

The priest threw me another look, faintly hostile. I knew how he felt; there was no real need, in his opinion, to have the will written down. Dozens of men every year disposed of their property by word of mouth – a nuncupative will as it was called – and when it came to the attesting of such unwritten testaments there was no word that carried so much weight as a priest's. I accuse Sir Andrew of nothing when I say that, had I not been there with my ready pen, he could have called two gaping oafs from kitchen or yard, listened to Martin Reed's wheezing expression of his last wishes and later on very easily proved that on his death bed the wool merchant had turned very pious and left most of his goods to Holy Church. That had been done a thousand times and would be again. The number of Chantries in the country served by idle, self-indulgent priests, who could not even remember the names of those for whom they were to sing Masses, and by whose bounty they lived, proves that.

In this case, here I was, seating myself sideways, awkwardly against the chest where I had set the writing things, leaving the table for the cloth, the wafer and the wine of the ritual.

Master Reed, in a voice that sounded like an ungreased wheel in the distance, said, 'First I want every man who's worked for me five years or more to have three shillings and fourpence; those less long, twenty pence.'

Before I could set down a word the priest said, 'A written will should be properly made. This is no way to begin. You commend your soul to Almighty God and then say that you are of good mind and memory.'

'You can both see. I'm short of breath. We'll get the main things down. Trim it up afterwards.' Master Reed signed to me to write, which I did hastily.

His habitual economy of words now served him well; the sentences, though barely audible, were brief and clear. Calling me his 'faithful servant and good friend', he left me the premises, the good will, tools and instruments which would enable me to carry on his business as wool merchant, weaver and smith. His two ships and his flocks were not included in this bequest, but he left me twenty pounds in cash for immediate expenses. Out of the profits of the business I was to pay, each year, three pounds to Sir Godfrey Blanchefleur, the elder, and ten to Anne Reed, widow of Richard Reed deceased, so long as they should live.

It was easy enough to keep pace with his dictation because of his frequent pauses to cough and gather breath. Having written that, I looked at him, hoping to convey my gratitude in a glance, but he was staring ahead, frowning. He drew a rattling breath and went on.

Everything else of which he was possessed, the house, his ships, his cash money, the sheep run at Minsham and the flocks, two house properties in Baildon Saltgate, the Great Field at Horringer, the freehold of 'God Spare Mariners', an inn at Bywater, were to go to his dearly beloved granddaughter, Maude Reed...

The name emerged in such an inconclusive way that for a second or two I was certain that he was going to add some conditional phrase. Holding the pen suspended, I looked at him again, and as I did so a bout of coughing racked him. When it was done, he said, 'That's all.'

Slowly I placed the full stop which would hold Maude in the nunnery. There was a little silence, broken by the priest's rasping voice, saying with genuine horror, 'Such a will a heathen might make. No mention of Holy Church, of alms or charity or so much as a Mass for your sinful soul. My son, I bid you think again. For your own sake.'

'What do you want me to say?'

'I!' Sir Andrew's voice conveyed his affront. 'I want nothing, except to ease your passage through Purgatory and give you credit at the Last Judgment. You, Martin Reed, like the young man who came to Our Lord, are a man of great possessions. I would not have you, like him, go sorrowful away when all the reckoning is made. And of this will I say that a Saracen who had never taken the Body and Blood of Christ upon his tongue might leave it behind.'

Master Reed had sunk a little further back into his pile of pillows and half closed his eyes.

'Sir Andrew,' I began, in an expostulatory voice.

'Be silent!' he said. 'You were brought in to write and well you have done it. I have his soul to care for. Martin, for your own sake, make a gift to the church, one of your many properties. One third to buy Masses for your soul; one third for the poor; and one third to be used at the priest's discretion. At Flaxham we have no bell.' He added the final words with a disarming simplicity.

'Then let it be the Minsham sheep run, that being nearest to you.'

'I will see that the Masses are faithfully said.'

I scratched the sheep run out of the list of properties that were to be Maude's, and thought how the Prioress would grudge it, could she but know. I added the bequest to those already written, with details of its disposal. Then a thought struck me.

'You have not named those who should execute your will, sir.'

'You,' he said, wearily. 'And Sir Andrew, here, if he is willing.'

'Right readily. And the bell, Martin, shall bear your name, with some reminder. "Pray for the soul of Martin Reed, whenever you my tongue shall heed" or something like that.'

'I thank you,' Martin Reed said, but he looked at me as he spoke, and one of his eyebrows lifted as I had seen it do when Mistress Reed spoke with extra haughtiness, or Walter made some unusually extravagant statement. And I thought to myself – This is not the way he would have willed it on the afternoon when he came back from Clevely. I put the quill into the inkhorn and tipped it a little, so that a thin black stream ran from corner to corner of the written sheet.

'Now look what I have done,' I said. 'I am very sorry. The chest is awkward to write at. Shall I now make a fair copy?'

'Yes,' said Sir Andrew firmly. 'And in the rewriting make a proper beginning. Write, "In the name of Almighty God Amen". And then go on, "I, Martin Reed, being of good mind and memory, make my testament in this wise". Can you bear that in mind? And first mention the gift to Flaxham Church, it will look better there than tagged on at the end.'

I looked again at my master. Save for two small dusky red patches over the cheek-bones, his face was the colour of a candle; his eyes were half closed.

'In all else, sir, this is as you wish?'

'Make a fair copy, Nicholas; while I make my peace with God.'

I bent down and lifted one of his big, work-worn hands and put my lips to it. I fumbled in my mind for some words – not my own – with which to refute the priest's attitude, and found them, spoke them haltingly. ' "What more can a man do than love mercy, do justice, and walk humbly before his God?" That you have always done, and God will know His own, sir.'

I picked up the writing things and went from the room as the priest settled his stole.

Downstairs in the office I rewrote the will in a neat, clear script, setting it down as I had been bidden, until I came to the point where, leaving Maude's name hanging in the air, Master Reed had paused. There I wrote in what I genuinely believed he would himself have added at any other time: 'on condition that she abandon all intention of becoming a nun.' He had wanted Maude to come home and marry and have children; those few added words would give her the chance to do so at least.

Then I thought – Nobody would make such a condition without providing against its non-acceptance. So I added that if Maude insisted upon becoming a professed religious, all her portion was to go to Flaxham Church. It hurt me to dispose so lightly of such a fortune, but the priest had just shown that, like many people who do not rely upon the written word, he had an excellent memory. That final sentence would blur his memory and stop his mouth. It also, in a curious way, cleared my conscience.

Two witnesses who had no interest in the will were needed. I fetched two men who were waiting in the forge. They made their crosses and I wrote their names below.

By midday Martin Reed was peacefully unconscious, and in that state he died, just before dawn on the following morning.

Interval

WHAT HE FOUND so hard to stomach was that in the end he brought about his own undoing; was punished for behaving well; sustained a hurt which would last a lifetime simply because he had shown a delicate consideration for another person's feelings and exercised self-restraint.

That he had, perhaps, challenged Fate by being too certain, somewhat arrogant, a trifle smug, never once occurred to him.

He had been right, surely, not to make an instant proposal of marriage when Maude, at last, came back to the Old Vine. She had suffered enough emotional strain, returning to Clevely, after three days of hard travel, to learn that her grandfather was dead and buried, and while that grief was still raw, coming home to learn of Walter's death and to be confronted by her idiot mother.

At Clevely the Prioress had lost no time in producing an aged copy of the Bull Periculoso of Pope Boniface the Eighth.

'Here it is, clearly set down in black and white, in the vulgar tongue for the benefit of the unlearned,' she said. 'A rule made one hundred and fifty years ago, which has been disregarded by the heads of many Houses with consequent disorder and ruin. Read it.'

It was a piece of stiff parchment which had been kept tightly rolled for many years. Under the Prioress' white, well-kept hands it opened a little and then tried to spring back into its roll.

'Take hold of it. It has no teeth. There...'

Maude read a sentence about forbidding, on pain of excommunication, any nun or sister to go outside the bounds of a monastery. She looked up with a puzzled frown. She and Dame Lucy had been *sent* to Ramsey.

'There,' said the Prioress, and the finger jabbed down upon the next sentence. 'Read it aloud.'

'Item,' Maude read, 'let no one be received as nun or sister until we have inquired more fully into the resources of the House.'

'It could hardly be clearer,' the cool voice said. 'A convent is not, as so many people suppose, a refuge for the indigent. The terms of your grandfather's will ensure that if you stay here you will have nothing. Not even the miserable five pounds a year that has hitherto been paid, and which he as good as promised me should be increased. Old men in their dotage,' she said savagely, 'change their minds with every wind. And the Flaxham priest, naturally, had an eye to his own advantage.'

Maude took her hands from the document, folded them in front of her in the approved manner and stood silent. There was nothing to say. She knew, in her heart, that her grandfather, although he had allowed her to live at Clevely, had done so against his will, and that had she become a nun it would have been with his disapproval. She had often wondered during the last year whether he had not known her better than she knew herself; and since the installation of the new Prioress her uncertainty and lack of contentment had grown daily. Now, after the long and wearing indecision, the choice had been made for her.

'There is no need to tell you,' the Prioress said, 'that this is a House virtually without resources. What I brought to it is already spent and not half of what is needful is yet done. If, in the circumstances, I allowed you to stay here, I should act in direct disobedience to this Papal Bull, and should myself deserve to be removed.'

She spoke as though she were repudiating some plea, refuting an argument. Maude wondered how often this scene would be re-enacted; upon how many women who were sure of their vocation, and who perhaps had no resources, even sequestrated ones like her own, this Papal Bull would be used like an axe. For herself it did not matter. She drew a long breath, lifted her head and said clearly, 'Madam, I am not asking you to keep me.'

She never guessed that a little humility at this point, a few tears, some pleading words, would have persuaded the Prioress to disregard Boniface the VIII's express command. She never guessed that she had been sent to Ramsey to make a study of the music, not because she had a better ear than most of the others, but because the Prioress hoped that the idea of improving the Clevely singing would forge another link, give her an aim and a purpose. Maude had taken less kindly than anyone except Dame Cecily, who was so old that she counted for little, to the new régime at Clevely, and Maude was, in fact, exactly the type of woman whom the Prioress wished to rule; educated, well-connected, on one side at least, sensible and rich.

Rich no longer. The Prioress' disappointment was commensurate with her hopes, which had ridden high after her interview with old Martin Reed; and since he was beyond her reproaches, she expended her anger upon Maude.

'I don't *mind*,' Maude told Nicholas in one of their many talks. 'I wasn't sure; I don't think I ever was sure, and Grandfather knew it. I think that is why he made that condition. As a test. All the same,' she frowned, and on her smooth white forehead the ghost of Martin's double horse-shoe cicatrice appeared, 'I was shocked. In the old days money never mattered at Clevely.'

'Then it was,' he said lightly, 'the only place on earth where it did not; and now there is none. Money always matters.'

'Not to Walter. He was the one person who never minded about it.'

He was tempted to retort sharply that even so it was money, some infinitesimally small sum of it, that had led to Walter's premature death. But he had seen that same darkening of the eyes as had once accompanied any mention of Melusine, and as on former occasions, all his impulse was to comfort and console. So he took her hand and told her gently that she must not grieve for Walter: Walter's life, short as it was, had held as much happiness as most people know in sixty years; he had always done exactly what he wanted, and nothing that he did not; he had loved nothing and nobody but his music, and that love had never failed him.

He could, even thus early, have gone on to speak of other forms of love, confessed his own. But he refrained.

Opportunities to step smoothly from the impersonal to the intimate abounded, seemed, indeed, to thrust themselves upon him. She spoke once, in an astonished way, of the fact that her grandfather had named no guardian.

'I expected to be somebody's ward, like poor Madge FitzHerbert,' she said. 'And when I left Clevely I made up my mind that nobody was going to marry me for my possessions.'

He realized that the omission had been an oversight: in his hasty rewriting of the will the matter of Maude's age had never entered his mind. He could not now say what was true, that Martin, in the making of his will, had visualized her under the guardianship and management of the Prioress of Clevely.

'Your mother is still living,' he pointed out, 'and I am here to look after everything for you. You need no guardian. And the notion of being married for your money is an absurdity. You are no Madge FitzHerbert. You are beautiful.'

Her face coloured and the pace of his heart-beat quickened. Now? Why not? So easy. You are beautiful and lovable and I love you; to marry you has been my one desire since the moment I saw you almost four years ago.

But he left it where it was. A compliment, accepted with a blush.

There had always been, at the core of his feeling for her, an element of the worshipful, novel to him in his experience of women, and therefore oddly enjoyable. There was also in his attitude something resembling that of the gourmet who, before setting about some particularly succulent dish, eyes it with pleasure, sniffs its savour with gloating. Some part of his restraint was also not far removed from fear. She was so innocently friendly; a word spoken too soon, some betraying gesture made before he had succeeded in endearing himself to her, might ruin all. He had come so far, waited so long, worked so cunningly, that in the end nothing but perfection would suffice.

He behaved – as he saw, looking back – in lunatic fashion. Not content with a dumb wooing, fetching and carrying, acting in all but the ultimate assertion of rights like an elderly man with a lovely and capricious mistress, he went to other lengths. He broke with Clemence, promising her a pension of five pounds a year, and bearing first her reproachful tears and then her vituperative anger with the utmost detachment, as though suddenly a wall of glass had reared itself between her and him. He rode home from Minsham whistling, and on the next day took himself into the confessional at St Mary's Church, and for some moderate penance and a contribution to the Poor Box, was absolved from all his sins of fornication.

Young men on the eve of knighthood made similar confessions, and washed themselves thoroughly and then kept vigil in churches all through the night. That thought occurred to him as he left the church, raising his eyes to the carved angels in the roof, the angels of whom Maude, at the age of twelve, had reminded him. A carving, once made, he thought, was finished, could never grow or change. *His* angel, while losing nothing that could deserve reverence, had developed all the qualities which would enable a man to say truly 'With my body I thee worship.' It occurred to him that on the night before his marriage he would keep vigil in this church, under the angel roof.

So he stepped out into the greenish April dusk at almost the same moment as a young man, thoroughly washed, confessed and absolved, went into the chapel of the Knights Hospitallers, at Dunwich, to keep his pre-knighting vigil.

The days lengthened; the trees shook out their young green; daisies and cowslips and lady's smocks gemmed the meadows. There had never been so sweet a spring as this one through which they rode, on her business, on his, or something which concerned them both. It was a matter for laughter that *his* pack-ponies on their comings and goings must use *her* front door and trot through the very heart of *her* house. And his certainty that he had done right, that he had carried out both Martin's wish and Maude's was proved beyond all doubt on the day when Sir Andrew, riding a bony mule, came into the Old Vine, and with the air of doing Maude a favour, said that if she cared to return to Clevely and take the vows she could: Flaxham Church, out of what would then fall into its hands, would endow her handsomely. The Prioress, upon whom he had called, was very anxious, he said, to have Maude back, providing her return was in accord with the Bull Periculoso. If she saw his real purpose Maude gave no sign of such awareness, but thanked him heartily and said she had no wish to return to Clevely.

'There are other houses,' he suggested.

'None where I am needed as I am here. I look after my mother.'

He argued at some length and then, finding her immovable, made a peevish complaint about the wording of the will.

'It was made hastily and badly.'

425

'You were present at its making, Sir Andrew,' Maude said mildly.

'Yes; and I said at the time that it was such a will as a heathen might make. And I had my mind set upon persuading your grandfather on another point, so that that condition slipped in without my noticing. Also I had a cold in my head and at such times I am a little hard of hearing. Of one thing I am *sure*, and that is that it was never Grandfather's intention to so make his will that you should renounce your vocation.'

'I think it was his intention to prove to me that I had no vocation.'

'Then why did you contemplate the religious life?'

She frowned thoughtfully.

'I was trying to run away from certain things in this world that I was unwilling to face.'

'And have they changed?'

It was impossible to explain how the balance had been adjusted, Clevely under the new régime another lost illusion, and the Old Vine, free of her mother's dislike, no longer a place to flee from. She said simply, 'The change has been in me.'

Some hot and hasty words about the uncertainty of purpose, the halting faith, the self-indulgence of this new generation, formed in his mind, but stopped short behind his teeth. She was his parishioner, and a wealthy one; it would serve him ill to alienate her. He had already ordered the new bell: there was that much gained; and now, to test her attitude, he said, 'I find that I made your grandfather a rash promise. I also was hasty that morning. The bell will cost more than I thought and I shall not be able to afford the engraving which was to remind all those who heard its voice to pray for his soul.'

She said eagerly that she would pay for that.

When he left, disappointed in his main objective, he looked forward to a future rich in little extortions. She had not taken advantage of his offer, but he was sure that in her heart she had appreciated it. She was convent-schooled and would be amenable. He remembered a proverb, current amongst the homely members of his flock – There were more ways of catching a coney than by chasing it, shouting.

Nicholas Freeman decided to declare himself on May the third, which at the Old Vine had always been the date of a humble, rather curious little family festival, known as 'Sparrow-grass Day'.

At the end of the garden, beyond the rose bushes and the apple trees and the herb plot, was a bed of asparagus, twenty years old. Richard had brought the first crowns back from one of his trips to Flanders; they had spread and flourished to such an extent that each year, at the height of its bearing, the bed gave at least two cuttings of such plenty that every man and boy in the dining hall could have ten or twelve green spikes as a vegetable with his supper dish. Martin Reed had convinced himself that the plant had medicinal qualities: it cleansed the blood. Earlier in the season, when the first shoots were ready for cutting but not in such number that they would 'go round', the asparagus presented a problem to a master of Martin Reed's nature: the square family table in the hall was always served with exactly the same food as any other. Luxuries were enjoyed later, in privacy. A cooked vegetable, however, could not be served after supper, casually from the livery cupboard; nor could the first, succulent green growth be wasted. So, for some years, in the last days of April, or the early ones of May, Martin and Richard, and later Anne and then the children, had observed Sparrowgrass Day, and had supper served at the table in the solar. Then someone had observed that it was on May the third that Martin had first approached Anne's father about her marrying Richard, and so the little feast day was fixed. Other delicacies, such as fresh fish hurried up from Bywater, were added to the table, and always jugs of good wine.

This year Nicholas intended to keep the festival and, because Maude's birthday had fallen during the days of mourning for her grandfather and gone unmarked, it could be a celebration of her birthday too. He had ridden into Colchester and bought her a present from the goldsmith's there. It was a reliquary pendant, hung on a thin gold chain. The pendant was a flat, slim oblong of gold which, upon pressure on a spring, opened into a triptych of pictures, beautifully worked in enamel, the centre picture showing the Crucifixion, the one to the left the Annunciation and the one on the right Christ's Ascension. When closed it measured an inch and a half by two, and was a masterpiece of delicate workmanship. It had cost every penny of his filchings and three pounds of his cash legacy.

He planned it all to the last detail. Mistress Reed could go to bed and eat – in the disgustingly slovenly way she had lately developed – her dish of asparagus there. He and Maude would sit in the solar, at a table with a good linen cloth, set near the window to catch the evening light. There would certainly be, to start with at least, the sadness inseparable from any family anniversary after a bereavement, and he would exert himself to talk as entertainingly as possible. The servant would serve the asparagus, and then the fish, and go, leaving the sweetmeats on the cupboard. When they were alone he would remind Maude of her forgotten birthday and produce his gift. After it had been admired he would fix the chain about her neck, drop his hands to her shoulders, turn her towards him and kiss her.

All this planning gave him the same half-incredulous pleasure as he had felt through the waiting time. He, Nick Freeman, whose approach to women had always been so forthright, setting a scene, preparing the very words he would say. It was amazing, but it was wonderful; he loved her, never having loved any woman before; therefore it must all be as different as he could make it.

The very day was exactly as he would have had it could he have ordered it as he had ordered the clothes he intended to wear that evening; a warm, fair day, full of the first scents of summer. The little pink monthly rose, always the first to come into bloom, was covered with half-open buds; the lilacs were in heavy flower. A bowl of the roses, he thought, closely massed together in the centre of the table, between the silver candlesticks. Giving this order to the maid, whom he had taken into his confidence, an odd thought occurred to him – it was almost as though he were a priest, arranging an altar! The thought provoked a smile, which still lingered in the corners of his mouth and in his eyes as he went on to have a word with Phyllis. Mistress Reed to be out of the solar and into bed by six o'clock.

Then, so that the whole thing might be a surprise to Maude, he sought her out with the suggestion that in the afternoon they should ride together. There was a clip of wool he wanted to inspect at Marly.

'I've never been there,' Maude said.

'You turn off at Flaxham and ride alongside the river. It is a pretty ride, especially now, with the hawthorns coming into bud.'

Before they left he took out his new clothes and laid them on the bed. Never in all his life had he had such clothes, because always every garment he had bought, even for best, had ahead of it years of servile office wear. His new tunic and hose were garments for a young, prosperous merchant, garments that Maude's own father might have worn: a tawny-yellow, slashed with buff, colours carefully chosen to enhance his dark good looks, and the easy cut of the tunic calculated to conceal the hint of threatening stoutness. He laid the pendant beside the clothes, ready to slip into his pouch when he changed.

They exchanged casual, unimportant remarks as they rode, until in the distance they could see the double arch of the ancient stone bridge, with its image perfectly reflected in the water below. On either bank of the river were the hawthorns covered with bright green leaves, just uncurling, and clusters of buds a little less white than the flowers into which presently they would break. Somewhere on the other side of the river a cuckoo called, and another answered.

Maude gave a great sigh which called her grandfather to Nicholas' mind.

'Beautiful!' she said. 'So beautiful. And when I think how nearly I missed it all.' The ecstatic note in her voice gave way to a kind of grating impatience. 'Oh, I know that the summer will pass and the bloom will fade and the leaves will fall, whereas the spiritual things, the devotion and the duties and the joys, go on unchanging whatever the season...and when one is old. I *know* that. In my mind. But my heart was never convinced. It would not be. I prayed and prayed for some sign, for some proof that what I knew I should do was the thing that was right for me. And nothing happened. Then, when the sign came, it pointed the other way.'

They had halted their horses, who after nuzzling one another dropped their heads and strained towards the green grass.

'I warned you,' he said. And she took that not as a reproach but as proof that he knew what she was talking about. That was what made him so delightful a companion; he did not need everything explained and underlined.

'I know. But when you are young what do you know about yourself? I mean...a dim-witted person might, for the best of reasons, wish to be a scholar, and try and try, and he would learn *something*; then one day he might be sent to feed pigs and realize that feeding pigs was what God meant him to do. You know why I went to Clevely; I told you. And for a long time it seemed right. Being cold and tired and hungry, salting the butter away in casks with the salt getting into the cracks of my hands was all helping, I thought. I offered my little sufferings so that Melusine...And then, all at once it was no good for me any more. Nothing I did was a gift; it was a tax, wrenched from me.'

'I could see that,' he said.

'There was one time when I was afraid I might go mad. Shall I tell you what I thought? I thought that if this went on much longer I should begin to hate Melusine. I thought she should never have done...never have got herself into such a situation in the first place; or, having let it happen, she should have married one of those silly young men who were always following her around. Wasn't that shocking? The one person who had been kind to me. The person who had taught me to read and write. To think such shameful things.'

'Thoughts walk in uninvited,' he said.

She turned to him with a look of bright relief.

'That *is* true, isn't it? I was in the chapel, at the end of a twenty-four hour fast. I was making a Novena. And that thought, as you say, walked in. And after that it all seemed such a waste. But I went on praying, and in the end there was a sign – the Bull Periculoso!'

'May Heaven reward Pope Boniface the Eighth,' he said lightly. But one day, or rather one night, one night very soon, when they lay spent with loving, breathless with loving, when she had tasted to the full all the joy she had so nearly missed, he would tell her to whom she owed it. The story of how the long dead Pope had had a little help from a humble living clerk would be worth telling.

The thought of being in bed with her, of her hair spread loose on the pillow, of the way he would handle and teach that virgin innocence moved him so much that once again he was astonished. He might have been a boy again, virgin himself, excited by the prospect of his first experience in the art of love.

'I think we should move on,' he said. 'We mustn't be late for supper. I have a surprise for you.'

They rode towards the bridge, she trying to extract from him some details about the surprise, he refusing to tell her, and both finding cause for laughter in this simple business because they were happy and it was a day for laughter.

How well, he thought, he had chosen his time. Her return to the world had combined with the natural resiliency of youth to enable her to throw off her sorrows. She was whole now, and happy, and his for the taking.

Presently he had another notion, as far-fetched as the earlier comparison of a supper table with an altar. They were already, he thought, like a married couple. The proposal, the acceptance, the ceremony would be nothing but formalities. The real bonds of affection and common interest and good companionship were already forged.

He looked back upon how he had come to Baildon, having been thrown out of the leather merchant's house in disgrace; upon how, before ever he had set eyes upon her, he had decided that to marry his master's granddaughter would be a desirable thing to do. How seldom in this life did one's desires and one's material advantages run alongside. How profoundly, how miraculously lucky he had been.

He fell silent and rode for some time indulging in these gloating, self-congratulatory thoughts which ignorant heathen everywhere and at all times have regarded as dangerous, likely to provoke the gods to jealousy and wrath.

The road by which he and Maude, at the end of their ride, approached the Old Vine, ran steeply down hill, and the road itself had been made, immemorial years ago, by heavily laden horses who, to ease the incline, had struggled not straight forward but from left to right and then from right to left. It had three sharp bends; and three times, riding downhill, one could catch, and then lose again, the sight of the house, the weaving sheds and stables, lying at the bottom of the slope, with, just beyond, the wall and South Gate of Baildon.

On this afternoon, as the view came first into sight, they could see two horsemen ride through the gateway; both men, one riding a tall horse, the other a heavier animal which bore, beside its rider, a sizeable bundle behind the saddle. They saw so much, and then the road turned and a clump of elms blocked out the view.

When they could next look down, the riders had almost reached the house and were visible in some detail. The one on the tall horse was young, his tanned face dark against his straw-coloured hair; the other man was older, and the bundle behind him, by its awkward angular shapes and the fact that it was enclosed in a soft, yellowish bag of goatskin, could be identified as a suit of armour packed for transit. Two squires on their way to join their master. The view was obscured again.

The road ran out on to the level and made its last turn. The two riders had halted by the great door of the Old Vine. The younger was studying the house, looking it over, up and down, from side to side. Perhaps because he was conscious of the new clothes lying spread upon his bed, Nicholas observed, between one blink of the eyelid and the next, the shabbiness of the scuffed, rubbed greasy leather jerkin worn by this young man. At the same time, not to be missed, was some indefinable hint of quality; in the way he sat in his saddle, in the turn of his head, as he looked the house over. This quality was oddly reflected in his mount: raw-boned and rough-coated, it yet bore the stamp of breeding.

Nicholas looked at Maude and was about to say – It seems we have visitors; for the young man, making a sign with his hand which his companion interpreted as an order to wait where he was, turned his horse and rode into the great door of the house. There was no time to make the remark, for Maude brought her hand down in a slap on her horse's rump and it shot forward. Nicholas caught one glimpse of a face he had never seen before, transformed, almost idiotic with joyful surprise.

His own horse, without urging, hurried after its companion and they clattered into the yard nose to tail.

The young man was in the act of dismounting, his eyes fixed on the back of the house in the same keen earnest scrutiny to which he had subjected the front.

He reached the ground and then, hearing the clatter of hoofs, turned about. Maude threw herself out of the saddle and cried, 'Henry!' Her face was red as a rose from chin to brow and his turned even darker. He said in a gruff, embarrassed way, 'I told you I should come.'

It was not what he had intended to say, nor the tone in which he had intended to speak. And just behind Maude a man, too old to be her twin brother, a neat good-looking man, was just dismounting.

Too full of sudden fear to mind his manners he seized Maude's hands and pulled off both her gloves. Only one ring, and that the one which he had pushed on to that finger more than four years ago.

'You've worn it…all this time?'

She nodded, and laughed, and said, 'It's still too big.'

Satisfied, he remembered what, through four hard years, he had kept in mind, as part of his goal. Still holding her hand he went on one knee and lifted her fingers to his lips.

'Sir Henry Rancon,' he said, so thickly that he seemed about to choke, 'now and forever at your service, demoiselle.'

'Last time,' she said, 'it was the other way round. You remember? Stand up, Sir Henry, and let me look at you.'

He had changed very little, except to grow; the shabby old jerkin was much too small. An old scar ran from one eyebrow to the edge of his badly cropped, dusty hair, and a newer one, hardly healed, showed just below the line of his jaw. She remembered the surprising softness of his lips and wondered…And was then aware that Nicholas had come to stand beside her. She turned to him, and with a smile that haunted him to the end of his life, dealt him his mortal wound.

'This was the surprise! Oh, Master Freeman, how did you guess?'

They had been on Christian name terms for at least a month.

Sometimes, during his almost meteoric rise to the upper ranks in the clerical hierarchy – for with money behind him, celibacy willingly embraced, and ruthless ambition as his motive power, nothing could stop him – he would ponder the irony of it all. Occasionally such musings ended with disconcerting thoughts about puppets and the strings they danced on, thoughts unsuitable in a churchman, tacitly dedicated to the theory of man's free will.

He suffered one such moment when, thirty years later, he was presented with his Cardinal's hat. He recalled then, as though it had been something he had dreamed, Maude's story of the Rune Stone at Beauclaire. That was easily to be dismissed as girlish fancy. Less easy to ignore was the memory of old Martin Reed saying mildly, out of his garnered experience, 'People do what they must.'

Norah Lofts

The House at Old Vine

Beginning in the fifteenth century and concluding at the time of the Restoration, this is the second volume in the 'House' trilogy. *The House at Old Vine* is a colourful account of a turbulent period in English history containing religious persecution, war, rebellion and social change. The house in Suffolk is a dramatic link between the six characters who inhabit it during this period and whose heartfelt stories we are told.

The House at Sunset

Spanning a period from the eighteenth century to the mid 1950s, this is the impressive concluding volume in Norah Lofts' 'House' trilogy. With skill and originality, Norah Lofts again presents a period in history from the perspective of those who have experienced it – people like the eccentric Felicity Hatton, living part of her life against the backdrop of 1740s London; or Mary Crisp enduring the horrors of the First World War. All are linked by the House.

OTHER TITLES BY NORAH LOFTS AVAILABLE DIRECT FROM HOUSE OF STRATUS

Quantity	£	$(US)	$(CAN)	€
THE HOUSE TRILOGY:				
THE HOUSE AT OLD VINE	6.99	12.95	19.95	13.50
THE HOUSE AT SUNSET	6.99	12.95	19.95	13.50

ALL HOUSE OF STRATUS BOOKS ARE AVAILABLE FROM GOOD BOOKSHOPS OR DIRECT FROM THE PUBLISHER:

Internet: www.houseofstratus.com including synopses and features.

Email: sales@houseofstratus.com
info@houseofstratus.com
(please quote author, title and credit card details.)

Tel: Order Line
0800 169 1780 (UK)
1 800 724 1100 (USA)
International
+44 (0) 1845 527700 (UK)
+01   845 463 1100 (USA)

Fax: +44 (0) 1845 527711 (UK)
+01   845 463 0018 (USA)
(please quote author, title and credit card details.)

Send to: House of Stratus Sales Department
Thirsk Industrial Park
York Road, Thirsk
North Yorkshire, YO7 3BX
UK

House of Stratus Inc.
2 Neptune Road
Poughkeepsie
NY 12601
USA

PAYMENT

Please tick currency you wish to use:

☐ £ (Sterling)   ☐ $ (US)   ☐ $ (CAN)   ☐ € (Euros)

Allow for shipping costs charged per order plus an amount per book as set out in the tables below:

CURRENCY/DESTINATION

	£(Sterling)	$(US)	$(CAN)	€(Euros)
Cost per order				
UK	1.50	2.25	3.50	2.50
Europe	3.00	4.50	6.75	5.00
North America	3.00	3.50	5.25	5.00
Rest of World	3.00	4.50	6.75	5.00
Additional cost per book				
UK	0.50	0.75	1.15	0.85
Europe	1.00	1.50	2.25	1.70
North America	1.00	1.00	1.50	1.70
Rest of World	1.50	2.25	3.50	3.00

PLEASE SEND CHEQUE OR INTERNATIONAL MONEY ORDER
payable to: HOUSE OF STRATUS LTD or HOUSE OF STRATUS INC. or card payment as indicated

STERLING EXAMPLE

Cost of book(s):..................... Example: 3 x books at £6.99 each: £20.97
Cost of order:..................... Example: £1.50 (Delivery to UK address)
Additional cost per book:.............. Example: 3 x £0.50: £1.50
Order total including shipping:........... Example: £23.97

VISA, MASTERCARD, SWITCH, AMEX:

☐☐☐☐☐☐☐☐☐☐☐☐☐☐☐☐☐☐

Issue number (Switch only):

☐☐☐

Start Date: **Expiry Date:**

☐☐/☐☐   ☐☐/☐☐

Signature: _____

NAME: _____

ADDRESS: _____

COUNTRY: _____

ZIP/POSTCODE: _____

Please allow 28 days for delivery. Despatch normally within 48 hours.

Prices subject to change without notice.
Please tick box if you do not wish to receive any additional information. ☐

House of Stratus publishes many other titles in this genre; please check our website (**www.houseofstratus.com**) for more details.